WESTERN

Rugged men looking for love...

Worth A Fortune

Nancy Robards Thompson

Her Hometown Secret

LeAnne Bristow

MILLS & BOON

Nancy Robards Thompson is acknowledged as the author of this work
WORTH A FORTUNE

First Published 2024
First Australian Paperback Edition 2024
ISBN 978 1 038 91052 3

HER HOMETOWN SECRET

First Published 2024
First Australian Paperback Edition 2024
ISBN 978 1 038 91052 3

Published by
Harlequin Mills & Boon
An imprint of Harlequin Enterprises (Australia) Pty Limited
(ABN 47 001 180 918), a subsidiary of HarperCollins
Publishers Australia Pty Limited
(ABN 36 009 913 517)
Level 19, 201 Elizabeth Street
SYDNEY NSW 2000 AUSTRALIA

Printed and bound in Australia by McPherson's Printing Group

Worth A Fortune

Nancy Robards Thompson

MILLS & BOON

Nationally bestselling author **Nancy Robards Thompson** holds a degree in journalism. She worked as a newspaper reporter until she realised reporting "just the facts" bored her silly. Now that she has much more content to report to her muse, Nancy loves writing women's fiction and romance full-time. Critics have deemed her work "funny, smart and observant." She resides in Florida with her husband and daughter. You can reach her at Facebook.com/nrobardsthompson.

Visit the Author Profile page
at millsandboon.com.au for more titles.

Dear Reader,

I love the Fortune family. Over the years, I've been fortunate enough to contribute to several seasons of their ongoing saga. Along the way, I've watched this larger-than-life family grow and change, but one thing remains constant. Every time I sit down to write a Fortunes book, it feels like coming home and reconnecting with family and old friends.

One of the things I love the most about *Worth a Fortune* is that there's a very light thread of mystery woven in among the romance. Haley Perry is determined to get to the bottom of how many people died when the Fortune Silver Mine collapsed nearly sixty years ago. If she does, it will be a huge boost to her career as an investigative journalist. However, it soon becomes clear that not only are Camden Fortune and his family standing in her way of learning the truth, but if she persists in solving the mystery, advancing her career might cost her her true love.

I hope you'll enjoy Haley and Camden's story as much as I loved writing it. Please keep in touch. I love to hear from readers.

NancyRobardsThompson.com

Instagram.com/NancyRThompson

Facebook.com/NRobardsThompson

Warmly,
Nancy

DEDICATION

This book is dedicated to Isaiah and Luke.
You're priceless.

CHAPTER ONE

To: Haley Perry
From: Edith Moore; features editor, Inspire Her Magazine
RE: A fun assignment for you

Good Morning, Haley,
As one of our favorite single journalists, you immediately came to mind when this story idea crossed my desk.

The bestselling self-help book *Five Easy Steps to Love*, by Jacqueline La Scala, claims you can make a stranger fall in love with you by doing these five things: 1) Sharing something personal about yourself. 2) Helping with something important to them. 3) Listening without judgment to an issue they're having. 4) Attending an event together. 5) Kissing after all the above.

We are dying to know if this is true!

I hope you'll take the story and run with it as only you can do. To that end, I've already put a copy of the book in the mail to you. You should receive it within the week.

Who knows—maybe you'll end up with more than a story.

Best,
Edith

HALEY WASN'T SURE which part of the woman's email was more offensive: *take the story and run with it like only you can do* or *maybe you'll end up with more than a story.*

Seriously?

Haley hit Reply and started typing:

My Dearest Edith,

Surely I am not the only writer who could do this assignment. In case you weren't aware, it is not a truth universally acknowledged, that a single woman in need of an income must be in want of a husband—

Haley stopped typing and stared at the screen. She was so irritated that she was channeling bad Jane Austen.

She hit the backspace key and watched the words disappear until there was nothing left but the blinking cursor on the blank white screen.

Truth be told, it wasn't the prospect of being single—or finding love, for that matter—that made her grumpy. It was that once again, Edith was tossing her a puff piece. She could've cushioned the blow with a simple *P.S. I chose you not only because you're single, but also because you do great work.*

Haley had gone to college in New York City and worked her way up from intern to staff writer at *Inspire Her Magazine.* The pandemic had hit and layoffs followed. Edith had promised to rehire her once the publication righted itself post-COVID.

In the meantime, the magazine had offered plenty of fluffy freelance pieces, such as this one, test-driving a self-help book that promised the secret formula for falling in love.

While Haley was barely scraping by as an independent journalist, she'd also discovered a keen interest in more serious pieces. When she'd pitched ideas about more meaningful women's issues to Edith, her former boss agreed that while they had the makings of worthwhile articles, they were keeping those types of stories in-house for the moment. She continued to toss Haley the equivalent of cotton candy when she was starving for a thick, juicy steak.

"How will I ever become an investigative journalist that people take seriously if I keep writing empty-headed fluff?" Haley complained to her cat, Nellie Bly. In response, the feline purred and wound figure eights around her legs. Haley reached down and stroked the animal's silky fur. "I know, I know. Pieces like this keep you in kitty treats—but did you ever consider that the more time I spend researching and writing pieces like this, the less time I have to devote to the work I want to do?"

However, *Inspire Her Magazine* had a great circulation, and it paid well. Plus, it kept her in touch with Edith. If she turned down assignments, plenty of writers would be lined up behind her, ready and willing to graciously accept the work...and possibly her former job, should it ever become available again.

She recalled what her former boss had said about them willing to do more meaningful pieces with their full-time staff. If she was able to get back on with the magazine, it would mean a steady salary and benefits while she proved herself a reliable investigative journalist.

Until that happened, Haley would have to work on her serious stories in between the fluffy pieces, which would not only pay the bills but also finance the research required for the big articles.

With that in mind, she took a deep breath and typed:

Thanks for thinking of me, Edith. I'll look for the book in the mail. You're right, maybe it will turn out to be more than just a story—

If the email had a soundtrack, that part would've been a needle scratching over vinyl.

She deleted the last line, then replaced it with a query

about word count and the deadline before closing with a businesslike, *All my best, Haley.*

As she hit Send, she had the fleeting thought that if this crazy piece actually did lead her to love and she got married, at least Edith would no longer have a reason to give her the single-girl drivel . Of course, if she married anyone around here, it would mean she'd have to give up on her hopes of moving back to New York City.

Chatelaine, Texas, wasn't so bad. Her sisters were here, and she enjoyed spending time with them, and…, well, that was about it. Maybe true love and a family of her own would fill the void that yawned inside her as she tried on the idea of living here indefinitely.

The problem was, love seemed so far out of reach right now, she couldn't really imagine it.

Instead, she pulled up her web browser and typed in the title of the self-help book Edith was sending and read the description, which told her nothing more than what the features editor had included in her email.

Haley suspected, at a steep $24.95 for the thin hardcover, *Five Easy Steps to Love* was nothing more than a good gimmick aimed at separating the lovelorn and lonely hearted from their hard-earned money.

She scoffed at the duplicity of the promise. If it only took five easy steps to fall in love, the entire world would be head over heels.

She knew from personal experience how foolish it was to trust the heart's fickle promises. She'd been a believer once and bore the scars to prove it. Now, she took care to be on her guard.

Immediately, she came up with her angle. She would disprove Jacqueline La Scala's theory. In fact, she'd find the hottest, most eligible bachelor in Chatelaine to test the bogus concept.

As she leaned back in her chair and considered her options, Nellie Bly jumped up in her lap. Haley stroked her. "I need to think about this, but right now, I'm going to work on the story I want to write before I get bogged down with the one that will pay the bills."

She opened the computer file titled Chatelaine Mine Disaster.

In 1965, fifty people died when a silver mine owned by the Fortune family collapsed. Rumor had it that two of the four brothers who owned the mine—Edgar and Elias Fortune—were to blame, but they lied and pinned the blame on mine foreman, Clint Wells, saying he was the one who'd ignored signs that the mine was unstable. The brothers claimed that Wells had neglected to keep them abreast of the situation. They swore they never would've let the miners work under such dangerous circumstances. Since Wells had died with his crew, he couldn't dispute the accusations.

From what Haley could piece together, the brothers had lied. She'd heard from numerous reliable sources that Edgar and Elias had known the mine was unsafe yet insisted on business as usual. They'd turned the story around, stirring up the sad and angry citizens of Chatelaine, and made the late foreman their scapegoat, ruining his reputation and leaving his grieving family to shoulder the blame. Out of self-preservation, Wells's wife, Gwenyth, and their eighteen-year-old daughter, Renee, had left town, never to be heard from again.

She scanned her list of facts and questions:

Four Fortune brothers had been involved with the mine. From what she could gather, Edgar and Elias Fortune were the ones who had pinned the blame on Clint Wells. The other two siblings, Walter and Wendell, had each held a stake in the mine but were less hands-on.

Walter had passed away in the year 2000.

Edgar had died of a heart attack fifteen years ago. He had left his good-sized fortune not to family members or the locals who had lost loved ones when the mine collapsed, but to every animal rescue in the state of Texas.

In a strange twist of fate, Elias Fortune's wife of the past ten years had arrived in town with the news that Elias had recently passed away. She had come to Chatelaine not only to make amends with the community and restore her late husband's good name, but she had also summoned Elias's grandchildren, nieces and nephew to Chatelaine to execute his will, which granted their most fervent wishes.

Why Chatelaine since they had been from all over? Maybe it was because the only living brother, Wendell Fortune—who had lived under an alias for decades as Martin Smith—had settled in town.

Another question was, what had happened to Gwenyth and Renee Wells?

And, on top of that, no one seemed to know where Elias and Edgar Fortune had gone after Gwenyth and Renee had left town. Haley had discovered that the Fortunes had thrown a lot of money at the problem, trying to make it go away, but it didn't happen as fast as they'd hoped, and eventually Elias and Edgar Fortune quietly slunk out of Chatelaine. There were rumors that claimed that after the fallout of the mining tragedy, Edgar and Elias had become estranged. Other rumors had the brothers dying in a boating accident in Mexico.

The reality was that both men had lived relatively long lives.

Haley was convinced that they'd run to dodge murder and tax-evasion charges. In the beginning, faking their own deaths would've been the perfect *get out of jail free* card, allowing them to escape punishment for their crimes.

That aside, one of the most nagging questions Haley

had yet to answer pertained to mysterious notes left in town that said fifty-one—not fifty—miners had died in the disaster.

Haley underlined Wendell's name in her notebook and, next to it, added the name Freya Fortune.

"I know they could answer my questions," she murmured. "But the cantankerous old fool refuses to help me out."

It was true. Every time she tried to approach Wendell, he always had some excuse not to talk to her. Either he was late for an appointment or he'd say *no comment*—or Haley's personal favorite was that one time when she had him cornered, and he'd claimed that his hearing aids were acting up and he couldn't hear her.

Did he think she was stupid?

Because the minute she'd walked away, he was yukking it up with the bartender at the Chatelaine Bar and Grill. Either his hearing aids had miraculously come back to life or he was lying. That was a no-brainer. Those Fortunes would stoop to nothing to protect each other.

Speaking of which…every time Freya Fortune saw her, she turned around and walked the other way.

Haley had to admit that on a personal level, she understood their being protective of their families. A decade ago, she'd been reunited with her sisters, and the love she felt for them was fierce. She would keep them safe at all costs. Then again, Lily and Tabitha weren't hiding information about a disaster caused by other family members that cost fifty—or was that fifty-one?—innocent people their lives.

Also, the three of them didn't have extended family, so it was sort of apples and oranges. All they had was each other.

Haley ran her finger down the list of Fortunes who might talk to her or at least point her in the right direction of solving the conundrum of the fifty-first miner. This town was swarming with Fortunes. They were like Baptist churches in the south—one on every corner.

The editor of the *Houston Chronicle* had said he would buy the story in a heartbeat because it involved the Fortunes. However, *because* it involved the Fortunes, the facts needed to be ironclad.

There was no room for error.

Her finger continued down the list and stopped on Camden Fortune's name.

"Well, hello there, hottie," she said.

Nellie Bly chirped as she nudged Haley's hand until she petted her.

"I wasn't talking to you, silly," she chuckled. "Although you are a beautiful girl. I was thinking of Camden Fortune."

A tall, dark and green eyed, long and muscular man with the most incredible mile-wide shoulders she'd ever seen.

Yes. If a person looked up the definition of *hot* in a dictionary, Camden Fortune's picture would be right there.

"He's the only Fortune in town who doesn't run in the other direction when he sees me coming. Well, other than West and Asa…and Bea and Esme. But for the sake of your aunties, I've decided they're off-limits. Now that we're family, I don't want to make things awkward."

She sighed. Her sister Lily had married Asa Fortune, and Tabitha was engaged—again—to her long-lost love, West, a prosecutor who'd faked his own death to protect Tabitha from a criminal he'd put away. After the thug had been killed in prison, West returned home to everyone's shock and delight.

"Even though our family ties should be all the more

reason they'd want to help me," Haley murmured as she nudged Nellie off her lap and stood up to shower and make herself presentable. "I'm family, too, and the only thing keeping me from selling this piece to the *Houston Chronicle* and taking a huge leap forward in my career is confirmation of whether or not fifty-one miners died in the 1965 disaster."

But while she loved her sisters too much to stress the family-bond theory, Camden was her new Plan B.

The two of them had undeniable chemistry. Unless she was imagining it—and she wasn't—every time they were around each other, the air sizzled.

It was curious, though, that despite all the flirting and chatting-up that had happened between them since Camden moved to Chatelaine after the first of the year, he'd never asked her out. Could it have anything to do with her being deemed a persona non grata by the majority of his family?

A ridiculous scene played out in her head in which there was a mandatory weekly Fortune family meeting where they collectively decided who was in the family's favor and who was outside the circle.

Haley sighed as she turned on the shower tap. Why didn't the Fortunes want the truth to come out? They must be hiding something. Because if they weren't, they certainly wouldn't be so hedgy and tightlipped about it.

Next year would mark the sixtieth anniversary of the Fortune Silver Mine disaster. Even if it took that long to get to the bottom of the story, Haley refused to give up until the truth came out.

If she had to do a little extra flirting with Camden Fortune, so be it. It was a hazard of the job.

And since she was *all* about the truth, she had to admit, she was looking forward to it.

"So that's all I need?" Camden Fortune said into the phone.

"Yes, sir," Shelia, the agent on the other end of the line, replied. "To recap, in addition to property and liability, the policy we've written for your business covers mortality, which essentially is life insurance on your horses. There's also loss-of-use coverage, which is similar to mortality insurance, but it's designed to compensate you for the loss of the horse in the event the animal is not able to compete or perform as intended. Finally, there's medical coverage, which covers expenses like one might insure a family member. Do you have any questions?"

Yes. Why the hell has it been so fuc—er—fricking difficult getting to this point?

Fricking. Yes, fricking.

Not the other word that had so easily rolled off his tongue in the past. If he was going to welcome kids to his camp in a few weeks, he needed to curb the language.

He also needed to watch his temper. It wasn't Shelia's fault the premium that covered the policy kept getting lost, waylaying what should've been a relatively simple process. Fortunately, it appeared that the money had finally landed in the proper place.

"I don't have any questions," Camden said. "You've been a big help, Shelia. Thanks so much for working with me to unravel this mess and see it through to the end."

"That's what I'm here for," she assured him. "Call if you need anything else. In the meantime, we are in receipt of the wire transfer, which means the policy will take effect at twelve a.m. tomorrow morning. Congratulations on your new business, Mr. Fortune."

After Camden hung up the phone, he pumped his fist in the air.

This was a dream come true. He considered calling his step-grandmother, Freya, who had made everything possible when she'd emailed Camden and his cousins to introduce herself and report that Elias Fortune, the grandfather he'd never known, had passed away and had named his grandchildren, nieces and nephew in his will. His widow, Freya—someone else they'd never met—was the executor of the will and was in charge of granting each of them a wish.

Camden's wish had been to open an equestrian school and summer camp that served underprivileged children. He wanted to give the kids the opportunity to learn the proper way to ride a horse, because safety shouldn't be reserved for the wealthy, who could afford extras.

He'd seen firsthand the dangers of children riding horses when they didn't know what they were doing. Safety shouldn't be a luxury. Especially when it came to children.

Now that the insurance debacle was out of the way, he had a lot to do before he could open his doors by August.

The first order of business was to unpack and put away the equipment that had been accumulating. He had decided not to open the boxes until the insurance situation was sorted…in case everything fell through.

He wasn't being negative—just being practical, given that everything seemed to be working against him, right down to the insurance policy he needed. Even so, he hadn't given up, and now his perseverance had paid off.

He smiled to himself and set his hat on his head, then left the office for the stables. Never had he ever considered unpacking tack as a way to celebrate, but right now, he couldn't think of anything else he'd rather do.

He was approaching the paddock when he heard a car's motor and the crunch of tires on the gravel drive. Putting his hand up to his eyes to shield them from the late-morning sun, he watched Haley Perry emerge from the red older-model Honda Civic.

As she walked toward him, he was already rethinking his declaration about unpacking being his preferred means of celebration. The way she looked in those cropped, low-slung blue jeans and white button-down blouse, which was tucked into the front of her jeans, leading his eyes up to where she'd left it unbuttoned to give an enticing glimpse of her cleavage, was titillating in itself. But the manner in which she'd left the shirt hanging loose in the back set him on fire and had him hungering to pull her close and run his hands along those inviting curves of hers.

The way her collar was popped up, he supposed the ensemble was a fashion statement. Hell, she could've been wearing a feed sack and she still would've been sexy.

"Hey there, Haley," he said. "To what do I owe this pleasure?"

He saw the notebook and pen in her hand—the only two things in the world that could've been the antidote to his attraction to her.

"I figured I'd find you here," she said . "I thought I'd pop in and say hello."

"Really?"

She nodded.

Her long brown hair was pulled back in a ponytail. The simple elegance of it accentuated her cheekbones and pretty hazel eyes. She was something to look at, but he knew she hadn't come all this way just to say hello.

"What really brings you out here this morning?" He nodded at the notebook. Her gaze dropped to look at it as if she'd forgotten she'd brought it.

She smiled that smile that made her dimples wink.

"I was hoping you would answer some questions for me."

Under any other circumstances, those dimples would

have been all it took to totally disarm him—but Camden knew better, so he strengthened his resolve.

"Haley, we've already been through this. I'm not answering any questions about my family."

He turned for the stables. Not entirely sure if he heard her footsteps or just sensed her following him.

"Camden, you're my only hope of getting to the bottom of this story, and—"

"No." He stuck out his hand behind him like a backward traffic cop. He felt kind of dumb for making such a dramatic gesture, but drastic times called for drastic measures.

"Look, I've got to get these boxes unpacked and all this tack put away," he said without facing her.

When she was silent for a few beats too long, he turned around and saw her clutching her notebook in both hands and staring down at it like she might start crying or something equally dramatic.

Oh, good lord.

"Haley, I'm sorry, but I've told you more than once that I don't want to answer questions about my family or the past. The Fortunes have finally come together again, and we don't need old scandals and terrible tragedies reviving the black mark on the family name."

She looked deflated as they stood there in awkward silence.

"What if I made it worth your while?" she asked, her right eyebrow arching. She bit down on her bottom lip.

"And what exactly did you have in mind?" he asked before he could stop himself.

She must've read his completely inappropriate mind, because she pulled herself up to her maximum height—which couldn't have been more than five-five—and glared at him.

"Well, certainly not *that*," she said.

"What?" he asked, feigning innocence. Yes, his mind had gone there—not that he'd betray his family for something untoward. Not that Haley would offer anything improper. They were friends. Okay, under other circumstances, they could've been more than friends. But even though she was hot as hell and exactly his type, he was too busy to get involved with her—with *any* woman.

He couldn't let down his defenses. Not when she was bound and determined to dig up a part of the past his family wanted to keep buried for reasons unknown to him.

Now she was looking at him like he'd said her cat was ugly.

"I don't know where your mind went, but I was going to offer to help you with the boxes. I thought we could talk while we work."

"Haley, what part of no—"

Now she was the one cutting him off with the traffic cop hand. "Camden, I get it. I understand. Your family is off-limits. But…there's actually something else that you can help me with. This morning, I got an assignment from *Inspire Her Magazine*. A self-help author named Jacqueline La Scala wrote a book called *Five Easy Steps to Love*. Maybe you've heard of it? It's all the rage right now."

He shook his head. "Nope, doesn't sound like my kind of read."

"Not my kind of book either," she admitted dryly. "That's why I intend to disprove her theory that all you have to do is follow the five simple steps she outlines in the book and you can make anyone fall in love with you."

He must've looked horrified, because she said, "What's that look for? Didn't you hear what I said? We are going to *disprove* her theory."

"Yeah, I know. I heard you."

It's not like the self-help book's claim could possibly

be true, and since she'd assured him she intended to prove it wrong…this experiment of hers might be kind of fun.

"Then what's the problem?"

The *problem* was, he'd stopped believing in love a long time ago. He sighed. What was it about Haley Perry that made her want to dredge up the past in so many different areas? But to her credit, she knew nothing about his lovelorn history. He intended to keep it that way. It was for the best. The reminder of his most recent disaster of a relationship was better than a bucket of water in the face… more like a cold shower, and it would keep him in check.

He gave himself a mental shake. Haley had been explaining the book's theory, and he'd zoned out.

"If you think about it," she said, "all of the steps—except the kiss, maybe—are the basis of friendship, not necessarily romantic love."

"What was that about a kiss?"

She smiled and a wicked gleam shone in her eyes. "What's the matter, Fortune? Don't tell me you're scared of a little peck between friends."

CHAPTER TWO

YESTERDAY, THE LOOK on Camden's face after Haley had mentioned there would be a kiss involved in the research had been priceless. There was nothing like watching a big, strong, handsome man squirm over the mere mention of a smooch. For a moment, she was afraid he might back out of the experiment altogether, but after a little cajoling, he'd finally come around.

Before she'd left the ranch, they had agreed to meet at the Chatelaine Bar and Grill, where they would tackle item one on the list: *Share something personal about yourself.*

Haley suspected Camden's initial reluctance had less to do with him not being into the Five Steps story and everything to do with it possibly segueing into questions about the fifty-first miner.

Being completely honest, if she could wear down Camden Fortune's resolve with a kiss, she'd be all over it. Or all over *him*... It was fun to think about it, but the likelihood of the two of them actually locking lips was slim to none.

That was another question she'd like to get to the bottom of—clearly he sensed the chemistry between them, but he'd never asked her out. Why not?

Maybe she could work that into the conversation tonight. But first, she needed to refocus and get her head in the game for the work she needed to get done this morning.

She was going to talk to Ruthann Richmond, the widow of Kenny Richmond, one of the miners who perished when the mine collapsed. She and her husband had been friendly with Gwenyth and Clint Wells. She was willing to talk to her and tell her everything she knew.

Haley parked her car in the driveway of 619 Blue Bonnet Street. The residence was a modest bungalow, with window boxes and a neat little front yard surrounded by a white picket fence. As she got out of the car and made her way toward the front door, which sported a wreath made of silk daisies and wooden cutouts of ducks wearing red calico bonnets, her first impression was that this was a happy house.

Not that she had expected Kenny Richmond's widow to have given in to such despair that she would've let the place go, but judging by the curb appeal, the house gave off a pleasant vibe—like a grandma's house that would be full of love and the scent of fresh-baked cookies.

She knocked on the door, noticing that the flowers in the window boxes were silk like the daisies in the wreath. Much easier to maintain than real flowers, she supposed, but from a distance, they had looked real. It was a good reminder that not everything was as it appeared.

"Hey there, darlin'," said the cheerful woman who answered the door. "It's good to see you again. Please come in."

Haley had been right about one thing: the entire house smelled like fresh-baked cookies. She breathed in deeply, and her mouth watered at the delicious aroma.

"Hi, Ruthann. It's so nice of you to let me come over. I appreciate it."

Haley met Ruthann when she'd been shopping at GreatStore, Chatelaine's lone big-box store. She'd only intended to run in to grab some things to make a quick dinner and had been standing next to Ruthann in the produce section. The older woman had commented that the cantaloupes were as sweet as candy and a good price to boot. She'd told Haley they were so yummy that she had come back to pick up a couple more. The two had struck up a conversation, which led to Haley learning that Ruthann was a widow who had never remarried after losing her husband in the 1965 Fortune Silver Mine disaster.

Haley's heart had pounded as she realized this might be her big break. Which meant she needed to play it cool so she wouldn't scare Ruthann off.

As she'd racked her brain, formulating a way to steer the conversation to a place where the woman would agree to let Haley interview her, Ruthann said, "I figured everyone has one great love in a lifetime, and Kenny was mine. Know what I mean?"

"If you say so." The words had slipped out before Haley could stop them, and she could've kicked herself.

"What? Don't tell me a pretty little girl like you has never been in love." Ruthann had sounded truly astonished.

In response, Haley had smiled and shrugged, embarrassed to admit that she'd certainly had her heart broken, but something like that was too personal to tell a total stranger. "I suppose I haven't met him yet, but I'm hopeful."

"That's the spirit," Ruthann had said. "Your Mr. Wonderful will come along soon enough. I admire you for not settling for Mr. Sort-of-Okay. You deserve better." A faraway look had entered her eyes. "That brings me back to my original point. When you've had Mr. Wonderful, it's hard to settle for less. Why tempt fate? Getting married again wasn't going to make me miss my Kenny any less. So I figured I'd be better off by myself."

"I'm so sorry—" Haley began.

"Please, don't be sad for me, honey. My kids and grandkids come to visit me all the time. Being alone isn't the same as being *lonely*. Especially when you're surrounded by good memories and a family that loves you."

As if the clouds parted and the sun came out, Ruthann had handed Haley the opening she needed. "I lost the love of my life when that mine collapsed. If not for those greedy Fortunes, my Kenny might still be alive today."

After extending her condolences, she had taken a deep breath and told Ruthann about the story she was working on, then asked if they could meet somewhere more private to talk about it.

"I would be happy to tell you everything I know," Ruthann had said. "But not here. The produce has been known to have ears, if you know what I mean. But I'll tell you what—Gwenyth Wells was one of my best friends, and I can guarantee you that her husband was made a scapegoat. And I don't care who hears that. Because it's the honest to God truth, but there's something else..."

Ruthann had been about to tell her when a man and a woman walked up to the other side of the produce island where the apples were stocked. They seemed to be in no hurry.

Shaking her head, Ruthann had whispered, "I can't talk about it here."

"Do you have time for a cup of coffee or lunch?"

Giddy over the possibility of a break in the story, Haley had instantly decided to scrimp on a few meals so she could buy Ruthann lunch in appreciation for doing the interview.

The woman had smiled and shook her head. " "Why don't you come over to my house sometime. I'll fix some lunch for us and give you an earful."

They decided on a day that worked best for both of them, and Ruthann gave Haley her address before the older woman was off to the checkout stands.

Even though Haley had grown up in Goldmine, Texas, a town slightly larger than Chatelaine and located about an hour north, she'd gone to college and worked in New York City. She was still surprised when people like Ruthann invited a stranger into their home. Nonetheless, she was grateful because it meant they could truly talk privately. Judging by Ruthann's hesitation to talk in the GreatStore, Haley hoped she had something juicy for her.

As Haley glanced around Ruthann's living room now, taking in the modestly furnished but sunny quarters, she thought it stood to reason that anyone who claimed cantaloupe tasted like candy would maintain a sweet and cheerful little house with flowers in the window boxes and ducks on her front door.

"I hope you're hungry," Ruthann said as she ushered Haley into the kitchen. "I whipped up some egg-salad sandwiches, a batch of chocolate chip cookies and a fresh pitcher of sweet tea for us to enjoy."

"That sounds delicious, but you shouldn't have gone to the trouble, Ruthann."

"Nonsense," the older woman demurred with a wave of her hand. "I have to cook for myself anyway. It's just as easy to make a double batch. Sit yourself down at the table, and I'll fix us each a plate."

"May I help with anything?"

"Nope. I made the egg salas earlier. Lunch is as good as ready."

They made small talk as they enjoyed the sandwiches and wavy potato chips Ruthann had added to the plates. After she had whisked away the detritus of lunch and returned with a platter of cookies, Haley opened her notebook and prepared to get down to business.

"Again, Ruthann, I'm so sorry about your loss."

The woman shrugged. "Thank you. As you know, it's

coming up on the sixtieth anniversary of losing him, and in some ways, it seems like yesterday. But in other ways, it feels like a lifetime ago."

Haley's heart squeezed at the sorrow on the woman's face.

"You must've been a young woman when you lost Kenny."

Ruthann nodded. "I was twenty-two years old when Kenny died. We got married right out of high school. He gave me the gift of two beautiful children before he left us. I see so much of him in our son, Kenneth, Jr."

Haley had already established such trust with Ruthann—enough that the older woman would invite her into her home and fix lunch for her. She knew instinctually that she needed to start slow, with softball questions, and work her way up to the more pointed bits, such as whether or not she had any clue about the notes that had been left around town hinting that fifty-one—not fifty—people had died when the mine collapsed. Did Ruthann know the identity of the fifty-first victim? And better yet, what was the juicy morsel she'd been reluctant to divulge in the store?

"Of course, you weren't even born when the mine collapsed," her hostess said. "In fact, your mama and daddy might not have even been born. Are your mama and them from around these parts?"

Haley swallowed, trying to buy some time. Not only did she not like to talk about herself, but it was also a tricky question. Even so, she answered, "Yes, my parents lived in Chatelaine briefly, but they were killed in a car accident when my sisters and I were very young. We grew up in foster care—one of my sisters was adopted. We reunited in the past decade."

Ruthann's eyes went wide. "Why, Haley Perry. Of course! You're one of the Perry triplets."

She reached out and covered Haley's hand with her own. "Honey, what happened to your mama and daddy was such a tragedy. Believe me, I know about tragedy. That's probably why we hit it off like we did. Like recognizing like."

That familiar hollow feeling yawned inside Haley as she searched for something to say. It was true—both she and Ruthann were two tragic kindred souls.

"You know what sets us apart from others?" she asked. "You and I haven't let our tragedies define us."

Ruthann nodded and nudged the plate of cookies closer to her guest.

"You are absolutely right," the older woman said. "And that is precisely why I intend to help you as much as I can."

"I appreciate that more than I can possibly say." She cleared her throat. "Speaking of which, do you know anything at all about these notes that keep turning up around town?" Haley asked as she helped herself to another sandwich quarter.

Ruthann cocked her head to the side as if she didn't understand the question. "Notes? I haven't heard anything about any notes. Or at least, I can't recall right off the top of my head. What did they say?"

"The first note was discovered last fall," Haley said. "All it said was *There were 51.* It was vague, but right away, I believed that whoever wrote that note was talking about the mine accident. They were suggesting there were fifty-one miners, not fifty." She blew out a frustrated breath. "But everyone I've asked about it has looked at me like I'm crazy since everyone—including the authorities—believes *fifty* people died. The official records say fifty, so others that I've talked to believe what the records say. But a couple of months ago, another note appeared. It was tacked up on the community bulletin board in the park.

It said *51 died in the mine.* It's pretty darn clear what the second note was talking about, don't you think?"

Ruthann furrowed her brow. "I want to agree with you, but honestly, I don't know what to think. Believe you me, if I could help you, I would. I'll tell you everything I know—but I've only ever heard that we lost fifty miners in that accident, not fifty-one."

She held up a finger. "The reason I remember is because it was such a round number. Fifty miners. And my Kenny was one of them. Those Fortunes pointed fingers at innocent people to deflect the blame when three of their fingers were pointing right back at their own guilty selves. The way they did us wasn't right."

Ruthann leaned in. "What I wanted to tell you when we were in the store was that I know for a fact that them Fortunes were to blame for the mine collapsing."

"How do you know? The people I've talked to have been split on the matter," Haley said. "Some believe that the foreman, Clint Wells, was the one who ignored safety protocols, but others think Edgar and Elias Fortune were ultimately responsible. What can you tell me?"

"A friend of my friend Enid told her that Freya Fortune herself said that her late husband, Elias Fortune, confessed on his deathbed that he and his brother made Clint Wells the scapegoat so they didn't have to shoulder the blame."

"Does this friend of Enid's have a name?"

Ruthann shook her head. "Enid wouldn't say. You know how it is—them Fortunes, with all their pomp and privilege, will put you in your place right quick if you cross 'em."

Haley considered telling the woman that not all of them were bad news. One of her sisters was married to a Fortune, and the other one was engaged to a member of that family, but she held her tongue. And found herself fighting back a wave of disappointment. This juicy secret that Ruthann hadn't been able to tell her in the store had ended up being a bit of a letdown.

"Did this friend go to the authorities about it?"

"Honey, the police couldn't do anything."

The woman had a point. After all, Edgar and Elias were dead.

"But if no one wants to talk about it, Clint Wells's name will never be cleared," Haley reminded her. "He lost his life, too. We owe that to him."

"I agree, and I think more people know about it than you might think. Of course, you could put it in this story you're writing."

She shook her head. "Not without proof positive that Freya said it."

"Why don't you ask Mrs. Fortune yourself?"

"I will if I can get close to her," Haley said. "But every time she sees me coming, she runs in the opposite direction."

"Sounds about right." Ruthann shrugged and stared off into the distance, but the disdain for the Fortunes was clear on the woman's face. Ruthann was sweet, but Haley had to wonder if her pleasant persona masked a personal vendetta.

The woman had lost her husband when the mine collapsed, and Gwenyth Wells had been a good friend to her. Therefore, it stood to reason that Ruthann wouldn't want to blame her friend's late husband. Would she be the type to make up a confession from Freya Fortune? If Haley could ever corner Freya, she would certainly ask her.

For now, she'd be smart to change tracks.

"Speaking of the authorities," Haley began, "I looked into getting ahold of the mine's personnel records. I believe that's what they used to account for everyone, but they told me that case has been sealed. That means the people can't access the records, but if the authorities wanted to reopen the case, they could."

"And?" Ruthann sat up straighter. "Are they going to do it?"

Haley scoffed. "Are you kidding? People don't even want to talk about it, much less reopen it."

The widow gave a weary sigh and slumped back in her chair. "Well, what do you expect? It was nearly sixty years ago. I wouldn't put it past the Fortunes to have done away with the payroll records themselves. Darlin,' when the Fortunes don't want something to happen, it's not going to happen. End of story. You'd might as well get used to it."

Haley nodded. "You wouldn't happen to have any photographs of your husband on the job or an old phone list of his associates, would you? I thought that since you were friends with Gwenyth and her husband was the foreman, she might've shared something like that."

"No, sweetie, sorry. If I'd ever had such a thing, I would've gotten rid of it ages ago. My house is small, and I don't have room for clutter."

Haley only had to take a look around the neat little house to know that was the truth.

With that, they'd come full circle, right back to where they'd started.

Fortunes: all the points; Haley: 0.

Even though the explosive bombshell that Ruthann had hinted at had turned out to be little more than a whisper of hearsay, Haley still believed there was more to this story than met the eye.

She scribbled in her notebook: *Did the officials cover for the Fortunes rather than serving the people of Chatelaine?*

She underlined the question and looked back at Ruthann.

"You and Gwenyth Wells were good friends," Haley said. "Have you heard from her since she left?"

"Honey, I already told you, Gwenyth was a widow. She and that daughter of hers were basically run out of town after the Fortunes pinned the blame on Clint. I have not seen or heard from either of them since. I believe nobody has."

Okay. The standard answer.

A couple of people Haley had interviewed had mentioned that their great-grandparents had known Gwenyth and no one had set eyes on the woman since she'd left all those years ago. It seemed that everyone around her who wasn't related to the Fortunes knew someone who'd died in the mining disaster or knew the Wells family, but no one seemed to have more info than that.

Ruthann crossed her arms and shifted in her seat. Haley got the distinct impression that was her cue to lighten up. Maybe a better tactic was to keep things more general. Ask open-ended questions and let Ruthann talk. Maybe she'd remember something she hadn't realized she'd forgotten.

Something with more weight than gossip coming from the friend of a friend.

They sat there in heavy silence as Haley wrote down in her notebook everything that Ruthann had told her.

"You know, it's kind of funny. The town seems to be growing even as we speak—what, with all those Fortunes coming back." The woman lowered her voice, and a conspiratorial look washed over her. "And rumor has it there are illegitimate children on both Walter and Wendell's parts. So who knows how many more will end up crawling out of the woodwork—but that's beside the point. As it is, I'm at constant war with myself. I resent those people for killing my Kenny and running off, but I wonder if it's fair of me to blame this new crop of them for something they had no part in because they share the same blood."

Haley had heard rumblings about illegitimate Fortunes, but she hadn't met any of them. Who knew what was true and what wasn't. Besides, there wasn't any indication that any of them could help her with the mine-disaster story. What was more important to her right now was how the family had closed ranks and refused to talk about the past.

This new breed of Fortunes may not have been actively involved in the accident and subsequent coverup, but they seemed pretty content to retreat into their comfortable, privileged lives while people like Ruthann and Gwenyth Wells suffered the consequences of Edgar and Elias Fortunes' careless actions.

Even Camden had clammed up when she'd asked him if he would help her with the mine exposé. Did silence equal complicity? Well, she intended to find out tonight when they met to complete the first task on the list: share something personal about yourself.

She was bound and determined to inspire that sexy cowboy to come clean and spill some family secrets.

CAMDEN HAD ALMOST suggested that Haley meet him at the Cowgirl Café, Chatelaine's newest casual-dining option, which had opened earlier that year. However, Bea Fortune was his cousin, and despite his mad craving for one of Bea's famous shrimp po'boys, if she saw him out with Haley Perry, word would get back to the rest of the family faster than he could say *Give me fries with that sandwich*.

That meant their only other favorable option for dinner was the Chatelaine Bar and Grill. It was a little bit fancier than Camden would've preferred, but what else was he going to do?

This wasn't a date, he reminded himself. It was dinner

with a friend. A friend he was helping out with a work assignment, which also happened to involve testing a theory about falling in love—or rather, *not* falling in love.

He groaned. Maybe he shouldn't have offered to be her guinea pig.

Well, it was too late now.

As Camden steered his truck into the lot, he spied Haley's red Honda Civic parked next to an empty space, which he claimed. He glanced at the clock on his dashboard to make sure he wasn't late. Actually, he was a couple of minutes early. Haley was sitting in her car, doing something on her phone. She looked up and smiled when he pulled in beside her.

Man, she sure was pretty.

For a second, he wondered if it had been a good idea for the two of them to meet tonight, because judging by his visceral reaction to her, she might be able to squeeze any information out of him that she wanted.

Well, since they were already here, he'd just have to be on his guard.

Steeling his resolve, he vowed to keep the conversation focused on this crazy self-help book story she was doing. At least they were on the same page where the book's philosophy was concerned—no pun intended. They were both determined to disprove the theory that it only took five simple steps to fall in love.

Neither one of them believed it was that easy.

He knew that from experience.

As he opened his truck's door, unfolded himself from the vehicle and tucked his plaid shirt into his jeans, he wondered what had happened to Haley to make her as jaded about love as he was. A smart, attractive woman like her shouldn't be single.

From what he knew of her, she was way too smart to

let herself get mixed up with a user the way he had. The memory sobered him up and hardened him to the vibe he felt as he met her at the back of their vehicles.

"Hello." There was a flirtatious note to her voice.

He felt his defenses slipping as he said, "Hey, you look nice."

Because she did look nice. Hayley had put on a pink dress that showed off her tan. She was wearing high heels and had even curled her hair.

If he didn't know better, he might be fool enough to think this *was* a date.

However, as dusk settled around them, he reminded himself it wasn't. He wasn't dating anyone right now. Not even casually. That was compliments of his ex-fiancée, Joanna, who had shattered his heart, shredded his trust and used the Fortune name to further her own ambitions.

Not that he would've minded helping her out. That was the rub. She'd been so dishonest, so underhanded, and when he'd questioned her…

He blinked the thought away. He was not about to let Joanna ruin this night—date or no date.

"You look pretty handsome yourself," Haley said in that easy way of hers as they walked toward the Chatelaine Bar and Grill's front door. As he held the door open and she walked in ahead of him, he caught an intoxicating whiff of her perfume.

Something that smelled like honey and sunshine…wildflowers on a warm summer day.

Yeah, if this had been a date, he'd have picked her up proper rather than meeting her here. When he dropped her off, he might even have gone in for a kiss. If she'd signaled that she wanted one.

"Well, look who it is," Damon Fortune Maloney, who

was a bartender at the Chatelaine Bar and Grill, remarked. He also happened to be Camden's cousin.

Come on, it was Chatelaine. There were five Fortunes for every person not related to them. Or at least it seemed that way.

The difference between Damon and Bea was that Damon wouldn't feel compelled to report a play-by-play to the rest of the family.

However, to be on the safe side, when Camden saw Damon give Haley a curious glance, he said, "Business dinner."

He started to add that he was helping her out with a story, but he thought better of it.

"Haley, this is my cousin, Damon Fortune Maloney. Damon, this is Haley Perry."

"Yes, we've met before," she said with a warm smile. "It's good to see you again, Damon."

Damon nodded. "Good to see you too."

His cousin shot him a look, which Camden took as a subtle warning. He wondered if Haley had tried to get information about the family out of Damon before she'd come knocking on Camden's door. He hadn't mentioned it, but the man tended to be circumspect by nature. If she had hit him up for answers about the Fortunes the same way she'd asked him, there was no doubt in Camden's mind that Damon would've stoically set her straight.

A fleeting thought crossed Camden's mind. Joanna had used him for her own purposes. Now Haley wanted something from him too. It wasn't exactly the same, but it was a good reminder for him to remain on his guard.

"So, table for two, then?" Damon asked.

"I don't know." Camden turned to Haley. "Would you rather eat at the bar? There are two empty seats in the middle."

She followed his gaze and frowned. “It’s a little noisy in here. Let’s get a table instead.”

It was only seven o’clock, but the country music playing through the sound system was loud, and the place was already rocking. He nodded and they followed Damon to the hostess stand.

“We need a table for two,” he said to a blonde and a brunette standing at the desk at the entrance. “This is my cousin. Please make sure you treat him and his friend right.”

“Of course,” they said in unison. The blonde held up two menus and motioned for them to follow.

The restaurant featured red leather banquet seating and wooden walls that gave the place a masculine, traditional feel. The photographs on the wall and various props paid homage to Chatelaine’s mining past.

Great. How come he’d never noticed that before? As many times as he’d been in the Chatelaine Bar and Grill, the decor had sort of faded into the background. Granted, he often came on Tuesdays. Not only was the place always packed, making it difficult to see anything but wall-to-wall people, but it was *Ladies Night.* He usually wasn’t looking at the interior decorations.

As they settled into a booth, sitting across from each other, he reasoned that he’d already made it clear that his family and the mining disaster were off-limits. Not that he’d have anything newsworthy about it to give her.

“Is this table okay?” asked the hostess, whose name was Brandy, according to her name tag.

Camden looked at Haley, who was looking at him, and they both nodded.

“This is great,” he said. “Thanks.”

“Very good,” Brandy replied. “Raymond will be your server. He’ll be right along to take your drink order.”

With that, the hostess left them alone.

For some asinine reason, Camden felt a little tongue tied. He rarely found himself at a loss for words. He had no idea what was going on with him tonight.

He was attracted to Haley. *That's* what was going on with him. It was that simple. Even if he'd been a bad judge of character in his last relationship, attraction didn't mean that he was looking to get serious again.

Nope. That wasn't going to happen anytime soon.

Even so, it didn't mean he'd sworn off women—only love and messy romantic entanglements.

He redoubled his resolve. What he was feeling tonight was just pure, unadulterated sexual desire. Haley Perry was a gorgeous woman, after all. If she was game, a fling while they were disproving this so-called love formula might be the release he needed.

"So, tell me how not to fall in love," he said, propping his forearms on the edge of the table and steepling his fingers.

Haley laughed.

"Well, okay then. Let's get right down to business."

He shrugged. "Did you want to talk about something else before we…'get down to business'…as you put it?"

She raised her right brow, and a wicked gleam sparkled in her hazel eyes. "Oh, I don't know." She bit her bottom lip and dropped her gaze to the table as she traced the woodgrain with a hot pink–polished fingernail. "I was thinking it might be nice to get to know each other a little better before we…you know…get down to it. I always like to take things slowly and build up to such an intimate moment. Don't you?"

She looked up at him, eyes smoldering through long, dark lashes.

Oh, fuc—

He had to clamp his mouth shut to keep the obscenity from escaping. But there was no stopping the way his body reacted to her. No pulling the curtain on the thought of his mouth on hers as he swept her up into his arms and whisked her off to his bed, where they'd "get down to it."

"Oh my gosh." A smile spread over her face. "I'm messing with you, Camden."

Oh, for f's sake.

"What do you mean, you're messing with me?" he asked as if he had no idea what she was talking about. "You don't want to talk about your assignment—how you want to disprove that self-help book?"

"Of course I do," she said. "I was trying to get you out of your own head. You seemed a little quiet there, Camden. I thought you might be feeling a little shy."

"That's very considerate of you," he retorted. "I'm a lot of things, but shy isn't one of them."

Their gazes snared, and there was that electric jolt he felt every time they connected—even when there was no physical touching involved.

"Howdy, folks. I'm Raymond. I'll be your server tonight."

The guy's presence seemed to surprise them both.

Clearly, the fact that they'd been having a moment didn't go unnoticed by Raymond. "Is this a bad time?" he asked. "I could come back in a minute."

"No!" they said together.

Camden added, "Your timing is perfect."

"We are so glad you're here, Raymond," Haley said, a little too brightly.

The waiter glanced back and forth between the two of them. "That's great. How about if I tell you about the specials and take your drink orders?"

By the time Raymond walked away from their table to

get a glass of red wine for Haley and a draft for Camden, whatever it was that had passed between them earlier was gone—extinguished like water thrown on a fire.

Obviously, he needed to get laid if his body was going to react like that to innuendo.

He watched her as she pulled a notebook and a paperback out of her purse. While the flames of the fire that Raymond had extinguished were under control, for him, the embers still burned.

It had been a long time since he had felt so physically pulled toward a woman—not that he was confusing lust with love.

In the same vein as learning the hard way not to touch a hot stove burner, maybe it wasn't such a good idea to have a fling with Haley Perry. He wasn't so sure he could trust himself around her.

CHAPTER THREE

"OKAY, LET'S DO THIS," Haley said after Raymond had taken their orders. "Let's start with the first point in *Five Easy Steps to Love*."

Camden stared back at her blankly. "Which is? You've read this book, but I have not."

"Fair enough," she said. "Point number one is to share something personal about yourself."

She gazed at him across the table, watching him as he pondered the question. "Something personal…" he murmured to himself. "Like how personal? That could go in a lot of different directions. It could be something from way back in my childhood, or it could be something more recent and less transformative but still personal."

"It's your choice." Haley shrugged. "It doesn't have to be complicated. Don't overthink it. Tell me the first thing that pops into your head."

She could practically see the wheels turning in his mind.

If he told her something that had impacted him as a child, she might glimpse another dimension of Camden Fortune and get another piece of the puzzle of what had made him the man he was today. Yet if he shared something personal that had happened recently, she'd get to know more about what was going on in his life right now.

Hmm... As far as she was concerned, it was a win-win.

"If you can't choose, why not tell me something from the past and something more recent?"

He frowned. "What do the rules say? I think I'm only supposed to tell you one thing."

Haley arched a brow at him. "Camden Fortune, I never knew you were such a rule follower."

The left side of his mouth quirked. "A rule follower? Hey, look, I'm trying to help you with this article. Seems like if you're going to disprove the theory, you'd want to follow her instructions to the tee." He shrugged. "It's your journalistic integrity on the line."

Her mouth fell open. "My *journalistic integrity*? Are you serious? Fine. If you want to play strictly by the rules, pick something and tell me. Don't take all day. This is not that hard."

His face had morphed into a full smile. He seemed to be getting a kick out of needling her, and she was playing right into his hands by getting rattled.

Pen in hand, poised on a page in her open notebook, she glanced up at him with a straight face.

"I'm ready when you are," she said.

"Okay, I've got something," he informed her. "Yesterday, right before you arrived at the ranch, I settled some insurance issues that had been standing in the way of my opening a free summer riding camp I want to start for underserved children."

Oh. Wow.

"It's for underserved children?"

He nodded.

Well, that was unexpected—and it certainly let the wind that had propelled her annoyance out of its sails.

"How long have you been planning this camp?"

"Oh, I don't know. For a while now."

"Does this place have a name?" she asked.

"Not yet. It's still in the beginning stages. Until I came into an inheritance, it always seemed like a pipe dream."

"Getting an inheritance is bittersweet," she said. "Basically, it boils down to exchanging someone you care about for a large check."

"I don't know about that..." He seemed as if he was going to say something, but maybe he thought better of it. "What I mean is, it's never easy to lose someone you love. There's no way any amount of money can replace them, but if you can do some good with the gift they left you... it takes some of the sting out of it."

"Why a free camp? What was your inspiration?"

There was another story behind that. She could smell it, and she wanted to know more.

He hesitated for a moment. "It's ironic that you mentioned doing something good with an inheritance. The inspiration behind the camp came when a childhood friend of mine, a kid named Josh Dunn, died in a riding accident. He had no business being on that horse because he'd never learned how to ride. So, I figure if I can teach kids about riding safety, it will be a way to honor Josh and keep others safe."

She was speechless, which didn't happen very often.

He folded his arms across his broad chest and broke the awkward silence. "Now it's your turn."

She blinked. "My turn to do what?"

"It's your turn to tell me something personal about you."

"Oh no." She shook her head. "That was a very moving story you just shared, Camden. It's touching that you would use your inheritance to help kids. But circling back to our purpose, it's of the utmost importance that I remain neutral in this story."

"But isn't this experiment of yours supposed to be a

two-way street? How can two people fall in love if only one participates?"

He clamped his mouth shut, like he wished he could reel in what he'd said.

"Why, Camden," she teased, "are you saying you want me to fall in love with you?"

At that moment, Raymond approached the table, carrying a big tray with their meals. They had both ordered the nightly special: steak cooked medium rare, with sautéed mushrooms and loaded baked potatoes.

"Saved by the dinner bell." Camden smiled victoriously.

"Excuse me?" their server asked, as if he'd misheard.

"Once again, your timing is perfect, Raymond," Camden assured him as he looked knowingly at Haley.

"Great." The waiter beamed. "I hope you're hungry. There's a lot of good food on this tray."

After they were situated with their food, Haley's question seemed to have evaporated into the restaurant's fragrant air. Or so she thought.

"Can you explain how this story is supposed to be a valid assessment of this author's work if you're looking at it so one-sidedly?"

"Sorry, I make it a practice not to discuss the particulars of my story with someone I'm interviewing. And I never let a person I'm writing about read the story before it's published."

"You don't?" he asked. "Why not?"

"No self-respecting journalist would ever do that. I mean, this is not an advertorial where I'm writing this to make you look good."

"You're not?" He quirked a brow. "Are you planning on making me look *bad*?"

"Of course not."

"Okay, I think I understand. You like to be in charge,

don't you?" Camden forked his first bite into his mouth and chewed.

Haley wanted to snort, but she took a sip of her wine. "You say that like it's a bad thing."

He swallowed the bite and wiped his mouth with a napkin. "Now you're editorializing. I did not say it was a bad thing."

"So you like take-charge women?"

"I happen to think it's sexy when a woman knows her own mind. What I was saying is, sharing is a two-way street. For this experiment to work, it needs to be mutual. I share something personal with you, and you share something personal with me."

He punctuated the statement by taking another bite.

"Nope." She shook her head.

He chewed and swallowed.

"What are you afraid of?" he taunted. "That I might actually fall in love with you if I knew you better?"

The thought made her entire body vibrate. Keeping her expression neutral, she looked him square in the eyes, hoping he couldn't tell the effect he was having on her.

"Nice try, Fortune," she said. "But this interview isn't about me. It's about you and how you make me feel."

She narrowed her eyes at him and tried not to think about how he had such an ability to get under her skin.

Which did not mean she was falling for him. Besides, the self-help author espoused that a person must go through all five steps before falling in love. They were barely into step one.

Granted, she found him hot as hell. Physically, Camden Fortune was exactly her type. The tall, well-built, rugged, outdoorsy type who seemed just out of her reach. Oh, how she loved a challenge. And there was the quick-witted banter they bandied back and forth. He was fun *and* challenging.

However, his propensity to deflect, to answer questions with a question, could easily be a convenient way to keep her from seeing the real him.

Add to that, when she'd thought she had him all figured out, he'd thrown her a curveball, saying he was investing his inheritance into a summer riding camp for underserved kids to honor his late friend. That said *a lot* about who he was as a person. There was no way a venture like that could be profitable, but he'd used the money to buy the land and the horses. That would be something he could benefit from for the rest of the year since the freebie was only a summer camp.

She thought about all those kids he'd be helping, and she found herself back at square one, finding him exceedingly attractive.

"So, essentially, it *is* about you," he mused, watching her in a way that felt as if he was peering right into her private thoughts.

"Don't be rude," she said. "I'm the one asking the questions and writing the article. If you would rather not participate, it's fine."

Oh, gosh. Why did she say that? It *wouldn't* be fine if he backed out. Because...well, who else would she interview? The truth was, he was the only person she wanted to do this experiment with.

Haley braced herself for him to say he was out, but he didn't. He simply sat there, quietly enjoying his dinner.

As she took another bite, she asked herself the very thing she'd feared he'd ask her after he'd answered the first question.

What am I feeling?

She wasn't sure.

She pondered what she'd tell him if she did share something personal; then she let herself taste the bitterness for a couple of seconds before she swallowed it. There was no sense in dwelling on the past.

THE NEXT AFTERNOON, as Camden mowed the back acres of his property, he couldn't get Haley's voice out of his head.

Are you saying you want me to fall in love with you?

Every time he thought of her saying it—and it had been playing over and over in his head on a continuous loop—he smiled. If anyone could see him as he steered the tractor mower over the land, they'd probably think he looked like an idiot grinning to himself.

Even if it wasn't true. He didn't want to fall in love with anyone. Though, if he was completely honest with himself, it wasn't the most repugnant thought in the world either, if he were capable of falling in love again—which he wasn't. But hypothetically, if he were, she could be a candidate.

It was no secret around town that the Perry sisters were hot. But his cousin Asa had married Haley's sister Lily, and his brother West was engaged to Haley's other sister Tabitha, because they'd found true happiness—true love — with them. That was worth much more than falling for a pretty face.

It seemed like Fortune men had a thing for Perry women.

As far as he was concerned, if he had his choice, he'd pursue Haley. He loved her independent streak and the way she knew her own mind.

Even though he couldn't help her out by answering her questions about his family's past, he respected her for not being deterred. That probably seemed like he was contradicting himself, but everyone had their own path, and she seemed to respect his position when he told her he couldn't talk about it.

Of course, he didn't know much about the mining disaster. It had happened nearly sixty years ago, after all. And everyone in town seemed to have pretty much moved on from it. So what if some crackpot had left a couple of notes around town? The family had collectively concluded that whoever it was had been trying to stir up trouble.

Freya had been particularly insistent that they ignore the rumors and focus on the future. Given that his step-grandmother hadn't asked for anything more after making his dream of starting the ranch come true, who was he to ignore her wishes? If all she wanted in return for her generosity was to bring the family together and honor Elias's dying wish, he would make sure he did his part to make that happen.

Even if it meant putting off Haley Perry.

Thank goodness for the other article she'd asked him to help her with. It was pretty clear they enjoyed each other's company, and helping her with the story for the women's magazine gave them a reason to see each other.

As Camden drove the tractor mower toward the barn, he saw West's car turn off the road and head down the long driveway toward the ranch.

Camden glanced at his phone to check the time. West was a few minutes early, and the mowing had taken longer than he had expected because he'd been so lost in his thoughts rather than concentrating on what he was doing.

His brother and the twins would either have to wait while he showered and cleaned up or they'd have to take him as he was. Even so, Camden parked the big green tractor, jumped down, quickly toweled off and pulled on a fresh white T-shirt from the stack he kept in a supply closet.

By the time he'd walked out of the barn to the parking area near the office, West had the boys out of their car seats and in their stroller.

"Look at you with that stroller," Camden said by way of greeting. "It's like you're the poster dude for father of the year."

West shrugged and smiled down at his babies. "I guess there are worse things that people could call me."

Despite the jabs, Camden was happy to see his brother and the twins. Actually, *happy* wasn't a strong-enough word for it. For nearly two years, the family had believed that West, a former district attorney, was dead, his life cut short by a thug he'd put in prison.

In reality, after the criminal had threatened to end the life of West's girlfriend, Tabitha, West had faked his own death to protect her.

It was only after the thug had died in prison that West felt it was safe enough to resurface. Now every day with him felt like their family had been granted the ultimate do-over or given a gift that kept giving.

This second chance had certainly been a lesson in never taking anyone you loved for granted.

Camden reached down and, one by one, tousled the babies' downy soft hair, and each one grinned up at him in turn. The one-year-old twin boys were a surprise to West, who'd had no idea that Tabitha had been pregnant before his "untimely death." Now the two of them were engaged and making up for lost time. They were the picture-perfect family. So much so that if Camden hung around West long enough, he might almost allow his jaded cynicism about love and marriage to fall away.

Almost.

"Fatherhood is pretty cool," West said as he pushed the

stroller toward Camden's house, which was set at a perpendicular angle from the office. "You ought to try it."

He grunted a noncommittal response.

"Seeing the way you are around Zach and Zane almost makes me believe you could buy into the tradition of love, marriage and babies," West said. "Not that it has to happen in that order."

"Or any order, for that matter," Camden grumbled as he opened the front door and motioned for West to push the stroller into the house.

"So what order are things happening with Haley Perry?" West asked.

Camden flinched at the mention of her name and walked into the kitchen.

"What are you talking about?" he said, turning to the refrigerator to search for snacks for the twins and beers for him and West—if he didn't throw his brother out for asking nosy questions.

"I heard through the grapevine that you had a date with Haley last night," West said.

"A date?" Camden said. "Nope."

"So you weren't out with Haley Perry?"

"We had dinner," he confirmed. "But it wasn't a date. Why does everyone have to jump to conclusions when they have no idea what the truth is?"

West raised his brows at Camden in a look that made him painfully aware that he might be protesting too much.

"According to my sources, you had dinner with Haley at the Chatelaine Bar and Grill. Yet you say it wasn't a date. I don't understand. I mean, you were out with *Haley Perry*. Every available guy with a beating heart in Chatelaine wants to date her."

Camden wasn't sure what to say. He didn't want to tell West that she had been poking around, asking questions about the mining disaster. Then again, the dinner had nothing to do with that. Haley had kept her word and hadn't brought up her investigation, but how was he supposed to explain the new article she was writing? He was squeamish about telling West details of the experiment.

When he didn't answer right away, West pushed. "Okay, if it wasn't a date, what was it?"

Camden lifted his hands, palms up. "It was two friends having a meal together."

A wry smile spread over his brother's face.

"That's not what I heard."

"What *did* you hear?" Camden asked.

Before the other man could answer, one of the babies started crying, and West bent down to pick him up, only to have the other boy start wailing.

"Here, hold Zach while I get Zane," he said, and plunked the baby into Camden's outstretched hands.

He loved his nephews, but he had to admit, it felt odd holding the child. It was as if he moved the wrong way, he might unintentionally break his little body.

No, paternal feelings did not come naturally to him at all.

Camden shifted from one foot to the other as the little red-faced guy squalled at the top of his lungs.

"*Shhh*, Zach," Camden coaxed. "It's okay. Your daddy will be right with you. In the meantime, I'm not going to hurt you."

At least, not on purpose, he thought as he eyed his brother, who was holding the other kid. The boys were dressed exactly alike. When he looked down to see if he could tell them apart, he realized he was still holding the baby at arm's length, away from his body.

"How in the world do you tell which is which?" Camden asked. "I'd have to put an ink dot on one of them so I could keep them straight.

West smiled, clearly enamored. "It was hard at first, but now I just know. They're unique little guys."

Camden would have to take West's word for it. He tried to mimic the way his brother cradled Zane to his chest and gently rocked the baby back and forth.

West looked so natural.

And so happy.

Camden, on the other hand, felt inept and out of his league. Praying he wouldn't drop Zach, he adjusted his grip on the baby's tiny leg.

After West returned Zane to the stroller, he looked up and smiled at Camden's awkward attempt to calm the baby.

Much to his surprise, Zach wasn't crying anymore.

"Look at you," West praised. "You might even give me a run for my money in the competition for father of the year."

"Heh." The response sounded more like a croak than a word. "Not if I can help it."

Camden handed the baby to his brother. West took him and set him in the stroller next to Zane.

"Why do you pretend to be so against settling down?" West's expression looked sincere, devoid of all earlier ribbing. "It's the best thing that's happened to me."

Camden drew in a slow, deep breath as he weighed his words carefully.

"You're lucky to have found Tabitha," he said. "If ever two people were meant for each other, you are. I haven't been so fortunate."

"Are you still brooding over Joanna?"

The mention of her name no longer packed the same

punch in the gut it used to carry. Instead, Camden felt nothing, which was exactly the way he wanted it.

After all, the opposite of love wasn't hate. It was *indifference.*

He'd fallen hard for Joanna. She'd used him and then moved on to greener pastures. But they'd been broken up for two years. He was happy he felt nothing for her.

All that was left was an instinctual warning at the sound of her name. It reminded him of what a fool he'd been for trusting her.

If she could pull the wool over his eyes, any woman could.

If he let them.

He didn't plan on letting anyone get that close ever again.

End of story.

"No, I'm not still 'brooding over Joanna.' I've moved on. Even so, it's going to be a while before I let myself trust anyone again."

Desperate to change the subject, Camden asked, "So, speaking of trust, Tabitha is okay with you taking the babies out and about like this? Or does she know you have them?"

West laughed. "Of course she knows. I wanted to give her some time with her sister. Which is how I know that you had dinner with Haley last night and that you've agreed to serve as her guinea pig for this experiment she'd doing. You must not be as against falling in love as you claim if you're willing to put it to the test."

Irritation needled Camden's temper.

This was getting old.

He frowned. Maybe West wasn't as good at picking up on nonverbal cues as he had thought. He was opening his mouth to tell him to knock it off when his brother said,

"Clearly, you don't want to talk about it. So this is the last thing I'll say..."

West gave him a look that was a little too smug for Camden's liking and continued. "You think you have a handle on everything—that no one's going to break through these iron walls you've erected around yourself. But sometimes love has a way of slipping in through the cracks when you least expect it. I know Joanna did a number on you, but I hope you won't let her take a chance at real love away from you. I'm just saying."

"I DON'T UNDERSTAND why you won't call it a date," Tabitha said as she topped off Haley's wineglass.

She shook her head. "Sorry, Tabs, it doesn't work that way. I can't wish something into fruition."

"So you're saying if you could wish it into being, you would?" Tabitha smiled over her wineglass and raised a perfectly groomed, knowing eyebrow at her sister.

"I didn't say that. You're taking my words out of context."

"The only context I care about pertains to you and Camden ending up together. You two are perfect for each other. Think about it. Lily is married to Asa, who is my cousin-in-law. Wouldn't it be fun if we were married to brothers? Our husbands would be best friends, and we're best friends. It would be awesome!"

"I don't know about that," Haley said. "It sounds nice, but too much togetherness doesn't always work out."

Tabitha tsked. "Of course it would work out like that."

One of the things she envied about her sister was her ability to believe that the fairy tale would come true. Despite everything they'd been through, Tabitha still managed to see the bright side. Even though Tabitha had been the only one of them to actually get adopted, her life hadn't been easy. Her adoptive parents had taken her in because her blond hair and green eyes suited their family's looks and made her appear to be their natural child. However, in reality, they'd been cold and stern. They gave her a good life, but they were also proof that no amount of money and social status could make a person loving and nurturing. After believing she'd lost West and having the miracle of miracles happen-West coming back from the dead so to speak—

maybe it wasn't so ridiculous that she believed she could literally wish the impossible into becoming reality.

Too bad Haley didn't share her sister's indomitable faith.

If Tabitha was the wide-eyed believer and Lily was the deep feeler, Haley was the jaded realist.

"I mean, you saw how interested West was in hearing about your date—"

"I told you, it wasn't a date."

"Okay, *business meeting.* Whatever. Call it what you want. He and I are both all for you and Cam getting together. Couldn't you tell how interested he was in getting the scoop before he and the babies left to go to Camden's ranch?"

Haley's stomach fluttered. She hadn't realized that was where West had been headed. He hadn't said anything about where he was going. She quickly replayed the conversation in her head, hoping she hadn't said anything that would lead him to believe her dinner with Camden had been anything other than what it was—a friendly evening out between…friends. One friend who was helping another out with a work project.

"I don't know about that," Haley said, picking up her wineglass. "The way I read it was that he was being cordial to your sister because he's a nice guy. You're lucky to have him."

"I know I am." Tabitha smiled and stared dreamily into the distance, sipping her wine.

Haley was certain her sister was going to let it drop, but then she said, "Camden is a nice guy too."

Yes, he was a nice guy. A nice guy who loved to flirt. And once he got an inkling that the object of his flirting was starting to take it seriously, he backed way off. Case in point was when she'd joked about him wanting her to fall in love with him. He'd backed way up. So fast that if their server hadn't picked that moment to deliver the food, Haley thought he might've hightailed it out of the restaurant.

If she was honest, she was a little bit disappointed that Camden was all flirt and no action. Now that both her sisters were happily committed, Haley felt like the odd duck out. More than she'd like to admit, it played on the old insecurities she thought she'd laid to rest after she and her sisters had discovered each other and reunited more than a decade ago.

She finally had blood relatives. No, more than that—she finally had *sisters*. Family who seemed to need her as much as she needed them. Now both Lily and Tabitha were branching out and starting their own lives. Sure, they were as close as ever, but Lily's and Tabitha's priorities were different. And they should be. But for once in her life, Haley wished she could fall in love and be the heart and center of someone's life.

Maybe she would find him someday—a man who loved her for who she was—a nontraditional, challenging, sometimes-headstrong woman who knew her own mind and wasn't afraid to say what everyone else was thinking. Sadly, it seemed that man wouldn't be Camden Fortune. Lily and Tabitha would have that closer-than-close relationship Tabitha had been talking about a moment ago. But Haley would be on the outside looking in.

That was the story of her life.

"What?" asked Tabitha.

"Nothing." Haley shrugged and blinked away the thoughts that were threatening to bring her down.

Every single thing she was thinking might be true, but feeling sorry for herself was a waste of time.

"Actually, there is something," Haley said.

Tabitha leaned in from her place on the sofa. Her green eyes were large with concern.

"What is it?"

She waved her hand. "Oh, no, it's nothing to worry about. At least, not for you. But I'm so close to being able to break this story about the 1965 mining disaster, I can feel it, but I need to get answers to a few missing pieces."

Tabitha's concern gave way to a grimace, and she looked uncomfortable.

"I know you can't help me," Haley said. "I won't ask you to betray your husband or do anything that might jeopardize your standing with your new family."

She paused and checked her tone to make sure she didn't sound petulant. The bigger part of her would never ask her sister to go against her new family, but the tiny abandoned child that still lived deep inside her wanted to cry, *What about me? I'm your family, too, and you know what this story means to me and my career.*

"Never mind. I don't want to put you in the middle—but I feel like I'm so close to a breakthrough."

Haley shook her head as if to dismiss the subject, but she noticed a certain look on Tabitha's face. A look that wasn't quite the stone wall Haley thought she'd sensed a moment ago.

"What?"

Looking pensive, Tabitha bit her bottom lip.

Haley held her breath, fearing if she said another word,

it would spoil the mood and Tabitha might decide against sharing whatever was clearly on her mind.

Finally, her sister said, “If I share something, do you promise to keep it to yourself?”

Haley nodded. She would never betray her sister’s confidence.

“This might not be anything, but…” Tabitha seemed to be weighing her words. Finally, she breathed in and exhaled resolutely.

“So, a while ago, West’s step-grandmother, Freya, stopped by with baby gifts, but I got the feeling that the gifts were an excuse for her to backtrack on something she’d said in passing another time when we were with her.”

“What did she say?” Haley asked curiously.

“She mentioned that she had a daughter and the two have been estranged—for decades. But when she dropped by with the baby gifts, she admitted she felt a little vulnerable after revealing that she and her daughter were on the outs.”

Tabitha paused and the sisters looked at each other.

“I mean, it might not be anything,” Tabitha said. “But honestly, it was the vibe she was giving off, more so than the fact that she and her daughter are estranged, that doesn’t quite sit right with me.”

“What did you say to her?” Haley asked.

“It was a little awkward and of course, we both wanted to make her feel better because she was clearly distressed about it. So we told her we were glad she’d opened up to us and that we were sorry about the estrangement. I mean, we both know what it’s like to be separated from the people you love.”

Tabitha gestured back and forth between Haley and herself and then made a sweeping motion with her hand, which Haley interpreted to include the sisters growing up apart and the time Tabitha and West had been separated.

"You said it was her vibe more than her words that didn't sit right with you? So what do you think? Were you picking up on something?"

Tabitha shook her head. "I don't know. I'd never say this to West—or anyone else, for that matter—but Freya is such an odd duck."

"I know she is," Haley said. "No offense to your fiancé—I think he's a great guy. But there have been so many problems in the Fortune family's history."

She almost asked Tabitha if she was having second thoughts about going through with the wedding. After all, by marrying him, she wasn't only getting West—she was getting the entire family. Haley wondered how much of her own angst she was projecting onto her sister, who was, after all, opening up to her.

Haley scooted to the edge of the couch and looked at her earnestly.

"Is it possible that her daughter could be the fifty-first miner those two notes that were left in town hinted at?"

"I hope not," Tabitha said. "Because that would mean her daughter was..."

Her sister grimaced rather than say the word *dead.*

"I don't think the daughter could be the fifty-first miner because Freya is relatively new to Chatelaine," Tabitha mused.

Who is leaving the notes? Haley wondered, but she wasn't about to ask the question because she felt like she was already skirting dangerously close to the edge of her sister's comfort zone.

Tabitha sighed. "Oh, and there was one other thing..." She shifted in her seat and glanced around the room, even though it was only the two of them. "I shouldn't be talking about this. You have to promise me that you won't tell anyone I told you."

Haley held up her hands. "You know you can trust me with anything, Tabs. I would never betray your confidence."

Her sister nodded. "I know. That's why I'm going to tell you this."

The sisters locked gazes, and Haley decided to let Tabitha speak first.

After a long moment, she said, "There was another weird Freya incident. She told West and me that she thought someone was following her."

Haley's eyes went wide. "Did she know who?"

Tabitha nodded. "Remember that woman named Morgana who showed up in town a few months ago? You, Lily and I were together, and she asked us to recommend a hotel?"

Haley nodded. "Yeah, remember how cagey she got after we introduced ourselves? She would only tell us her first name."

"Yes," said Tabitha. "Turns out her last name is Mills."

"Is she the one following Freya?" Haley scooted to the edge of her seat. "That day, I told you there was something going on with her. Didn't I?"

"You're a reporter," Tabitha deadpanned. "You think everyone has a secret."

Haley shrugged. "Most people do—but tell me about Morgana Mills."

"Not only did she check into the Chatelaine Motel, but she also got a job there."

"That's where Freya lives, right?"

This wasn't really explosive information. The Chatelaine Motel was the only lodging in town, but there was a good reason for that. Chatelaine wasn't exactly a tourist hot spot. People usually came to town and stayed for a reason.

"Yes." Tabitha raised her brows. "I don't know Morgana well, but others say she's been cagey with them about why she's in town—not that she owes anyone an explanation. But Freya swore Morgana has been watching her. Freya says every time she looks over her shoulder, there's Morgana. Someone told Freya that the woman had been asking questions about the old mine collapse."

Haley's mouth fell open. "The mine collapse? Hey, back off. That's *my* story! Do you think she's a reporter?"

"Who knows."

"What does West think? Have you two discussed it?"

"He says the truth always comes out."

"Yeah, one way or another," Haley said, feeling territorial and more motivated than ever to get to the bottom of the story before Morgana scooped her.

Tabitha held up her hand. "Wait, this is the most important part. West told me he is convinced Freya is hiding something."

CHAPTER FOUR

HALEY SPENT A restless night tossing and turning, mentally sifting through the unexpected windfall of information Tabitha had shared with her. Finally, as darkness surrendered to dawn, she gave up the futile attempt of going back to sleep and got out of bed.

After showering and dressing in her favorite pair of jeans and a cotton button-down, Haley pulled her wet hair into a ponytail and settled at her kitchen table with a piece of toast, a cup of coffee and her notebook. She'd written down all that Tabitha had shared with her, leaving out the attribution of where she'd learned the news in case anyone got ahold of her notebook. It was unlikely, but in a town where the Fortunes vastly outnumbered the rest, one could never be too careful.

First and foremost, she would never betray her sister's confidence. However, why would Tabitha have shared this information if she hadn't intended for Haley to use it for her story? She would simply have to be careful and strategic in what she did with it.

Gazing over her coffee cup, she spied the framed photo of their mother standing behind a triplet stroller, which held Haley and her sisters. She had paused on the Chatelaine Dude Ranch's family trail at the point where it curved in an S-shape around an old oak tree. Her mother was smiling at the camera as if she didn't have a care in the world.

According to Val Hensen—the former owner of the

ranch, who had snapped the photo all those years ago—the picture had been taken the day before the accident that had killed Haley's parents. It was the only photo they had of their mother. They'd never seen a picture of their father.

Haley thought about what it would be like to protect a loved one at all costs. She tried to imagine how she would feel if the tables were turned. What if a reporter caught a whiff of a story that would potentially ruin her parents' reputation?

Would she protect her parents, who were long gone, or would she understand the journalist's need to tell the story?

Of course, if her parents' had cost fifty—and maybe fifty-one—people their lives, wouldn't the community and the families of the victims deserve to know the truth?

After mulling it over for a few moments as she drank a second cup of coffee, she still believed the truth outweighed the need to protect the wrongdoers.

It was common decency.

She decided her next order of business would be to go to the Chatelaine Motel to talk to Freya Fortune. If she got there early, maybe she could accidentally-on-purpose bump into the old woman and strike up a conversation with her.

Of course, she needed to be prepared. Because she was sure the first question out of Freya's mouth would be what on earth Haley was doing at the Chatelaine Motel at that hour of the morning. For that matter, she realized, her jeans and casual blouse wouldn't cut it if she was going to get the woman—who always looked nice—to open up to her.

As she changed into a tailored skirt and a dressier blouse, Haley racked her brain, trying to come up with a plausible reason she just happened to be in Freya Fortune's neighborhood.

That might be tricky.

Maybe she could say she was headed to the Cowgirl Café and ask Freya to join her. No, that wouldn't work. It wasn't in her budget to treat Freya to breakfast. Even if Haley had the discretionary funds at her disposal, it would look fishy inviting a woman she barely knew—for that matter, a woman who had studiously avoided her—to breakfast.

As she got into her car, she pondered the logistics of pretending she was making a delivery. She could knock on Freya's door with flowers from a secret admirer… Or maybe muffins?

The problem with that was the GreatStore didn't open until nine o'clock. It was only seven thirty. By the time the place opened, there was a good possibility Freya would already be out and about. Plus, wouldn't deliveries like that usually go through the motel's office? Even if she didn't follow protocol, what was she supposed to do after she handed over the supposed special delivery? It's not as if that would soften the woman and suddenly inspire her to invite Haley inside and spill her guts.

Realizing she was fresh out of options as she turned into the Chatelaine Motel's parking lot, she accepted the reality that her only choice was the straightforward approach. She needed to be up front and tell Freya she was working on a story about the 1965 mine disaster and that she would like to interview her.

The Chatelaine Motel was an older motor lodge at the tail end of the main street that ran through town. Because of its location, it was a bit removed from where the action was—if you could say that Chatelaine had any *action*. It was the only game in town when it came to lodging.

The two-story motel was comprised of fourteen rooms, all of which were accessible from an outside corridor.

There was an office, where owner Hal Appleby worked and checked in new guests.

Despite the peeling paint, there was something comforting about its kitschy seventies vibe, and from what Haley understood, the place was clean and well managed.

As she drove past the office, she saw a warm light glowing through the windows and caught a glimpse of Hal, who was sitting at the front desk, looking down at something in front of him.

Haley scanned the row of vehicles parked in the spaces facing the building. Freya's newer-model Mercedes Benz was parked directly in front of her first-floor unit. Haley steered her car into the first empty space she could find.

Her heart was thudding as she sat there listening to the pings and ticks of her car's engine. She put her hand on her chest and drew in a deep breath.

Why was she so scared? This was a core part of an investigative reporter's job. In fact, if she had a prosperous career, she'd be dealing with people who were bigger, badder and much scarier than Freya Fortune.

In all fairness, the eighty-something woman was formidable. She was tall and in good shape for her age. She wore her hair in a stylish ash-blond bob with bangs. Not only did she always look as if she'd just stepped out of the salon, she dressed very well. Haley cringed at her near wardrobe mistake and smoothed the fabric of her navy blue skirt.

She could do this.

Freya wasn't an ogre. In fact, to hear Tabitha and Lily tell it, the woman came across as a warm and loving stepgranny when she was around her relatives.

However, to Haley, she'd been an ice queen. Was knocking on this woman's door uninvited *really* a good idea?

She swallowed hard as she pondered the question.

Technically, Freya hadn't even been in Chatelaine

when the mining accident happened—or at least as far as Haley knew.

In fact, the woman had only been married to Elias Fortune for a decade before he died. What could she possibly know about the disaster?

Then again, Elias Fortune was one of the owners of the mine. Maybe he had confided in his wife. Plus, loving step-granny aside, even Tabitha and West thought something was not necessarily on the up-and-up with the woman.

First, there was her estranged daughter…and then there was the way she had wigged out when she thought Morgana Mills was following her.

Yes, there was definitely a story here. And if Freya was indeed hiding something, Haley intended to find out.

Haley jotted down several questions she wanted to ask Freya—in case her mind went blank when she was looking at the whites of the woman's eyes. Then she killed the engine, took a final fortifying breath and got out of the car.

She knocked on the door to unit five and waited.

She could hear a bird chirping over the sounds of traffic chugging to life on Main Street. As she was mentally rehearsing what she would say when Freya opened the door, Haley thought she saw the curtains flutter out of the corner of her eye. But when she looked, they'd stopped moving. Had someone—Freya—been peeking out to see who was calling? Given how still the curtains were now, it certainly hadn't been the air conditioner making them move. Despite the fact that in an outdated place like this, the AC was usually located right under the front window.

Haley knocked again.

And waited.

"Well, Freya, bad news," she murmured. "Your car is here. So I know you're in there, and I have all day. You've got to come out sometime."

The door to unit four—next door to Freya's place—opened, and Morgana Mills stepped out.

Haley hadn't seen her since the day she and her sisters had met her, but she instantly recognized the pretty, tall young woman with medium-length brown hair and startling green eyes.

"Excuse me?" she said to Haley. "Did you say something?"

Haley glanced at Freya's door and then back at the woman, who was pushing a cleaning cart out of the unit. "Oh, no, I was talking to myself. It's a bad habit. But wait—I know you. You're Morgana Mills, aren't you?"

Morgana seemed surprised by the question. Her gaze lingered on her cart, and she seemed to weigh her words before finally saying, "I am. Are you a guest here? Do you need something?"

"No, I'm not a guest. My name is Haley Perry. We met a few months ago when you first got to town. I was with my sisters, and you asked us about places to stay."

Haley held out her hand, and Morgana eyed it as if it might be a trick. Finally, she gave it a perfunctory shake before stepping back behind her cart, as if seeking refuge.

"Is there something I can do for you?" Morgana asked, glancing hesitantly from Freya's door to Haley.

Haley smiled. "I hope so. I'd love to buy you a cup of coffee. Do you have time now?"

"Oh, thanks, but no. I just started my shift, and I can't take a break for a while." After a beat of silence, she asked cautiously, "Why would you want to buy me coffee?"

"Fair question," Haley said. "I heard that you've been inquiring about the 1965 Fortune mine disaster, and I was curious to know why. Are you a reporter?"

Morgana's eyes widened, and Haley saw the woman's throat work as she swallowed.

"No, I'm not a reporter." Morgana held up her hands. "Look, I don't mean any harm. I'm new to Chatelaine, and I'm interested in the town's history. That's all."

She looked a little frightened for someone claiming to be a history buff.

"It's okay," Haley assured her. "I *am* a reporter, and I'm working on a story about the mine and was wondering if we could compare notes."

"Oh… Well…" Morgana looked as if she was about to say something, but the door to one of the rooms located farther down the corridor opened, and a woman in a white terry bathrobe stepped out.

"Excuse me, miss? May I trouble you for some extra towels?"

"Certainly," Morgana called, then turned back to Haley. "Sorry, I have to get back to work. I can't afford to get fired."

As Morgana maneuvered the cart in the direction of the woman, Haley called out, "Can I meet you later when you take your break?"

Morgana quickened her pace and didn't look back.

"Well, shoot," Haley murmured as she watched Morgana interact with the guest and then disappear into another room.

She considered whether or not to knock on Freya's door again.

It probably wasn't a good idea. She didn't want to get Morgana in trouble for talking when she was supposed to be working. If Freya had seen or heard them, she might tell Hal Appleby. If Morgana got fired and Hal barred Haley from the property, it would make it more difficult to get in touch with Freya.

If she left now, she could come back another time.

And she *would* be back.

Freya was in that motel room and wasn't answering the door. And this Morgana Mills woman… Suffice to say, it didn't take an investigative journalist to deduce that she was up to something. Morgana and Freya had information that could further Haley's story, and she intended to get them to talk.

Resigned, she got into her car and was putting the key in the ignition when her phone rang. The name on the display screen was Camden Fortune.

Her heart kicked into high gear.

"Camden, hi," she said, doing her best to hold her voice steady.

"Hey there." His timbre was as smooth as velvet and twice as lush. She wanted to wrap herself in it. "Do you have a minute?" he asked.

"For you? Always." It was so much fun to flirt with him. Like second nature.

"So, I was thinking…" he began.

What? That you've decided you're madly in love with me and can't live without me?

"That's always a good thing to do," she said. "Thinking, I mean. Thinking is always good."

His chuckle was a low rumble, and she felt it in her solar plexus.

"Yeah, well, with you, I always have to be one step ahead."

"You do?"

Why not walk beside me? Or better yet, lie beside me? Or on top of me...that would be very nice...

She bit her bottom lip against the heat that was simmering in her most intimate places.

Camden Fortune, if you only knew what you do to me.

"I went out and picked up a copy of that book you're testing out. I was thinking about step number two: *help with something important to the person.* I have to be honest, I'm not quite sure who is supposed to help whom—if I'm supposed to help you with something or if you're supposed to help me. But I thought if you were free tonight, maybe you could stop by and take a look at the brochure mock-ups for Camp JD. Our *Five Easy Steps to Love* project aside, I value your professional opinion as a writer, and I'd love for you to take a look."

"You named the camp?" she asked.

"I did. The official name is the Josh Dunn Camp at Chatelaine Stables. Camp JD for short. After talking to you last night, I realized that since Josh was the inspiration for the camp, it made sense to name it after him. What do you think?"

"I think it's wonderful, Camden," she said. "I'll bet Josh would be very honored."

"So..." He drew out the word. "Are you free tonight? If so, I'll cook dinner for you. It won't be anything fancy. I was going to throw some chicken on the grill."

"Sounds delicious," she said. "How about if I bring my famous potato salad?"

"Since you're helping me out with the brochure, I wasn't expecting you to bring anything," he said. "But since you say it's your *famous* potato salad, how can I say no?"

Actually, she'd made the potato salad only once for a potluck, but her friends had raved about it. She'd gotten the recipe off a food blogger's website, but Camden didn't need to know that. As far as he was concerned, it was Haley Perry's famous potato salad.

That was her story, and she was sticking to it.

Now she hoped she could find the recipe again.

"If this dish of yours is so famous, why haven't I heard of it?"

"You haven't invited me to dinner before tonight."

"Touché. To give you fair warning, if it's as good as you say, I might fall in love with it. Then I'm going to expect you to share your recipe. Are you prepared for that?"

"But if I gave you the recipe, then it'll no longer be Haley Perry's Famous Potato Salad. So, to give *you* fair warning, you'd better guard your heart."

She cringed a little at the awkwardness of the conversation, but when he laughed, there was nothing awkward about the rich sound, and Haley's stomach flip-flopped.

"I'll see you tonight," she said, feeling a little breathless and off-balance—the way only Camden Fortune seemed to make her feel.

"Yeah, I'm looking forward to it."

As she hung up the phone, she smiled and did a little victory shimmy.

THAT EVENING, CAMDEN was sitting on the front porch when Haley arrived, carrying a covered glass bowl.

He stood to greet her. "That's your famous potato salad?"

"The real deal," she answered as he took the bowl from her and motioned for her to come into the house. "Don't be fooled by imitations."

"Good to know," he said as he put the bowl in the refrigerator. "I'll be on my guard."

He drank her in as she stood in his kitchen. She was wearing a Ramones T-shirt and a pair of jeans that looked soft and faded and hugged her curves in a way that made him envious. He loved the way she always seemed so at home in her own skin, so natural and at ease.

"What?" she asked, and he realized he'd been staring at her too long.

He smiled and deflected. "The chicken is on the grill, and it needs to cook a little longer," he said. "Do you want to see the barn? I've put everything away since you were here last."

"I'd love to see it."

"How about a beer for the tour?" he offered.

Haley nodded. "Sure, thanks."

He took two cold bottles from the fridge, opened them and handed one to her. He motioned for her to follow him out the kitchen door, where they fell into step as they walked to the other side of the ranch where the camp stables were located.

"Where are the horses?" she asked.

He frowned and looked around. "Aw, man. I knew I forgot something. No, seriously, they're at the stables on the other end of the ranch."

As he pointed out the camp's features—the stalls, the tack and feed rooms within the stable, the indoor arena where he would give lessons, and the outdoor riding area—he tried to see everything through her eyes.

"This is tremendous," she gushed. "The kids are going to love it!"

He beamed with pride, but sobered when he remembered how it had all come to be.

"Ever since Josh's accident, it's been my dream to start a program that offers riding classes for kids during the year. They'll pay on a sliding scale, whatever their families can afford. But the summer camp that teaches kids how to ride safely will be free to all kids. Everyone deserves to learn the basics so they can be safe. Especially in this area, where there are so many horses. I don't want another child or family to suffer what Josh and his folks went through after he was thrown."

"I can't imagine how difficult that was for his family," she said. "How old was he?"

"He was ten. We both were. He was my best friend. We

did everything together, like you do when you're a kid. It was so difficult to understand how he could be here one minute and gone the next."

His throat became tight and he didn't know if he could say more without getting emotional. He'd better get used to it because by naming the camp after Josh, he'd be telling his buddy's story a lot. It needed to be told.

"It's so good of you to do this," she said. "But I have to say, horses are expensive. If the majority of your lessons and camps are for those without the ability to pay, how are you going to keep your doors open? If you don't mind me asking, that is. I mean, if that's not too personal."

She shrugged, looking a little embarrassed by the question.

"I don't mind you asking," he said. "Of course, I'll apply for grants and I will shamelessly beg for donations. So if you know anyone with a pile of money that they're not using, I could put it to good use."

She laughed, "I think you'd be in a better position to know people like that. Especially those who enjoy horses."

"Do you ride?" he asked curiously.

She shook her head. "No, I never learned. If I'm completely honest, I'm actually a little bit afraid of horses. Don't judge."

She pulled a face.

"No judgment here," he promised. "It's smart to have a healthy equestrian fear if you don't know how to handle them. Riding is like any sport. It's physical and it requires a number of learned skills and practice. It's like someone who doesn't know how to ski—it would be unsafe to leave them to their own devices at the top of a black diamond mountain."

She nodded. "A lot of the kids I went to school with were into horses, but I never learned how to ride."

"Why not?" he asked.

She shrugged and shook her head. "I never had the opportunity."

"I could teach you," he offered.

She looked taken aback. "Oh, well, thanks, but..." She looked at him then looked away. "There's not much in my budget for riding lessons these days."

"I wouldn't charge you," he said as they started walking back toward the house.

"Don't be ridiculous," she protested. "You'll be giving away plenty of freebies. You don't need to waste your time on me."

"No time I spent with you would be wasted time."

That hadn't quite come out the way it had sounded in his head.

She blinked. "Well, thank you. It's nice of you to say that."

"Before you leave here tonight, let's get a riding lesson on the books. Think of it as giving me an opportunity to try out my program. A dress rehearsal, of sorts." He paused. "But we should head back to the house now. I need to check on the chicken."

As they walked, she glanced over at him shyly; it was a look he wasn't used to seeing on her face.

"I'm not used to accepting things for free," she admitted. "What if we did a trade of some kind?"

"A trade? What do you mean?"

"What if you taught me how to ride and I wrote a story about Camp JD at the Chatelaine Stables? Maybe it would help you attract some sponsors or donors? Or even kids in need of lessons? I could pitch it to Devin Street. You know him, don't you? He's the owner and editor of the *Chatelaine Daily News*. He seems to love to do human-interest stories like this. I'll bet you he'll go for it."

"I know Devin. He's engaged to my cousin Bea."

"Of course," she said, flushing slightly. "I should have realized that."

"But you'd do that for me?" Camden asked. "Write an article about the camp?"

"I said it would be a *trade*. Riding lessons for a feature story. So it's not like either one of us would be giving away the goods."

He liked that about Haley Perry. She wasn't looking for a handout, and she didn't give much away—in the figurative or literal sense. There wasn't a single guy this side of Austin who didn't want to date her, but she had the reputation of keeping most men at arm's length.

Last night, Haley had been reluctant to share anything personal about herself. But he got the sense that growing up, she might not have had a lot of extras. Such as horseback riding lessons.

He knew from experience that not having everything handed to you developed a certain type of character that no amount of money could buy.

Although, sometimes a modest upbringing caused some people to carry a chip on their shoulders. His ex, Joanna, was a case in point. She seemed to think the world owed her everything and more. She had been out for anything she could get. He'd been a fool and fallen in love with her. She'd broken up with him as soon as she'd figured out he was a Fortune in name only and he didn't have the privilege some of his cousins enjoyed.

Haley Perry, on the other hand, was a breath of fresh air. She wouldn't even accept a few horseback riding–safety pointers without offering something of value in return. He had nothing but respect for this woman, and out of respect for her, he pushed the memories of Joanna back into the compartment where he'd relegated her since their breakup.

"I can't believe I didn't ask you this last night, but where are you from?" Haley asked.

"My brothers and I were born and raised in Cave Creek, Texas. Have you ever heard of it?"

"I have, but I couldn't find it on a map."

He grinned. "Well, there ya go. That's why we couldn't wait to get the hell out of there once we came of age."

The only time they'd returned to Cave Creek was for their parents' funerals five years ago, but as soon as it was over, they'd all scattered and gone back to where they'd started their new lives.

"Where did you end up?" she asked.

"After college, I went to Dallas, which was the exact opposite of Cave Creek, but it didn't take long for me to discover that I'm not cut out for big cities like that."

"I know what you mean," she said. "I grew up in Goldmine, and I went to college in New York City. I was determined to make it as a big-city reporter. I got a job with the same magazine that I'm freelancing for now, but when the pandemic hit, they laid off a lot of people. I was one of the casualties." She shrugged, but he sensed that she was trying to make light of the situation for his sake. "That's when I started freelancing. Since I can do that from anywhere, I figured I might as well move back to Texas to be closer to my sisters and my mom. But enough about me. Did you come here from Dallas?"

He laughed and shook his head. "Nope. I moved to Waxahachie, which is about thirty miles outside of Dallas. I worked on a ranch that breeds quarter horses. I started out as a ranch hand and worked my way up to foreman after a few years. At the time, it seemed like the best of both worlds. I was doing the work I loved, but I also had proximity to Dallas if I wanted something more, which wasn't very often.

"The only reason I left that job was because of the letter I received from Freya summoning my brother, cousins and me to Chatelaine, where she promised to grant us our most fervent wish."

Her face brightened. "Oh, yeah?"

Haley had such a great smile.

"Yeah, It was pretty much a no-brainer. I'd always wanted a ranch of my own where I could start a camp and do my part to teach kids how to ride." He shook his head, but all the while, he couldn't tear his gaze from Haley. She was so damn pretty.

"It was a dream come true, and I have Freya to thank for making it possible. It was like winning the lottery. Hey, it's a little muggy out here," he said as they approached the house. "Go inside and cool off while I turn the chicken. Then I'll show you the mock-up for the brochure I'm putting together."

CHAPTER FIVE

HALEY COULD NOT believe that Camden had brought up Freya.

It was the opening she'd been waiting for. Even though her sisters had told her all about Freya's largess and how the woman had summoned the Fortune five to Chatelaine to have their wishes granted, Haley wanted to hear Camden's take. Maybe he would end up telling her something she didn't know. That's why she needed to jump at this opportunity and ask as many questions as she could before he clammed up.

After he'd started the grill and set up his laptop on the kitchen island to show her the brochure he'd laid out using a template, she said, "So, let me get this straight. Freya called out of the blue claiming to be your step-grandmother?"

Camden nodded.

"She asked you all to come to Chatelaine and promised to grant you each a wish?"

"Yep," he said, but he'd turned his attention to the computer screen.

"But at this point, none of you had ever met her?"

He sighed and raised his brows. "Right."

"Oh, that's not weird at all." She grimaced. "It sounds like the plot of a movie where someone gets swindled."

Camden turned his palms up and gave a half shrug.

"I know," he said. "It sounds crazy. Things like that

never happen to my cousins and me—or at least not me. I don't have a history of being lucky."

Haley gave him a dubious look. "Come on, you're a Fortune. You were born lucky."

Camden laughed. "Despite the Fortune last name, I never grew up with any of the perks. So this sudden windfall was unexpected. For all of us. I thought I'd be working for someone else for the rest of my life. That's one of the reasons that it's important to me to pay forward my good fortune and help others."

He was a good guy. There was no doubt about it.

Haley didn't feel quite so virtuous as she racked her brain for a way to turn the conversation back to Freya, but keeping him talking about the Fortunes was a necessary means to an end.

"So you'd never met this woman, and out of the blue she tracked you down. Didn't you worry that her offer might be a scam? I mean, come on. It has all the makings of a con job. I would've been skeptical as all get out."

"Sure. All of us were suspicious at first, but her only stipulation was that we all come to Chatelaine. We figured there was strength in numbers since there were five of us—or four, actually, since my brother Bear refused Freya's call. And at that time, we thought West was dead." He glanced back at the computer, clearly wanting to change the subject. "We're not dumb. Before my family and I uprooted our lives, we vetted her, and everything checked out."

Haley nodded and bit the insides of her cheeks to keep from blurting out that she knew for a fact West thought there was something fishy about Freya.

But she'd promised Tabitha she wouldn't say anything to anyone about what she'd told her in confidence. Haley wasn't about to betray her sister—and of course, West had no part in the Freya-vetting process and hadn't gotten his wish granted because everyone thought he was dead.

After his miraculous comeback, Freya had been willing to grant him a wish, but he'd said the only thing he wanted was to be a good father.

Tabitha had mentioned that Freya doted on the twins and spoiled them with gifts, the amount of money she'd spent on the babies paled in comparison to what his brother and cousins had received.

West was a good guy. He had always done right by Tabitha. And he was smart. He seemed to sense when people had motives, which probably stemmed from him being a lawyer and dealing with all sorts.

Haley wished she'd asked Tabitha if West's gut feeling that something was fishy about Freya had played into his essentially refusing her offer to grant him a wish.

She made a mental note to ask Tabitha about it later. In the meantime, she needed to keep Camden talking about Freya because this might be the only opportunity she'd have to ask him questions.

"Here, take a look at this and tell me what you think," Camden said.

Haley looked at the computer page and scrolled down to glance at the rest of the brochure. "It looks fine, but why don't you have any photos of the ranch? These look like stock photos."

"That's because they *are* stock photos," he said. "I haven't had a chance to hire a photographer."

"I think you should," she told him. "You've done a nice job with the place."

"Thanks," he said. "I'll look into hiring someone. What do you think of the wording?"

"It's a little difficult to read it on the computer. Can you print it out?"

"Sure."

As Camden keyed in the commands to print the brochure, Haley steered the conversation back to Freya. She had to keep him talking.

"Now that you've had a chance to get to know her, what do you think of your step-grandmother, Freya?"

Camden made a face. "What do I think of her? I don't know what you mean."

"I mean, she was married to your grandfather, Elias, who you never knew, right?"

Camden nodded, then narrowed his eyes at her. She could hear the printer working in the distance.

"Right." Camden's voice was flat.

Uh-oh. She was losing him. She needed to turn this around and fast.

"I'm curious about what she's like," Haley said.

"Why does it matter?"

"Because it's interesting, Camden," she replied. "Think about it. Freya knew your grandfather. She had a life with him. Have you asked questions about him? Was she willing to share anything to help you get to know him better?"

He ran a hand through his hair, looking away from her for a moment toward the living room, where the printer had finished its job.

Finally, he said, "Is this Haley Perry the reporter asking or Haley my...*friend* wanting to know?"

Her heart twisted a little at the word *friend* because she feared that she'd already been friend-zoned. But they *were* friends. What else was he supposed to call her? She certainly wasn't his girlfriend.

They hadn't even kissed.

All of a sudden, she realized she wanted to kiss him. In an *epic* way. She wanted to crawl across the kitchen island, put her hands on each side of his face, and cover her mouth with his and—

Yeah, that's not happening.

She swallowed hard, trying to wash away the thought, digging deep for something else.

"I guess what I'm asking is… I think I told you that my parents died when I was a baby. I have no memories of them. Val Hensen gave my sister Lily a photo of our mother with the three of us. Do you know Val?"

"Of course I do. She's the one who sold the Chatelaine Dude Ranch to my cousin Asa."

"Lily asked questions about the photo, but Val didn't have a lot of information to offer… But if my sisters and I met someone who knew our parents well—" she raised a brow at Camden "—like your grandfather's wife surely knew your grandfather, I wouldn't be able to stop asking questions."

He mirrored her expression, raising a brow at her. "You like to ask questions, don't you? That's one of the things that makes you a good reporter."

She rolled her eyes and looked away. On one hand, the quip felt like a personal dig, but on the other hand, it felt as if he was deflecting and trying to change the subject. She decided the best thing to do was to not let him make this about her.

"Don't you want to know about your grandfather?"

Camden shrugged and crossed his arms. "In a lot of ways, he doesn't even seem like a real person to me. I never knew him. He's shrouded in mystery."

Yes! Now we're getting somewhere.

"You mean the mystery of the mining accident?"

Camden's eyes flashed, and he exhaled. "Yeah, right. It always comes back to the mining accident, doesn't it?"

She saw his walls go up and lock into place.

"I need to check on the chicken." His voice was flat.

He hooked a thumb toward the living room. "Make yourself at home. If you still want to look at the brochure, the printer is in there. If not, don't worry about it."

Without another word, he disappeared out the kitchen door.

Okay, then.

Clearly, that was the end of that.

As Haley walked into the living room, she juggled myriad emotions. She felt bad for asking the question, but she felt worse about tossing out the tidbit about her parents' death like bait.

She was ashamed of herself because they were worth more than that.

Looking around the living room, she located the printer and picked up the brochure. She sat down on the couch and tried to read the copy, but when she got to the bottom of the first paragraph, she realized she hadn't comprehended a single word. And it wasn't because the writing was bad.

All she could focus on was this icky, tarry feeling churning in the pit of her stomach that she had not only spent her parents' history like spare change but that she had also broken Camden's trust in the process.

The conundrum was, if she was ever going to get to the bottom of the mining exposé, she had to ask uncomfortable questions. Because she never knew when she'd catch someone with their guard down—or, as with Tabitha last night, catch them when they were ready to share.

But she did not need to use her parents to get what she wanted.

As she sat there, Haley spied a framed photo on the bookshelf. She crossed the room and picked it up. It was a family picture, like the ones they took at church or in a department-store portrait studio. A man and a woman stood behind three young dark-haired boys, beaming at the camera. Haley picked out Camden right away. There was no mistaking those intense green eyes set under that dark brow. The boy to his left had to be West, which meant the third one must be their oldest brother, Bearington—or Bear, as everyone called him. Haley had never met him, since he'd yet to set foot in Chatelaine.

She felt a bittersweet smile turn up the corners of her mouth as that old familiar pang of curiosity laced with the longing that seeped into her when she saw a traditional family.

A family like this was an experience she'd never known. Even though her foster mom, Ramona, had been loving and had worked hard to give Haley a good life, it had just been the two of them. No father figure, no siblings, only the hollowness—a feeling that fate had robbed her of one of the most fundamental foundations of life when her parents had been killed and she and her sisters had been separated as infants.

However, the unfortunate experience had also made her strong and independent, qualities that served her well as an adult. As she returned the photo to its place, she made a mental note to ask Camden about Bear. Or better yet, she should read the brochure and offer him some feedback. That would be a nice, neutral starting point for their dinner conversation.

Much better than pulling at the thread about how Camden was missing his chance to learn more about his grandfather. But in all honesty, she couldn't understand his reluctance to talk about a man he didn't even know.

Then again, maybe he was bluffing. Maybe he knew more than he was letting on and didn't want to share it with her. The same way she wished she wouldn't have blurted out that bit about her parents.

She heard the kitchen door open and close and then the sound of Camden setting the plate of chicken on the quartz countertop.

She joined him in the kitchen.

"That smells delicious," she said.

"There's nothing like barbequed chicken." His tone was lighter than before he'd gone outside, but he wouldn't meet her gaze.

"I'd like to take the printout of the brochure home with me, where I can concentrate," she told him. "I'm not good at doing things like that on the fly."

"Thanks," he said. "There's no hurry."

"In that case, why don't I set the table?" she offered.

Regardless of whether or not he would help her with the Fortune silver-mine story, she enjoyed spending time with him, and she wanted to salvage this night with hopes that it might lead to more time together in the near future.

"That would be great," he said, startling her out of her thoughts. Then she realized he was pointing to a drawer as he basted the chicken with fresh barbeque sauce. "The silverware is right there. The chicken needs to rest for about ten minutes."

He made a tinfoil tent for the bird and set a timer on the stove. As they moved around the kitchen in weighted silence, she gathered everything she needed for the table.

"Want another beer or a glass of wine?" he asked.

"I'd love some wine, thanks."

He opened a bottle and poured the merlot into two goblets. As he handed one to her, she steeled herself and looked him straight in the eyes to see if she could sense any remnants of resentment.

But as they clinked glasses, something else passed between them—something hot and electric. Like a bolt of lightning that was both beautiful and dangerous.

She tore her gaze away, her heart thudding, and her thoughts jumbled as she tried to get back on stable ground.

"Camden, I'm sorry if I pushed too hard a few minutes ago. I know you are protective of your family. I get that—or at least, I get the concept of your loyalty. I think. I love my sisters and my mom, Ramona, but family loyalty like yours is kind of a foreign concept to me. Because you have such a big family."

She bit down on her bottom lip, forcing herself to stop talking before she said too much…again.

They stood there in silence for what felt like ages.

Finally, he said, "How can I understand what family does or doesn't mean to you when you won't tell me, Haley?"

This wasn't what she'd expected him to say. Maybe she'd been bracing herself for him to tell her to mind her own business…anything but *this.*

"I told you that my parents died when I was a baby and I have no memories of them. I don't usually share stuff like that…" Her voice broke. She gave him a one-shoulder shrug and looked away, hating how she felt so vulnerable.

He reached out and put a finger under her chin and gently tilted her face upward until she looked him in the eyes.

"I want to know more about you." His voice was a low, sexy rasp.

"Says he who won't share his life with me," she whispered.

"I want to know what made you the woman you are today."

Her bravado faded as a million thoughts raced through her head.

She remembered herself as a little child. How Ramona had worked as an art teacher at a private school so Haley could get a good education. But she'd been a scholarship kid, and some of the kids used to bully her. She couldn't bring herself to tell Ramona about it. Haley had been afraid that the school's administration would side with the kids who paid tuition and Ramona would lose her job. They never had much money with Ramona working, and Haley feared if she cost her foster mom her job, she might not be able to get another one. It would be her fault, and Ramona might lose custody of her—or worse yet, give her up voluntarily and put her into the foster system.

Growing up, she'd lived with the perpetual feeling that her life was a house of cards and one wrong step would bring it all tumbling down. The kids she went to school with—the ones with strong, influential families and lots of money—had the power to do that. That was one of the reasons she was still uncomfortable around rich people.

Even though Camden hadn't grown up with privilege, he was fully a Fortune now.

Everyone knew the Fortunes were powerful. They protected their own. Like the kids who had never let Haley forget that she didn't belong.

Wendell and Freya Fortune had made it clear they were determined to keep this secret that threatened their family.

It wasn't right that people got away with murder because they had the money to cover up their messes.

But Camden didn't want to hear this.

He probably wouldn't be interested in hearing that even if going toe to toe with the Fortune family opened up Haley's old wounds—made her feel like she wasn't welcome in Chatelaine. But no matter what it took, she refused to back down. She *would* get to the bottom of what happened the night the mine collapsed and make sure everyone knew the truth.

So, Camden was right. It did all come back to the story of the mining disaster. To the possible fifty-first person—nameless and unrecognized as if his or her life had been worthless.

Just like the rich kids had made her feel worthless.

Haley closed her eyes against the sting of gathering tears and turned away, trying to regain her composure.

"Hey, it's okay," Camden soothed. "I didn't mean to upset you. I want to know more about you. You can tell me when you're ready. If you want to..."

She turned back to him, amazed by his gentle tone, unsure what to say. He didn't want to hear how, even now at twenty-nine years old, she still struggled with belonging.

That was one of the reasons she prided herself on being the one to ask the questions and listening to people tell their stories.

Her truth was too difficult, and every time she relived it, a little piece of her died.

She needed to leave it in the past

Taking a deep breath, she tucked a strand of hair behind her ear with one hand and folded the other arm across her chest. Camden was still looking at her. His eyes were dark and hooded, and his lips were parted ever so slightly. She couldn't remember anyone ever looking at her the way he was looking at her now.

The next thing she knew, he had closed the distance between them and was pulling her into his arms. Despite her better judgment, she melted into him. A faint voice in the back of her mind sounded an alarm, reminding her if she wasn't careful, she would mess up everything. But she couldn't make herself pull away.

His arms felt like a sanctuary.

Camden's thumb traced a path along her jawline and up to the corner of her mouth until he'd found the center of her bottom lip; then he paused, as if he was offering her the chance to walk away.

She snared his gaze, telegraphing exactly what she wanted.

He slid his hands down the sides of her body, tracing her curves until his arms closed around her waist. His lips gently brushed hers. A sharp inhale escaped as she opened her mouth, inviting him.

He kissed her deeper, pulled her closer.

Her hands were in his hair, fusing his mouth to hers, and they devoured each other as if their life breath depended on this connection. Camden walked her backward until she gently bumped into the kitchen island. His hips pressed into hers, and all the lines and contours of their bodies meshed.

Haley had no idea how long they stood there ravishing each other's mouths, exploring each other's bodies, but he had slipped his hands under her T-shirt and had started to tug it up and out of the way when the kitchen timer sounded.

He let her shirt fall back into place, and they ripped their mouths away from each other, gasping for air.

Camden pressed his forehead against hers.

"Excuse me," he said thickly. "I need to get that."

The spell was broken. Alarms were sounding in her head.

This could *not* happen.

Camden was a Fortune.

She was the outsider.

"I'm sorry," she said as she moved toward the door. "I just realized that…um… I need to go. I'm sorry, Camden."

WHEN HALEY NEEDED to focus on work, she could put frivolities like a kiss out of her mind.

But kissing Camden Fortune hadn't felt frivolous.

That's why she'd run.

As she descended the stairs that led from the breezeway

of her apartment down to the alley behind Main Street, she could still feel the tingle of his kiss on her lips. She bit her bottom lip, hoping to make it stop, but it buzzed like a bee.

Bees stung if you weren't careful.

As she cleared the last step, she took a deep breath. This was nothing a good walk in the park wouldn't cure. Getting some exercise would help her clear her head and reframe her thoughts so she could focus on the story she needed to crack. If she didn't make a major breakthrough soon, she feared the editor of the *Houston Chronicle* that she'd been talking to might lose interest in the story.

Worse yet, another writer might scoop her story, but given how tight-lipped the Fortunes were, that was unlikely. Still, stranger things had happened. The sooner she confirmed the name of the fifty-first miner, the better.

Reflexively, her fingers went to her lips, and she reminded herself that time was definitely of the essence, which meant she had no time to obsess over Camden Fortune.

Or the fact that at this moment, they had no plans to meet again. Why? Because she'd run away like a scared rabbit. Of course, they still had three points left to explore for the *Five Easy Steps to Love* article, if he didn't think she was an idiot.

Either way, the ball was in her court.

Way to make it awkward, Haley.

She forced herself to focus on the mining story. This stroll she was taking was more than a walk in the park. It was a reconnaissance mission.

A couple of months ago, Asa Fortune, Lily's husband, had been out for a late-night drive when he'd witnessed a mysterious person pinning something to the community bulletin board.

It had been a foggy night, and the way the person

seemed to startle and then disappear into the mist had piqued Asa's curiosity. He'd gotten out of the car to take a closer look and discovered that the note asserted that not fifty, but fifty-one people had died in the 1965 Fortune silver-mine disaster.

This morning, Haley would retrace Asa's steps.

As she walked toward the area where her brother-in-law had found the note, she took her phone out of her wristlet and pulled up the photo he'd snapped of the strange missive. Lily had texted it to Haley thinking it might help her with the story.

Haley enlarged the photo and read the note: 51 died in the mine. Where are the records? What became of Gwenyth Wells?

"Yeah, where *is* Gwenyth Wells?" she murmured. "That seems to be the million-dollar question."

Since no one else wanted to talk about the accident or the missing woman.

"Probably because she might be the one person who could shed some light on whether fifty or fifty-one people lost their lives that night."

That was the theme that kept coming up in these mysterious notes. The first one, which had been found last fall, was a bit more succinct. It had said *There were 51.*

Simply put.

Even though the Fortune family didn't want to talk about it, even after all these years, clearly someone else did. Haley wished that person—or people, whoever they were—would make themselves known. Maybe they could work together to get to the bottom of this mystery.

Hmm... Maybe she should leave a note on the same community bulletin board where the person had left the note Asa had found and ask him or her to get in touch... She rolled her eyes. Yeah, and if she left her phone number, she'd probably get crank calls from every crackpot this side of the Rio Grande.

However, she could leave an email address. That way she could pick and choose who she answered.

She pulled a small notebook and pen from her wristlet and started writing a note asking for anyone with information about the 1965 Fortune mine disaster to contact her via her work email address, all the while pondering why the note poster had chosen to remain anonymous and leave such cryptic messages. Was he or she afraid of retribution? With a renewed purpose, she picked up her pace and collided—*hard*—with someone as she turned the corner onto Main Street. The impact caused Haley's notebook and pen to fly out of her hands.

It was Val Hensen, the former owner of the Chatelaine Dude Ranch, the place her brother-in-law, Asa—speak of the devil—now owned.

"Oh, Val! I'm so sorry," Haley said as she reached out and touched the older woman's arm. "I should've been watching where I was going. Are you okay?"

"I am just fine, honey," she assured her.

Wiry and spry, Val was in good shape for a woman in her seventies. Her short gray hair and penetrating dark eyes gave her a perpetual mischievous look. "It was as much my fault as it was yours. You okay?"

Haley nodded, and Val beat her to bending down and picking up her notebook and pen.

Val glanced at the message Haley had been writing and raised a black-and-gray-brindled brow. "Looks like we both have a lot on our minds today. I don't mean to be nosy, but why are you looking to get in touch with the person who left that note about the mining disaster?"

Haley took the notebook and closed it. "Because I'm trying to get a break on this story, and no one wants to help me by sharing what really happened that day. Yet clearly some people who don't want to be identified believe there's more to the story than the Fortunes are willing to divulge. It seems like the family wants to rewrite history. Or erase it altogether."

Val's eyes narrowed and her mouth flattened into a thin line. She seemed to assess Haley, who steeled herself for the usual upbraiding she received when she asked the wrong person the wrong questions.

As Haley opened her mouth to excuse herself, Val said, "Come on, let's take a walk."

The older woman looked around, and Haley wondered if she was afraid to be seen with her since so many knew her as the pesky reporter who poked her nose in everyone's business. But then she realized Val was simply looking both ways before she stepped off the sidewalk and into the road that ran between the Main Street shops and the park.

Haley didn't know Val very well other than she was the one who had finally sold the ranch to Asa after some hesitation over some false allegations about his reputation—mainly that he had been a player and a hard partier.

As was often the case, Haley probably knew more about Val than Val knew about her. One of the most important things Haley knew about the woman had nothing to do with the Fortunes. It was *personal*.

Val was probably one of the last people to see Haley's mother and father alive. Lily had discovered this. As Val was packing her things and preparing to move out of the Chatelaine Ranch after selling it to Asa, she came across the photo of Haley's mother and the three baby girls in the triplet stroller that was now sitting on Haley's desk.

Lily had told Haley and Tabitha that Val had said that their family had been to the ranch's petting zoo the day before the accident that killed their parents. Val had told

Lily she remembered the woman because of the triplets. They were hard to forget. A few days later, Val had heard the sad news that the parents had been killed in the accident and the baby girls had been put into foster care.

If Haley had a dime for every time she'd closed her eyes and willed herself to remember that day, she'd be a rich woman. Instead of wealth, she was bereft because, try as she might, she didn't have a single memory of that day or her parents.

Lily swore she could remember them. But Haley…she wasn't so fortunate.

Her heart ached at the thought, and she wanted so badly to ask Val to recount the story because maybe there was something she hadn't told Lily that she'd remembered after giving Tabitha the photograph, but Haley couldn't force the words out of her throat. They were bottled up, along with the raw hurt and anger she felt over being dealt such an unfair lot in life.

Instead, she heard herself asking, "Val, do you know anything about how many people died in the mining accident?"

The woman slanted a glance at her but remained silent.

"Or, if not that, do you know anything about what happened to Gwenyth Wells?"

After they stepped into the grassy park, Val stopped and pinned Haley with a look that was both pointed and full of pity.

"Honey, I don't know what happened to Gwenyth, and I doubt that you'll find many people who want to talk about her. Rumor had it, her husband was to blame for operating the mine under unsafe circumstances—"

"But haven't they since proven that Clint Wells was a scapegoat and the Fortunes were at fault?" Haley interjected.

Val sighed. "They did, but by that time, the damage

had been done. People can be real ugly in times like that. Some of them made life hard on Gwenyth and that girl of hers. I don't blame the two of them for leaving town and not looking back."

Haley sighed. "It seems like what should've happened was the people who treated her badly should've apologized and righted the wrongs they caused."

Val shook her head. "Honey, nothing like that disaster had ever happened around these parts before the mine collapsed. The ones who treated Gwenyth poorly were in shock. I know it's hard to excuse bad behavior, but they weren't thinking straight. They were grieving, and then they were trying to put their lives back together."

Haley nodded. She understood that irrational urge to lash out over a loss that seemed so unfair.

"You'd think that after the authorities discovered Edgar and Elias Fortune were to blame, the family would do everything in their power to right the wrongs caused by their relatives rather than closing ranks and obscuring the truth."

Val shrugged. "That's not for me to say."

Haley shook her head. "Think about it. If Freya Fortune is doling out money couldn't she have put back a little for Gwenyth? Or even a fund to make restitution to those hurt by Edgar and Elias's greed? Shouldn't she have done that?"

Val tilted her head to the side. "Darlin', it's not my place to pass judgment on Freya. She's here to fulfill Elias's will. Honestly, she's been nothing but lovely to me."

"Lovely?" Haley made a face. "What do you mean?"

Val pursed her lips and seemed to weigh her words.

Finally, she said, "Consider this—it must be very hard on Freya Fortune, Elias's widow, to be in the town where Elias was once a golden boy and then fell hard from grace. I think in her own way, Freya is trying to make it up to the community."

Haley snorted. “If she was trying to make it up to the community, don’t you think one of the best ways to do that would be to go on record about what really happened? Maybe she could be transparent and help get to the bottom of the mystery about how many people actually died in the mine accident. Because clearly there’s still a question about it.”

Val crossed her arms and shook her head. “I think that’s up to the authorities. Freya wasn’t even in Chatelaine when the mine collapsed. She didn’t even know Elias at that point. I think it’s admirable that she’s doing as much as she’s done. Maybe in time she’ll be able to do more. For now, I’m glad Freya has the Fortune grands and Wendell as her new family. She’s still working hard to earn their trust.”

“How exactly is she doing that?”

“Well, she’s brought all of Elias’s family to Chatelaine when they were scattered hither and yon. Freya rolled up her sleeves and helped out in the kitchen on Bea’s big opening night, and she was such a comfort to Bea when the night turned into a disaster.”

Val gave her head a quick shake as if trying to do away with the bad memory.

Yeah, right. That was all good and well.

But no matter how Haley sliced it, something seemed slightly off about Freya.

“Okay, so she forced Elias’s family to come back to the place from which he ran away because he was disgraced, and she showered them with money and granted wishes. That’s not exactly altruistic. I don’t know. The woman won’t even give me the time of day. The way I see it is, if you’re not a Fortune, she has no use for you.”

Val held up a slender finger. “Now that’s not entirely true. As I said, she’s been lovely to me.”

Haley clucked her tongue. "What? Did she deign to speak to you?"

Val recoiled.

Instantly, Haley wished she could take back the words. If Val thought Freya was *lovely*, Haley wasn't doing herself any favors talking smack about her. Before Haley could apologize, Val said, "She's not just throwing money at her step-family. Before she granted their wishes, she made sure they used the opportunity for good."

Is that true? Haley wondered.

Of course, Camden's riding camp was the epitome of good, but it had been his dream long before Freya came around granting wishes.

"How so?" Haley asked Val. "I heard that she summoned them to Chatelaine to grant their wishes. I've not heard anything about her largesse being designed to help the greater good."

Val made a face that led Haley to believe the woman knew more than what she was saying.

"Can you give me an example of how Freya has helped Chatelaine in general?" Haley urged.

"Well..." Val pursed her lips. "I know that Asa Fortune recently became your brother-in-law, but before he found your sister, Lily, he was a bit of a gadabout."

"Really?" Haley said. "I think someone started a rumor, and he got a bad rap. I mean, he was single and he loved the ladies. What's wrong with playing the field? Wasn't that his right?"

Val shook her head. "It wasn't a matter of playing the field, dear. Asa was..." Val's eyes grew large, and her hand fluttered to her throat. "Let's just say, he was *something else.* And I know that for a fact because Freya is the one who warned me about him. She knew my principles, and she wanted to make sure I knew what was what before I sold my ranch to him. One day, Freya gave me an earful in the supermarket about how he had four girlfriends at once."

"It's not a crime for a single man to date around," Haley said resolutely.

Val waved off Haley's retort as if shooing away a stink. Clearly, there was no sense in arguing the point further. Thank goodness they'd reached the community bulletin board.

Haley walked closer and scanned the various notes and notices. A weather-beaten paper fluttered in the breeze.

She smoothed it with her hand before reading the note, which had been scrawled in bold black ink. It was waterlogged and the worse for wear, but it was still legible.

51 died in the mine.
Where are the records?
What became of Gwenyth Wells?

DESPITE HER PLAN to retrace Asa's steps, she hadn't expected the note to still be hanging on the board. It had been up there for at least three months. Haley had assumed someone would've removed it, but there it was—a bit worn and torn, but the message was the same as in the photo Lily had shared with her.

As Haley pried loose a thumbtack and posted her own note to the bulletin board, she scanned the other messages that had been left. None of them had anything to do with her story. She returned her attention to the original note she'd come to see. She had to be overlooking something that would lead her to Gwenyth Wells—or better yet, to the identity of the fifty-first miner.

She heard Val gasp.

Haley followed the woman's gaze and saw Wendell and

Freya Fortune walking across the park from the opposite direction from which she and Val had come.

"What I told you about Freya...how she told me about Asa's girlfriends..." Val's voice was quiet. She glanced toward Freya and Wendell, who were now about fifteen yards away.

"Please, keep that between you and me," she whispered. "After he met Lily, he was a changed man, and that is all that matters now."

"Yes, he's a good husband to my sister," Haley said, but Val had already turned her attention to Freya and Wendell.

"Hello, hello!" she called to them. "Are you two out for a stroll on this beautiful morning?"

As Freya approached, she eyed Haley with all the enthusiasm she might have mustered if she'd stumbled upon last week's garbage. Wendell lagged a few paces behind.

"I'm getting in my steps," Freya said cautiously. "How are you today, Val?"

"Well, I was out for my walk, and I ran into Haley."

Before Freya could reply, Wendell let loose a string of curse words and quickened his pace toward the community bulletin board.

"Why the hell is this still up there?" He reached in front of Haley and ripped the note about the miners and Gwenyth Wells off the board. "I thought Asa said he took that thing down."

As he crumpled it in his fist and stuffed it in his pocket, Haley held her breath, waiting for him to rip down her note too.

After a few more choice words, he looked at her pointedly. "Those damn idiots and snoops. They don't know when to leave well enough alone."

He didn't seem to notice her note.

Despite Wendell's mood, this was her opportunity to

introduce herself and maybe ask some questions. "It is a curious note, isn't it? Mr. Fortune, Mrs. Fortune, I'm—"

"I know who you are," Wendell growled. "You're Haley Perry. As I said, you don't know when to leave well enough alone, do you?"

He walked away, and Freya followed without another word or backward glance.

"That was…interesting," Haley said when they were out of earshot. "Wendell Fortune knows who I am. I'm not sure if that's good or bad."

Val shifted from one foot to the other. "You mind yourself, Haley. Stop stirring things up. No good can come of it."

The woman shook her head. "I'd best run. I have things to do."

"Take good care, Val," Haley said as she watched Val walk away.

She knew Asa hadn't been an angel before Lily, but she also knew for a fact that he believed someone had been trying to sabotage him with rumors and a smeared reputation to keep Val from selling him the ranch.

Now Haley knew that Freya was the one who had been feeding Val the rumors.

It was another piece of the puzzle that she filed away. While it felt important—especially in light of what Tabitha had said about West not trusting Freya—she didn't quite know what to do with it.

At least not yet.

CHAPTER SIX

HALEY TOOK HER time walking back to her apartment.

Her mind ping-ponged back and forth between Val sharing how Freya had gossiped and Wendell telling her off. She wanted to call Camden and inform him of what she'd learned. This seemed like enough to prove she wasn't barking up the wrong tree. There was a story here, and the citizens of Chatelaine deserved to read it.

But after running out on him last night, wouldn't it be weird to call him as if nothing had happened and launch into more scuttlebutt about his family and the things they might be hiding?

She sighed.

She'd have to think about it…and the best way to handle it.

Val had asked Haley to keep the info about Freya dishing about Asa being a ladies' man to herself. Technically, she hadn't agreed. While she usually respected a source's request for talking off the record, she certainly hadn't coerced Val into talking. The woman had volunteered the information, and she'd known darn good and well that she was talking to a reporter. Not to mention, what was that little distancing sidestep Val had done when she saw Freya and Wendell walking toward them? Clearly, the woman had been embarrassed to have been caught fraternizing with the enemy reporter.

That made Haley feel less beholden to Val.

Plus, Asa was her brother-in-law. Didn't he deserve to know that Freya was the one who had tried to sabotage his chances of buying the ranch? She had concocted rumors—no, not just rumors. She'd *misrepresented* Asa to Val.

Wasn't that enough to confirm West's gut feeling that something unseemly was going on? There was definitely something off about Freya Fortune.

She was deep in her head when she stepped off the grass and onto the sidewalk parallel to Main Street. That's when she saw Devin Street, owner and editor of the *Chatelaine Daily News*, walk out of the Cowgirl Café.

"Just the person I wanted to see," she murmured as she waited for a car to pass before she crossed the street, picking up her pace to catch up with Devin. He was holding a paper bag, which might have been his lunch. It couldn't have been later than ten thirty. A little early for that, but his fiancée, Bea Fortune, owned the place. Maybe he'd stopped in for a midmorning snack.

Lucky Bea. At well over six-feet tall, with broad shoulders and serious dark eyes, Devin was a handsome guy, but that was beside the point. Haley was going to do a quick pitch about the Camp JD at the Chatelaine Stables story. If he acted even remotely interested in it, she'd have a legitimate reason to call Camden.

Of course, there was always the *Five Easy Steps to Love* project that they needed to finish, but with that one, he was doing her a favor by being her guinea pig...and so far, they hadn't exactly disproved the author's theory.

Her stomach flipped at the thought, and she drew in a deep breath to offset the sensation.

That kiss had thrown a monkey wrench into the experiment. It wasn't supposed to happen until step five. They hadn't even made it through step two. She'd only given the brochure a cursory glance. She'd promised Camden she'd take it home and go over it when she could concentrate. But they'd gotten carried away. Things had gotten emotional.

And she'd hightailed it out of there like her life depended on it.

The next time they talked about it, they'd get back on track. In the meantime, she'd see what Devin thought about the Camp JD story.

"Hey, Devin," she called out.

He stopped and did a double take, as if he'd just noticed her.

"Hi, Haley. What's going on?"

"I'm out for a walk. How's everything at the paper?"

"It's going well." He tucked the bag under his arm, which Haley took as a sign that he wasn't in a big hurry. "You know how it is. It's rarely a busy news day in Chatelaine."

"Well, you know, it doesn't necessarily have to be slow," she said.

He raised a brow. "Oh, yeah? How do you figure?"

"I have a story for you," she said.

He smiled. "Of course you do. Are you saying you have new info on the mining exposé?"

After Haley had moved back to Chatelaine, the first place she'd applied for a job was the *Chatelaine Daily News*, but Devin ran the paper with a skeleton staff and didn't have a permanent position for her. However, he had said he would be interested in taking her on as a stringer and paying her for freelance articles from time to time.

She'd already been through the paper's archives—or "the morgue," as journalists called it—looking for info on the mine disaster. She'd only found basic information.

She shrugged. "I'm still interviewing people," she said. "Though I did hear through the grapevine that both Walter and Wendell Fortune allegedly have a slew of illegitimate children out there."

His brows knit. "What does that have to do with the mining disaster?"

"I don't know, Devin." The exasperation was clear in her voice. She took a deep breath and prepared to soften her tone. "I can't get anyone to talk to me."

She told him about running into Wendell and Freya at the community bulletin board, and how Wendell had flown into a rage, ripped the note off and told her she needed to mind her own business. And that Freya seemed to dodge her.

Devin sighed. "Can you blame either of them for not wanting to talk about it? It happened a long time ago, and it still brings shame to the Fortune name."

"Oh. Okay, Devin. I see how it is. You're engaged to Bea Fortune, and I get there might be a conflict of interest here. But I wanted you to know that I believe I'm close to a breakthrough." She looked him square in the eye. "Are you even interested in publishing the story when I have something ready to print?"

When he didn't answer her immediately, she said, "Look, don't worry about it. An editor at the *Houston Chronicle* is interested—"

"Haley, I didn't say I wasn't interested in the story. What I mean is, I can empathize with Wendell and Freya."

She started to say, *Of course you do*, but she bit back the words. She still needed to pitch the story about Camp JD, which was the original reason she'd wanted to talk to Devin. However, when it came to the mine-disaster exposé, she was tired of people blocking her at every turn.

Devin was going on about how it couldn't be easy to remember *that terrible day* and the aftermath, how *it hurt so many families.*

That was exactly the reason the story needed to be told. If everything was brought out into the sunshine, everyone could heal.

"You're the second person today who has been talking about the mine and the Fortunes," he said.

Wait, what?

"Who else was talking about it?" Haley asked.

He opened his mouth, then shut it fast, as if thinking twice about answering her question.

"Devin, tell me," she insisted.

When he didn't answer her, she said, "It was Morgana Mills, wasn't it?"

His face was impassive. "I will neither confirm nor deny that."

"Well, you just did," Haley said. "You better not have told her more than you've told me."

"Haley, come on. I've shared with you everything I know." "What about these notes, Devin?"

Devin shrugged. "I don't know. Those notes and the identity of the person—or people—leaving them have stumped everyone. Wendell assured me he would look into it, but he doubted it would amount to anything. Probably just someone trying to stir up trouble."

"And?" Haley prodded. "Did he look into it?"

Devin shook his head. His expression was guarded. "I don't know."

Like everyone else who had a connection to a Fortune, Haley could almost see his walls go up around his willingness to share. It was starting to feel as if everyone in her orbit had a Fortune connection that prohibited them from talking—but that didn't mean she had to accept it.

"Does your *I don't know* mean you don't know anything new or you just don't want to talk about it?"

Devin sighed once more. "I haven't asked him. I've been busy, and when I've been around him, he's been moody."

Haley thought about how Wendell had told her off at the community bulletin board. "I guess one has to wonder if it's because he's at his wits' end because he's plagued by false allegations or whether it's his anger deflecting his guilt."

Devin held up his hands. Haley had a feeling she was wearing him down.

"When Freya first arrived in Chatelaine with Elias's will, she seemed open about being here to make amends for what happened," he confided. "Because of that, it seemed like everyone in town was talking about the mine disaster again, but pretty soon, it got to be too much. I guess they felt like they had to do some damage control."

"Yeah, but good luck putting the genie back in the bottle," Haley said. "Even though I don't love the fact that a stranger who is interested in the exact story I've been working on has come to town, doesn't the fact that she's here say that there might be more to this story than the Fortunes are letting on?"

Devin held up his hands. "I don't know. But I didn't tell Morgana anything I haven't told you, okay? That's because I don't know about this possible fifty-first miner. I don't know what became of Gwenyth Wells and her daughter either. And because I don't know either of those things, I don't want to keep poking at old wounds—"

"What kind of newspaperman are you, Devin? This is an important story. It is a *Chatelaine* story, and it affects every single person in this town. This is their history. If you don't care about the truth, other people do. I know I certainly do. We all deserve to know the truth."

Haley clamped her mouth shut, already regretting losing her cool. Much to her surprise, Devin was nodding and watching her with an expression that she almost believed was…respect?

Haley held his gaze, determined not to speak first.

Finally, he said, "You have a point. Since it impacts Chatelaine and its citizens, the mining story belongs here. That means we should be the first to publish it. There's a very good chance that other papers and wire services will pick it up after we do."

Haley felt her brows pull together. Her heart thudded as the possibilities raced through her mind. "What exactly are you saying, Devin? That you'll buy my story?"

"I'm saying you reminded me of how my father used to say that the newspaper has an obligation to the people. I agree. However, you need to get to the bottom of these rumors about the fifty-first miner, and then we'll discuss publishing the story and your compensation."

Haley exhaled.

"Of course," she said. "Everyone wants the big story once all the hard work is done. However, if you're not willing to take a chance on me—because there *is* a story here, Devin, and I guarantee I will get to the bottom of it—it will cost you even more once I've nailed down everything."

She forced herself to stop short of spelling out that she *would* sell to the highest bidder.

Even though she was irritated, she knew baiting him with that wasn't the right thing to do. She would like the exposé to be published in the *Chatelaine Daily News* first, but since he was being obstinate about helping her because he was Fortune adjacent, he didn't need to know she wanted to give him first crack at the story.

They stared at each other for a moment, but then an idea dawned.

"Devin, if—and this is only an *if* at this point—I do let the *Chatelaine Daily News* have first crack at publishing the story, it's only fair that you have some skin in the game too. You can't expect me to do all the hard work and hand it over to you for the glory."

Devin started to say something, but Haley held up her hand. "Here's how it's going to be, Devin. You need to give me a token of good will in the form of leads and information."

He pulled a face that suggested it was an impossible exchange.

"Those are my terms, Devin. You are quite possibly sitting on a goldmine of helpful information. If you help me by feeding me leads, I'll help you by giving you the first chance to buy my story. *Capisce?*"

He grimaced and raked his hand over his close-cropped dark hair before shaking his head and letting loose a dry chuckle.

"Haley Perry, you drive a hard bargain. I can't guarantee anything, but I am impressed with your journalistic instincts and integrity. That's what it takes to be a good investigative reporter. It's too bad I'm not hiring right now, because if I were, I'd offer you a job on the spot."

"Remember that when something opens up." She raised her chin. "That is, if I'm still available."

"Yeah, yeah, yeah." He laughed again. "By that time you'll be winning Pulitzer Prizes and the *Chatelaine Daily News* will be a speck in your rearview mirror. I'll talk to you later, Haley."

"I hope so. I'll be looking for those leads. Oh, and, Devin—one more thing."

She pitched him the Camp JD story.

"Sure, why not?" he said. "We could all use an inspirational story these days. Keep it under one thousand words, and have it to me by Wednesday. I'll carve out a spot for it in the weekend edition."

As he walked away, waving over his shoulder, Haley resisted the urge to do a fist pump over this small victory, but inside she was happy dancing as she walked back to her apartment. Before she ascended the steps, her phone sounded the arrival of a text. She fished it out of her wristlet.

Camden Fortune: We got a little sidetracked last night. You up for a do-over of point #2 on your self-help book exposé?

Her heart raced and she smiled to herself. This day just kept getting better and better.

Haley: What did you have in mind?

CAMDEN SMILED WHEN Haley's answer popped up on his phone. It had to be a good sign that she'd replied so fast.

Things had gotten out of hand between them the previous evening. Now that he suspected she wasn't upset—wouldn't ghost him over a kiss…and a damn-good kiss, at that—his tune had changed from one of tentative regret to sorry, not sorry.

But now what?

What exactly *did* he have in mind?

There wasn't a simple answer. At the base level, he wanted to pick up where they'd left off before she'd run away. No, more than that—he wanted to finish what they'd started.

But then what?

He was not in the place to get involved with a woman right now. He had way too much on his plate getting Camp JD ready for a summer opening. Plus, he'd learned his lesson with Joanna. She'd shamelessly used him for what she could get.

Haley was not Joanna, though. Haley was smart and had drive and determination to make her own way in this world—but she was on a mission, with or without his help.

It was too bad that Haley's getting ahead involved dragging his family through the mud over something that happened so long ago.

Still, the bottom line remained: he couldn't stop thinking about her.

Camden paced the length of the floor. Sunlight streamed through the windows of his office, highlighting the sketches and blueprints that were scattered across his desk, depicting various ideas for the children's barn he needed to whip into shape by August.

He had a lot of work to do. He should keep his head down until after the camp was up and running.

His text tone sounded again.

Haley: Good news! I ran into Devin Street and he agreed to run the article on Camp JD in the weekend edition.

Camden's mouth fell open. He read the text again to make sure he'd gotten it right. Yep. Devin Street wanted to run the article.

Rather than texting her back, he dialed Haley's number.

She picked up on the second ring.

"Hey, Camden."

She sounded slightly breathless. Or maybe he was projecting because he was feeling a little winded by the excitement himself.

"This is great," he said."

"Yeah, I ran into him as he was coming out of the Cowgirl Café, and I pitched the story. He loved it."

Camden raked his fingers through his hair. He couldn't stop smiling.

"I owe you a lot more than riding lessons," he said. "I could never afford this kind of publicity, Haley. You're amazing, you know that?"

Joanna had never gone out of her way to do a single thing like this for him.

He needed to stop comparing the two women right now.

As soon as he acknowledged the thought, he realized Haley had been silent a few beats too long. The initial elation was tempered by uncertainty.

"Are you there?" he asked.

"I'm here," she said. "You don't owe me anything, Camden. If anything, it's another freelance job for me. It's a win-win. But I do need to interview you ASAP because I have to turn in the story by Wednesday for it to make it into the weekend edition."

"Come over tonight," he suggested. "That is, if you're not busy. I mean, you might have a date."

"I don't have a date tonight." He couldn't quite read her voice.

"What time?" she added.

"Whenever you can get here. Now?"

"No, not now," she laughed. "I need to finish looking over your brochure so we can cross item number two off the list for the *Five Easy Steps* article. I have to wrap that one pretty soon. We still have to get through the last three steps, and I need to leave myself enough time to write the piece."

He started to say that they'd already kissed. That technically, they could cross that one off the list. But if they took the steps in order, it meant he would get to kiss her again. Electric heat rushed through his body, pooling in his center. Even though it shouldn't have caught him by surprise, it did.

"I guess we got a little sidetracked last night," he admitted.

"Yep."

He wasn't sure if he should say it wouldn't happen again, because he didn't like to lie, and he couldn't be certain it *wouldn't* happen again.

He decided to throw the ball in her court. "You said you needed to formally interview me. How do you want to work that?"

"I know you've already shown me around the property," she said. "But maybe we should start over. Give me another tour of the children's barn and all the components of Camp JD, and I'll take notes this time. Let's focus on how you'll be serving underprivileged kids in the community. I think Devin liked that angle."

"Sounds good to me," he said.

"I need to get to work on your brochure. So I'll let you go."

He wanted to say, *Don't ever let me go.* The feeling bubbled up as if it was a byproduct of the carnal rush that had coursed through him a moment ago. Instead, he took a deep breath and said, "Okay, see you soon."

AS CAMDEN STEPPED out of the barn, he saw Haley's red Honda Civic make its way toward him. He hadn't realized it, but he hadn't been one hundred percent sure that she would show up until he saw her car turn off the highway and head up the drive that led to the Chatelaine Stables.

He gave himself a mental shake. It was a sort of lingering PTSD after being disappointed in the past.

But he knew it wasn't Haley's fault. She'd never let him down.

At least, he hoped she wouldn't.

The thought that she would be there in a matter of seconds—that he'd be able to see her pretty face, smell her perfume, try to sort the kaleidoscope of colors in those hazel eyes of hers—had excitement coursing through him.

Then he noticed another car following at a modest distance behind her. Who was that? Not only was he not expecting anyone else, but he also didn't want anyone infringing on the limited time he'd have with her tonight.

Even so, as Haley parked and emerged from her car—wearing a yellow blouse with white flowers and a pair of skintight jeans that hugged her curves in all the places he wanted to touch—Camden couldn't contain the smile he felt stretching across his face. Until the buzzkill of the other car, a newer-model blue SUV, parked next to Haley. He didn't recognize the vehicle, and because of the glare of the setting sun reflecting off the car's windshield, he couldn't see who was behind the wheel.

When Lily Perry Fortune stepped out, the harsh words Camden had been gathering for the interloper dissipated like water on a hot stone.

Had Haley brought Lily as a chaperone? *Huh*. He sifted through his feelings as he watched the sisters walk toward him. He was disappointed, but if Haley wasn't comfortable being alone with him, having Lily here was for the best.

Sort of.

"So, what's going on, Camden?" Lily's eyes sparkled with curiosity as she glanced at the barn and then back at Camden and her sister. "Haley was a little cryptic today when she asked me to come with her, but she said you needed me?"

He didn't quite know what to say. Luckily, Haley jumped in.

"I was thinking about how Camp JD is for underserved

children, and you'd mentioned that foster kids would be among them. Then I figured there was no better adviser for learning what would make foster children comfortable than talking to a former foster child. Lily can take the tour with us and help you fine-tune the details to best serve the children. Plus, it will make a great angle for the story."

"Smart." His gaze snagged Haley's, and his heart beat a little faster. "I appreciate both of you making the time to come over. You both can offer a unique perspective. Lily, you know what it's like to be in the foster care system, and I want to make sure the camp provides a safe and nurturing environment for all the kids, but especially the foster children. Haley, maybe you can offer pointers on what might help kids who've never been around horses?"

Haley nodded and her expression softened as she and Lily exchanged glances.

"I told you he was a good guy." Lily raised a brow at her sister and smiled in a knowing way.

Haley murmured through gritted teeth, "I never said he wasn't."

"I hate to interrupt this enchanting discourse," Camden chimed in. "Especially when it's about me—"

Haley snorted.

"Aw, come on Haley," Camden said. "I'm not so bad."

This time she refused to meet his gaze.

"On that note," he continued, "Lily, would you like the grand tour?"

"You bet." Lily flashed him a smile. "This is such an exciting project, Camden. I am happy to help you in any way I can. I'm sure Haley feels the same way."

"Of course I do," she said as she pulled a small notebook and pen out of her purse. "You two go on and pretend like I'm not here. I'll take notes, and after you're finished showing my sister around, I'll ask any questions I might have."

"Great. Let's start over here and walk through the process like the kids would." Camden guided them toward the office where the kids would check-in every morning.

He pointed out the lockers where the campers could secure their belongings, the first aid station, and the restroom facilities.

Next, he led them to the barn he would use for the equestrian school. As they stepped inside, Lily gasped. "Everything is gorgeous. It's all so new. I'm in awe!"

He pointed out the spacious stalls, the neatly organized tack room. Camden looked around and tried to see it through the women's eyes. The scent of new construction and fresh hay hung in the air. The horses nickered contentedly in their stalls.

Yesterday, he'd moved the horses from the other barns on the property to their new digs on this side of the ranch. It was starting to come together. Pride coursed through him.

"We have plenty of storage for horse-care products, maintenance equipment and other necessary items," he said. "The kids will be actively involved in caring for the horses. You know, mucking out the stalls and such. It's not glamorous, but it's as important for them to learn responsibility as well as proper riding technique."

He watched as Haley's gaze scanned the room, glancing over a child-size mounting block and the colorful murals on the walls before she wrote something in her notebook.

"Let me know if you have any questions," he told her.

Haley glanced up, and their gazes snared. "Thanks. I'll have plenty of questions for you later on, but right now, I want you to give us the complete tour."

Something in her expression hinted that the questions might not be exclusively about the camp. Or maybe he was reading into things. Then she smiled.

Maybe not...

"In that case," he said, "right this way…"

They left the barn, and he showed off the indoor arena, the paddock and a special elevated outdoor viewing area.

"I had an observation deck built so the children and visitors can watch the horses grazing. The kids can interact with each other or simply get a feel for what they'll be doing by watching what's going on."

Finally, when they'd come full circle and were back in the office, he asked, "So. What do you think?"

"Camden, it's all truly amazing," Lily said. "When I was in foster care, I would've loved a place like this—a haven where I could feel safe and cared for."

Camden smiled. "That's exactly what I hope to create here. I want every child who walks through these doors to feel a sense of belonging and take comfort in the company of these gentle creatures."

Lily nodded as she approached the whiteboards on the walls near his desk, her fingers tracing the sketches.

"The only suggestion I have is, in addition to the outdoor viewing area, maybe there should be a quiet place away from the horses where kids can catch their breath if they start to feel overwhelmed," she said. "Sometimes kids who have been in and out of foster care can be a little skittish about new things. A quiet area would allow them to ease into the situation on their own terms. They can stand up on the observation deck and watch and decide if they want to participate. If not, they can retreat to the quiet room." She paused. "And don't be offended if some kids take a while to warm up. At least they'll get a taste of what it's like to be around horses."

Lily turned to him. "Not to be nosy, but do you have the funding for something like that? I realize that not only would an observation deck require extra money to construct it, but you might also need extra staff to supervise since kids shouldn't be left alone."

He nodded. "I could talk to Freya and see if there's any money left in her wish budget." Reflexively, he looked at Haley. Last night, the tension between them had started when Freya's name came up. He'd hoped they could start fresh tonight.

Maybe they could, because she continued to write in her notebook as if the mention of his step-grandmother hadn't registered.

"Keep me posted," Lily said. "If Freya can't help, I would be honored to help you make it happen. I want every child who visits this camp to feel the love and kindness that they deserve."

She glanced at her watch. "Oh, look at the time! I have to run. I told Asa I'd meet him at the Chatelaine Bar and Grill at seven. Thank you for the tour, Camden. You're doing something truly remarkable here. I mean it when I said I want to help in any way I can."

Lily's voice was soft and full of warmth, but the minute she looked at her sister, her eyes sparkled. "And you, my dear sister—call me tomorrow."

Haley and Camden watched Lily's SUV pull out of the parking area and head down the dirt drive toward the highway.

"You've been quiet," he remarked. "Is everything okay?"

"Yes. Fine." Haley clipped her pen to her notebook, and then her gaze met his.

He debated whether he should bring up last night—the tension over Freya and then the kiss—but the question felt a little too pointed.

"Do you have any questions about the camp?" he asked instead.

"Only about a million," she said. "Oh, but before I forget, I brought your brochure back."

She pulled a piece of paper from her notebook. "I made a few suggestions about the copy and the photos."

Haley held out the paper, and he accepted it.

"It's just my opinion." She shrugged. "Take it or leave it."

"I value your opinion," he said.

The corners of Haley's mouth turned up, but the smile didn't quite reach her eyes.

"Do you have time to come in for a glass of wine?" he asked. "We could go over your notes on the brochure, and I could answer your questions about the camp for the article."

Even though he thought she'd brought Lily along as a chaperone, they'd come in separate cars, and Haley wasn't exactly rushing to get away.

"Sure," she said. "That way, we can cross item number two off the list."

They drove to his house in their own vehicles.

As they parked and she followed him to the porch, he had an odd sense of déjà vu.

He'd been irritated when she wouldn't stop asking questions about Freya, and the next thing he knew, they were kissing, and then she'd run away.

He was afraid he'd ruined everything, but she'd agreed to come over. Granted, she had two stories she had to write—the *Five Easy Steps to Love* piece and the local-interest bit about Camp JD—and she needed to talk to him about them.

This felt like a do-over, a chance to make things right.

As long as she understood that he couldn't talk about Freya—or any of his family, for that matter. Family was everything to him.

Even so, he couldn't stop thinking about Haley when they weren't together. And when he was with her, the world felt...right. He didn't know where things were going with her—or if they were going anywhere.

But he was eager to find out. In true do-over fashion, they ended up in the kitchen, where everything had gone down last night.

As he opened a bottle of wine, she set her phone, keys and notes about the brochure on the island and excused herself to the bathroom.

"I'll be right back," she said. "Don't drink all the wine without me."

Happy that she was starting to act more like herself again, Camden poured two glasses of wine. He seated himself at the island, and as he reached for the paper with her notes about the brochure, a text popped up on her phone.

He hadn't meant to read it, but it was right in his line of sight. When he saw it was from Devin Street, he thought it might be about the piece she was writing about the camp, but it wasn't.

Devin Street: I have a lead on the mine exposé. Call me.

The screen went dark, and he knew he had no right to touch her phone, but before he could stop himself, he'd picked it up so he could make sure he'd read it right.

That's when she walked back into the kitchen.

Sitting there holding her phone, he probably looked guilty as hell. And he was. He had no right, but what was done was done, and she'd caught him red-handed.

As she watched him set the phone down, her expression darkened.

"What are you doing?" She picked up the device, and her eyebrows arched as she read Devin's message and then looked back at Camden.

"Um?" Her free hand was on her hip.

"I'm sorry," he said. "There's no excuse. I was reaching for the brochure notes when your text tone sounded.

It was in my line of sight, and then it went dark. And I… I wasn't sure I'd read the message right. So I picked up your phone."

He grimaced. "I apologize."

"Well, Nosy Parker, are you happy now?"

He hesitated, weighing his words, and fighting the absurdly inappropriate impulse to laugh at what she'd just called him. *Nosy Parker.* Who even said things like that?

Haley did. That was one of the many reasons she was unique, and why he was falling for her, despite her dogged determination to write this exposé about his family.

"You know what?" she said. "Scratch that question because if this is going to happen—this thing between you and me—you need to know up front that I am going to keep working on the mine-disaster story because it's a part of Chatelaine's history and people deserve to know the truth. But I will not ask you any questions about it or about your family. That's not why I'm here today. That's not what I want from you—"

"What *do* you want from me, Haley?"

"I don't want anything from you, Camden. I just want…you."

CHAPTER SEVEN

HALEY STOOD THERE, the weight of his question pressing on her, the desire between them flaring so intensely, her brain couldn't form words.

She wasn't sure who moved first, but suddenly, they were in each other's arms.

Without another word, his mouth was on hers. Her hands were in his hair, pulling him closer, until their bodies were flush and perfectly aligned. She could feel his body responding to hers, to them…together.

At last.

Until this very moment, she hadn't realized how much she wanted him. It was as if she knew she couldn't handle the letdown if it didn't happen.

But it was happening, and all thoughts except for the way he felt, the way he tasted and how good he smelled melted away. It was as if they were the only two people in the world.

He tasted like the wine, blackberries mixed with a hint of cocoa and clove…and there was something else, something unique—that indefinable flavor that brought her back to last night when they'd kissed.

Only this time she had no desire to run.

On the contrary. Suddenly, she realized, she'd been desperate for this man since the first time she'd laid eyes on him. He seemed both familiar and forbidden, and she wanted him so badly, she feared she wouldn't be able to draw her next breath without him.

The thought made her heart stutter and almost brought her back to her senses, but when his lips found her ear and trailed down to tease the sensitive spot at the base of her neck, she knew she was a goner.

She shuddered with pleasure.

"You okay?" His voice was quiet and raspy and sexy as hell. His hot breath was on her neck, and she was putty in his hands.

"I have never been better in my entire life," she whispered.

He pulled her even closer. "I wanted to make sure. I don't want to do anything you don't want—"

She covered his mouth with hers and swallowed the words.

He moved his hands to her hips, cupping her bottom and pulling her closer, and she arched against him. Her body tingled as his hands slid up and dipped into the waistband of her jeans, finding the hem of her blouse and pulling it free.

He slipped his hands underneath the fabric. She reveled in the way his fingers lingered on her stomach, inching their way up until he cupped her breasts. She shivered at the feel of his touch on her body.

"I've wanted this—I've wanted *you*—for so long," he rasped. "Sometimes I can't even think straight because you're all I can think about."

Ohh. She could fall so hard for this man, and he could easily break her heart into a thousand shards that were so fragmented, she'd never be able to put them back together again.

However, when his lips found hers again, and he was kissing her with such a slow and burning passion, she could almost believe he was making promises of what was next to come.

Her head was so muddled, and her body was singing at his touch. She wasn't sure whether those promises were about what would happen when they made love—or their relationship in the days after.

"Why don't we go into the bedroom?" His breathing was heavy. Both his hands were on her waist, and his forehead was resting on hers. His eyes were searching hers as he awaited her answer. This was her chance to run, but she wasn't going to do that again.

"Yes." She managed to find the word and make it intelligible.

He picked her up and carried her through the living room and down the hall, turning into the first room on the right—his bedroom.

Kissing her neck, her cheeks, her eyes and then finally returning to her lips, he gently laid her down on his bed and eased his body down on top of her.

CAMDEN HAD NEVER felt such overwhelming longing in his entire life. He wanted to show Haley how much he ached for her, how much he'd craved this moment. He wanted to demonstrate with his lips and hands and body why they would be so right together.

In the back of his mind, however, something objected. It warned him to slow down, to not lead her on, to not make promises—spoken or implied—that he couldn't keep. Yet that flicker of caution dissipated into nothingness when the part of his body that ached for her settled into the recess of her, fitting together as if they were made for each other.

He wasn't going to think about anything else right now other than how damn right she felt and how much he wanted her.

He rolled to the side, giving himself room to tug her blouse up and over her head. He made quick work of getting her bra—a pink lacy feminine thing—out of the way, freeing her breasts. The gorgeous sight of her made his own body swell and harden. He touched her breasts, cupping them, loving the feel of her curves, so supple under his hands, savoring their fullness before teasing her hard nipples. When he lowered his head and suckled, she gasped.

The sexy sound and the sight of her losing herself in his touch almost undid him.

His need to make love to her sent a hungry shudder racking his whole body. But that was nothing compared to the feel of her hand on the front of his jeans. She teased his erection through the layers of his pants and boxers. The sensation was almost more than he could bear. Suddenly, he needed them both to be naked so that he could bury himself inside her.

But he needed to slow down.

He wanted to savor the moment. He took his time undoing the button on her jeans. In one swift, gentle motion, he lifted her so that he could remove them.

Haley unbuttoned his jeans and slid down the zipper. He moved so that she could push his pants and boxers down. They fell away, freeing him.

She lay beneath him, the most beautiful woman he'd ever seen in his life. Hadn't every single day since the first day he'd met her been leading to his moment? He had been crazy to think he could ever resist her.

Then they were kissing deeply again, tongues thrusting, a merging of souls that begged for their bodies to become one.

When he was sure she was ready, he buried himself inside her.

That's when he knew without a doubt that he needed her in his life.

Always.

As they made love, slowly and softly, time slipped by.

It was irrelevant. It didn't even exist.

Until sometime later, after they were spent and satiated, lying together in each other's arms, when he asked, "Where exactly does this fit into the *Five Easy Steps to Love* challenge?"

It dawned on him that in the past, the mere mention of the word *love* would've sent him running from intimacy. He pulled her closer, needing to feel her warmth, craving the way her body fit just right with his.

She turned onto her side, facing him, and snuggled closer. *"Hmm*...that's a good question."

"The book says it's important to take the steps in order," he reminded her. "We can check off step two, but we still need to do step three—*Listen without judgment to an issue the other is having.* And step four—*Attend an event together.* Each step informs the next and builds intimacy."

She lifted up and braced herself on her elbow, looking at him like he'd said something completely mind blowing. "Are you really reading the book? I mean, you said you picked up a copy, but I didn't think you'd actually read it."

"Why not? I'm a reader. Do you think I'm not?"

"No, I'm glad you're a reader. Men who read are sexy." She ran her hand over his bare chest. "Especially when they look like this."

"Why, Haley Perry, are you *objectifying* me? Because if you are, I don't mind."

She flashed him a wicked grin. "Are you trying to make that the issue that would count as step three?"

"Hell no," he said. "We just finished step two. I want

to drag this out as long as possible so we can have more nights like this."

"Oh, yeah?" she asked, her lips hovering a fraction of an inch above his.

"Yeah. I want to make sure I do my part. I'm conscientious like that."

She lowered her head and kissed him long and slow.

Haley's fingers found their way to the nape of Camden's neck, tangling in his hair as they deepened the kiss. It was a fervent, desperate connection, fueled by the intensity of emotions and the hope that their bond might be stronger than any doubts and differences they faced. The weight of their uncertainties faded into the background, leaving only warmth and tenderness.

His body responded.

Time seemed to stand still as they made love again.

After they went over the edge together for a second time, they remained entwined, foreheads pressed together as they caught their breath.

To HALEY, THE world around them seemed distant and insignificant in the wake of their intense connection.

Intense yet tender.

Somehow, amid the chaos and uncertainty that had once threatened to keep them apart, her feelings for him had bloomed.

Of course, that left her wide open for heartache.

Haley tried not to acknowledge the flicker of fear—that this was a one-night thing. That Camden would pretend like he didn't even know her.

No, that wasn't him.

It would be more likely he would ask her to put down the mine-disaster exposé.

Would he ask her to choose?

She refused to dwell on the unknown. Instead, she focused on relaxing and living in the moment. There would be enough time for worry in the days to come.

Or maybe this was the start of something really good.

As Camden held her tight and his breathing took on the slow, steady, relaxed rhythm of a person who was content and satiated, Haley stopped thinking and drifted off to sleep in his arms.

THE NEXT MORNING, Camden woke Haley with a kiss and a hot cup of coffee. This was the first time in a long while that he'd awakened with a woman in his bed.

It was his doing.

In the middle of the night, she'd tried to leave, but he'd talked her into staying.

But this morning, things looked a little different in the light of day. Even though he wouldn't undo last night if given the chance, the reality of their situation loomed like a specter.

"Thanks for the coffee." She was sitting up with the bedsheet tucked under her arms, sipping from her cup. "Did you sleep well?"

His heart and his head were at war. She was so sexy, it was all he could do to keep from undressing and crawling back in bed with her, but it wasn't that easy. Once she uncovered all the information she needed, she was going to write that story about his family, reopening old wounds.

"What are you thinking about?" Her hand was on his arm.

She'd been honest with him yesterday. He needed to be honest with her now.

"I'm thinking about that phone call you have to make to Devin Street for the lead on the mining story he has for you."

"Oh, that," she said.

Haley set her coffee on the nightstand and crossed her arms tightly over her chest. All the tension that had vanished last night when they'd made love returned. He didn't even have to touch her to know. He could see it practically radiating off her body.

He knew he had struck a nerve.

"Well, um, I won't know what he has for me until I call him. I was going to do that after I got home—but, Camden, last night I told you that I was going to write that story. I won't involve you, but..."

She trailed off. Holding the sheet in place against her with one hand, she examined her fingernails on the other, as if weighing her words.

Finally, she said, "Something you need to know about me is, I love my work. However, even though I actually do enjoy writing these puff pieces, I want the opportunity to do something with more substance."

He nodded. "When did you know you wanted to do this?"

"I grew up thinking my foster mom, Ramona, had adopted me," she said. "She led me to believe she had. I mean, she was a good mother, but she misled me, and for the longest time, it felt like such a betrayal. Because she wasn't forthright with me, I missed out on knowing my sisters—or at least Lily." She swallowed hard. "Tabitha was legally adopted, and her parents didn't want her to have anything to do with Lily and me. But poor Lily grew up bouncing around the foster care system, and I can't help but think if I'd known that I, too, was a foster kid and that I had a sister, her life might've been better. And to be honest, I might not have felt so alone."

He wasn't quite sure what this had to do with investigative reporting, but it felt insensitive to ask. Instead, he lowered himself onto the bed next to her.

As if she'd read his mind, she said, "I found out that Ramona never initiated the adoption when I was applying for colleges. I found my birth certificate, and it listed Laura and Brent Perry as my parents. If Ramona had adopted me like she'd said she had, she would've been listed as my parent. The first thing I did after learning my birth parents' names was do an internet search. That's when I learned that they died in a car accident in Chatelaine and that I was a triplet. It seemed like the more research I did, the more I learned, and it became clear that knowledge was power.

"And that sometimes, withholding information because you think it's for the best—like Ramona withheld my past—isn't the right thing to do. From that moment on, the truth—or getting to the bottom of the truth—mattered more to me than anything else."

Her eyes were dark with a sadness that made his heart ache.

"But I thought you and Ramona were still close," he said.

"We are," she replied. "We eventually got past it. She's a good woman, really."

"Why did she lie to you?"

Haley shrugged. "She didn't mean to hurt me. I know that now. After my parents died, my sisters and I were placed in foster care, which you know. We were only ten months old. Ramona had always wanted a baby, and her best friend worked for the foster care system and was handling our case. Thanks to her, Ramona was my first foster mother. I guess her friend sort of let my case 'fall through the cracks.'" She put air quotes around that last part. "And since Ramona was a single woman and I was a baby, she was afraid that if she tried to legally adopt me, the system would take me away from her and put me into a more traditional family."

"So did the friend break the law?" he asked. "A corrupt foster system seems like a meatier story than…"

Her eyes flashed, and he sat there with her, grappling with the consequences of his thoughtless words.

Camden reached out and placed a gentle hand on Haley's arm, hoping to comfort her. But she recoiled, shrugging off his touch, her gaze fixed upon him with a mixture of hurt and defiance.

"Haley," he began, his voice laced with regret, "I didn't mean it that way. Sometimes, in our eagerness to uncover the truth, we can overlook important things or think we see connections that may not truly exist. I worry that you're interpreting things through the lens of what you want to find rather than what is actually there."

She glared at him. "Look, I don't have a wealthy family gifting me with my heart's desire," she huffed.

He stared at her, astonished.

"I'm sorry, Camden. That came out wrong. You are using the gift Freya gave you in the best-possible way—but you haven't even heard the rest of my story, and you've already formed your own conclusion."

She started to get out of bed, but he was blocking her way.

"I'm sorry," he said. "Will you please tell me the rest? I promise to listen… In fact, I will listen without judgment."

He raised a brow at her, and to his relief, she smiled.

"I see what you did there," she said. "For the record, Ramona's friend did not break the law. The thing with foster care and adoption is, everyone wants the babies. The older a child gets, the harder it is for them to find a permanent home. Ramona's friend ran interference when I was a baby, but when I got to be school age, I was a less-desirable adoptee. Even so, as an unmarried woman, Ramona was terrified that the system would take me away from her."

Haley shook her head. "Ramona never believed that a piece of paper would change anything. That's why she never married. After I found out that she'd never initiated the adoption, she said that a piece of paper signed by a bunch of stuffed shirts wouldn't make her love me anymore than she did. Seeking adoption might have opened the door for the system to put me in another home or a group home that would've been far worse than living with an unconventional single mother."

She had a point.

"How did you and Ramona patch things up?"

"I was mad at her for the better part of a year, during which, I went away to college. And after I got over myself, I realized that she'd made a lot of sacrifices for me. She only had good intentions. So, does that still sound like the makings of an exposé?"

He shook his head. "No, it doesn't."

"I wish you could see that sometimes, in telling the truth, people are set free," she said. "That's how the truth impacted me. It hurt at first, but then it made things better. I also learned that it's so important to not let eagerness cloud judgment. That's how I'm approaching the story about the mine disaster. You need to understand that, Camden. I'm not doing this story because I want to hurt people.

"I have to write this story because not only does my livelihood depend on it, but I need to get to the truth. And I really hope you won't make me choose between my work and…us."

HALEY STEERED HER car into a parking spot at the GreatStore and killed the engine. She sat there for a moment, closed her eyes and relived last night—for the millionth time.

Camden's lips on hers, his hands on her body…in the most intimate places.

The way they'd fit so perfectly.

After she'd left his house and returned to her own apartment, after she'd showered and dressed for the day and set out with the intention of getting some work done, she could still feel him like a phantom touch nudging her, shadowing her, making it impossible to not think about him.

After their night together, she felt close to him. She wanted him. But they hadn't resolved the issue of whether or not he would expect her to give up the mine exposé, which, essentially, boiled down to her choosing between her work and him.

Normally, that would be a no-brainer. She did not let men get between her and her work. She'd drawn those lines, bold and black. Nobody crossed them.

But this morning, everything looked an unfamiliar shade of gray.

She'd never been so confused in her life.

Part of her wanted to drive back to his ranch and stay there until they'd resolved everything, but the rational part of her mind, the part she couldn't shut down, reminded her that she had things to do. Plus, she'd already shared way too much with him. She leaned forward and rested her forehead on the steering wheel. Not just her body, but all that personal stuff this morning. Thank goodness she'd stopped short of explaining that the reason she was so career focused was, before she'd moved to Chatelaine from New York, she'd put all her eggs in the boyfriend basket, only to have the bottom fall out of it. She'd lost almost everything.

At least, everything she'd worked for.

All because she'd put her trust in a man rather than focusing on her career.

It was a major setback that she was still trying to dig herself out of.

While she rarely went for casual sex—okay, she *never* went for casual sex—Camden was only her second lover. And she'd been in a committed relationship with the other one…until everything had blown up.

She should've known better than to give in to her attraction to Camden Fortune, but trying to resist him had been about as futile as a magnet rejecting steel.

How could she simultaneously need to be in his arms and in the next breath, want to run as far away from him as she could?

She sat in her car for a moment, gripping the steering wheel, resting her forehead on her hands, desperately trying to get herself together. She needed to compartmentalize her feelings for Camden—they were growing out of control…like kudzu. She had to focus on this new lead Devin had provided.

As soon as she'd gotten home that morning, she'd called the newsman at the office, and he told her that Doris Edwards might be able to provide some insight into the mining disaster. She was a Chatelaine native and had lost her brother, Roger, in the accident.

Doris was one of the few Chatelaine natives she hadn't interviewed. It was worth a shot, even though most of them hadn't been able to tell her much. The common consensus was that they had no clue about a potential fifty-first miner.

A wave of doubt washed over Haley. It stood to reason that if fifty-one people—rather than fifty—had died in the accident, wouldn't that person have had loved ones or friends who would've reported him or her missing?

Maybe she was barking down the wrong mine shaft. She sighed. Was it possible everything about this story was already out in the open? Like Wendell had said, maybe she should leave well enough alone.

She sat with the thought for a moment, mulling it over, seeing how it resonated. On one hand, she didn't blame the current generation of Fortunes for not wanting to reopen the case. It wasn't their fault, and it couldn't be easy for them to remember that terrible day and the aftermath. That would be a good reason for Gwenyth Wells and her daughter to want to remain out of the fray too. Haley could imagine that she'd worked hard to put her life back together again and start over. Even though everyone knew her late husband was not to blame for the disaster, it would be hard to return to a place where people had turned on her.

In many ways, Haley could relate to Gwenyth's moving on. Losing her birth parents at such a tender age was sad, but she'd gotten past it. She hadn't wanted to wallow in the sadness. And despite Ramona's mistakes, her lies of omission, she'd given her a loving home.

She couldn't blame Gwenyth for wanting to move on too.

Haley shuddered at the thought of what Gwenyth Wells must've gone through, shouldering the blame for a tragedy that she and her husband weren't responsible for—but people needed a scapegoat, and her late husband had been it. She and her poor daughter had been left to bear the brunt of it.

It wasn't right.

Justice had never been served.

That's what kept driving Haley back to the story.

Not only for justice for the Wellses. *Someone* believed one more person, other than those who had already been accounted for, had lost their life because of Elias and Edgar Fortune's carelessness and greed.

That was why this story needed to be told.

Haley flipped through her notebook, going over what she'd already learned before she made a list of what she wanted to ask Doris Edwards.

Maybe the fifty-first person was related to the person leaving the notes. But why now, nearly sixty years later? Why hadn't anyone reported the extra person missing before now? If they had proof, why not go to the authorities rather than leaving cryptic messages around town?

Was the person afraid of the Fortunes? Or maybe they didn't trust the police to look into any evidence they had.

She'd received a couple of crackpot responses to the note she'd left on the community bulletin board yesterday, but nothing of substance to give insight into the unanswered questions.

She hoped Doris Edwards could give her some direction. If not, it wouldn't hurt to try to talk to Morgana Mills again—but first things first.

Once inside the store, Haley adjusted her notepad and approached the GreatStore's "Ask Me," table where a friendly-looking elderly woman wearing a name tag that read *Doris Edwards* sat, working on a crossword puzzle. The table was adorned with sales flyers, credit card applications and store directories, indicating Doris's role in assisting shoppers with their inquiries.

"Hi, Doris, I'm Haley Perry. I was wondering if you could help me."

With a warm, welcoming smile on her face, Doris looked up from her puzzle book and nodded. "That's what I'm here for, honey. What can I do for you today?"

"I'm a local reporter," Haley told her. "And as the sixtieth anniversary of the Chatelaine mine disaster approaches, I am doing a story about it. I heard you knew Gwenyth Wells, and I was hoping you would talk to me about her."

"Lord have mercy." Doris put her hand over her heart, a sad look of recollection clouding her watery gray eyes. "I haven't heard that name in a month of Sundays—but yes, I knew Gwenyth well enough to say hello around town back in the '60s when she lived here. You know, she was the widow of the mine foreman when it collapsed. People were real ugly and took out all their pain on her because they thought her husband was responsible." She shook her head. "I declare. I haven't seen or heard anything about Gwenyth Wells in an age."

Haley leaned closer, captivated by the connection. "Do you remember anything about her or her family?"

Doris tapped her chin thoughtfully. "I remember she had a daughter, about eighteen years old at the time, but I can't recall her name. It's been so long, you see."

Doris glanced around as if to see who was nearby and might overhear their conversation. Then she leaned in and lowered her voice. "You know, her husband died that day too. He wasn't to blame. It was those Fortunes."

Her mouth flattened into a line.

"Speaking of which, I did see that Freya Fortune deigned herself to come in here a few months ago." Doris's voice was flat. "She bought a wig, of all things. I was watching because I was curious what a woman with all her money would buy in a place like this. The wig she picked out was short and mousy brown. I couldn't understand why she thought she'd look good in it. She has such pretty ash blond hair. Looks like she spends a fortune on it. That wig would have made her kind of dowdy. The color was all wrong for her."

Doris held up a finger. "Come to think of it, she also purchased a cane that day, but I haven't seen her use it around town. Her leg or hip must be better."

A surge of excitement coursed through Haley's veins as she recalled Esme Fortune mentioning that the volunteer who had been helping in the nursery at County General Hospital earlier that year, the night Esme and Ryder Hayes's babies were switched, had short, mousy brown hair and walked with a cane.

Could Freya have been at the hospital that night? If so, why would she go incognito and pose as a volunteer? Did she have something to do with the baby swap? The same way she'd been responsible for filling Val Hensen's head full of lies about Asa and nearly ruining his chance to buy the dude ranch? The same dude ranch that her largesse had made possible for him to purchase?

None of this made any sense. If this was all true, it would mean she was undermining the very people she claimed to be making amends with for the sake of her late husband Elias.

Haley's mind was buzzing, but she forced herself to focus on everything Doris was saying so she could write it down verbatim. Then two separate parties approached the desk. They were tolerant for a moment, but then the man who was next in line cleared his throat and began shuffling from foot to foot, a clear indication that his patience was wearing thin.

Finally, he said, "Can someone else help me? I want to open an account, but I don't have all day."

Doris held up a hand. "I'll be right with you, sir." To Haley, she said, "Listen, honey, it's been fun chatting with you, but I have to get back to work. You take care now, you hear?"

"I understand, Doris. Thank you for your time."

As she walked toward the exit, Doris called out, "Honey, what did you say your name was again?"

"Haley. Haley Perry." She went back to the desk and handed Doris a business card with her phone number and email address.

The woman looked down at the card in her hands and studied it. "Haley Perry. Why does your name sound so familiar?"

As the woman pursed her lips and squinted at her, Haley had a sinking feeling that maybe Doris was having second thoughts about spilling her guts about the Fortunes. It wouldn't be the first time it had happened. Haley called it interviewee's remorse.

Oh well. She couldn't take any of it back. The toothpaste was out of the tube, and Doris had offered some exciting new information. A potential bombshell, in fact, if it turned out that Freya was the one who had been at County General Hospital the night the babies were switched.

"Are you going to help me, or are you going to stand here and chitchat all day?" grumbled the man who wanted to open the new account.

"Of course, sir," Doris said. "To open an account for you, I'll need to see your driver's license and a credit card."

"Thanks again," Haley said. "Please let me know if you think of anything else."

Doris waved, but her full attention was trained on the man.

Haley's heart was pounding as she walked away, sorting through the strange and unsettling information Doris had dished out.

While all the pieces didn't quite fit together to reveal the entire picture, she could see clear as day that Freya Fortune, the woman who had so studiously avoided her, was the missing link in this investigation.

Haley had no other choice. She had to confront Freya

and get the answers directly from the source—but first, she wanted to be up front with Camden and let him know what she'd learned. She owed him that much.

CHAPTER EIGHT

CAMDEN SAT HUNCHED over his desk, staring at the same invoice he'd been looking at for the past hour. Again, he'd reached the bottom of the page and hadn't a clue what he'd read. This had happened so many times, he'd lost count.

He rubbed his eyes with the hand that wasn't holding the paper and cursed his lack of concentration.

All he could think about was what Haley had said before she'd left his bed this morning. Were they really going to pretend like they were going on with their lives as if nothing had happened last night?

Well, if that was the case, he was doing a piss-poor job of it.

He leaned back in his chair and raked a hand through his hair, taking a deep breath, trying to get a whiff of her—her shampoo, her perfume, her body.

She was like a drug. His kryptonite.

And she'd left him with a kiss and what was tantamount to an ultimatum.

I have to write that story, Camden. I hope you won't make me choose between my work and...us.

In other words, he had to choose between loyalty to his family and her. Because if she reopened this sad chapter in his grandfather's and uncle's lives, it would essentially mean Freya would be dragged into it by proxy.

The woman had been nothing but kind and generous to him. It wasn't just the money—she had reached out to his brother and cousins and him and welcomed all of them into the Fortune family. She'd given them a chance to heal, a chance to come back together and be a family—without the continuous upheaval and drama their parents had caused, the screaming and yelling and storming out. That was the example his parents had set for relationships. Those were dark days, and they still played a big part in his ambivalence to commit.

He'd momentarily lost his head over Joanna, and she'd proven relationships were nothing but trouble.

This tug-of-war with Haley didn't bode well.

Despite all that, he wanted things to work with her.

If Haley felt for him even a fraction of what he was feeling for her, shouldn't it make her more sympathetic about not dragging Freya through the mud?

The sound of someone opening the office door pulled Camden's thoughts back into the real world. Maybe Haley had come back to talk about things, to work out something equitable that would make both of them happy.

"Hey, Camden."

But it was West. Not Haley.

His brother removed his black Stetson and set it on one of the chairs in front of Camden's desk. He slid into the other one, propping his booted foot on his jean-clad knee. "I have the final draft of the articles of incorporation. I brought you a hard copy to look over. I've already emailed the file to you. Did you get it?"

Camden met him with a blank stare. "Oh, no. I haven't checked my email this morning."

West narrowed his eyes at him. "Rough night?"

Camden laughed and threw back the last swallow of coffee in his mug.

He and West had gotten close over the month he'd been back.

Nothing like getting a second chance with someone you thought was dead. It was still surreal.

Camden rose to refill his coffee cup. Maybe a big dose of caffeine would pull him out of this funk.

"Want coffee?" he asked his brother as he shuffled over to the drip pot on the bookshelf.

"Is it fresh?" West asked.

"Beggars can't be choosers."

"Who peed in your Cheerios?" West said.

Camden scowled. "Yes, it's fresh. I made it this morning. And it's strong."

"You're in a mood," his brother remarked. "What's wrong with you? I thought you'd be in a good place after we got the insurance all straightened out. Have you hit more snags with the camp?"

Camden handed him a navy blue mug with yellow fish painted on it. "Naw, everything is good with the camp. It's…my love life that's…"

He wanted to say his love life was *in the shitter*, but that wasn't exactly true. It didn't have to be, if he could find it in himself to look the other way while Haley dug up dirt on his family.

"Are you still seeing Haley?" West asked.

Camden shrugged.

"Tabitha said last night she thought things were going well. She was talking about the wedding and putting the two of you together in the bridesmaid–groomsman pairings. Should I tell her not to?" He gnawed on his lower lip. "I guess Haley could be paired with Bear. That is, if he decides to grace us with his presence for the wedding."

"No, don't ask her to change anything. If things don't work out, I'm sure we can act like adults for your big day."

"You want to talk about it?" West sipped his coffee and watched Camden over the cup's rim.

His brother was smart and levelheaded. God knew that he and Tabitha had been through it, but they had managed to not only stay together in the end but also come through it even stronger. And at one point, their problems had literally been a matter of life and death after the thug West had put behind bars threatened Tabitha's life.

Camden traced a coffee stain on his desk blotter, took a deep breath and laid out all his reservations about his relationship with Haley.

"Family has to come first," he concluded after he'd gotten it all out. "Especially now that we're all back together."

Even though West was nodding slowly, Camden could sense the *yeah, but...*coming.

"One of the things I love the most about you is your fierce sense of loyalty," West said. "That's such a great attribute, and those who earn your trust are damn lucky."

"But?" Camden prodded.

"But I'm not convinced that Freya deserves that trust."

Camden flinched. "Dude, she made it possible for me to buy this ranch."

"I know she did, and I'm happy for you to have it. But she's not as altruistic as a lot of people are making her out to be. I mean, it was our grandfather's money, not hers. It's our inheritance. There's something about her that doesn't sit right with me. I get the feeling that there's an ulterior motive hidden behind her generosity.

"I hope I'm wrong, but Haley is great. It would be a damn shame if you throw things away with her only to regret it later when we meet the real Freya Fortune."

"Can you tell me what it is about her that's given you pause?"

West ran his hand over his chin and looked up at the ceiling. Finally, he shook his head. "I don't know. I can't put it into words. All I know is that since I passed the bar,

I've met a lot of individuals, and it's helped me develop a sort of sixth sense about people. That's what's telling me that Freya is hiding something. And exposé or no exposé, that same sixth sense is telling me that you'd be an idiot to let Haley get away out of loyalty to Freya."

AFTER HER MEETING with Doris Edwards, Haley went back to her apartment and thought about what to do with the information Doris had shared.

Even though she and Camden had left things unsettlingly open ended that morning, she knew she had to tell him what Doris said before she shared it with anyone else. Based on what the older woman had told her, Freya might be implicated in the baby swap. Camden deserved to hear it from her rather than learning secondhand that she knew about it and hadn't told him.

Heart pounding, she dialed his number. He picked up on the second ring.

"Hey, it's me," she said.

"Hey, you. How was your morning?" There was no hesitancy in his voice. In fact, he sounded like he was glad she'd called.

"It was interesting," she said. "That's why I'm calling.

"Yeah, about this morning..." he began.

Was that regret she detected in his tone?

"You don't owe anyone any apologies or explanations for protecting your family, but I hope you understand that my career is important to me. On that note, I need to tell you something."

Ugh. She was sounding like gloom and doom personified.

"Oh, yeah? Sounds serious," he said. "What is it?"

"I'd rather tell you in person. Can you meet me this morning? If so, we could check off point three in the *Five*

Steps to Love project. You know, listening without judgment to an issue the other person is having."

She laughed, hoping to lighten up a bit so she didn't sound like the bearer of bad news—even though essentially, that's what she would be delivering.

"I think we've already crossed that one off the list with what you told me this morning," Camden said, his voice husky. "After last night… I think we've more than proven Jacqueline La Scala's theory works.

Wait. Did he say they'd proven her theory? That he'd fallen in love? She was tempted to ask him to clarify, but by the time her brain formed the words, the window had passed. It would sound like a weird afterthought.

Instead, she steeled herself and said, "Well, we still have to get through steps four and five before we can form a legitimate conclusion."

"Speaking of," he said. "Step four is to attend an event together. Do you have a date to the big engagement party?"

He was talking about the double engagement party for Tabitha and West and Bea and Davin at the Chatelaine Dude Ranch that weekend.

"As a matter of fact, I don't."

"What do you say we go together and cross item number four off the list?" he said. "Then if you kiss me, we will have done everything in order, and you can write your story."

Heat flooded her body as she pondered what he'd said a moment ago about more than proving Jacqueline La Scala's theory…and last night…

Oh, last night.

Her toes curled in her sandals.

"That sounds like a plan," she said. "But first, I have something important to talk to you about."

Doubts about whether or not he would want to keep

those plans after she'd shared what Doris Edwards had said were like a turning a fire hose on her hot daydream.

A half hour later, Camden sat down beside her on a bench in the park across from her apartment.

"Thanks for meeting me," Haley told him.

"Yeah, of course."

"Are you hungry?" she asked. "I picked up a po' boy from the Cowgirl Café. Those sandwiches are big enough to split. Sometimes I can get three meals out of one."

She was nervous, which was why she was rambling on about stretching one sandwich into multiple meals.

"Go ahead and eat what you want, and save the rest for later," he said.

She gave him the side-eye. "I am not going to sit here and hog down on a messy sub while you watch. Here. Eat."

Bea had cut the sandwich and wrapped the halves separately. Haley handed him one of the two.

"Thank you," he said. "If I'd known you wanted to have a picnic, I would've contributed something. There's still a little bit of your famous potato salad left in my refrigerator. We never got to share it since other things...kind of got in the way."

They exchanged meaningful looks.

He was right. So much had happened since he'd invited her over that first time. Now she was about to potentially blow up all the progress they'd made.

But maybe everything she'd learned from Doris could wait until they'd finished their sandwiches. It was such a gorgeous spring day. Not too warm. In fact, it was so nice sitting on this bench, having a picnic in the shade of the big Texas red oak. She had an overwhelming impulse to backpedal and tell him never mind, she'd been kidding about the heavy stuff. Really, all she'd wanted was to have lunch with him.

Yeah.

No.

She needed to tell him the truth.

"I didn't want it to go to waste, so I've been enjoying it." He was still going on about the potato salad. "I can see why people call it your famous recipe. It's delicious."

"Thanks, but full disclosure—it's not my recipe. It's Ina Garten's. I got it online. I might as well tell you that, too, since I asked you to meet me here so I could come clean about something else. But I'm glad you like it. I did use less dill than she called for. So, in that sense, it *is* my recipe. Adapted from Ina's."

Oh, God, Haley, get to the point.

"What do you need to come clean about?"

As she took a deep breath and tried to figure out where to start, he must've sensed her anxiety. He set the sandwich on the bench space between them, bent forward and braced his forearms on his knees. Clasping his hands together, he looked at her and waited for her to speak.

Her brain was a jumble of nerves, and it was hard to think straight.

"I'm going to cut to the chase because I want to be completely transparent with you, Camden. I know you're very fond of Freya, but since I've been working on the mine story, I've heard some things I think you need to know..."

She sighed and tried to figure out where to start.

He fidgeted on the bench, then asked with a resigned tone, "What have you heard?"

She wrapped up her sandwich and stuffed it back into the paper bag and shifted so that she was facing him. Then she took a deep breath and told him what she'd learned from Val Hensen about Freya's lies about Asa.

"He's your cousin and my brother-in-law," Haley said. "I know he was no angel before he met Lily, but he was single and within his right to date whomever he wanted. It didn't matter if he was seeing a different woman every night. Maybe he was, but Val said that Freya made it sound like twenty-four-seven Sodom and Gomorrah. Asa might be a lot of things, but you know that's not him."

"But that would mean Freya was sabotaging his chances at buying the dude ranch," Camden muttered. "Why would she do that? She wanted him to have it."

"I don't know, Camden. I get the feeling that Freya has tried to sabotage you and your cousins. Asa had troubles. Then someone tried to sabotage Bea—"

"Freya cares about us," he insisted. "Or at least, she cares enough to carry out my grandfather's last wishes for us to get our inheritance. The best way she could've hurt us would've been to withhold the money. But she's the one who is granting our wishes."

"Legally, she had to give you the money. She's the executor of the will."

The tension was radiating off him in waves. Haley bit down on her bottom lip and forced herself to lay it all out.

"Think about it, Camden. You even had trouble with the wish Freya granted you. All that mysterious red tape surrounding the insurance for the camp. You told me yourself that at one point you thought it was going to cost you your dream. Then the issue went away as quickly as it started. Since Freya was the one who was supposed to pay for the policies, don't you think it's likely that she created that headache?"

Camden looked at her like she'd called his benevolent step-granny a whore. Then he rested his head on his balled fists.

"Freya said she paid the premium. We have no proof that she didn't. Just as we have no proof that she did anything to sabotage Bea's restaurant opening or that she said anything about Asa."

"Val Hensen told me point-blank that Freya was the one who informed her that Asa was a player and tried to talk her out of selling the dude ranch to him. Look, I'm not doing this to stir up trouble. Put aside your skepticism and weigh the facts. Will you at least do that?"

He looked at her like she was speaking a foreign language.

"First, there's your cousin Asa. He was all set to buy the Chatelaine Dude Ranch until Val Hensen got wind that Asa was a wild ladies' man and had quite a few girlfriends. Then Bea had trouble on the opening night of the Cowgirl Café. And you had problems with the insurance."

She ticked the points off on her fingers, but paused before playing her final card.

"I interviewed a woman named Doris Edwards, who works at GreatStore. She told me that Freya purchased a short brown wig and a cane around the time that Esme and Ryder's babies were switched at County General Hospital."

Camden's brows knit. "I don't understand."

"*Short mousy-brown hair. Walking with a cane.* That matches the description of the woman who was hanging around the hospital the night the babies were switched. Don't you see the common factor in all of these mishaps is Freya?"

"You don't have solid proof that my step-grandmother didn't pay the insurance premium. She said she did. And there's also no evidence that she was the one who sabotaged Bea's opening night. If anyone caused trouble for Bea, it was Devin Street, by running that bad review. We know that Bea has more than forgiven him. She's going to marry him. Are you sure you understood Val and Doris right?"

Camden's tone wasn't accusatory; it was almost deflated.

"If you want, you can ask them yourself," Haley said. "Val lives near me. We could go knock on her door. Doris seems sharp as can be—and you have to admit, a woman as fit and pretty as Freya purchasing a wig and cane would kind of stand out."

Camden put a hand on Haley's arm and gave her a meaningful look. She could see the wheels turning in his mind.

"Haley, I'm not trying to be difficult, but you can't blame people for things because it supports your theory. I know you're…eager to write this exposé, but even you have to admit, what you've told me is all circumstantial evidence."

She shrugged his hand off and crossed her arms.

"Will you listen to me, please?" he said. "I listened to you when you were delivering what was hard for me to hear."

She gave him a one-shoulder shrug. "Sure. Go for it."

"I hope you know I think the world of you, but I also think you're so…determined to get to the bottom of this exposé that you're reading much more into everything than what's really there. It's like forcing two puzzle pieces together that don't fit. They might look like they go together. You might want them to go together. But if they don't, they're not going to give you the picture you're looking for. This morning you told me it was important to not let eagerness cloud judgment. You said you didn't want to hurt people, but you keep grasping at straws, people will get hurt."

IF LOOKS COULD KILL, he would've been a dead man.

"You said I'm *eager* to write this exposé, huh?" Haley said.

He gave a one-shoulder shrug of his own and nodded, fearing he might've gone too far.

She shook her head. "*Eager* is not the word you really wanted to use, was it?"

Uh-oh.

Sensing a trap, Camden narrowed his eyes.

"You almost said I was *desperate*, didn't you?"

The truth was, he *had* almost said *desperate*, but he had thought better of it. It was uncanny how she could almost read his mind.

He hadn't meant anything derogatory by it, but after the bombshell West had dropped on him earlier—telling him that he, too, believed there was something off about Freya—Camden wasn't sure what to believe anymore.

He did know that he wanted to be damn sure of the facts before he blamed Freya for the accusations Haley was making. His grandfather's widow had been so good to him. She'd brought his family back together and had given so many of them a fresh start.

"It's semantics, Haley," he said.

If anyone was desperate, it was him. He was desperate to pull her close, desperate to taste her lips again. Desperate to make love to her and wake up beside her. But with the accusations she was making, it made him feel as if he were living in two parallel universes: one that made him whole and one that tore apart everything he'd never known he needed until now.

"You're not desperate. You're..."

Ambitious? Nah, that might sound wrong too. He didn't think there was anything wrong with ambition...as long as what the person aspired to didn't hurt anyone else. Right now he aspired to feel Haley in his arms. To run his hands along her curves and revel in how she fit just right against his body—

"I'm what?" She raised her chin and looked him straight in the eyes. "Am I an inconvenient truth?"

Camden shook his head and raked a hand through his hair. "Haley..."

"Because when you put everything together and factor in what I learned from Val Hensen about Freya saying such disparaging things about Asa and Doris Edwards, revealing that Freya bought a mousy-brown wig and a cane, and witnesses saying the mysterious volunteer who was at the hospital the night the babies were switched had mousy-brown hair and walked with a cane. You have to admit that it's all a remarkable coincidence. Just because the truth doesn't fit your narrative, Camden, doesn't make me desperate—"

"You're not desperate. That's why I didn't say it. I really wanted to say you're *beautiful*."

The words were out before he could stop them.

Her eyes narrowed, and she crossed her arms even tighter, her body language reflecting her resistance to his words.

"You're also tenacious, strong and smart as hell," Camden continued, his tone softening. "I understand your suspicions about Freya, but I hope you can understand that this is a lot for me to process. This is about my family. We can't jump to conclusions without concrete evidence. We need to think it through and consider alternative explanations and not let emotions cloud our judgment."

Haley looked at him, her expression softening. He thought he saw a flicker of doubt cross her features, but he couldn't be sure. Even so, Camden reached out, and she didn't pull away when he took her hand.

"I'm not saying you're wrong, Haley. I'm just asking you to be cautious and thorough in your investigation. We need to approach this with an open mind, examining every angle before we draw conclusions that can hurt people."

Her gaze searched his face. Her emotions seemed

to shift from defiance to vulnerability. She took a deep breath, and in that moment, Camden could see that she was willing to listen to reason, willing to consider his perspective.

That was all he wanted.

"Let's go talk to Val and Doris, and they can tell you exactly what they told me," she said. "Maybe then you'll believe me."

Had he mentioned she was tenacious?

"I'M SO GLAD you came back!" Doris practically sang as Haley and Camden approached the "Ask Me" desk.

"Why? Did you remember something?" Haley murmured.

First, they'd knocked on Val Hensen's door, but she wasn't at home. So they'd come to the GreatStore with the hope of catching Doris before she took her break.

"I sure did. I remembered why your name sounded so familiar. You're one of the Perry girls."

Doris slapped her hands together. She made it sound like Haley and her sisters were part of a girl band and Doris was their biggest fan.

Haley nodded, but she was determined that the conversation was not going down that alley. Anytime anyone discovered that she was one of the poor, pitiful triplets whose parents had died and left them orphaned at such a tender age, the conversation always turned maudlin. The night of her parents' death was the last subject she wanted to get into in front of Camden. Especially when he seemed to be on board with getting to the bottom of what was happening with Freya.

"Doris, I want to introduce you to Camden Fortune," Haley said.

"Hi, Doris." Camden smiled. "It's nice to meet you."

"Well, hello there, good lookin'," she replied. "So, you're one of those hoity-toity Fortunes, are you? I suppose you're okay, if you're friends with Haley. You sure are a handsome guy."

She waggled her eyebrows at Haley, and Haley knew she needed to move quickly if she didn't want to lose control of this conversation. The best way to steer matters was to be direct.

"Yes, Camden is a member of the Fortune family," Haley said. "In fact, Freya Fortune is Camden's step-grandmother. I was telling him what you told me about Freya buying the wig and cane a couple of months ago."

Doris held up her hands. "Hey, look. I don't want no trouble." She turned to Camden and hooked a thumb toward Haley. "She was the one who came in asking questions. I told her what I saw. There ain't no law against that."

"It's okay, Doris," Camden reassured her. "I can promise you that we're not here to cause you any trouble, but if you could tell me exactly what you told Haley—or better yet, what you saw the day Freya was in here—I'd appreciate it. We're trying to get to the bottom of some things that have happened."

The area around the "Ask Me" desk wasn't very busy. "Okay, I can talk as long as I don't get a customer. If anyone needs my help, I'll have to tend to them."

"That's perfectly understandable," Camden said.

Haley was happy he was taking charge. Doris seemed to like him, and it boded well that she would keep talking.

"Haley mentioned that you said Freya was in the store back in January," he told her. "Are you sure it was Freya who bought the wig and cane?"

"Of course. My memory is great. Sometimes it might take me a minute to pull up the details from the annals, but believe me, it's all stored in this old steel trap of mine."

Doris tapped her index finger on her temple. "Case in point is when I remembered that Haley was one of the Perry triplets." She turned to Haley. "How are you and your sisters doing?"

"We're fine, thank you for asking."

"You know your folks lived a few houses down from me." She shook her head. "Such a sad, sad turn of events."

Haley froze. She wasn't going to do this now. She wasn't going to stand here and discuss her parents with a complete stranger. It was upsetting. Maybe someday when she was alone, she'd offer to buy Doris a cup of coffee and ask her all about her parents. But right now wasn't the time. "Doris, have you seen Freya in here since she made the purchase you told me about?"

The woman shook her head. "Nope. Not in the store. I see her around town with that old man Wendell Fortune, but they never speak to the locals. They usually have their heads together. You suppose there's something going on between them? They sure seem cozy."

"Not that I know of," Camden said. "Especially since she was married to Wendell's brother."

"Say, speaking of brothers, how's your brother these days?" Doris asked. "Where is he keeping himself?"

For a split second, she thought Doris was asking Camden about West, but then she realized Doris was staring right at her. Haley laughed. "Oh, no, sorry, I don't have a brother. It's just my sisters and me. The Perry triplets—or that's what everyone calls us."

A nervous laugh escaped.

"Correction—you were the Perry quadruplets, darlin.' Three fraternal girls and the cutest baby boy you've ever seen."

"I'm sorry, Doris. I think you have confused my sisters and me with another family—"

"I beg your pardon, missy, but I know this for a *fact*. I would never forget something like that. You and your folks lived right down the street. How often does a person encounter a set of quadruplets? That's something you don't forget."

Haley was too busy drowning in a sea of humiliation for dragging Camden here to continue arguing with Doris. Clearly, the woman was confused.

Camden must've been internally punching the air after proving his point.

Doris tsked and shook her head. "I'll never forget how hard it was raining that night. Your folks knocked on my door in the middle of the night and asked if I'd keep you girls while they took your brother to the emergency room. I suppose they were rushing because they were worried about that baby boy. I think he was pretty sick. They were such a sweet, young couple. So much promise.

"They were new to town, so no one knew much about them. The authorities tried, but no one could locate any next of kin, and I suppose that's why y'all got split up as you did. So you gals stayed local. Whatever happened to the boy? What was his name?"

Haley did not have a brother.

Lily seemed to have a good handle on their birth parents and had been eager to share all she knew. She would've mentioned it. It would've been *huge* news.

Then again, she'd grown up believing she didn't have any siblings and later she'd learned she had two sisters.

Could they have a brother out there somewhere?

An instrumental rendition of Bon Jovi's "Livin' on a Prayer" played over the store's sound system, and Haley suddenly felt acutely aware of her senses. The florescent lights seemed brighter. The music seemed louder. The smell of produce and the perfumes from the adjacent beauty department seemed to mingle and merge, making her feel lightheaded. Then it was as if she had floated up and out of her body and was watching the scene unfold below.

Until Doris nodded to a woman who approached the counter and said to Haley and Camden, "Okey-doke, kiddos. Nice talking to ya, but I gotta get back to work."

It was just as well. Doris was convinced that she was right, but Haley knew she was wrong.

She gave her head a quick shake.

If the woman was confused, that meant everything she'd said about Freya earlier was now in question. It might all be a figment of her imagination.

She couldn't bear to look at Camden, who didn't say *I told you so*—well, not out loud, anyway—as they walked to his truck.

"That was weird," she said, steeling herself for him to say he was right. That she needed to be cautious and thorough and approach everything with an open mind before she drew conclusions that could hurt people.

Instead, he asked quietly, "Are you okay?"

No, she wasn't. She was ashamed of herself for jumping to conclusions. She was shaken by Doris claiming to know her parents and asserting she and her sisters had a brother out there somewhere.

If they did have a brother, it would be great…in theory. In a perfect world, where all children are loved and wanted and well cared for. But where had he been all these years? What had he been through? Had he been happy, or had he been through the ringer, like so many orphaned children?

Or maybe he'd died that night with her parents. If so, why had the newspaper articles only mentioned her parents and the triplets?

Triplets. Not quadruplets.

"You seem pretty shaken," Camden said as they stood in the parking lot.

"Yeah, I'm, uh…" She pressed her hands to her eyes. "I'm sorry, Camden. I guess you were right. I do need to be careful before I accuse people."

He didn't answer, but nodded instead.

Something about the gesture seemed smug. She wished he'd come right out and say *I told you so* rather than giving off such a self-satisfied air.

"Why don't you just go ahead and say it?" she asked.

"Say what?"

"Really? So, you're going to gloat?"

He looked confused.

"I'm don't know what to say right now."

"Aren't you just itching to say I told you so?" she said.

He shook his head. "What good would that do?"

"I don't know," she said. "It just seems appropriate right now."

She'd been working on this story for months, knocking on doors that weren't opening. Was this a sign that those doors were meant to remain permanently shut or maybe there was nothing of substance behind them at all?

Or was it simply an indication that she did indeed need to be more careful with her research…or at least, careful about what she shared with Camden before she had ironclad proof?

He stood there looking at her, arms crossed, a perplexed frown on his handsome face.

All she could think was that she wished she could rewind time to this morning and skip the confessional and not bring him into the Doris debacle.

Then they could go to the engagement party on Saturday night and pick up where they'd left off.

Do-overs weren't an option. The only choice she had was to move forward.

Freya would be at the party. That would be a good time to get the story straight from the horse's mouth.

But first, she needed to talk to her sisters.

"I need to run," she said. "I promised Tabitha and Bea that I'd help this afternoon with the final arrangements for the engagement party."

Since Lily would be there, too, Haley decided to call an emergency sisters' meeting so they could talk about this supposed brother before Bea arrived.

"Okay, I guess I'll see you Saturday night, then?" Camden paused and she wondered if he was giving her a chance to back out. Or maybe he wanted to back out…

She nodded rather than asking, afraid that she wouldn't like his answer.

"I'll be in touch about what time you want me to pick you up."

He didn't kiss her goodbye.

As Haley watched him walk away from her, she felt the connection that had been so strong between them last night slip farther away with each step he took. For a moment, she wasn't sure what she regretted more, looking like a fool after her best lead went up in smoke or watching the man she was falling in love with walk away.

Even though she hated admitting it to herself, her heart knew the truth.

Her biggest regret would be losing Camden, but she didn't know how to stop that from happening.

CHAPTER NINE

"SHE SAID WHAT?" Tabitha asked as she popped the cork on a bottle of cava. The sound seemed like the appropriate punctuation on the news that they might have a fourth sibling out there.

"We do *not* have a brother," Lily huffed as Tabitha made quick order of filling and distributing the delicate crystal flutes—an early wedding present from one of the Fortunes, no doubt.

Haley had gotten used to the new reality that every event that even hinted at Tabitha's wedding involved some kind of bubbly.

But she didn't mind.

In fact, since she'd had a chance to digest the possibility that they might have a brother—as slim as it was—and separate it from what Doris had told her about Freya's coincidental purchase of the cane and wig, Haley almost let herself pretend this afternoon's cava was a toast to this brother they'd never met.

Of course, she needed to let her sisters catch up with her thought process. They'd barely had time to comprehend the bombshell.

"How could we have a brother?" Tabitha asked as she held out her glass for the sisters to clink before she settled herself on the sofa next to Haley.

"Think about it," Lily said. "If there was a boy baby,

why hasn't anyone mentioned him in nearly three decades? It can't be true. Can it?"

"I'd love for it to be true," Haley said. "But where has he been all these years? How come Doris is the only person who knows about him?"

"And why was he not in that picture of us with our mom?" Haley added. "The one Val gave to Lily and she shared with us?"

Tabitha got up and plucked the photo off the shelf where she kept it and presented it as if it was evidence that supported her theory.

"Look at us," she said. "We're triplets. There is no trace of a brother."

"Let me see it," Lily insisted.

Tabitha walked over to the armchair where Lily was sitting and handed it to her.

Lily studied it as if she might actually see the baby boy hidden in the brush along the winding path like the character in *Where's Waldo.* "I'm going to call Val," she said. "She's the one who found this picture. Maybe if I ask her, it will jog her memory. Our father's not in this photo. Who knows, he might be holding our brother."

"If there were four of us," Tabitha pondered, "why would they have a triplet stroller and not one for four babies?"

No one had an answer for that.

Lily pulled her phone out of her purse and placed the call and switched it over to speakerphone, allowing Haley and Tabitha to hear. Val answered on the third ring.

"Hello?" she said.

"Hi, Val, it's Lily Perry Fortune. How are you?"

"I'm just fine, dear. And you?"

"I'm doing well, thanks. I'm here with my sisters—

you're on speaker so they can hear—and we have a question for you."

"Oh, well. Hello, ladies."

Haley and Tabitha responded.

"I hope I can help," Val said. "What's your question?"

"Remember the photograph you gave me of our mother pushing us in the stroller shortly before the accident?" Lily asked.

"Of course I do."

"Do you have any recollection of us having a brother, which might make us quadruplets rather than triplets."

The extended silence on Val's end made Haley wonder if the call had dropped. Lily must have had the same concern, too, because she asked, "Val? Are you still there?"

"Yes, I'm here. However, I don't recall seeing another baby with your folks. Not in addition to you and your sisters. I don't remember a fourth baby. I wouldn't stake my life on it. Honey, that was so long ago… I could be wrong."

"In the photo, our mom is pushing my sisters and me in a stroller for triplets. Do you remember what our father was doing? Was he holding another baby or maybe pushing him in another stroller?"

There was more silence, followed by a sigh.

"I can't recall anything like that, but as I said, it was so long ago."

The sisters exchanged disappointed glances.

"Hi, Val. It's Haley."

"Hello, dear."

"I have another question for you."

"Fire away. Maybe it will give me a chance to redeem myself since I wasn't much help to Lily."

"Do you know Doris Edwards, the woman who works the 'Ask Me' desk at the GreatStore?"

"Yes, I do. I think everyone in town knows Doris—or

at least, everyone who shops there. She's a spitfire, but she's good as gold. What about her?"

"I was talking to her about something else earlier today, and she's the one who said we had a brother. How reliable is her memory?"

"I've never had any reason to think there was anything wrong with her. She certainly knows every nook and cranny in the store, which I find remarkable, given the size of that place."

"Val, Doris said she lived close to my parents."

Haley repeated what Doris had said about the night of the accident.

"Honestly, honey, I didn't even realize your folks lived in town. When they stopped by the dude ranch, I thought they were just passing through. We used to get a fair number of visitors back in the day."

"Doris told me they were new to town and didn't know many people," Haley explained. "It sounded like they might've kept to themselves. Every account of the accident that I've found only mentions our parents, and my sisters and me as survivors, but not a male child."

"I don't know what to tell you, dear," Val said. "You might want to contact someone at County General Hospital and see if they can look into the records for you. That might be your best bet."

"I tried that when I first started looking into information about our parents," Haley said. "The person in County General Hospital's records told me that the HIPAA Privacy Rule protects health information for fifty years after someone dies."

"Well, that's too bad," Val replied softly. "I honestly don't know what else to tell you…"

Haley considered sharing what Doris had said about Freya's strange purchases, but then she remembered what

Camden had said about not casting doubt on someone's reputation unless she was one hundred percent positive that the information was true.

She sighed inwardly. She missed him and wished she could go to him now to make sure everything was okay between the two of them. But she needed to focus on the possibility that they had a brother. If they found their brother, not only would it be a reason to celebrate, but it would also mean that Doris wasn't the addled old woman she appeared to be-confused about their supposed brother *and* about Freya's purchase. However, until she knew for certain, Camden was right, telling others would be tantamount to spreading gossip.

Or *would* it?

Would asking questions to verify or debunk Freya's actions really be a bad thing?

Even so, Val wasn't the person to ask. Given her reaction when they'd run into Freya in the park the other day, Haley didn't want to chance speaking candidly, because the woman clearly had a soft spot for Freya.

After they got off the phone, Tabitha said, "I've always wanted to do one of those at-home DNA tests. You know, like the 411 Me kit that Esme used to help her baby find out about his father's side of the family. I've never done it, because I was so happy to be reunited with you all. But now that I have kids, I've been thinking that it might not be such a bad idea to do one to see if we have extended family out there. You never know. If we do have a brother, maybe he's done one too. It might be the first step in finding him."

As Lily and Tabitha chattered excitedly about the possibilities of doing a DNA test, Haley listened quietly. She knew the tests were expensive, and it wasn't in her budget.

Lily pulled up the 411 Me website on her phone.

"It looks like they're about $199," she said. "But they offer free delivery. Want to do it?"

"Yes, let's do!" Tabitha said.

As both she and Lily pulled credit cards from their purses, Haley felt like an outsider. She composed a refusal speech in her head that didn't make her sound too pitiful.

"They should be delivered within the week," Lily said after they'd placed their orders.

"You'll have to keep me posted," Haley told them. "I mean, since we're triplets, we don't need for all three of us to do the tests."

"Yes, but it's more fun if we do it together," Tabitha said.

"Look, guys, I can't—" Haley started, but Lily interrupted.

"That's why I got one for you, Haley."

She didn't know what to say, except, "Lily, I wish you wouldn't have. You know I can't afford it."

She stopped short of saying *You of all people know what it's like to barely be able to make ends meet. I'm not married to a Fortune.*

Visions of making love to Camden flashed in her head, wiped out by how she'd ruined everything with him by accusing Freya. Well, she wouldn't always be this poor. She was actively working toward her dream, which would bring in more money.

The last thing she needed was another man who wasn't supportive.

Haley cleared her throat. "Well, thank you. I'll pay you back as soon as I'm able."

"You don't have to pay me back, Haley," said Lily. "It's a gift. It brings me a lot of joy to treat you."

Haley hesitated. The way Lily had framed it, so that it wasn't about Haley being broke, but about one sister treating another sister to something special, she would be ungracious if she made it about finances.

"That's so nice of you, Lily," Haley said. "Thank you. It will be fun to do our DNA tests together."

Eager to change the subject, Haley added, "I need to talk to you both about a couple of other things before Bea arrives," she said to her sisters. "But please promise me you'll keep them close to your chest. Camden is already upset with me because I wanted to believe Doris. He is choosing to ignore what Val said about Freya—"

"Excuse me," Tabitha burst out, her green eyes sparkling. "Did you and Camden have your first fight?"

"Wait, where have I been?" Lily said. "Are you and Camden a *couple*?"

Haley ached inside. She wanted it so badly to be true, but it wasn't. If she said they were a couple—as if thinking positively could will it to be so—it could turn out to be another case of her jumping to conclusions without considering all the facts.

Camden was a complicated man.

"He has been helping me with a story I'm writing."

When Lily raised her eyebrows, Haley rushed to say, "No, not the one about the mine disaster. Please! Don't even mention that around him. He's not having it. Not *his family*. Even though there is evidence to the contrary that Freya isn't as dedicated to her stepfamily as certain people would like to believe."

"Do tell," Lily said.

She told them about Doris's allegations about Freya's purchase and how the wig and cane were eerily similar to the description of the volunteer at the hospital the night the babies had been switched. Then she confided about how Val had said Freya had nearly tanked Asa's purchase of the Chatelaine Dude Ranch.

Lily's right brow shot up. "Do you mind if I share that with Asa?"

"Not at all. Though I do need to warn you that Val and I ran into Freya and Wendell moments after she told me what Freya had done, and Val immediately kissed up to Freya. So tread cautiously. Freya seems to hold sway over a lot of people in town."

"However, West didn't know about any of this and he's thought there was something off about the woman since the day he met her," Tabitha said. "His people instincts are pretty good. He can smell bull even when it's dressed in cashmere and pearls."

"He doesn't trust her, does he?" Haley said.

"Nope."

"You said Camden went with you to talk to Doris," Lily said. "What did he think about that?"

"It's complicated." Haley told them about Camden's guarded reaction. "After Doris insisted we have a brother, she lost all credibility with him."

Lily shook her head. "That's too bad. My gut tends to think Freya is…a little controlling, to put it mildly. Even so, I can't help but wonder why would Freya dress in a disguise and go to the hospital?"

"Doris was insinuating Freya was at the hospital in that getup the same night Esme and Ryder's babies were swapped," Haley said.

"Why would Freya do something like that?" Lily asked.

"I have no idea, but I'll lay it all out for you the way I see it," Haley said. "The babies were switched when Freya first got to town. Doris swears she saw Freya buy a wig and a cane right before the switch happened. I've never known Freya to wear a wig or seen her use a cane, have you?"

Her sisters shook their heads.

"No, she's in pretty good shape," Tabitha said as she

picked up the bottle of cava and topped off everyone's glasses. "I have no idea what she'd need with a cane."

"Exactly. Next, we know for a fact that she was talking smack about Asa behind his back, nearly ruining his chance to buy the dude ranch," Haley continued. "Then we all know how disastrous everything turned out the night Bea opened the Cowgirl Café. Freya was there, though in all fairness, we have no proof she had anything to do with the sabotage. Then, get this—Camden nearly gave up on opening Camp JD because of troubles with the insurance policy. Freya swore she'd paid the first premium, but lo and behold, the payment kept getting lost. But then West got involved, and everything eventually righted itself."

The sisters sat in silence, looking at each other.

"Do I need to ask what's the common denominator of this equation?" Haley asked.

The doorbell rang. "That's probably Bea," said Tabitha.

"Look, I'm not going to say anything to her about this. Camden's already angry enough at me. And after the brother curveball, I don't know if Doris is a credible source. Freya could be implicated in the baby swap if word gets around about her disguise purchase."

"If she had anything to do with it, she should be," Lily retorted. "Switching two babies isn't a prank. It could've had real, long-term consequences."

"And if she didn't do it and the finger is pointed at her," Haley said, "that could have real, long-term consequences too. I get what he's saying—I need to be careful until I have proof. I know I can trust you two, and I appreciate you letting me talk it out."

The doorbell rang again. As Tabitha walked toward it, she said over her shoulder, "Just because *you* can't ask questions doesn't mean I can't."

LATER, AS THE four women sat around Tabitha's dining room table, putting the final touches on the favors for the double engagement party, Haley listened to Tabitha, Lily and Bea talk about wedding preparations. While the women chatted, her mind drifted back to Camden and how they'd left things.

Things between them had seemed so good. In fact, for a few precious hours, everything had been perfect—passionate and intense, leaving her longing for more—but then everything had turned on a dime.

Why did it always have to come down to choosing between a deeper connection with a man and her career? She wouldn't be surprised if he decided they shouldn't go to the party together. If that happened, she'd remind him that she needed to finish the research for the article. They'd go to the party together, and if he didn't want to be there with her, it would prove her theory that the book and its five easy steps were a bunch of nonsense.

A sudden wave of sadness crashed down on her. She didn't want the book to be a bunch of nonsense. Because she wanted Camden and her feelings for him to be the real deal.

If he wasn't—if they weren't—that would be heartbreaking.

Haley was lost in thought when Tabitha's voice broke through her reverie. "Haley, are you okay?" Concern was etched on her face.

She blinked, offering a wistful smile. "Yeah, sure. I'm so happy for you, Bea and Lily. You've all found Mr. Right."

Bea chuckled, nudging Tabitha playfully. "Well, since your sisters are married to Fortune men-or, in Tabitha's case, about to be — maybe you should set your sights on one too. Speaking of which, I think we all know of one very eligible Fortune bachelor, and rumor has it that the two of you have been seen around town together on more than one occasion."

Haley rolled her eyes. "Oh, really? And who might that be?"

Bea exchanged a knowing look with Tabitha and Lily before speaking. "It's my cousin Camden. But did I really have to tell you?"

Warmth bloomed on Haley's cheeks.

She decided to play it off as a casual friendship. "Oh, Camden has been helping me with an article I'm doing for *Inspire Her* magazine. He's acting as my guinea pig for a story that disproves the theory of a self-help book that promises anyone can fall in love if they follow the five steps outlined in the book."

Curiosity danced in Lily's eyes. "You didn't tell me this. Which step are you two on?"

Haley hesitated for a moment, contemplating whether to divulge the truth about their passionate night together. "We've completed the first three steps, but…we've gone a little off-script."

Bea and Tabitha gasped in unison, their eyes widening with excitement.

"Okay, Haley, spill!" Bea exclaimed. "'Off script' as in, writing your own steps toward an engagement party of your own?"

Haley blushed, feeling both embarrassed and regretful for having said too much.

"The whole purpose of the experiment and story is to disprove the book's theory, and so far we're right on track."

"But you said you went off course," Lily prodded. "What did you mean?"

"We're both so busy, we took a little too long with step two, and we decided to repeat it. You know, to get it right."

"Is that so?" Bea seemed to be struggling not to smile. She locked eyes with Lily and then slid her gaze to Tabitha before looking at Haley. "Rumor has it, a red Honda that looked suspiciously like your car was spotted leaving Camden's ranch very early this morning."

Haley knew her face was as red as her vehicle, but that didn't mean she had to spill her guts. She didn't even know what to say.

"I have no idea what you're talking about," she said. And she didn't. The situation was so darn confusing.

"And even if I did, I wouldn't kiss and tell," she added.

She took a deep breath and looked down at her hands. "Camden Fortune is hot—there's no denying it. But the truth is, he's a little too intense for me. He's so tightly wound, and I think he's looking for a woman who's not quite as career driven as I am. We're not a good match."

The reality cut her to the quick, but it was true. No matter how badly she wished she could change the facts, to make their lives fit together as well as their bodies did, it was best not to kid herself. She'd tried to ignore the truth once and it had led to heartbreak.

Her sisters and Bea must've sensed a kernel of truth in it because the conversation ended like a dropped mic.

Thank goodness for Tabitha, who held true to her promise.

"So, Bea, did they ever get to the bottom of who tried to sabotage the Cowgirl Café's big opening night?"

Bea's face hardened and she shook her head.

"It was clearly an act of sabotage, but they have no idea who's behind it," she said. "The police have no leads."

"There was no security footage?" Lily asked.

"Nope," Bea replied. "It sure would have helped, but the system wasn't installed yet."

"Do you have a gut feeling about who might've done it?" Tabitha asked.

Bea shook her head, then shrugged as if she wanted to say more.

"What?" Haley urged. "You can talk to us."

"Yeah, we're family," Lily said.

"I keep coming back to how the alarm-installation appointment was mysteriously canceled. It was a strange coincidence. I had so much on my plate getting ready for the grand opening, it was the last thing I was worried about. Little did I know it should've been at the top of my list."

"I didn't hear about the appointment being canceled," Tabitha murmured.

"I didn't either," Haley said. "It almost sounds like it was part of a sabotage plan. Who knew about the appointment?"

Bea stared at the bag of candy-coated mints she'd filled and sighed. "That's the weird thing. Esme, Freya and I were the only ones who knew about the appointment."

Lily and Tabitha looked at Haley. She could practically read her sisters' minds. They were saying, *See! There ya go!*

Haley looked away before Bea caught on to their triplet telepathy.

"I know Esme would never harm you," Haley said. "She's your sister. You two are close."

"I don't think Freya would do anything like that either," Bea said, picking up on the unspoken suggestion.

"Why not?" Lily asked. "What do we really know about her? I recently learned that she was the one who gave Val an earful about Asa being such a man-whore and nearly cost him the ranch."

Bea shrugged. "Yes, but did you ever consider that situation is what brought you and Asa together? Not that you wouldn't have found your way to each other, but I'm not above saying my dear brother needed a wake-up call." She sighed. "In a similar way, Freya was super encouraging about me embracing my feelings for Devin. The only thing that bothers me about Freya is, she still brings up what happened on opening night. She keeps driving home the point that she can't imagine who would want to sabotage me. I wish she'd stop mentioning that night to other people too. I worry that customers might wonder if the food is safe. It's bad for business. But other than that, she seems to have a good heart."

Hmm... That's exactly how Val had justified Freya's gossiping about Asa.

Did she have a good heart? Haley wondered. Or was she the devil in disguise?

CHAPTER TEN

Haley Perry: I'll meet you at the party. Tabatha and Bea need some last-minute help. See you there.

CAMDEN STARED AT the text message again as he sat in his truck in the parking lot at the Chatelaine Dude Ranch. Actually, he was checking to make sure he hadn't missed another message from Haley saying she'd changed her mind or, worse yet, was cutting him loose for the night. The latter wasn't likely to happen, though, since the engagement party was for her sister and his brother and cousin.

He exhaled a forced breath. Saying she'd meet him there was the next best thing to cutting him loose.

Camden hated the way he and Haley had left things since visiting Doris Edwards at the GreatStore together. They were in the middle of a stalemate that had gone on for days in the wake of Doris's kooky revelation.

It was hard to fathom that Haley believed she had a brother out there somewhere. She had even admitted that Doris didn't know what she was talking about when it came to her own family. He didn't understand why she wouldn't give his family the same slack.

Rather than discussing it, they had avoided each other since the incident.

Tonight was about the engaged couples, but Camden decided he wasn't leaving the party until they'd talked things out. If she didn't want to see him and she told him that tonight, that was one thing, but he wasn't going to let a misunderstanding over something they didn't want to deal with come between them.

He let himself out of the truck and walked toward the new event center Asa and Lily had recently opened and had offered the couples for tonight's party. It was about a quarter after seven. The party was already in full swing. When Camden opened the door, the convivial sounds of guests—some dancing, others talking—floated over music played by a country music band stationed on a small platform at the opposite end of the barn.

Asa had invited him to tour the new building earlier, but Camden had been so busy, he hadn't made it over. He'd figured he'd see it tonight. He glanced around, taking in the place. He'd call it *rustic chic*, with its exposed wood and candlelight. Twinkling white lights hung from the rafters, giving the place a fairy-tale feel. After all that West and Tabitha had been through, they deserved a fairy-tale happy ending. Bea and Devin too.

"If I'd known a party was all it took to get you over here, I would've thrown one sooner," Asa quipped. "What do you think?"

He was standing with Uncle Wendell and their stepgrandmother, Freya.

"It looks great," Camden said, and greeted Asa with a handshake before dipping in for a man hug. Wendell offered a perfunctory handshake, and Camden greeted Freya with a quick kiss on the cheek. "Good to see you all."

"Camden, dear," Freya said. "Tell me, is there any truth to the rumor I've heard about you seeing that woman reporter who has been asking so many questions about our family?"

Rumors, huh?

She was one to talk.

For a beat, Camden wanted to ask Freya if what Val had said about her starting gossip about Asa and what Doris had said about the wig and the cane was true. And, for that matter, if everything was on the up and up, why did it bother her that Haley was asking questions? Why not answer her inquiries and put an end to all the speculation? But he didn't feel like getting into it with her. Not tonight. Not here.

"Are you talking about Haley Perry?" he asked.

"Is that her name?" Freya's chin tilted up. She was literally looking down her nose at him.

"Haley and I have been seeing each other," he said. "Why?"

He was showing great restraint not asking why it was her business.

Freya grimaced. "I would hope that you'd tell her to stop sticking her nose into places where it doesn't belong."

Camden shook his head. "I haven't experienced that with her."

It wasn't exactly the truth. Haley's curiosity about the Fortune family might very well spell the demise of their short-lived relationship, but he wasn't about to let Freya know that. He found the woman's elevated sense of entitlement even more off-putting than Haley's exposé. And more than anything, he was tired of secrets and people picking at each other and talking behind each other's backs.

He wished they could take a big step back. He wanted to rewind—or maybe fast-forward was a more apt wish—past all the crap so that he could bring Haley back into his bed and they could see if this thing between them was real… or if she was just another woman out to make a buck off the Fortune family's name.

Freya was scowling at him in a way that couldn't have been worse if he'd vocalized his thoughts.

"Look," he said. "She's a reporter. Reporters ask questions. It's what they do. It's not my business to tell her how to conduct *her* business."

Now Freya was looking at him as if she smelled something foul. "Well, young man, I would highly suggest that you make it your business. For the sake of your family."

Camden realized he was either going to explode or go completely still. He made a conscious choice of the latter.

He smiled, though he was sure it didn't reach his eyes. "I'll take that into consideration. Have a nice night."

Freya's nostrils flared. "Well, I never!"

She turned on her sensible heel and walked away. Wendell rolled his eyes and shook his head as if he was tired of her histrionics too. "I suppose I'd better go after her before she takes her mood out on the next unsuspecting person who crosses her path."

Camden and Asa watched them walk away.

"What the hell was that about?" his cousin asked.

Before he could stop himself, Camden said, "I heard that Freya was the one who told Val Hensen about your… exploits and almost cost you the ranch."

Asa's expression went from confused to dubious. "Why would she do something like that? It doesn't make sense."

"It doesn't, does it?" Camden said. "But it came from Val Hensen herself. So there must be something to it."

Asa ran a hand through his hair. "Yeah, but I suppose it all turned out okay in the end. I got the ranch and I got the girl."

Camden followed his cousin's gaze across the room to where his wife, Lily, stood talking to Haley. Camden's stomach did a strange flip that made him shift. Haley looked gorgeous in a maxi dress—wasn't that what they called those long dresses that weren't gowns? The flowery fabric looked soft and touchable, making him want to trace its V-neck down to where it dipped into her cleavage.

"I guess it's one of those glass half-empty or half-full kind of things," Asa mused, but Camden's gaze was pinned on Haley. "I have to give Freya full credit for me ending up with Lily."

Camden could hear his cousin talking but was barely registering his words because Haley had caught him looking at her and raised a hand in greeting, those kissable lips curving up in a melancholy smile.

"It's like this," Asa continued, "I thought I'd lost Lily, and when that happened, I realized nothing else mattered without her. None of this."

Out of his peripheral vision, Camden saw the man make a sweeping gesture as Camden raised his hand in greeting back to Haley.

"I ran into Freya while I was trying to figure out my head and heart, and where Lily fit into my life. I ended up confessing everything to her about the marriage," Asa admitted. "Freya told me it was very clear I loved Lily—not as a friend but as a woman, as a wife. She told me to go get my woman. That's what I did, and after that, everything fell into place. So I can't be too mad at her if she originally tried to fill Val's head with nonsense. None of it matters now."

The band transitioned into a slow song, and Camden murmured, "That's great. I'm happy for you two." He cleared his throat. "Listen, man, can I catch up with you later? I need to go talk to someone."

When he reached Haley, he said, "Dance with me." He took her hand and led her to the dance floor.

The minute he pulled her into his arms and she melted into him, all his doubts vanished.

"Did you help your sisters and Bea get everything set up?" he asked.

"I did." She smiled up at him, and he felt that zing. "Now we get to enjoy the party."

"The place looks great."

"Thanks," she said.

"How have you been?" he asked.

"Busy. Between the party and finishing the Camp JD article, which should be in tomorrow's paper, life's been hectic, but it's all good."

He thought about saying that he felt bad about the way they'd left things the other day after leaving the GreatStore, but in this moment, it didn't seem right to rehash something that seemed to have worked itself out.

It dawned on him that what Asa had said was right. Sometimes it took nearly losing someone to make you realize how much you cared. There was no such thing as a perfect relationship, but as long as both partners were willing to work on things, talk problems out…

He pulled back enough so he could look her in the eyes.

"Are we okay?" he asked.

She blinked, as if his question caught her off guard, but recaptured his gaze.

"Are we?" she repeated cautiously.

He was about to say, *I hope so,* when he saw his brothers, West and Bearington, near the bar. Bear was emotional as he hugged West because this was the first time he'd seen him since he'd learned he was still alive.

Camden got it. The miracle of West being here after they thought they'd lost him brought tears to Camden's eyes when he thought about it. The sight of how emotional his brother was as he hugged West was threatening to do a number on Camden too.

Plus, this second-chance theme was starting to feel like the universe was sending him a message.

Haley turned to see what he was looking at.

"Who's that with West?"

"That's my brother Bearington—Bear. We haven't seen him in…years. And he's here."

Haley stopped dancing. "Go," she urged.

"The song's not over," Camden protested.

She smiled softly. "There will be other songs."

"Yeah?"

"Yeah. Now, go. I'm going to see if Tabitha and Bea need help with anything. I'll catch up with you in a bit."

"West, I think my eyes are playing tricks on me," Camden said as he approached his brothers. He gestured to Bear. "This guy looks like someone I used to know. It's good to see you, man."

Bear and Camden bypassed the handshake and went in for a hug.

"Where have you been keeping yourself?"

Bear shrugged. "I've been out of the country, working on a big oil deal. It paid off. Your big brother is an oil baron. I finally struck it rich."

The fact that Bear had made his dreams come true filled him with pride. The brothers had come from humble backgrounds, but Bear had always acted as if he had more to prove since he had been adopted as a toddler.

As far as Camden and West were concerned, Bear being adopted was never an issue. He was their brother as equally as Camden and West were brothers. But as Bear had gotten older and had learned the truth about where he'd come from, he'd grown more and more restless, more of a loner.

Freya approached the trio.

"And who is this?" she asked.

West introduced them.

"Ahh, the prodigal son," she said.

"No." Bear shook his head. "A prodigal is a person who leaves home and behaves recklessly. That's not me."

Freya stiffened. "Well, I meant it in the sense that you'd been away and now you're back. Funny how they always return when money is being doled out."

Freya laughed, but the men didn't humor her by joining in.

When Camden had encountered her when he first arrived at the party, he'd been willing to write off his reaction to Freya sticking her nose into his business—into *Haley's* business—as irritability owed to things feeling wonky with Haley. But now, no. She was being high-handed and downright smug because she held the purse strings.

"I have no idea what you're talking about," Bear said. "But I can assure you I'm not looking for a handout. I can make my own way, thanks."

"I was speaking of the inheritance left to you by your grandfather," Freya replied archly. "No one said anything about a handout. The money belongs to you and your brothers and cousins. I'm simply here to fulfill Elias's wishes. But I can see you all have some catching up to do. If you'll excuse me..."

The brothers watched her walk away.

"So that's the infamous Freya Fortune," Bear said. "Seems like controlling the purse strings has put her on a bit of a power trip."

"You have no idea," Camden grumbled. "But she's right on one accord. The money belongs to us. It's not a handout."

Camden brought Bear up to speed on how Freya had offered to grant them all wishes funded by their inheritance. His wish come true had been Camp JD. He was unashamed that he'd invested his inheritance in the ranch and facilities that would serve children.

"I've always gotten a weird vibe from the woman," West said. "I know you all vetted her, but she shows up out of the blue with her checkbook. Something doesn't feel right. Call it a gut feeling honed after dealing with all kinds of people on both sides of the law."

He shrugged.

"At least she's doing the right thing by distributing the funds like Elias stipulated," West added.

"I'll probably donate my share," Bear said. "Somehow I get the feeling that even though she's here to fulfill the will, it might come with strings."

"How could it?" Camden's bristly feeling was back. "You're lucky you're both in a position to turn down the legacy. I accepted it because the money is ours."

"No one is saying any different," Bear insisted. "I'm just not interested in this Freya Fortune or Elias Fortune's wish-granting crap. I never knew the old man. He didn't seem to care that he'd never been a part of our lives. Did he really think throwing money at us now would make him the benevolent grandfather? Nah."

Bear swatted the air.

"It seems like she's dredging up a part of the past that I don't want anything to do with."

"I'm not so big on the thought of opening past wounds either," Camden said. "But there's something to be said for getting everything out in the open rather than keeping it buried."

"I'm not so sure about that," Bear said.

There was a lot that his brother didn't know, such as how Freya had put off a lot of people and how she wouldn't sit down and have a frank discussion with Haley. If she had nothing to hide, why not talk to her and say as much?

Camden figured there would be plenty of time to bring Bear up to speed. But not now. Not tonight. This night was about celebrating once-in-a-lifetime love and family and second chances.

They'd sort out Freya and any ulterior motives she might have soon enough.

"THANKS FOR YOUR HELP, Haley," Bea said as she handed over another platter of shrimp cocktail for Haley to set out. "We're a little in the weeds here. In hindsight, I probably should've let another restaurant cater tonight, but the businesswoman in me couldn't pass on the job."

Haley had a suspicion that Bea felt like she was still paying penance for the Cowgirl Café's disastrous opening night, but she wasn't about to bring it up. Instead, she was making herself useful by helping out. Two staff members had called in with the flu, leaving them shorthanded.

"It will be fine as long as you remember that you are one of the guests of honor tonight." Haley gestured around the event center's professional kitchen. "I know where everything is, and if I have any questions, I can ask one of your waiters."

Bea frowned. "I don't want you to be stuck in the kitchen all night."

"I won't be," she promised. "In fact, as soon as we replenish the buffet, I'm sure things will slow down and your staff will be able to handle it."

Bea breathed an audible sigh. "You're right." She untied the chef's apron she'd put on to protect her pretty green silk dress, smoothed the fabric over her hips and asked, "Do I look okay? I don't know why I'm so nervous."

"You look gorgeous," Haley said. "But there's just one thing..."

"What?" Bea's blue eyes were huge.

"You've still got your work-face on." Haley grinned.

It took a moment, but realization finally dawned and she returned Haley's smile. "Point taken. I am going out and joining the party."

"And you're going to have fun," Haley added sternly.

"And I'm going to have fun."

After her friend left the kitchen, Haley asked Joe, a waiter who had returned with an empty tray, "What else do we need out there?"

"We're good," he said. "I called a couple of friends who want to make some extra cash. One arrived a few minutes ago. She's filling in at the bar. My friend Mike should be here in fifteen minutes or so. I need to take out a cheese-and-fruit tray to replace this one, and then we can all take a breath. Thanks for pitching in. It got a little harried there for a minute."

Joe removed the cheese tray from the refrigerator, took the shrimp cocktail platter from Haley's hands, and left the kitchen. As Haley removed the apron she'd borrowed, she heard the tap-tap of high heels behind her and turned to scold Bea for retreating to the kitchen.

Only it wasn't Bea. It was Freya, looking as out of place amid the stainless steel counters and appliances as a gemstone among rocks.

"Oh." Freya looked Haley up and down and clearly found her lacking.

That only made Haley even more determined to show the woman how unfazed she was. "Do you need something?"

"Are you working in the kitchen for extra money tonight?" Freya's sneer made it clear the question was a dig.

Haley had gone to school with people like this. They looked down on anyone who hadn't been born into privilege. People like Freya thought regular folks like Haley were beneath them. If Haley had learned one thing over the years, it was that she couldn't give them the satisfaction of letting them know their careless words hurt.

"Not tonight." Haley infused as much sunshine as she could into her voice. "This party is for my sister Tabitha and my friend Bea. Since you mentioned it, I might see if Bea needs some extra hands in the future. There's no shame in earning an honest buck."

Freya replied with a gesture that was caught between a one-shoulder shrug and an eye roll. Haley knew she'd be playing right into Freya's hands if she gave the woman the slightest inkling that she'd gotten to her. Instead, she decided to beat her at her own game.

"Speaking of honesty," Haley said, "would you answer some questions for me? I'm working on a story about the Fortune mine that collapsed in 1965. I thought since you were married to Elias, you might be able to set the record straight about a few things."

Freya's nostrils flared. "This is hardly the time or place for something like that."

"I know," Haley agreed. "And normally, I wouldn't dream of trying to interview someone at a party like this, but you've been so difficult to pin down. I thought that since I had you here, you might answer a few questions."

Freya leveled her with a frosty glare.

"Or if you'd rather, we could set an appointment. Any day that works best for you. It would be so good if you could set the record straight about a few questions about the mine and some other things that have come up."

"I'll set the record straight right now." Freya pointed a French manicured finger at Haley. "I will not talk about my family to a reporter. Not now. Not tomorrow. Not next year. You might as well put down whatever story you think you're going to tell or—"

"Or what?" Haley looked Freya right in the eye and matched her menacing tone.

When the woman hesitated, Haley repeated, "Or what? If you think I need you for this story, then you'd better think again. All your running away and deflecting does is make me sure that you're hiding something."

Freya's face was stone cold.

"You listen to me and you listen good." She took a step forward into Haley's personal space. "You have no idea what you're doing with your muckraking. If you don't stop it, I will pull funding from Camden's ranch."

"You're the executor of Elias's will," Haley reminded her. "The money that bought Camden's ranch is his inheritance. It does not belong to you. You can't touch it."

Freya smiled in a way that made Haley believe she was about to play her ace. "As the executor of my husband's will, I have certain duties. Elias made me promise to protect the Fortune family after he was gone. I intend to honor his wishes at all costs. If Camden chooses to keep company with someone who threatens our family's good name, then I do have the power to cancel his inheritance. You don't believe me? Just try me."

Haley blinked. She hated to show an ounce of insecurity, but the truth was, she didn't know how Elias Fortune's estate had been set up. Was there such a stipulation in the will that would allow the hand that gives to also take away?

Camden had worked so hard to make this riding school a reality. She wouldn't be able to live with herself if he lost everything because of her. It was true that the only reason the Fortunes—or more specifically, Elias Fortune—would need to be protected by someone like Freya was if there was something he needed to be protected from.

As if reading Haley's mind, Freya said, "I'm only going to say this once, so you'd better listen to me. If you care about Camden, then you'll mind your own business. In fact, let's take that one step further—I don't want you to see him anymore. If you do, then I can promise you life will get very rough for him."

Freya turned and walked out of the kitchen without giving Haley a chance for rebuttal.

Actually, that was a good thing because Haley didn't know what to say. Her head was spinning. She cared for Camden. *Deeply.* But what was she supposed to do? If she told him about Freya's ultimatum, Freya might take back the ranch. Could she really do that?

Haley wasn't sure. West was a lawyer. He might know. He would have some insight into the specifics of their grandfather's will. Maybe he could take legal steps so that Freya couldn't hold them hostage, the way she was trying to do with Camden... That was a conversation for another day.

The last thing Tabitha and West needed was more drama in the middle of their engagement party.

Right now, the best thing Haley could do would be to leave the party. It was a shame to let a bully like Freya think she'd won by driving her out, but the woman was sure to be watching Haley's every move tonight.

Haley sighed. Even though things had gone sideways with Camden, she still had to write the *Five Easy Steps to Love* story. Technically, they'd completed all the steps. The kiss had come out of order, but it was done.

With a heavy heart, Haley let herself out the kitchen door and stepped into the warm June night. This theory that two people could fall in love by taking La Scala's five prescribed steps together...had worked.

She had fallen in love with Camden Fortune, but that would have to remain her secret.

After Haley got home, she wanted nothing more than

to go to bed and nurse her broken heart, but instead, she worked through the night, writing the *Five Easy Steps to Love* article for *Inspire Her Magazine.*

Despite her original angle of disproving the book's theory, she'd ended up pouring her heart into a different piece about how the steps had worked for her. She was careful to not identify Camden or speculate on his feelings. People would have to draw their own conclusions about whether or not it had worked for him as well.

Haley already felt too vulnerable after spilling her feelings on the page. Maybe Edith would let her use a pseudonym for this one.

She'd ask her later.

Right now, she was too exhausted to make a case for it.

She just wanted to sleep.

First, Haley emailed the article to Edith and then sank into her bed.

Despite her exhaustion, the tears she'd been holding back since Freya had leveled the final blow to her relationship with Camden poured like a dam that had been breached.

She was done with the five steps story. She never had to think about it or Camden Fortune again....She could leave him to his ranch and his riding school...

The next thing Haley knew, she was jolted awake by the sound of a ringing phone.

It took a moment, but all too soon, everything that had happened the night before landed like a kick in the stomach.

She groped for her phone on the nightstand and saw that Edith was calling.

Haley sat up in bed and cleared the sleep from her throat before answering.

"Hi, Edith. Did you get my story?"

"Good morning, Haley. I did get it..." The woman's

voice trailed off. The tender feeling in her belly gave way to butterflies. Edith sounded strange.

"Is everything okay?" Haley asked.

"Yes," Edith said. "For the most part. But, Haley, we're all dying to know how your guy feels. You left him out, and frankly, the article feels a little incomplete."

Incomplete? Ha. If you only knew.

"Haley, are you there?"

"Yes. I'm here. I was, uh… I was up late finishing the piece." She swung her legs over the side of the bed and rubbed her eyes. "I was totally knocked out until the phone rang."

"I'm sorry to wake you. I would offer to call you back, but I have some other news for you that I think you're going to want to hear, and I can't wait to tell you."

"What is it?"

"First, I need your word that you'll flesh out the *Five Steps* story to include how your guy faired in this experiment. I'm hoping he didn't feel the same way—I'm sorry, Haley. I don't want you to get hurt, but if he doesn't feel the same way, then I'm sure you'll be more inclined to move back to the city. Haley, I got the green light to hire another staff writer!"

Haley's heart pounded. Her job. It was exactly what she needed. A valid excuse to get out of Chatelaine. That way she wouldn't have to avoid Camden, and Freya would have no reason to foreclose on the property or whatever evil power the woman was able to lord over him.

She made another mental note to talk to West and tell him what Freya had said.

"Haley?" Edith prodded.

"That's great, Edith. Thanks." Haley did her best to muster all the enthusiasm she wasn't feeling. She'd waited so long for this day, for the steady paycheck and benefits that came with the job. Of course, it meant that she'd mostly be writing puff pieces, and she'd have to let go of the Fortune mine-disaster story because if she couldn't get people to talk in a place where she would get right in their faces, she wouldn't have better luck long distance.

"Of course, we will have to go through the formalities of interviewing for the position, but I am the one who gets to make the final decision since the writer will report to me," Edith added. "For the sake of appearances, it's important that you finish up the freelance story before we fly you up to interview. Everyone in the department has read it, and while they agree that what you've given us is good, as I said, it feels unfinished. We all know you'll make it right. Do you think you can finish the article in, say, three days? We'd love to fly you up at the end of next week."

Haley stood up and squeezed her eyes shut against the realization that she would have to talk to Camden to get his take.

Maybe they could meet somewhere that Freya wouldn't see them…

No. That was ridiculous. That would mean meeting out of town because that's the only way they'd be guaranteed to avoid her or anyone seeing them together and telling her.

Screw it.

Not only was she giving up the story about the mine disaster, but she was also leaving town. She would meet Camden here in Chatelaine, face-to-face, one last time. If Freya had a problem with it… Despite the way her heart twisted at the thought of Camden losing his dream, she knew he could handle Freya. If Freya took away Camden's dream that would do so much for so many deserving kids—that would be on her.

She would reveal herself.

"Absolutely. I'll have the revised copy back to you in three days or less," she said. "Thanks for this opportunity, Edith. It will be good to get back to the city."

CHAPTER ELEVEN

HALEY HAD LEFT the party without saying goodbye.

Camden had been grousing over it since he'd discovered she was gone.

When they'd danced, he thought everything was fine between them.

All morning, different scenarios had been running in his head.

Had he done something to upset her?

Maybe she'd been more upset than he'd realized about the way they'd left things after talking to Doris Edwards at the GreatStore.

Then again, maybe after seeing all his family gathered in one place she had realized the Fortune—and all their egos, ambitions and energy—were more than she wanted to take on.

Hell, sometimes he felt that way about them himself.

Regardless, they needed to talk. He wanted her to know that they could work this out. Because he didn't want to lose her.

He dialed her number, and she picked up on the first ring.

"Camden," she said.

"Hey. So you're alive. That's good. But last night, one minute you were there and the next you were gone?"

"Sorry about that," she said softly. "I should've told you I was leaving. I wasn't feeling like myself last night and—"

"Did I do something to upset you?"

"You? No, you didn't do anything like that."

"Did someone else?"

She was silent a few beats too long, but then she said, "Listen, I'm glad you called. I need to tell you something. My boss at the magazine in New York offered me my old job back."

His heart plummeted. "Are you going to take it?"

"Yes, I am. It will be good to have some stability again. You know, a regular salary that I can count on, and benefits. All the things that grown-ups are supposed to have, and since I'm closing in on thirty, I guess it's time that I start acting like a grown-up and stop chasing dreams." She hesitated. "Oh, but good news for you. That means I won't continue with the mine-collapse story. So your family won't have to worry about a pesky reporter sticking her nose in where it doesn't belong."

He couldn't believe what he was hearing. "You're giving up on it? After all the work you've done?"

"Camden, I thought you'd be happy about that. And I'm sure Freya and Wendell will be elated."

"I don't care what they think."

"Yes, you do. They're your family. I will not say another word about your family… I promise."

"You're really going?" he asked.

"I am."

After a pause, she said, "It's for the best, Camden."

"When are you leaving?"

"The sooner, the better. The job is available immediately. I need to get up there and find a place to live and arrange to move my things. But in the midst of everything, I need to finish the *Five Steps* piece. Do you have time to meet me later today or tomorrow to wrap it up? Full disclosure, I've already written my side, and I thought I could get by without yours, but my editor—who is the one rehiring me—called me on it."

He was trying to give her the benefit of the doubt, but she was being so cavalier about everything. Like it was nothing. Like *they* were nothing.

"We haven't finished all the steps," Camden said gruffly.

"Technically, we have. Sure, they were out of order, but I won't subject you to step five—"

"The kiss," he said.

"Right, we've done that. We can wrap things up. I won't take up any more of your time with it."

Why was she being so cold?

"What? So you're just done with it? With me? That's it? You write your article and move off to New York City?"

"Well, yeah, I guess so. Though I wouldn't necessarily put it that way."

"How would you put it, Haley? Or do I need to wait and read your article like everyone else?"

"Camden—"

"Look, write whatever you want. Make up something for me that matches what you said about yourself. Then you can be done with it."

She'd told him up front that she was out to disprove the book's theory. Why had he expected anything different?

"You want me to write something for you that matches what I said? But you don't know what I said."

He didn't need to hear her say it. The writing was on the wall. She'd left the party early last night. He'd been her guinea pig to test the theory for her assignment. He couldn't help her with her damn exposé. She was done with him.

Not so dissimilar from how Joanna had used him. Actually, when he boiled it down to the bone, it was the same.

Both of them had used him to get ahead and had walked away when he was no longer useful.

"Camden, I don't even know what point I'm trying to prove anymore. So I need to ask you to, um, go on the record. For the story. After going through the five steps... did you fall in love with me?"

Her words rang in his head, reverberating over and over again.

He desperately wanted to say, *Yes. I love you. I think I've loved you from the first moment I saw you.*

I thought you were different from every woman I'd ever met.

But the bile from the realization that she didn't love him, that he'd allowed himself to be used again, cauterized the words, searing them to the back of his throat.

He must be some special kind of idiot to love a woman who could walk away so easily.

"Write whatever proves your point, Haley," Camden bit out. "There's no need for us to get together. I have to go. Good luck in New York."

HALEY WAS BLAMING everything on exhaustion.

She might have been able to go back to sleep after Edith had called, but not after that devastating phone call with Camden.

Since then, everything she'd done wrong in their relationship had played on an endless loop in her brain.

She should've told him in person that she was leaving rather than blurting it out over the phone, but clearly, the sad silver lining-and what an oxymoron that was-now they wouldn't have to risk Freya seeing them together.

She couldn't help but wonder if Freya was telling the truth about having Camden under her thumb. She was probably full of crap. But now they wouldn't have to take the chance ruining everything for Camden, who, come to think of it, technically hadn't answered her when she'd asked him if he loved her.

As she sat waiting for Morgana Mills to meet her for lunch at the Chatelaine Bar and Grill, Haley wondered if seeing her today was the best idea. Her mind was barely functioning on the four and a half hours of sleep she'd managed to get in before everything had blown up. It wasn't all bad… Of course, getting her old job back wasn't bad. And getting Morgana Mills to agree to meet her for lunch so that she could hand off the story to her was a good thing.

Freya's highhandedness had made Haley realize she wasn't ready to dump the mine-disaster exposé. Since she wouldn't be able to work on it herself, she'd decided the next best thing would be to turn over everything she'd learned to Morgana. Let her have the scoop.

Heh. Nice work if you can get it.

At first, Morgana had refused Haley's lunch invitation. Frankly, Haley had been surprised that the young woman had even taken her call. After Haley had assured Morgana that she was willing to turn over everything and Morgana did not have to reveal her reasons or connection to the story, the woman agreed.

Despite being bone tired, Haley was afraid that lightning wouldn't strike twice, and she knew she'd better grab this opportunity to unload her research. The sooner, the better.

Camden and the other Fortunes wouldn't be happy about it.

He wouldn't say he didn't love me.

Yeah, but he wouldn't say he did either.

She shook away the thoughts and motioned to the server.

"My lunch companion should be here any minute, but while I wait, could I please have a cup of coffee?"

While Haley waited for Morgana and her liquid energy to arrive, she took out her phone and began composing a text to West. After several false starts—at first not wanting to reveal too much, but her fuzzy, sleep-deprived brain finally wrapped around the fact that she had to give West a reason for asking about Freya's role as the executor of Elias's will—she decided to give him a full account of everything that Freya had said last night.

As she finished composing the text, Morgana arrived and Haley pushed Send before reading it over. Regret washed over her. Had she said too much? She probably should've waited to read it through before sending it.

No. It was done. West, his brothers and his cousins needed to know everything that Freya had said and done the night before.

But maybe she should've gone to Tabitha first.

She rubbed her temples. Maybe she should just stop second-guessing herself.

"I'm so sorry I'm late," Morgana said as she slid into the booth across from Haley.

"You're not late. You're right on time. Excuse me, I need to send a quick text."

She fired off a message to both her sisters sharing the good news about getting her old job back. They should hear it from her and not through the Fortune grapevine.

Let's celebrate ASAP since I'll be leaving soon.

She pressed Send and then turned off her phone ahead of the barrage of messages she was bound to get from Tabitha and Lily. She would answer all their questions soon enough. Right now, she needed to give Morgana Mills her undivided attention.

As Morgana got settled, the server delivered Haley's coffee and took Morgana's drink order.

"Apparently, I'm late enough for you to have already ordered a drink."

"I was up all night working on a story. This isn't a drink—this is *life support.* If I don't get some caffeine in my system, I might fall asleep in my lunch. On that note, here…"

With both hands, Haley offered Morgana a large manila envelope. At first, her dining companion peered at it as if assessing whether or not it might be full of spiders and snakes rather than the information Haley had promised.

Finally, she accepted it.

"Why are you doing this?" Morgana asked.

"I told you when I called, I have accepted a job offer in New York City. I can't live and work there and continue to research the story. And I'm not going to lie—I have hit a brick wall. Those Fortunes are a tough lot. They stick together and protect one another. I guess I can't blame them."

Her heavy heart thudded. Every beat that slammed against her chest seemed to say, *Camden. Camden. Camden.* She wished she could ignore it, or make it change its sad tune, but how did that old saying go? The heart wants what the heart wants.

Suddenly, Haley had the strangest feeling. It was as if she was being watched and it pulled her attention away from her heart's despairing of Camden. She glanced to her left just in time to see Wendell Fortune staring at her and Morgana. When he saw her looking, he frowned and walked toward the restaurant's exit and disappeared out the door.

"That was weird," Morgana said.

"Well, get used to it. They will try their darndest to intimidate you and throw you off the trail."

The server returned to take their orders.

"Get anything you want. This is on me," Haley said, before ordering the lobster salad. After all, she was celebrating. She finally had a modicum of financial security—not that she could eat lobster every day. But today it felt appropriate—more like self-care than a celebration. In a matter of days, this place would be in her rearview mirror. While she'd miss her sisters, she wouldn't miss the Fortunes making her feel like an outcast. Her sisters had their own families now. It was time that Haley got on with her own life.

After Morgana placed her order—a burger and truffle fries—and the server had left, she said, "Off what trail?"

It took Haley a moment to understand that Morgana was asking what trail had she been on that the Fortunes were trying to throw her off of.

She explained as best as she could all through lunch. Haley managed to wrap up as they finished eating. She had to admit that she felt a pang of regret handing off all her hard work.

But it was for the best. She was getting ready to start a new chapter of her life. One that was far away from Camden Fortune and his family. It was going to take a long time to get over him, but she'd have work to keep her busy. Work and Manhattan. That was all a girl needed.

Or at least, that's what she told herself.

"You have my cell number," Haley said. "Feel free to call me anytime, even if it's simply to bounce around ideas and theories. I know you're going to do a great job with this."

She was so tempted to ask Morgana why she was interested in the story and what she was going to do with it, but she'd promised her she wouldn't. Maybe the woman would feel more comfortable about opening up after they'd known each other longer. After Haley was in a different state 1,800 miles away. For now, she needed to go home and try to grab a few hours of sleep before she sorted out what to write for Camden's *Five Easy Steps to Love* experience.

Her heart continued its requiem: *Camden. Camden. Camden.*

When Haley turned her head to look for the server so she could request the check, she saw Wendell Fortune lumbering toward their table as if on a mission.

She didn't even have time to say anything to Morgana before he was hulking over them. Well, apparently, Morgana was about to get a baptism by Fortune fire. Haley steeled herself, prepared to tell Wendell that it was a free country. That she and Morgana had as much right to be there as he did, but before she spoke, she saw that his face had softened and he was holding what looked like a stack of letters bound by a stretched-out rubber band.

"Since you're both interested in the mine collapse—and the truth—I have something for you." He placed the bundle of letters on the edge of the table, away from their lunch dishes.

"Hello, Mr. Fortune," Haley said. "What's this?"

As he drew in a slow, deep breath, his eyes swam with tears.

"I'm not ready to talk about it, but I will say this much—these letters are from my daughter, Ariella. She was, um, illegitimate, and I did not do right by her. You see, she fell in love with a young man who was penniless and didn't have any kind of future ahead of him. I did not approve of him, and I forbade her to see him."

Haley's heart was pounding and her head was spinning, but at least she had enough of her wits about her to ask, "Would you like to sit down? We could have dessert."

Wendell gave his head a single gruff shake.

"No. It's all in here. There's a letter in here that I could never bring myself to open. I reckon it will tell you everything you need to know."

With that, he turned around and walked away without looking back.

"IS THIS AN INTERVENTION?" Camden asked when he walked into the living room of West and Tabitha's house and saw Tabitha, Lily, Asa, Bea, Esme and Bear were there too. Of course, Tabitha lived there, but when West had said he needed to talk to Camden about something important, he thought it would be just the two of them.

"Why?" Bear smirked. "Do you need one?"

"No," said Camden. It left like a lie. His heart could use a Haley intervention. Or more aptly, a Haley exorcism since the phantom of her, of what could've been, had latched onto his heart and wouldn't let go. "I didn't realize this would be a family meeting. I thought West had some Camp JD business to discuss with me."

"I do," West said. "But it turns out the business concerns all of us."

Tabitha smiled at him and handed him a glass of iced tea. "Bea brought chocolate chip cookies. Help yourself."

"Thanks," Camden replied, his stomach a knot of nerves. "Maybe later. What's going on?"

Judging by the way they were slanting sidelong glances at him, he felt like he was the last to know whatever was happening.

"A couple of hours ago, I got a text from Haley," West said.

The revenant squeezed his heart harder at the mention of her name.

"Yeah? I know she's leaving, but what can you do?" He

shrugged, hoping he looked more unconcerned than he felt. "You didn't need to call a family meeting."

"It's more complicated than that," West told him.

That's the truth.

"How so?"

"Apparently, Haley spoke with Freya last night at the party, and Freya told her that there was a provision in Elias's will that allowed her to rescind our inheritances at her discretion."

Camden flinched and glanced at Bea and Asa. Judging by their lack of surprise, this wasn't the first time they'd heard this news.

West didn't wait for Camden to ask questions. "I don't handle estate law, so I made a few phone calls and had some colleagues look over the will. It's pretty straightforward. They couldn't find anything that would give her that kind of power."

"That's good, then?" Camden said cautiously.

"Have you talked to Haley today?" Bea interjected. "I'm curious to know more about the context of their conversation. We've all tried to contact her, but our calls go straight to voicemail, and she's not returning our texts."

"That's not like her," Tabitha said.

"Maybe she's busy preparing for her big move," Camden told them, struggling to keep his voice neutral. "I know she had a story to finish up on deadline. Maybe she turned off her phone?"

"I stopped by her apartment on my way over, but she wasn't there," Lily added. "I was hoping she'd join us and tell us what happened last night. She left the party early, and I don't know why."

"She did," Camden said. "I spoke to her this morning, and she definitely didn't seem like herself, but she didn't mention Freya. I wonder if she said something else to upset Haley?"

The doorbell rang and West stood to answer it.

"We can ask Freya ourselves. I invited her to join us. That should be her now. Rather than speculating, I figured that it wouldn't be such a bad thing to include her in this conversation."

Everyone sat silently, listening to West and Freya exchanging greetings in the foyer.

She seemed as surprised as Camden had been to see everyone gathered in the living room.

Her hand fluttered to her pearls. "What's this?"

"We thought we should have a family meeting," West explained. "But first, have a seat. Would you like a glass of tea and some of Bea's chocolate chip cookies? They're delicious."

Before Freya could answer, Tabitha was handing the woman her refreshments. Freya seemed to relax a little and bit into one of the cookies.

"You're right," she said as she dabbed at the corners of her mouth with a napkin. "They are the best chocolate chip cookies I've ever tasted. Bea, you must share your recipe."

Bea smiled. Camden thought it looked a little forced.

"It's come to our attention that there might be a question about the terms of Elias's will." West held up the paperwork as if he were presenting an exhibit in court. "I'm sure it's a misunderstanding, but we wanted to talk about it with you so that we're all on the same page."

"Oh?" Freya seemed genuinely clueless to what West was referring to. She set the cookie down on her plate, which was resting on her lap, and trained her full attention on West. "Please, do go on."

While West was filling her in on the claim that *someone* had heard her say that she had the ability to rescind their inheritances if she saw fit and that colleagues specializing in estate law had assured him the will contained no such clause, Camden scrutinized her reaction.

It was dawning on him that this issue with the will might be what was fueling Haley's sudden coolness.

"I believe you're speaking of Haley Perry," Freya said, a soft smile curving up the corners of her mouth. "She and I spoke last night. I'm so sorry, but I think she completely misconstrued what I said."

"You didn't tell her that unless she stayed away from Camden that Camden would forfeit the ranch?" West asked.

Camden started. His brother had left that detail out of the mix when he'd brought him up to speed. As red-hot pin pricks of fury needled him, he had enough of his wits about him to realize it was probably a good thing West had waited until now to mention it.

When he stopped seeing red, Camden glanced over at Freya, whose mouth had fallen open in utter surprise.

"Is that what she told you? Because that's not at all what I said. That's the problem with reporters. They're always taking things out of context."

"What exactly *did* you say?" Camden demanded.

Freya turned to him and blinked, as if seeing him for the first time.

"Well, let's see. It started off quite a lovely conversation, but when she started pushing me about our family—which is inappropriate at any time and quite rude at a party—I had to put her in her place and tell her once and for all that she needed to abandon the nonsense of this fifty-first miner. Not only is there no story there, but the mine disaster happened nearly sixty years ago. She's hurting a lot of people by ripping open old wounds that have long since healed. I don't know what part of *I have nothing to tell you* she couldn't understand."

"Well, you'll be happy to know that she's decided to drop the story," Esme informed her. "She has accepted a job at a magazine that's headquartered in Manhattan. She'll be moving soon."

"Freya, I have a question for you," Camden said. "If there's truly nothing to this story, why wouldn't you sit down with her over a cup of coffee and tell her? Why all the cat and mouse games?"

Freya's lips curved into an indulgent smile. "Contrary to what you all might believe, I have a very busy life. Essentially, last night at the party, we accomplished that. I told her she was tilting at windmills. I didn't mean to upset her. Especially if she was going to twist my words. But what can you do?"

"While we have you here, I have a couple more questions that don't have anything to do with the mine story, but they're still important," Camden told her.

The woman nodded and took a rather large bite of cookie.

"Val Hensen said that you were the one who had told her that Asa was a ladies' man, nearly causing her to refuse to sell to him."

She nodded adamantly as she motioned to her full mouth, indicating she would speak after she'd swallowed the cookie.

"Why would you do that?" Camden asked.

Freya washed the cookie down with a gulp of tea. As she blotted the corners of her mouth, she replied, "Because it was true. You can't deny it. And I'd like to think that because of it, he realized it was time to settle down."

She turned to Lily. "Lily dear, you can't deny that everything turned out for the best. You got the ranch, and you and Asa are together. You're a beautiful couple."

"There's also talk that you purchased a short brown wig and cane at GreatStore around the time that Esme and Ryder's babies were switched," Camden continued.

Freya narrowed her eyes at him. "What exactly are you alleging, son?"

"Why would you think that I was making an allegation?" he said. "It's a simple question. I thought while we were clearing the air, we might as well get this out in the open too."

Freya rolled her eyes. "This, no doubt, comes from your little girlfriend?"

"No. This comes straight from the source who claims to have witnessed you making the purchase."

"I can assure you they are wrong. When have you ever seen me wear a brown wig? Clearly, I do not require the assistance of a cane to get around. I am perfectly able to move on my own."

"If it's not true," Bear chimed in, "then why is your nose all out of joint?"

Freya glared at him. She set her half-full tea glass and cookie plate on the coffee table and stood up.

"Why? Because this feels very accusatory and quite like a personal attack." Her eyes filled with tears. "I have tried to be nothing but nice and accommodating to you all. I took care to track each of you down and see to it that you received the inheritance that was rightfully yours. I find this all very hurtful."

Camden wanted to ask if she'd also had a role in sabotaging the Cowgirl Café's opening night and if she truly had put through the insurance payments for Camp JD, but it felt like it would be tantamount to bullying. That's not what his questions were meant to accomplish.

He needed to hear from her that she had nothing to hide.

What did it matter now, though? Bea's restaurant had survived. He was well on his way toward opening his riding camp. It was probably best to drop it.

"We didn't mean to upset you," Asa said gently. "We just needed answers. Now we have them. We're all good here."

Freya sniffed and nodded. "When my late husband, Elias, was on his deathbed, he made me promise that I would look after you kids and protect his family and the Fortune name. That's all I wanted to do. So, if you'll excuse me..."

Tabitha walked Freya to the door. The others sat in silence, listening as Tabitha tried to soothe the woman's ruffled feathers.

"Please know we didn't mean to hurt your feelings, Freya," Tabitha said. "I hope we can put everything behind us."

Freya's response was too faint for Camden to hear, but the one thing he knew for sure was that he needed to talk to Haley. If she'd believed he might lose everything if Freya saw them together, her sudden change of heart—about him and the mining story—made so much sense.

It appeared that she had sacrificed what she wanted so that he could realize his dream.

A woman like Haley came along once in a lifetime.

He wasn't about to let her go.

CHAPTER TWELVE

WHEN HALEY ASKED the server at the Chatelaine Bar and Grill for the check, she learned that Wendell had taken care of it.

She and Morgana looked at each other, trying to make sense of the turn of events. Wendell had not only treated them to lunch, but he had also turned over a treasure trove of intel that might answer a lot of questions.

Suddenly, Haley was wide awake as she contemplated how she'd handed off the story in which some of the answers had finally appeared. As if sensing her uncertainty, Morgana invited Haley to go back to her room at the Chatelaine Motel. They spent hours reading through the stack of letters from Wendell's secret daughter.

In the letters, Ariella had written about her love for the destitute miner, Merle, whom Wendell had forbidden her to see.

They were stunned.

"If she was illegitimate and basically Wendell's dirty little secret—which, it seems, he took great pains to keep on the down low—what right did he have to tell her who she could and couldn't love?" Morgana asked.

"Well, you've met Wendell," Haley reminded her. "I think that explains a lot."

They both fell silent when they got to the letter where Ariella admitted that she and Merle had a baby and that she had hidden the child, but it was time her father knew the truth.

Attached to this letter was a note from Wendell, addressed to Haley and Morgana:

I am an old man and I've finally decided it's time I came clean about my past. I admit I am ashamed of myself for being so scandalized by Ariella's behavior and choices that I washed my hands of her. After I learned that she'd gone and gotten herself pregnant by that boy, I never read the final letter she sent. Now, I still can't bring myself to open it. But I give you two permission to open and read it. It's right here with all the others.

"This letter talking about the baby appears to be the last one," Haley said. "Did the unopened letter get mixed in with the others? Did we miss it?"

Morgana took care to pick up each letter and set it aside, but there was no sign of the missive Wendell had mentioned.

"Is this some kind of a joke?" Morgana asked. "Basically, he said that the unopened letter would crack everything open. Where is it?"

Haley shook her head. "Welcome to the wonderful world of the Fortunes. When you think you've figured out everything, you realize you're back to square one."

Morgana rolled her eyes.

Haley put a hand on her arm. "I'm sorry. That may have been too harsh. Clearly, Wendell is torn up over the choices he made. I'm actually sad for him. I wonder what happened to Ariella."

"That's what the mystery letter was supposed to tell us," Morgana grumbled.

"I know," Haley said. "But do you think that he would've told us all this if he was going to withhold the ending? Maybe the letter fell out when he wrote the note to us."

Haley shrugged. The fatigue had returned and it suddenly felt overwhelming.

"I will leave it to you to ask him," she said. "I officially wash my hands of this story. Though you have to promise me you'll tell me how it ends."

Morgana walked her to the door and hugged her.

"I promise I will. Good luck with your new—er—*old* job. New York is an exciting place."

Apropos of nothing, Haley was tempted to joke that just because she'd turned over the story didn't mean she was relinquishing Camden. It didn't make a lick of sense. Morgana didn't know him, and Haley knew she had no right to call dibs on a man to whom she had no claim.

Even if she loved him.

She'd realized it too late.

Outside in the motel's parking lot, the asphalt was steamy from the late-afternoon sun. Haley fanned herself with her hand as she walked toward her car. It didn't do any good, but the motion helped keep her awake.

She heard the sound of footsteps and looked up, but the sun was in her eyes. She startled because, for a moment, she thought it was Camden.

When she shaded her eyes to see better, she almost groaned with disappointment when she realized it wasn't Camden but his brother Bear.

Bear. It was a funny name since he wasn't a big bear of a guy. But that's not where the name came from. His full name was Bearington, which sounded almost regal.

"Hey," he said as he walked by.

She hadn't gotten a chance to officially meet him since Freya had preempted her return to the party.

"Hello," she answered.

He seemed nice enough, but it was just as well that they'd never met—never *would* meet—since she was leaving. If he stuck around, she might be formally introduced to him at a family thing when she visited her sisters. For that matter, she'd probably run into Camden at those functions too.

She'd cross that bridge if she came to it.

As she opened her car door, she heard Bear say, "Aren't you my brother's girlfriend, Haley Perry?"

The word *girlfriend* was like a slap. She was instantly wide awake once again.

Her traitorous heart mourned, *Camden! Camden! Camden!*

She couldn't say yes. She wasn't Camden's girlfriend. Instead, she settled on, "I'm Haley Perry. You're Camden's brother, aren't you?"

"Yeah, I am. He's been trying to get in touch with you all day."

That's when she remembered she'd turned her phone off at lunch. She pulled it out of her bag and switched it on.

"I had a meeting today, and I turned it off," she said. "Thanks for reminding me."

She flinched when she saw the notice that she had forty-two messages.

"Sure—but give him a call, okay? He needs to talk to you."

CAMDEN HAD FINISHED feeding the horses when the text from Bear came through.

I'm talking to your girl in the parking lot of the Chatelaine motel.

Camden quickly typed back.

Stall her. I'll be right there.

He was in his truck in less than a minute. As he drove down the dirt drive toward the highway, he noticed a spray of wildflowers in the open field.

Sunny-yellow chocolate daisies were swaying in the warm breeze as if they hadn't a care in the world. He hopped out of the truck's cab and gathered a big bunch, cutting them with his pocketknife. They looked a little ragtag, but that's how his heart felt.

These were heartfelt. He hoped Haley would be able to see that.

And the message they conveyed. He loved her, and he had to at least try to get her to stay.

But if going to New York was something she needed to do, they could make it work too.

Five minutes later, he pulled into the Chatelaine Motel's parking lot. The space next to her car was free. He wheeled his truck in and killed the engine.

As his boots hit the asphalt, he could see her beautiful face was full of questions and maybe a little panicked. She looked at Camden and then at Bear.

"I texted him," Bear said with a shrug.

"Why did you do that, Bear?" She shook her head and glanced back at the motel rooms. "I have to go. She can't see me with you, Camden."

As she tried to get into her car, Camden grabbed her hand. "Who shouldn't see me with you?"

Again, Haley shook her head. "Don't, Camden. Okay? I'm leaving in a few days. I don't want to mess everything up for you now."

"You're not going to mess anything up," Camden assured her. "If you're talking about Freya, I know what she said to you, and she was wrong."

"Are you sure about that?" Haley asked. "I don't know if I'd take a chance, unless you know for sure."

Suddenly, she looked to her left, and all the color drained from her face. Both Camden and Bear turned around to see what she was looking at. Freya had stealthily walked up and was standing there.

"He *does* know for sure," she said. "I was mistaken, and when I saw you out here, I came out to apologize to you. I've been wrong about a lot of things lately, and it's time I started doing the right thing. Bear, why don't we leave Haley and Camden alone? I'm sure they have a lot of things to talk about."

"Sounds good to me," Bear agreed. "I've got to make some calls. I'll get out of your hair."

Freya started to walk away with Bear, but she turned around. "Camden, Haley is a good woman. She's worth fighting for."

Haley and Camden stood in stunned silence until Bear drove off and Freya disappeared into her room at the motel.

"What just happened?" Haley asked. "I feel like I'm living in some alternate universe."

"Freya got it wrong," Camden confirmed. "We had a family meeting earlier today, and my brothers and cousins decided rather than guessing Freya's motives, we would ask her directly."

Haley's brows shot up. "I hear that's the best way to get to the bottom of things. A very wise man once told me it was better to go to the source rather than speculate."

"Oh, yeah?" His heart did a strange two-step in his chest, and he had to fight the urge to pull her into his arms.

"Yeah. How did Freya take it?" she asked.

"At first, she was defensive, but eventually she came

around. She said her only motive was that she promised my grandad on his deathbed that she would always protect the Fortune name."

Haley nodded. "I'm sure she'll be happy to know that I won't be asking questions about the mining story anymore, but—"

"Haley, while we're talking about being straightforward, I need to talk to you about some things."

"Oh, well, if it's about me handing the mine story off to Morgana Mills, you'll have to talk to her about that. It's out of my control now. You might want to talk to Wendell too. He seems to have had a change of heart. I had lunch with Morgana earlier today, and Wendell gave us a stack of letters." She held up her hands. "I'm not going to get in the middle of that."

"If Wendell is supplying details, then who am I to get in the way?" he said, racking his brain for an opening to tell her how he felt.

"Morgana is awfully pretty, you know," Haley said. "I'm sure she'll want to get your take on the story."

"I don't know what she looks like, and frankly, I don't care because I can only see you." He exhaled slowly and looked into her eyes. "You're the only one, Haley. I love you. I fell in love with you that first day you came to the ranch and you roped me into helping you with that crazy *Five Steps* story. If you still want my take on the story, it didn't take five steps for me to fall in love with you. It didn't even take one. I took one look at you, and I knew I'd already fallen."

She stood stock-still, her arms hanging down by her side. She almost looked frozen.

"Will you say something?" Camden shook his head. "It's okay if you don't feel the same way. I had to tell you my side…for the story. Maybe what was good about the five-step process was that my heart was so hard that I needed to go through that crazy program with you before I would let myself believe. But I do now. Haley, I love you, and as far as I'm concerned, the five steps worked."

Haley opened her mouth as if to say something but closed it, clamping her lips between her teeth. Finally, after what seemed like an eternity, she asked softly, "Are those for me?"

She pointed to the flowers. He looked down at them in his hands. They looked all but wrung out because he'd been nervously twisting them as he talked to her.

"Yes. I picked them for you because they reminded me of you, but I've kind of crushed the life out of them. You want to come back to the ranch with me, and I'll pick you some more?"

She nodded. "Yes, I would. I would love that. How did you know that wildflowers are my favorite flowers?"

"The same way I knew that I love you," he confessed.

"Good, because I love you too," she said, taking the bunch of flowers from him and wrapping her arms around his neck. He pulled her in close and kissed her in a way meant to leave no doubt about how he felt about her.

HALEY AWOKE WITH a start. It took her a moment to realize she was in Camden's bed. After they'd gotten back to his house, they'd made love, and she'd drifted off to sleep in his arms.

Hands over her head, she stretched, feeling it from her fingertips all the way down to her toes. As she took a deep breath, she realized that something smelled delicious. Her stomach growled. A subsequent clang hinted that Camden was cooking something.

The inky night visible through the open window shutters cast shadows. As she reached for her phone on the nightstand, she saw the vase of freshly picked wildflowers.

Oh, Camden. Suddenly, she was nearly overcome with

emotion as the realization of how much she loved this man flooded through her.

She loved him and he loved her. Freya wasn't going to get in their way.

If Edith was serious about rehiring her, maybe she'd let her telecommute. A lot of people were doing that. And if it wasn't an option…she'd have to think about it. Her heart insisted she didn't want to live in New York if Camden was in Chatelaine.

They'd have to talk about it, but in the meantime, she wanted to know what smelled so good.

After a quick shower, she had just pulled on her clothes when her phone rang. Devin Street's name flashed on the screen. She hadn't had a chance to tell him that she'd handed off the story to Morgana, and he was probably calling with another tip. She'd put the two of them in touch.

"Hi, Devin, what's up?"

"I guess I could ask you the same thing." His voice was tinged with amusement.

It had become a reflex to steel herself against admonishments and unwanted advice about what she should do with the mine story. Her guard went up.

"What do you mean?" she asked, sitting down on the side of Camden's bed. *Her* side of the bed.

"Rumor has it you're moving back to New York."

"That's a good possibility." She smoothed her hand over the sheets, and a memory of their lovemaking washed over her. Her hands in his hair. His lips on her body. A wave of sadness nearly did her in. If she and Camden could make this work, she didn't want to leave him. Her heart broke even thinking about it. "How did you know?"

"Bea told me. Your sisters told her."

"Of course," Haley said. "But it's not exactly an offer… yet," she clarified. "I have to go up at the end of the week and interview. But it's really just a formality. It's for my old job and I'll be working for my old boss, who is fabulous."

"So it's not a promotion or anything?" Devin asked.

"No, but I'll be a staff writer. The job offers a salary and benefits."

"So I still have a chance, then?" Devin asked.

"Excuse me?" Haley said, unsure of exactly what he meant.

"I talked to my accountant today," Devin said. "Advertising revenue is finally at a place where I can afford to hire a managing editor for the paper."

"What?" Haley exclaimed.

Camden walked into the room.

"Is everything okay?" he asked.

She nodded and mouthed, *Yes, I think so.* He started to leave the room.

"No, Camden, stay," she whispered.

"Is Camden there?" Devin asked.

"Yes, he is."

"Well, that's a good sign." Devin made her an offer. "It's probably not the salary you'd get at the magazine, but it does come with benefits, and the cost of living here is a lot lower than in Manhattan. Technically, it would be a promotion, if you compare the titles *staff writer* to *managing editor.* There might even be opportunities for you to do some investigative pieces here, but it would be up to you to find the stories."

She told him that she'd handed the mine exposé over to Morgana and didn't feel right about taking it back. "Well, maybe you can edit it, if it turns out to be something we want to publish. Haley, I'm not going to lie. This is a good opportunity for me to grow the paper in the direction I've wanted to go for a long time. Hiring you would be the cherry on top.

"Think about it. I know you have a lot to consider, but is it possible to have an answer for me tomorrow?"

She wanted to tell him right now that the answer was yes, but she needed to talk to Camden first. She needed to make sure that he hadn't simply been caught up in the moment.

"Sure, Devin. I'll call you tomorrow."

She disconnected the call and told Camden about Devin's offer.

"How do you feel about it?" he asked cautiously.

"I feel...like I want to know how you feel about the possibility of me staying in Chatelaine." She held her breath, awaiting his answer.

"To put it bluntly, I would give my right arm if you would stay. I love you, Haley, but I want you to do what makes you happy."

Now it seemed like he was the one holding his breath.

"You love me that much?"

He nodded. "Like my life depends on it...on you."

"I love you, too, Camden. More than words can say."

"Does that mean I get to be the first to congratulate the *Chatelaine Daily New*'s first managing editor?"

She nodded, tears springing to her eyes. She'd never known she could be this happy.

"I believe you owe me some riding lessons," she said. "Maybe you can test out the camp's curriculum on me."

"You've got a deal."

Camden pulled her into his arms and kissed her soundly.

He pulled away a moment later. "Hey, step five is a kiss. We finally made it through all the steps in order. I hope you give that author one hell of a ringing endorsement for her *Five Easy Steps to Love* book."

* * * * *

Don't miss the stories in this mini series!

THE FORTUNES OF TEXAS: DIGGING FOR SECRETS

Follow the lives and loves of a complex family with a rich history and deep ties in the Lone Star State.

Worth A Fortune

NANCY ROBARDS THOMPSON

May 2024

Fortune's Convenient Cinderella

MAKENNA LEE

June 2024

Her Hometown Secret

LeAnne Bristow

MILLS & BOON

LeAnne Bristow writes sweet and inspirational romance set in small towns. When she isn't arguing with characters in her head, she enjoys hunting, camping and fishing with her family. Her day job is reading specialist, but her most important job is teaching her grandkids how to catch lizards and love the Arizona desert as much as she does.

Visit the Author Profile page
at millsandboon.com.au for more titles.

Dear Reader,

Of all the characters in Coronado, Arizona, Emily is probably the one I can most relate to. Like Emily, I was a single mom for a short period. While my boyfriend at the time (now my husband of thirty years) was serving in the US Army and was a little busy with Operation Desert Storm, I was juggling college, work and learning to be a mum. I have to say, I think Emily was better at it than I was.

I love picking up a book and discovering a little piece of myself in the story, and I hope that you find someone in Coronado that you relate to. If you do, I would love to hear your story.

I love connecting with readers. You can find me at leannebristow.com, Facebook.com/authorleannebristow and Instagram.com/authorleannebristow or email me at leanne@leannebristow.com.

Blessings,

LeAnne

DEDICATION

This book is dedicated to my grandchildren, who remind me every day how blessed I am to be their "Moo-Moo."

CHAPTER ONE

EMILY BECK LEANED back in her chair and glanced at the clock on the wall. It was too quiet. Even though her tiny office was in the back corner of the hardware store, she could usually hear her grandfather piddling around out front. And she hadn't heard a peep from her eleven-month-old son since she put him down for a nap. That was over an hour ago. What worried her most was that she hadn't been interrupted by her grandfather at least a half dozen times.

She pushed away from the desk and walked to the doorway to look out at the store. Her grandfather wasn't sitting on his stool behind the counter. The cowbells hanging on the entrance door hadn't rung all morning, so she knew he wasn't busy with a customer. They hadn't had a customer since reopening after New Year's. Of course, colder-than-average temperatures kept most people at home. The streets were pretty clear, but few people actually lived in town. If she didn't live just down the street, she wouldn't risk driving on the icy mountain roads, either.

Only one side of the store was lit up by the bright fluorescent ceiling lights. The other side was dark and empty. The sight was gloomy, but she understood her grandfather's reasoning. It was senseless to keep the entire space lit up when most of the inventory fit inside the smaller area.

Emily pressed her lips together and sighed. It was hard to see the business her grandparents had poured their heart and soul into slowly failing. Coronado had never been a booming community, but for over forty years, business had been steady. But the last five years had been hard on all the businesses left in the small town. Customers could find and order things faster online and often for less money than local shops could sell them for.

She walked down the center aisle, toward the front of the store, her eyes scanning the side aisles for her grandfather. Where could he be? He hadn't left the store. She walked back toward her office when she heard a noise from the room next door. She tiptoed to the door and peeked inside.

Her grandfather was holding her son. The baby's arms were wrapped around his neck as the old man swayed back and forth, one hand supporting the baby's diapered bottom, the other hand patting his back. Her grandfather's crackly voice sang in a soft tone, "'Hush, little baby, don't say a word. Granddad's gonna buy you a mockingbird.'"

Emily's throat tightened. That was the song her grandmother had sung to her when she was little and couldn't sleep. She could still feel Granny's rough hand patting her back as she crooned to her.

It felt odd to use this room as Wyatt's nursery away from home. Once upon a time, the space had been used as a workshop for her grandfather's projects. He would spend hours building or fixing things for customers. Now his hands were too gnarled from arthritis to do the projects he used to love.

The workshop had been cleaned out long ago and used for storage. When she'd started helping him in the store last summer, he'd converted the room to a nursery and playroom for Wyatt. He'd started on it before she'd even begun working for him. It was a gesture that still made her emotional. Almost as emotional as the scene she watched now.

Wyatt lifted his head and patted the old man's face.

Granddad caught the baby's hand in his mouth and pretended to eat it, which sent Wyatt into a fit of giggles. Granddad's face lit up and he blew raspberries against the baby's chubby cheek. The bond that had formed between the two was something she never would have anticipated but for which she would be eternally grateful.

After Granny had died, Granddad had shut himself off from the world. Running the hardware store was the only thing that had gotten him out of the house. And even then he was only a shell of his former self. He'd become a cranky, bitter old man who didn't want anyone around, especially her. But Emily had made a promise to her grandmother, and she'd refused to walk away, even though he'd told her in no uncertain terms that he would like her to.

The first time he'd held Wyatt, his world had seemed to shift. Suddenly he had something to live for again. He started eating better, paying closer attention to his health, and began attending church and community functions again. Maybe he realized that he was the only male figure Wyatt had in his life, so he wanted to stick around for as long as possible. Whatever it was, Emily loved that her grandfather was almost back to his old self.

She leaned against the door frame and watched them play. A few moments later, her grandfather caught her eye. He shifted the baby to his hip. "Are you done already?"

"Not even close," she said. "Some of the numbers aren't matching up. I want to double-check the ledger."

He nodded, and she stepped back as he walked past her toward the counter. She held her hands out toward Wyatt, but he buried his face in her grandfather's neck. Her grandfather grinned.

He sat Wyatt on the edge of the counter and held him in place with one hand while he reached under the first shelf and retrieved the black notebook that held every transaction he had made. Scooping Wyatt off the counter, he handed it to her with a frown. "I may have forgotten to put a few purchases in the computer."

Emily sighed. Of course he had. But after almost fifty years of writing everything down in his ledger, she couldn't expect him to switch his entire system overnight. "It's okay," she said as she took the book from him. "As long as you have them in here."

The bells on the front door rang, and Emily and her grandfather exchanged a hopeful glance. They both turned to look at the doorway at the same time. Her best friend stomped mud and snow off her boots at the entrance. When Abbie's husband entered a few moments later, Emily's stomach dropped.

She nodded at her son. "Grandpa, why don't you take Wyatt to the playroom?"

He gave her an odd look but obliged by taking Wyatt to the back room. Emily willed her heart rate to slow down and greeted her friend with a smile. "Hi, Abbie. What brings you to town?"

"We needed to go grocery shopping in Springerville, and I wanted to stop by and see how everything was running."

It wasn't an unusual comment. After all, Abbie was the one who had set up the computer program for the store and trained Emily how to use the software.

"If I could get Granddad to remember to enter everything in the computer, it would go a lot better," Emily joked.

Abbie shrugged. "Sorry, my expertise is software. I don't think I can change fifty-year-old habits."

"Me, neither." She glanced back at the nursery. "If you're heading to Springerville, you better get going. It might snow again later, and you don't want to get home too late."

"We already went," Abbie said. "I'm at your disposal for the rest of the afternoon."

Normally, Emily would jump at the chance to spend a few hours with her friend. All the snowfall hampered traveling back and forth on the road to the Double S Ranch, and they hadn't seen each other for several weeks. But it was hard to relax with Abbie's husband standing there.

"That's great!" She glanced at Noah. "Thanks for dropping her off for a while."

He gave her a crooked smile, one that looked all too familiar. "Sorry. You're stuck with me, too."

"Oh." Panic clawed at her chest. She glanced at the nursery again. Noah hadn't seen Wyatt for several months. Since then, Wyatt's resemblance to his father had gotten more noticeable.

Abbie laughed. "Don't worry, he's got a list of questions for your grandpa, so he'll stay out of our hair."

Noah glanced over Emily's shoulder. "Where is Denny?"

Her brow furrowed. "He's in the back. I'll get him."

If she took Wyatt into the office with her, Noah would be so busy with her grandfather, he wouldn't have time to notice her son. She turned toward the nursery.

"That's okay," Noah said. "I'll find him."

When he stepped past the counter, her heart rate sped up another notch. Before she could beat him to the nursery door, Granddad stepped out of the room and she let out a sigh of relief.

Her grandfather gave her a sheepish grin. "I think the baby needs to be changed."

Never had Emily been so grateful for the fact that her

grandfather refused to change a dirty diaper. "Okay. Noah was just looking for you."

She stepped inside the nursery and closed the door behind her. Leaning against the wall, she took a deep breath and willed her heart to slow down. Until Noah was out of the store, she wouldn't be able to relax.

Her mind raced. When Abbie was here, they usually stayed in her office. It was much too small for Noah and her grandfather to join them, so as long as she stayed in her office, she was probably safe. With the plan formulated, she turned her attention to her son.

"Hey, little man." She scooped him up from the playpen. Odd. Wyatt didn't smell dirty. She lifted the baby up and sniffed.

She turned him around and pulled the back of his pants out so she could peek. Nope. She blew a raspberry on his cheek. "You must have the toots."

Wyatt wrapped his chubby fingers in her hair and giggled, showing off deep dimples identical to his father's. Emily rested her forehead against his. How long could she hide her son from the Sterling family? The better question was, why did she feel like she needed to? Who was she really protecting?

Steeling herself, she opened the door.

Her grandfather sat at the counter, flipping through a magazine. His blue eyes looked up at her. "They're gone."

"What?" She frowned. "Why?"

"I told them I was closing the store early today because you and I have an appointment."

She raised one eyebrow. "Your appointment isn't until Monday. Are you feeling okay?"

"I feel fine," he said. "I didn't say it was a doctor appointment."

Her chest tightened. "Then what is it?" Other than his

arthritic hands, her grandfather rarely complained. How had she not known something was wrong?

"This is a different kind of appointment." He gave her a serious look. "It's more of a come-to-Jesus meeting."

Emily swallowed. "You knew Wyatt didn't need his diaper changed."

He nodded. "When you told me you were pregnant, I kept my mouth shut because you're a grown woman and your private life is your own. But I love that boy more than anything, and he deserves to have a father."

She bit her tongue. He remembered things a little differently than she did. He didn't speak to her for months after he found out she was pregnant. All because she refused to tell him or anyone else who the baby's father was. Wyatt was six months old before Granddad started speaking to her again. But since he'd let Wyatt into his life, his world had centered around the baby.

"I can understand why you're keeping it a secret, with Abbie being your friend and all." Her grandfather put his hands on his knees and leaned forward. "But that all happened before she moved here."

Her mouth dropped open. "What are you talking about?"

He pointed at Wyatt. "When are you gonna tell Noah he has a son?"

"Noah?" Emily gasped. "Noah's not Wyatt's father! Why would you think that?"

Granddad crossed his arms and raised one eyebrow. "I wasn't born yesterday. Wyatt's got the same cleft chin, the same dimples and the same dark brown eyes as the Sterlings. Aside from that, you get all uptight and nervous every time Noah is around."

She shook her head. If her grandfather thought that, how

long would it be before other people did, too? "Noah's not his father, Granddad. Luke is."

"Luke?" His eyes widened. "Now, that makes a lot more sense. His dimples are a lot deeper than Noah's. Regardless, don't you think it's time he knew?"

"He does know." Emily lifted her chin. "He's known since before Wyatt was born."

"And he ran off to Nashville anyway?" Anger flashed in his eyes.

She swallowed. "No. It happened the night before he left. I didn't know I was pregnant until six weeks later."

His bushy white eyebrows drew together. "Well, I know you didn't go to Nashville to talk to him. So, how did you tell him? I hope it wasn't with one of those text messages your generation likes so much. You told him in person, right?"

"I tried. But he was always too busy to talk." She didn't know if Luke had been telling the truth or trying to avoid her. It didn't matter anyway. "When I couldn't keep him on the phone, I resorted to the messaging system of your generation. I wrote him a letter."

"And you're sure he got it?" He looked skeptical.

"Oh yes. I'm sure." She pressed a kiss to Wyatt's head. "He never responded. And he never told his family, either. That's why I get nervous around Noah. One day he's going to look at Wyatt and notice the resemblance, and I'm not sure what to say."

"You just tell the truth, darlin'," Granddad said. "You hold your head up high. It's Luke Sterling who ought to be ashamed of himself."

LUKE STERLING TURNED his bar stool away from the bar and scanned the crowd. He didn't normally hang out at a bar unless he was playing. Of all the bars he'd performed at in Nashville, he liked this one the best. It was a small country-and-western bar on the outskirts of Nashville, so it wasn't as rowdy as some of the ones closer to Broadway.

Last night, after he'd finished his set, Kain, the bartender, gave him a message from his old roommate. He was looking forward to seeing Quint after almost a year.

He glanced at his watch. Quint's band was scheduled to play in an hour, so he had to get there soon. If Quint didn't hurry, they wouldn't have time to talk until after Quint was done playing, and there was no way he was hanging out at the bar that long. Not that he had anyplace else to be, but the bars in Nashville had a totally different flavor than the tavern back home in Coronado, Arizona.

The Watering Hole was the place to relax after a long day of work, play pool with your buddies, listen to some good music and have a few drinks. The bars in Nashville weren't nearly as laid-back. It seemed like everything was a competition. Whether it was how they dressed, how they moved on the dance floor or how they drank, everyone wanted to outdo everyone else.

A curvy brunette slid into the empty seat next to him.

"Hi there, cowboy." She flashed him a brilliant smile. "Didn't I see you onstage last night?"

He took a drink of his soda and nodded without looking at her.

"You're good." She tossed her long hair over her shoulder and leaned against the bar.

Luke kept his eyes on the door. "Thank you."

She nudged him. "Buy me a beer?"

"I'm not your type."

She laughed. "How do you know?"

"I have a girlfriend."

"I won't tell if you don't."

He pushed his Stetson hat back and looked her in the eye. "That answer is exactly why I'm not your type."

She raised one eyebrow. "Your loss," she said before tossing her hair back and disappearing into the crowd.

He let out a sigh of relief and turned back to the bar and signaled to Kain. Yep. This was definitely not his scene. The only time he liked being at the bar was when he was performing. Any other time, he steered clear. The music was too loud. There were too many people. And the performers weren't the only ones putting on a show.

Kain slid another soda to him. "Girlfriend?"

"What?" Luke gave him a look of fake innocence. "I could have a girlfriend."

"But you don't."

An image of Emily flashed in Luke's mind. She wasn't his girlfriend, so why did memories of her intrude on every date he'd attempted to go on in the past year? *Because she should have been.* He'd messed that up, though. She'd called him a few times after he'd moved to Nashville, but he either avoided the call or told her he was busy and would call her later. He never did. Not because he didn't want to talk to her. He did. Too much.

If he allowed himself the luxury of a long conversation with Emily, he would be back in his truck headed for Arizona before the phone call ended. He missed her, but there was nothing for him in Arizona. He swallowed the bitterness that rose in his throat every time he thought of her. How long did she wait after he left to find someone else?

A familiar face entered the bar. Luke stood up. "Quint's here. I'm going to leave as soon as I'm done. Have a good night."

"Maybe you do have a secret girlfriend. I've never seen anyone turn down as many dates as you do." Kain shook his head. "And you're going home early. That's just wrong."

Luke shrugged. "I have to work in the morning."

He scanned the crowd, looking for the man who'd just walked in. Quint spotted him and wove through the people to get to him.

"Hey, stranger." Luke reached out to shake the man's hand.

Quint ignored his hand and pulled Luke in for a hug. "Good to see you, man!"

Luke followed him to an empty table close to the stage. "How was the tour?"

Quint leaned his guitar case against the table. For the next ten minutes, he barely stopped talking long enough to catch his breath. Luke didn't mind. If he'd just returned from a cross-country tour, he'd talk about it to anyone who'd listen, too.

Quint finally paused long enough to take a drink of the beer Kain had sent over to him. "I'm really sorry about the apartment."

Luke shook his head. "It's okay. It was your cousin's apartment, and he wasn't obligated to let me stay there after you left."

"I still feel bad about how it played out. You were living in your truck when we met. Please tell me you found a place."

"Yeah, I got a place not too far from the airport."

"I see that you still play here. Where else do you play?"

"Here and there. Every other weekend I play with Gil's band, and my agent is pitching some of my songs."

"That's not much." Quint frowned. "How do you manage to pay the bills?"

"I work for Schecter's Heating and Cooling." It wasn't as exciting as touring with a band, but Luke was proud of his job.

"That's rough, man. I'm sorry."

"Don't be," Luke said. "I love my job, and my boss gives me time off when I need to meet with my agent or go to a gig. And it pays a lot more than playing part-time with a band."

Quint looked skeptical. "Part-time musicians never make it. You gotta get more aggressive."

Luke grinned. "I like not having to live in my truck. If it's meant to be, it'll happen. And if it doesn't, I'm okay with that, too."

"So you've given up." Quint shook his head. "I've heard your songs. You've got a gift."

"I appreciate that. My agent likes my songs, too, which is why he hasn't canned me yet." He waved at a passing waitress and asked for a water bottle. "Thanks for letting me know you were back in town. Here's my new number. Give me a call sometime, and we'll catch up."

Quint nodded to someone at the back of the bar. "Yeah, I better go help set up."

Luke stood up to leave, but Quint stopped him. "Wait. I have some stuff of yours."

He waited while Quint opened his guitar case. He pulled out a stack of letters. "My cousin didn't have your forwarding address, so he just put them on my dresser. I found them when I got home last week."

"Thanks." Luke doubted there was anything important in the mail that was over a year old.

He weaved his way through the crowd and exited the building. It was still early, but the parking lot was already full. He twirled his keys on his finger as he made his way to where he'd parked. A car moved slowly behind him, following him all the way to his pickup truck. The driver probably wanted to snag his parking space as soon as he could pull out. Sure enough, the car stopped when he got into the cab of the truck.

Another vehicle approaching the opposite direction stopped as well. Luke shook his head. Both drivers were waiting for the opportunity to claim his spot. The person who got it would depend on which direction he turned when he backed out.

He tossed the mail onto the seat and started the engine. Both drivers watched him patiently. How long would the two of them wait if he just sat in his truck? If either had honked or yelled something through their window at him, the decision would've been easy. That would be the driver who didn't get his coveted spot.

Luke glanced at both drivers. His truck was in the last row between the parking lot and the street. The traffic wasn't too bad, especially on a Thursday night. In another few hours, it was likely to be bumper-to-bumper.

He put the truck into four-wheel drive and surprised both drivers. Instead of backing out, he drove straight over the curb, across the sidewalk and onto the street. He didn't glance back to see who won the race to the empty spot.

It took almost a half hour to get back to his apartment. Thanks to his job with Schecter's, he was able to afford a decent apartment in a good neighborhood. It wasn't in the heart of Nashville, but that was fine with him. He'd grown up on a ranch, and while he had no desire to be a rancher like his brother, he wasn't fond of city life.

Maybe Quint was right. Maybe he needed to get more proactive about his music career. For the most part, he let his agent book his gigs. He'd become complacent. He enjoyed his work at the HVAC company but that wasn't what had brought him to Nashville. It was time to refocus on his career.

He unlocked the door to his place. It wasn't fancy, but he didn't require much. He hung his keys on the hook by the door and flipped through the mail Quint had given him. As expected, most of it was junk mail or so outdated it no longer mattered. The bills had all been paid—that was one thing he never fell behind on, whether they came in the mail or not.

A plain white envelope with his name scrawled across the front stopped him cold. The return address was from Coronado, Arizona.

Why had Emily sent him a letter? He swallowed. Was this his Dear John letter? Whatever it said didn't matter now, not after a year and a half. He dropped the envelope, along with the rest of the mail, into the trash can on his way into the bedroom.

He took off his cowboy hat, changed from his jeans to a pair of pajama pants and picked up his guitar from the corner next to his bed. He went back into the living room and sat on the sofa. His fingers plucked the strings without conscious thought. Music had always been the best counselor, and he chose what to play to match his current mood. He wasn't playing for an audience. He played for himself.

As he strummed, his eyes drifted to the only picture on his wall, a family photo taken at his mother's wedding last October. His mother and her new husband beamed at each other, and he and his older brother, Noah, stood on either side of them.

He was glad that his mom had found happiness after all these years. Gerald was a great guy who not only adored his mother but had helped Noah establish some great contacts that had saved their ranch from being foreclosed on.

At the wedding, Luke had met Abbie, Noah's girlfriend at the time. The two of them had gotten married right after Thanksgiving. Luke's agent had booked him for several performances for the kickoff to the Christmas season in Nashville, so he wasn't able to make it to their wedding.

While he felt bad about not getting to be his brother's

best man, he was also relieved he couldn't go. Abbie's maid of honor was Emily. The same Emily he had a hard time getting out of his head. The same Emily who had a child with someone else not even a year after he left.

CHAPTER TWO

IT WAS LATE when Luke got home from work Friday evening. He balanced Chinese takeout in one hand and unlocked the door to his apartment with the other. His stomach growled, but he set the containers on the counter. He was too sweaty and grimy to enjoy his dinner, and he wanted to relax while he ate.

Fifteen minutes later, he sat on the bar stool at the counter that separated the living room from the kitchen, eager to enjoy some kung pao chicken. While he chewed, he opened his fortune cookie and unrolled the slip of paper. *Good news will be brought to you by mail.* His gaze drifted to the trash can, where he'd dumped the mail the night before.

His gaze kept drifting to the fortune. Finally, he set his fork down. Until he put his curiosity to rest, he wouldn't be able to enjoy his meal, no matter how hungry he was.

Leaning over the trash can, he searched until he retrieved the plain white envelope with Emily's name and address on it. He tore off the end of the envelope and dumped the contents onto the counter. One folded piece of notebook paper and another smaller slip of paper. He picked up the smaller one and turned it over.

His breath caught in his throat. While he couldn't tell exactly what the black-and-white smudges on the picture were, he recognized it as a photo from an ultrasound. He stared hard at the white blob in the picture. He looked at the date: July 15. He did a rough calculation in his head. The date was eight weeks after he'd left Coronado. His hands began to shake, and he opened Emily's letter.

Luke,
First, I want you to know that I'm proud of you for chasing your dreams. Second, I don't want or expect anything from you. I'm sorry to do this over a letter, but you've been dodging my calls for two weeks and now the calls don't go through at all. I'm pregnant. And yes, it's yours. I just thought you had a right to know.

We never made each other any promises, and I'm just as much to blame as you are for what happened that night. I expect you'll let me know if you want to be involved, but don't do it out of guilt. I'll...we'll... be fine without you.
Emily

He picked up the ultrasound picture again. He had a child. His heart pounded, and his throat was dry. Did he have a son or a daughter? Did the baby have his dark features or Emily's blond hair and blue eyes? And why hadn't someone else told him? His brother's wife was Emily's best friend, yet they had never said anything to him. Noah never even asked him if he was the father of Emily's baby.

Maybe Noah thought the baby was better off without him? No, he dismissed the thought before guilt could set in. From the time he'd been old enough to notice girls, Noah had warned him about the importance of taking responsibility for his actions. If he was man enough to create a baby, he'd better be man enough to take care of it. Unlike their own dad. If Noah knew that he was the baby's father, he would've come to Nashville and dragged him home by his ear if he had to.

Was it possible that Emily hadn't told anyone? His chest tightened. Gossip traveled fast in small towns, and Coronado was no exception. He was certain that Emily had been subjected to a certain amount of shame and ridicule. Why would she endure that alone?

He needed to talk to her. Social media was out as a form of communication. He didn't have any accounts, and unless Emily had changed in the last year and a half, she didn't, either.

He went to the bedroom to retrieve his phone from the charger and scrolled through his contacts just to make sure he didn't have Emily's number already. As he suspected, it wasn't there. When his phone was stolen shortly after moving to Nashville, he'd lost most of his contacts. A few of his friends got his new number from Noah and texted him, but most of them had never been replaced, Emily included. If he wanted her number, he was going to have to do something that risked opening a can of worms. He would have to contact his brother's wife.

He scrolled through his contacts again and stared at his sister-in-law's name. Taking a deep breath, he hit Call.

On the third ring, his brother answered Abbie's phone. "Luke? What's wrong?"

"Nothing," he lied. "Where's your wife?"

In the background, he heard muffled voices, and then Abbie's voice came on the line. "Sorry about that, Luke. Noah thought something must be wrong for you to be calling me. Are you okay?"

"Yes, but I wondered if you could give me Emily's number." He held his breath and prayed she wouldn't ask any questions.

"Um…sure." There was a pause. "I just sent it. Are you sure everything's okay?"

Luke pulled the phone away from his ear to verify that he'd received her text. "Everything is fine. Talk to you later."

Before she could ask more questions—or worse, put his brother back on the line—he disconnected the call. For several seconds, he stared at Emily's contact information. His heart raced as he hit the call button.

The phone hadn't rung when he heard an automated message. "The person you are calling does not accept calls from unknown numbers. Please state your name and the purpose of the call."

He swallowed. "This is Luke Sterling. I need to talk to you. Please call me back." He left his phone number, even though he knew she would see it.

For good measure, he sent a text message with the same message to her number.

His food was cold now, but he didn't have much of an appetite anymore, despite the fact that he'd worked through lunch. He closed the containers and put the food in the refrigerator.

He walked to the living room and sat down with the ultrasound picture still in his hand. After a few minutes of staring at it, he was able to make out the head and body. A child. His child.

Having a family was the last thing Luke wanted. He didn't know anything about being a father. His brother was the closest thing to a father figure he'd ever had. After watching Noah give up everything to take care of their grandfather and the ranch, Luke had sworn he would never be trapped by anything…especially a family.

What about Emily? Luke tried to remember if she'd ever told him what her dreams were. She hadn't come from the perfect family, either. It was one of the things they had in common. Her parents had prioritized careers above their daughter and sent her to live with her grandparents. While she'd never been outspoken about her future plans and dreams, Luke was certain raising a family hadn't been one of them. What had she had to give up because of their recklessness? Did she still work at the tavern? Who took care of the baby while she worked?

His palms began to sweat. It cost a lot of money to raise a child. He knew because his grandfather reminded his mother every time she came home. It was part of the reason she was always gone. Until recently, he thought she'd left to escape the constant criticism of his grandfather. It turned out that she was working. Every dime she made went to their grandfather.

Emily had a grumpy grandfather, too. His fists clenched. He didn't know anything about being a father, but he could make sure Emily had enough money so that she didn't become indebted to her grandfather or anyone else.

The tension in his shoulders relaxed a little. He wouldn't make a very good father, but he could certainly be a good provider. At least better than his father was.

His cell phone chimed with an incoming message. He read the reply from Emily.

I'm working right now. What do you want?

Texting was not the mode of communication he wanted to use to find out about his child.

I would rather talk. Can you call me when you're off work?

That answered his question about the tavern. The Watering Hole was the only place in town open on Friday night.

It'll be late.

He couldn't blame her for not wanting to talk to him. She must think he'd ignored her letter.

It doesn't matter. I'll wait.

He held his breath, waiting for the response.

Fine.

Should he ask about the baby? No. Not over text.

His emotions were a jumble and he couldn't sit still. He paced around the small apartment. Was a phone conversation really going to be enough? Before he could second-guess himself, he picked up his phone and called his boss.

Jay Schecter answered on the second ring. "Hey, Luke. What's up?"

Luke cleared his throat. "Something has come up, and I need to take a few days off."

"Did you get a gig?" Jay had always been very supportive of Luke's ambitions.

"No," Luke said. "Something came up back home."

"Oh." The concern in Jay's voice was evident. "I hope everyone is okay."

Luke took a deep breath. He needed to talk to someone about this. "Actually, I'm the one who's not okay. I just found out I have a kid."

"That's rough." After a moment of silence, Jay began to rattle off questions. "Why are you just now finding out? How old is it? Are you sure it's yours?"

"Slow down. I don't know the answers myself." Luke picked up the ultrasound picture from the side table next to the sofa. "My old roommate gave me some mail that has been at his apartment for a year. There was a letter in it from…her." Could he even call Emily a girlfriend? They'd never dated, and they'd only been together the one time.

Jay let out a noise that sounded like a snort. "Don't let her pin anything on you. You make sure it's your kid."

"It is." There wasn't a reason to question it. Emily wouldn't lie to him.

Jay let out a whistle. "What are you going to do?"

"I don't know yet. I have to go see her."

"You're not coming back, are you?"

Luke laughed. "You're not getting rid of me that easy. There's nothing for me in Coronado. I just need a few days to get things settled."

"Glad to hear that. You're a good service tech, and I'd hate to lose you."

"Thanks," Luke said. "I'll be back as soon as I can."

He ended the call and went to pack his clothes.

"Good night, Emily. Thanks for staying late tonight."

Emily nodded at the owner of the Watering Hole. "No problem, Freddy. See you tomorrow."

She wrapped her scarf around her neck and trudged through the snow from the bar to her car. She held her breath as she slid the key into the ignition and cranked the engine. Her older-model car wasn't a fan of the cold weather, and sometimes it wouldn't start right away.

She let out a sigh of relief as the engine sputtered and came to life. She didn't bother turning on the heat. It wouldn't warm up enough to matter in the short time it would take her to drive home. She did, however, need to let the engine run for a few minutes. If she tried to put it in gear too soon, it would die.

While she waited, she pulled her phone out of her purse and stared at the last message. She hadn't heard from Luke in a year and a half, so why now? Was he finally getting curious about his son?

He had said to call him when she got off work. Even if it was late. It was two o'clock in the morning in Nashville. She wasn't calling anyone at that time. Whatever he wanted could wait until morning.

She shifted the car into Drive and slowly pulled out of the parking lot. It hadn't snowed today, but that didn't mean the roads weren't slick and icy. She was anxious to get home but not so anxious that she wanted to slide off the road and walk.

The single-wide trailer that she rented was dark when she pulled up to it. Her aunt Tricia babysat for her on the evenings that she worked at the tavern. Most of the time, Tricia left as soon as Emily got off, but she rarely worked this late.

Emily unlocked the front door and opened it as quietly as she could. The television was on, but Tricia was asleep on the sofa. Emily locked the door and tiptoed over to where her aunt was curled up under a thick quilt. Emily picked up the remote and turned off the TV.

"You're home late," Tricia murmured.

"I know," Emily whispered. "I'm sorry. The other waitress called in sick and I couldn't leave Freddy shorthanded."

"It's okay." Tricia yawned. "Is it snowing?"

"No. Why don't you sleep in my bed?" Her sofa was comfortable, but the bed was better.

"Oh no," Tricia said. "I'll get up as soon as it's light outside and head over to Dad's for a while anyway. I wouldn't want to disturb you."

"You won't disturb me. Wyatt will be up before six no matter what."

"Yes, and if I know you, you'll put him in bed with you

and go back to sleep until at least nine." Tricia fluffed the pillow she'd taken off Emily's bed. "I'll be fine right here."

Emily nodded.

Tricia frowned at her. "What's wrong?"

She sighed. Tricia was the only person, aside from her grandfather, who knew that Luke was Wyatt's father. "I got a message from Luke tonight."

Immediately, Tricia's eyes opened and she sat up straight. "What? Why?"

"I don't know."

Tricia tossed the quilt back and motioned for Emily to sit next to her. "Tell me exactly what happened."

Emily plopped onto the sofa next to her surrogate mother. Tricia wrapped one arm around her as she pulled out her phone and showed her the text messages.

"Did you call him?" Tricia handed the phone back to her.

"No." She yawned. "Whatever he wants can wait until morning."

Tricia pressed a kiss to her forehead. "Get some sleep."

Emily stood up. "Good night."

She tiptoed into the bedroom she shared with her son. Her full-size bed was pushed against one wall, and Wyatt's crib was along the opposite wall, leaving only a narrow walkway between them. The night-light on the wall cast just enough light for her to see Wyatt sprawled out in his crib. His teddy bear was tucked underneath his arm, and the pacifier had fallen out of his mouth and lay next to him.

Emily sat on the bed and put her elbows on the edge of the crib. She let her chin rest on top of her hands and stared at the sleeping form of her son. He looked so much like Luke. His smile. His eyes. Even his laugh was just like Luke's.

If Luke hadn't left, would they be together? Her chest

felt heavy. If he hadn't been leaving, that night wouldn't have happened, and Wyatt wouldn't be here now. She had known Luke for ten years. In all that time, he'd never suspected that she'd been in love with him from the first time she'd seen him. In high school, they'd been friends, but in a town the size of Coronado, everyone was "friends."

It wasn't until she started working at the tavern with him that they really got to know each other. Every night after the bar closed, he would stay and help her clean up. They talked. They sang. They danced. But it never went further than that...until the night he stopped at her house on his way out of town for good.

She missed Luke. But she wouldn't trade Wyatt for a lifetime of friendship with him. She crawled under the covers and fell asleep with memories of Luke floating through her mind.

CHAPTER THREE

EMILY LIFTED A blanket in front of her face, then dropped it down. "Peekaboo!"

Wyatt's little body shook with giggles. She loved Saturdays. She didn't have to rush around in the morning to get to the hardware store on time. The entire day was spent at home with Wyatt. She usually worked at the tavern on Saturday nights, but she didn't leave until Wyatt was fed, bathed and in bed.

She glanced at her phone lying on the arm of the sofa. She still hadn't returned Luke's call. Most of the morning had been spent debating what to say to him. By 10:00 a.m., she decided to wait. If it was important enough, he'd call her back.

"It's almost lunchtime, little man," she said. "What do you want to try today?"

Wyatt scooted across the rug and picked up a rattle. He rolled onto his back and put the end of the toy in his mouth. Drool covered his chin.

Emily left him to play and walked to the kitchen. One good thing about having a small house, she could fix lunch and never lose sight of him. The kitchen, dining room and living room weren't really separate, but rather one large room. The kitchen and dining area were on one end, while the living room was in the center of the house. A narrow hallway on the opposite side of the house led to the only bedroom. The bathroom was tucked between the living room and the bedroom.

Overall, the trailer was less than six hundred square feet, but it was okay for now. Her grandfather paid her enough for working at the hardware store to make ends meet, but the money she made at the tavern went straight into her savings account. Emily almost had enough money saved up for a down payment on a home of her own. If she was very careful with her money, she'd be able to buy a house this summer, provided she could find anything affordable.

Coronado was a popular vacation spot for people living in the Phoenix area to escape the desert heat. Which was great for the small town's economy. Not so great for residents who wanted to buy a home. City people looking for a vacation property in the area were willing to pay much higher prices for that luxury. As a result, many of the nicer residences were vastly out of her price range. The ones that were in her price range usually needed so much work, they weren't worth the money.

She was dicing up some bananas when someone knocked on her door. It was probably her grandfather. When things were slow on Saturdays, he'd close the hardware store for lunch and come to her place to play with Wyatt. Her stomach growled. He usually brought food, too.

She wiped her hands off on a kitchen towel and went to the front door. "I hope you brought lunch. I'm starving."

Her heart leaped to her throat. The man on the other side of her door wasn't her elderly grandfather.

"Sorry." Luke Sterling stood outside. "I didn't bring food. Are you expecting someone?"

"No." Her heart pounded so hard she could hear it in her ears. "What are you doing here?"

He glanced around. "Can I come in?"

She swallowed. Was he worried that someone would see him here? She stepped back and allowed him to come inside. As soon as she shut the door, she repeated her question. "What are you doing here?"

"I—" He paused.

At least he had the decency to look uncomfortable. She crossed her arms and waited.

"I know you may not believe this, but I just got your letter two days ago."

"You're right," she said. "I don't believe you."

"It's true." His voice came out in a breathless rush. "A buddy was letting me rent a room from him, but his band went on tour, so I had to move out. Your letter must have come after I found a new place, and the mail never got forwarded. He got back last week and just gave it to me."

Emily's heart rate started to slow down. Could it be true? And if it was, what happened now? She took a measured breath. "Okay. I believe you. I still don't know why you're here."

"I would have been here sooner if I'd known." Anger flashed in his brown eyes. "I should have known. You should've made sure I knew."

Her breath hitched as she fought the urge to kick him out of her house. She gritted her teeth. "I tried. Or did you forget how you dodged my calls?"

His gaze narrowed. "I wasn't dodging your calls."

She crossed her arms and cocked her head. "Really? So you just happened to be walking into a big meeting every time I called?"

"You should have told me it was important."

"I did." Heat rushed through her body, and she lifted her chin. "Don't you dare try to blame me."

"Well—" His face fell, and he let out a loud sigh. "You're right. I'm sorry."

"You really didn't know that I had a baby?" Had she meant so little to him that he'd never bothered to ask about her? Hadn't his brother told her she had a child?

"Noah told me you were pregnant," he answered her unspoken question. "He said the father bailed when he found out and you were going to raise it alone."

So he did know. "And you didn't question the timing?"

"The only thing I questioned was how quickly you moved on after I left."

She let out a sarcastic laugh. "Right. Because what we shared was so special you couldn't wait to get out of here the next morning."

The lines around his eyes tightened. "I just meant that I know you're not the type to sleep around, and you weren't dating anyone when I left. I figured whoever he was, he must have really swept you off your feet."

His words calmed her a little. At least he had a higher opinion of her than her grandfather had when he'd found out.

"Noah thought you were dating a guy from Springerville," he said. "I never dreamed in a million years the baby was mine."

When he'd come to Coronado for his mother's wedding, she'd thought he might have been curious enough about his child to come see her, but he didn't. Now that she knew he didn't know about Wyatt, it just meant that he hadn't missed her enough to want to see her.

But he was here now. Her stomach felt like a lead ball settled in it. Now he knew, and he was here to find out about his child. Not about her.

They stood in silence for a moment. Finally, she took a breath. "Would you like to meet him?"

"Him?" Luke's face softened. "I have a son."

Emily paused. He really didn't know.

She stepped away from the door and moved into the living area. Wyatt had managed to scoot around to the end of the sofa. He was reaching for a small ball that had rolled under the end table. She picked him up and put him on her hip. When she looked back at Luke, the blood seemed to have drained from his face.

"He looks just like me." Luke's voice was barely more than a whisper.

Emily nodded. "He's got your chin, eyes and dimples, but his attitude is all his own."

Luke didn't laugh. He didn't say anything. Instead, he looked very uncomfortable.

She took a step toward him, thinking he would want to hold Wyatt. Instead, a look of panic crossed his face, and he backed away.

Emily stiffened. "Don't worry. I haven't told anyone who his father is. You can go back to Nashville with a clean slate. If you leave now, no one will know that you were here, and no one can judge you."

LUKE FLINCHED AS if he'd been gut punched. Heat flooded his face. What kind of man did she think he was? He gritted his teeth. "Do you think that's what I'm worried about?"

Emily lifted her chin. "You seemed awfully nervous at the door."

"You acted like you were expecting someone. I was wondering if we were about to be interrupted." He waited to see if she would deny it.

Instead, she shifted the baby to her other hip. "So now what?"

"I don't know," he admitted.

She pressed her lips together. "Let me know when you figure it out."

He didn't like the trace of sarcasm in her voice. "Give me a break. I found out less than forty-eight hours ago that your baby was mine. I got here as fast as I could."

Something flickered in her blue eyes. "You would have known if you'd ever bothered to return my calls."

He gave her a sharp look. "I was home for my mother's wedding in October. You could have talked to me then. Made sure I knew."

Emily let out a huff. "Why would I? I hadn't seen or talked to you in over a year. For all I knew, you received my letter and wanted nothing to do with either one of us."

"You know me better than that." He swallowed. "Or at least I thought you did."

Her face pinched. "You're right. I had nine months to prepare for this. I guess you're allowed to have a few days."

"Thanks." His gaze drifted to the little boy on her hip, and his heart pounded harder.

What was he supposed to do now? For the past year, music had been the focus of his life. Truthfully, it had been his focus for the last eight years.

From the day he graduated high school, he'd had only two dreams. The first was getting out of Coronado. The second was his music. He was so close to getting everything he wanted. How was he supposed to juggle a music career and a family? He was going to have to give up a lot. But she was going to have to meet him halfway.

He took a deep breath. "I hope you don't want a big wedding. I have to get back to Nashville, so a courthouse ceremony is all we have time for."

A low chuckle rumbled out from deep within Emily, and she didn't try to hide her laughter. "You're kidding, right?"

Tightness stretched through his chest and shoulders. He didn't know what he'd expected from his impromptu wedding proposal. Certainly not laughter. "Not at all."

She bit her bottom lip. "If I wasn't standing here, holding your son, would you have asked me to marry you?"

Luke swallowed. They both knew the answer to that question.

Emily's gaze narrowed. "It's not that I don't appreciate your willingness, but we're fine, really. If you want to be part of his life, that's great, but I'm not going to marry you to reduce your feelings of guilt."

"Guilt has nothing to do with it," Luke said. "He's my son. He's my responsibility."

While he wasn't ready for a family, he wasn't about to abandon her like his father had done to them.

"Look," she said, "we were friends for a long time before Wyatt was conceived. We never made each other promises or had any expectations. There's no reason for that change."

So what did she want from him? Did she already have someone in her life? Someone who didn't care she had another man's child? Was that who she'd thought was at her door with lunch? He couldn't ask her because it was none of his business, despite the flare of jealousy burning in his gut.

He looked at the little boy and was again amazed at how much Wyatt looked like him. "Just tell me what I'm supposed to do?"

Wyatt stared back at him with open curiosity. Three fingers were in his mouth, and his chin was wet with drool. He yawned and rubbed his face on Emily's shoulder.

She took a deep breath. "We'll figure it out. But if you'll excuse us, I need to feed him and put him down for a nap."

Obviously, she wanted him to leave. Again, he wondered if she was trying to get rid of him before someone else showed up.

He hooked his thumbs in the front belt loops of his

jeans. “All right. I’ll leave. You have the number to the ranch, right?” Cell phones were useless at the ranch. The only place cell phones worked was in town.

“Yes.”

He started to open the door but paused and turned back to her. “I just want you to know that I’m not going to skip out on you. I’m going to take care of him—of both of you.”

“I know that.” She stroked the back of the baby’s head as he squirmed against her.

“I’ll be back.” He opened the door. “And I’m sorry I wasn’t here for you.”

Her face softened and she smiled at him. “I’m sorry you didn’t find out until now. You’re here now. That’s what matters.”

He closed the door behind him and went to the SUV he’d rented at the airport. While he waited for the cab to heat up, he stared at the tiny home in front of him.

Aside from being small, the trailer was old. He glanced up and down the street. Unlike other houses on the street, her yard was free from clutter. The neighbor on one side had a car up on blocks that hadn’t been touched in years. A variety of car-related parts were strewn around the yard, covered in snow.

A wobbly fence divided her yard from the neighbor on the other side. Through the fence, three large dogs trotted around. He doubted the fence would stop them if they wanted to get out. What would happen when his son wanted to play in the yard? Would Wyatt be safe? And would he be around to do anything about it?

CHAPTER FOUR

LUKE BACKED SLOWLY out of the yard. His brother didn't know he was in town, so he was in no hurry to get to the ranch. He turned onto the main street of the small town. The roads were empty, except for a couple of cars parked in front of the Bear's Den Diner. Christmas lights still decorated the lampposts, even though it was already almost a month since the New Year.

This was the slowest time of the year for Coronado. The little town was a hot spot in the summer for families that wanted to escape the Arizona heat. In the fall, every hotel room and every cabin was booked by hunters hoping to bag a deer, elk or turkey.

Winter was his favorite time. He loved to snowboard, and the ski resort was only an hour away. Occasionally, when the resort at Sunrise was full, people would stay in Coronado, but for the most part, the town was pretty empty.

It took longer than usual to navigate the road to the ranch. His brother hadn't left the ranch today, at least not judging by the amount of snow on the road.

The Double S brand hung on the archway to the entrance of the ranch. The sign was new. So were the fences. And the sight of horses grazing in the pastures was new, too. Luke's chest swelled with pride. His brother was well on his way to rebuilding the ranch.

He parked next to Noah's beat-up ranch truck, which

was definitely not new, and retrieved his duffel bag from the back seat. Tom greeted him as he stepped onto the front porch. He bent down to scratch the cat behind his ears.

The front door opened. “Luke?”

He stood up. “Hi, Abbie.”

She grinned and gave him a hug. “What are you doing here?”

“I was in the neighborhood, so I thought I’d drop by.” He shrugged. “Do you mind if I crash here for a few days?”

She shook her head. “You don’t have to ask. This is your home, too. Come in. Where’s your stuff?”

“Right here.” He held up the duffel bag. “Where’s Noah?”

“He’s hauling a load of cattle to El Paso for the Maxwells. He won’t be back until late this evening.” She looked around. “Where’s your guitar?”

For as long as he could remember, he’d taken his guitar everywhere. “I didn’t bring it.”

“What’s wrong?”

“Nothing. I’m here for a few days, so I didn’t want to bother with it on the airplane.”

Abbie looked skeptical but didn’t question him. “You know where your room is. I have to check the oven.”

The smell of baking bread made his stomach growl. He hadn’t eaten anything except a couple bites of Chinese food the night before. It seemed like a lifetime ago.

His room was the last one at the end of the hall on the second floor. Noah’s room used to be the first one, but now that he was married, he and Abbie had the main bedroom on the first floor.

He pushed the door open. It hadn’t changed since he’d left for Nashville. His pictures still hung on the wall where he’d left them. His favorite bedspread was still on the double bed. Some of his clothes were still in the closet. He tossed his duffel bag on the floor and sat on the edge of the bed.

It was strange to be in the home where he'd spent most of his childhood. He expected a wave of nostalgia to sweep over him, but it didn't. When he'd been here for his mother's wedding, he'd only been able to stay for one night. He arrived the morning of the wedding and had left early the next morning. There hadn't been time for him to reminisce about his childhood.

More than anything, he was hit with the sense that he didn't belong here. But he knew that already. Noah had taken to ranch life like a fish to water. He loved everything about it, from getting up before dawn to check on the animals to repairing fences all day long.

Luke could cowboy with the best of them. He was an excellent roper. He could mend fences, deworm cattle and stay on a bucking horse. But it was never in his blood like it was Noah's.

He looked around the bedroom. While he was here, he would pack up his things and put them in storage. He didn't want to send them to Nashville. For some reason, it didn't feel like home, either. Regardless, someday Noah and Abbie would start a family, and they might need this room.

With that decision made, he went back down the stairs to beg Abbie for a piece of her homemade bread.

When he got to the kitchen, Abbie had a plate of food waiting for him. His mouth watered at the sight of the chicken-fried steak, mashed potatoes and buttered corn.

"How did you know I was hungry?" He took the plate to the small table in the breakfast nook.

Abbie laughed. "Are you kidding? I heard your stomach growl as soon as you walked in the door."

He held up the slice of bread. "Your bread is so good that it would make a full man's stomach rumble."

"Well, thank you," she said. She pulled a chair out from the table and sat across from him. "As happy as I am to see you, why are you really here?"

He waited until he swallowed the mouthful of food. "Why does something need to be wrong? Maybe I just wanted to come home and visit people."

"People?" She arched one eyebrow. "People like Emily, maybe?"

Luke froze. He set his fork down. "You know?"

"Don't look so surprised," she said. "Only a fool wouldn't see the resemblance. Or Noah. He refuses to believe that you would walk out on your son, so why did you?"

"I didn't walk out on him," Luke said. "I only found out two days ago."

Abbie's eyes narrowed. "You don't expect me to believe that, do you?"

Quickly, he retold the story of how Emily's letter had been lost and returned. "My phone got stolen not long after I moved to Nashville. I don't know how many times she tried to call me before she gave up and mailed that letter."

Her face softened as she listened. "That's why you wanted her number. My opinion of you just climbed a few notches." She folded her arms on the table and leaned on them. "Emily knows all this?"

He nodded. "I just left her house."

"So you met Wyatt."

"Mmm-hmm." He scooped a bite of food into his mouth. His insides were still in a jumble from seeing the little boy who looked like him.

Abbie seemed to sense that he wasn't ready to talk about

it yet, so she stood up and began tidying the kitchen while he finished his food.

Luke took one last bite of mashed potatoes and carried the plate to the sink to rinse off. Abbie was Emily's best friend. She probably knew the answers to some of the questions that had plagued him since leaving Emily's house.

"Does Emily have a boyfriend?"

Abbie laughed. "She is a single mother with two jobs. When would she have time to find a boyfriend?"

"Two jobs?" Guilt punched him in the chest. Emily needed two jobs to provide for their son. "I know she works at the Watering Hole. Where else does she work?"

"She only works at the tavern part-time now. Her main job is working at the hardware store for her grandfather."

"I thought he wouldn't speak to her." He had never been able to figure out the relationship between Emily and her grandfather.

Abbie grinned. "He's over it. His world revolves around Wyatt now."

Luke was happy to hear that. When Emily's grandmother died, her grandpa didn't handle it very well. He even kicked Emily out of the house for a while.

If Emily worked during the day for her grandfather and worked nights at the tavern, when did she have time to see her son? "What does she do with Wyatt while she works?"

"She takes him to the hardware store with her. Mr. Morgan converted his old workshop into a nursery and playroom for Wyatt." Abbie cocked her head to one side and gave him a curious look. "Why did you want to know if she had a boyfriend? Do you doubt that baby is yours?"

"No. He's definitely mine. I just wondered if that's why she turned down my proposal."

Abbie's eyes widened. "You proposed?"

Luke nodded. "Seemed like the right thing to do."

"That's why she turned you down." Abbie picked up his empty plate.

"What do you mean?"

"No girl wants a guilt proposal," she said. "What good is a marriage without love?"

He wiped his mouth with the napkin and stood up. "Thanks for lunch."

Abbie didn't say a word as he exited the kitchen and went back up to his room to start going through things.

As he removed everything from the walls and emptied out his closet, he sorted things into two piles: one for storage and one for trash. So far, the trash pile was the biggest. Mostly because he had no reason to keep the mementos from his childhood. He'd worked too hard to get out of Coronado; he didn't want to take part of it to Nashville with him. Next time he went to town, he would look for some boxes to pack the things he wanted to keep.

He had been at it for several hours when Abbie pushed his door open. "I found some of your baby pictures last month. It's really amazing how much Wyatt looks like you."

She stepped into the room holding a photo album and looked at the mess he'd created. "What are you doing?"

"Sorting things. I'll have this room packed up before I leave so you can do whatever you want with it."

Abbie's green eyes widened. "But this is your room."

"It was my room," he said. "Not anymore."

Her brow crinkled. She set the book on his dresser. "I'm going to the barn to feed the horses, then I'll cook dinner."

Luke didn't open the photo album. "I have a better idea. I'll go feed the horses, and you start dinner."

She grinned. "Deal."

He put his jacket on and bundled up against the cold. Snow crunched under his feet as he headed to the barn. Inside was nice and warm. Luke looked around. He'd never seen so many horses in the barn.

One horse nickered at him. Luke went over to the palomino filly. "Hey, Jasper. I can't believe you remember me."

He patted her neck and rubbed her nose before feeding the others. Some of the other horses poked their heads over the stalls to look at him, but most of them ignored his presence.

By the time he got back to the house, Abby had supper ready. "I hope you like spaghetti," she said.

"I love it." He joined her at the table. "I didn't realize you had so many horses."

Abbie laughed. "You should see how many are out in the pastures. The barn only has the ones they are working on training."

"Noah does all that alone?"

"Caden, my sister's husband, helps a lot. Especially with breaking them." She handed him a piece of garlic bread. "He's been talking about hiring a ranch hand, so I know he'll be glad to have you back."

Luke almost dropped his fork. "I'm not back."

"Oh." Her mouth pressed into a thin line. "Is Emily willing to move to Nashville?"

Luke's stomach knotted. "Why would she do that? I told you she turned down my proposal."

Abbie bit her bottom lip. "That doesn't mean you can't get back together."

He and Emily had never been together in the first place. Wyatt was the result of a one-night stand. Not that he didn't have feelings for Emily. He cared about her. If he hadn't left, their friendship might have developed into something more. He left because there was nothing for him in Coronado then. There still wasn't.

He frowned. "I don't know what we're going to do. We haven't really talked about it yet."

The look Abbie gave him made him feel like a little boy who had been caught with his hand in the cookie jar. The knots in his stomach got worse. He could only imagine the questions his brother would throw at him. He needed to talk to Emily and see what she expected from him before he talked to his brother.

He stood up, his appetite gone. "Thank you for supper. I'm going to town to talk to Emily."

"Weren't you just over there this morning?"

"I was. But she had to put the baby down for a nap, so I left. We didn't really get anything settled. I have the feeling I need to do that before I talk to Noah."

Abbie nodded. "When will you be back?"

"Probably before Noah gets home."

"DARLING, WHEN ARE you going to quit this dead-end job and run away with me?"

Emily laughed. "And leave all this? Not on your life." She set the pitcher of beer on the table. "Anything else?"

Corbin Munroe winked at her. "You let me know if you change your mind."

"If I do that, you'll run from here so fast all we'll see is dust." She took his money and counted out his change before moving to the next table.

Corbin was a regular face at the Watering Hole. His flirting was all in good fun because everyone knew he was head over heels in love with himself. At fiftysomething years old, he was a confirmed bachelor. And oddly enough, despite his own propensity for flirting, he was the first one to step in if he felt someone was being disrespectful to the waitresses.

For the first time in weeks, the sun had come out, so

people were taking advantage of it by getting out of the house. The tavern had been crowded since six o'clock. The band would start playing soon, so it was likely to get even busier. Emily didn't mind, though. The night went faster when she didn't have time to sit around. Tips were a lot better, too. She couldn't complain about that.

She stopped to clean off an empty table when she saw Luke enter the bar. Her heart began to race. Why was he here? She balanced the tray above her shoulder and hurried back to the bar. When she turned around, he had sat at an empty table, but his eyes were on her.

Butterflies danced in her stomach, and she stepped around the end of the bar to get a drink of water.

"Is that Luke Sterling?" Freddy asked.

"The one and only," Emily answered.

Freddy stepped out from behind the bar and walked over to his table. Luke stood up and shook his hand, and they talked for a few moments before Freddy returned. "Give Luke a round on the house."

She nodded and smoothed her shirt down over her hips. Why hadn't she worn that loose sweater she liked so much? At least it covered up the extra padding around her middle. She'd never been petite, but having a baby added a little more to her curves than she liked.

She poured Luke a beer and took it to his table. "Freddy wanted you to have this."

Luke gave Freddy a two-fingered salute. Then he leaned closer to her and whispered, "Can I let you in on a secret?"

"What?"

"I don't drink." Luke gave her a sheepish grin.

She bit her lip. "That's not a secret. It's been a while. Freddy just forgot."

She'd always wondered how someone who spent most

of his time in bars didn't drink. After Luke left, Noah started bartending at the Watering Hole, so she asked him.

Noah told her that in high school, one of Luke's friends had stolen some beer from his dad's truck. The boys had gone up to Crescent Lake and polished it off. In their drunken stupor, they'd decided to see if they could swim across the narrow lake. The other boy had quit before going very far because the water was so cold, but Luke made it halfway across the three-hundred-yard stretch of water before exhaustion and muscle cramps hit him. A fisherman sitting on the bank heard Luke's friend calling for help and was able to get a boat to him in time. After that, Luke's declaration to never drink again was only reinforced every time he played music in a bar and saw firsthand how alcohol affected some people.

"What are you doing here?" she asked him.

"I went by your house, and your aunt answered the door. She told me you were here."

Emily tapped her pencil on the notepad in her hand. "Every Thursday, Friday and Saturday night, just like always."

"And your aunt watches Wyatt every time?"

"No. Tricia has to work on Friday mornings, so Millie watches him on Thursdays." She tucked her pencil behind her ear. "Why were you looking for me?"

"I wanted to talk to you, but I guess this really isn't the best place for that."

The butterflies turned into angry bees. He knew it would be impossible to talk at the tavern. The music was too loud, there were too many people, and she was too busy. He was checking up on her. Her heart raced. Did he want to prove that she wasn't a good mother so he could take her son away from her?

She swallowed the lump building in her throat. Luke

wouldn't do that. How many times had he told her he never wanted kids? And she was a good mother, so she had nothing to worry about. "I'll be home all afternoon tomorrow. We can talk then."

"Afternoon?" He cocked his head. "You have plans in the morning."

"It's Sunday," she said. "We go to church with Granddad."

"Oh, that's right." He slid the untouched beer toward her. "Maybe you can give this to someone else."

Corbin was walking back from the restroom and must have overheard. "Thanks, mate." He reached down and took the beer. "You be good to my girl here."

Emily rolled her eyes. "I'll see you tomorrow, after church, then."

"Yes." Luke stood up and put his cowboy hat back on.

He didn't seem to be in a huge hurry to leave, but Emily pretended not to notice him and went to clean a table. She was, however, keenly aware of his every move.

He stopped and chatted with Freddy for a moment before heading toward the door. As he was walking out, band members started coming in, getting ready to set up for the evening. It was the same band Luke played with before he left for Nashville.

Out of the corner of her eye, she saw Dan Tippetts shake Luke's hand. They stood and chatted for a minute, then Luke turned around and went back to the table where he had been sitting before.

She ignored him and tried to go back to work. He waved her down as she walked by.

"Can I get a soda?"

She pressed her lips together. "I thought you were leaving."

He nodded toward the band. "I told Dan I'd stay and listen to their set."

She didn't rush to get his soda but stopped and took orders at another table first. On the outside, she tried to be all business, but her insides quivered like a scared cat. And that was exactly what she was. It wouldn't be long before the entire town knew that Luke was Wyatt's father. That alone was enough to throw her back into the center of the town's gossip.

But that wasn't what scared her. What scared her was the way Luke made her feel every time he looked at her. She doubted he shared any of the feelings she had for him. Still, she felt his eyes on her throughout the night.

The band had warmed up and was getting ready to start. Dan stepped up to the microphone. "We've got a little surprise for y'all tonight. Coronado's own prodigal cowboy is back for a limited time. I bet if we cheer loud enough, we can coax him into coming up and singing a song with us. What do you say, folks? Let's give it up for Luke Sterling!"

The tavern erupted in applause, and Luke's face turned red. After a few moments, he made his way up to the stage and took the microphone from Dan. The band started playing a George Strait tune, and Luke started singing.

The sound of his smooth baritone voice filled the tavern and sent goose bumps down Emily's arms. She loved to listen to him sing. Before he left for Nashville, he would practice after the bar closed, and she was the first one to hear the songs he wrote. Thanks to years of piano lessons forced on her by her parents, she had some musical background, too, and they even sang together on occasion. Never in front of people, though.

She sighed. It seemed everything about the two of them had been behind closed doors. How shocked would everyone be when their secret got out?

Luke sang a few more songs and then excused himself. But he didn't leave. He went back to his table.

Emily stopped on her way to get another round of drinks for a group at the back. She put a water bottle in front of him. "Your soda is probably watered down by now. I'll get you a new one."

"That's okay, water is fine." His brown eyes sparkled with energy.

She envied the way he seemed to come to life when he was onstage. When she was a little girl, her mother had entered her in a children's beauty pageant. She completely froze when she got up on the stage for the talent portion. Her mother had been mortified and never entered her again.

At the bar, she told Freddy, "I need three beers, a Moscow mule and a shot of tequila for table seven."

"Nice to see Luke onstage again," Freddy said. "How long's he going to be in town?"

Emily avoided looking him in the eye. "How should I know?"

Freddy gave her a pointed look. "He's here to see his son, isn't he?"

Her mouth dropped open. "Did he tell you that?"

He laughed. "No. But I've suspected it since the first time I saw that baby."

She placed the drinks on her tray and headed for table seven. The men at the table weren't from Coronado, so she didn't know them. They were loud and rowdy, and she hoped they left soon.

"Here you are, boys." She smiled pleasantly and set the drinks on the table.

One of the men winked at her. "I like my women with a little meat on their bones, and you're just about the prettiest thing I've seen in this town. How 'bout a dance?"

She kept her voice calm. "Sorry, I'm working."

The other men at the table laughed. "She shot you down."

He followed her to the next table. "Just one dance."

"I told you, I'm working."

He grabbed her arm. "Take a break."

Emily covered the hand on her arm with her own. She leaned closer to him and kept her voice low. "If you don't take your hands off me, you might lose that arm."

He let go and stepped back. "Fine. Don't say I didn't give you a chance."

She hurried to the bar as quickly as she could. Freddy noticed the exchange. "Everything all right?"

She nodded. As long as Freddy was around, she wasn't worried. He always had her back and wouldn't hesitate to throw out anyone who crossed the line.

On her next trip past the table, the man hollered at her and waved her over. She took a deep breath. "What can I do for you?"

"We need another round," the man said, "and I need your number."

"Your drinks are coming right up."

A few minutes later, she returned with a round of drinks, and the man again asked her for her number. She picked up a napkin and wrote the number for the tavern on it. When she slid it to him, the other men at the table all whooped and slapped him on the back.

Emily scanned the crowd until she made eye contact with Caroline, the other waitress. Caroline arched one eyebrow, and Emily tilted her head toward the table. Caroline nodded, and Emily relaxed. For the rest of the evening, Caroline would serve that table.

The almost forty-year-old woman not only had a way of handling drunks, but she was a force to be reckoned with. More than once, Emily had seen her physically remove rowdy customers.

A little later, the crowd started to clear out, and she

took a break to run to the restroom. When she came out, the man was waiting for her. She sighed. She thought by trading tables with Caroline, the man would get the hint.

"How about that dance now, beautiful?" His words were slurred.

Before she could answer, a hand clamped on the man's shoulder. "Do you need something?"

The man whirled around to face Luke. "Yeah. I need you to mind your own business."

Luke stepped closer to him. "It so happens that she *is* my business."

The man lifted his chin. "You feeling froggy?"

Luke looked him dead in the eye. "Jump."

Emily wasted no time stepping between them. "All right, gentlemen. Break it up."

Luke didn't budge, so she nudged the other man toward his table. By the time she got the man back to his table and warned his friends that she wouldn't serve him any more alcohol, Luke had disappeared.

CHAPTER FIVE

Luke pulled his jacket a little tighter around him. The cold was just uncomfortable enough to keep him awake. If it got much colder, he'd give in and turn on the SUV's engine until it warmed up inside. How much longer would Emily be?

He could go back into the tavern where it was warm and wait for Emily, but he didn't trust himself. For over a year, he and Emily had worked together at the Watering Hole, and it had never bothered him to see Emily flirt with customers. To be fair, she hadn't really flirted with the man inside the tavern tonight. She had a way of talking to obnoxious customers while putting them in their place. He, on the other hand, wanted to clock the guy who'd been bugging her.

As long as Freddy was inside, he knew Emily was safe. The trouble was, Freddy often left early and let the employees close the place down. Luke would stay until Emily left, even if that meant sitting in the cold until 2:00 a.m.

A motorcycle pulled into the parking lot. It was awfully cold to be on a bike this time of year. Luke did a double take when he saw what looked like a dog perched in front of the driver.

It was a dog.

The dog jumped down and waited for the man to dismount. The man tucked his helmet under his arm and headed for the front door.

As he was about to pass Luke's SUV, Luke realized who he was and rolled down his window. "Caden?"

The red-haired man squinted in the dark. "Oh hey, Luke. I didn't know you were in town."

Luke shook the man's hand. "I'm just here for a few days. Who's your copilot?"

"This is Max," Caden said. "I better get inside. Freddy's got a group of ice fishermen in there that need a ride home."

Noah had told him that Stacy's husband had become the tavern's guardian angel. Whenever someone was too drunk to drive, Caden took them home. He had, on occasion, also helped Freddy escort rowdy patrons out of the bar.

"You're taking them home on a motorcycle?"

"Nah. Some people risk drinking and driving because they don't want to leave their vehicle here overnight. So I drive them home in their vehicle."

Luke frowned. "Can't they just drive somewhere after you get them home?"

"Not if they don't have their keys." Caden grinned. "Sometimes I leave them with someone else at home. If they're staying at a motel, I leave the keys with the manager. If neither of those options work, I hide the keys and leave them my phone number. They have to call me the next day to find out where their keys are."

"How do you get back to your bike?"

"I jog."

Luke had worked at the tavern long enough to know that not everyone lived close by. "What if they live far out?"

"I don't mind. If it's too far, I call Stacy to come pick me up. That doesn't happen very often." He nodded toward the door. "I better get going. One of them was getting a little rowdy."

Luke stiffened. "Want some help?"

"I imagine Caroline's got it taken care of, but it's always nice to have backup."

"Caroline?" Luke didn't recognize the name.

Caden laughed. "She's the bouncer."

Luke opened the door to his SUV and got out. "Since when did Freddy get a bouncer?"

"She's not really a bouncer, she's a waitress, but I wouldn't mess with her."

Before they got to the front door, it opened. The man who had harassed Emily earlier that evening was being led out by the tall woman he'd seen waiting on tables inside. The man's arm was twisted behind his back, and his face had a pained expression.

"Oh look," she said sweetly. "Your cab is here."

The man's two companions followed behind them. Neither of them looked happy with their friend.

"Thanks, Caroline." Caden reached out and took the keys from one of the men. "All right, boys, where to?"

When the men told him they were renting a cabin at Beaverhead Lodge, Caden frowned and glanced back at Luke. "I hate to ask you this, but that's a little farther than I want to jog, especially in the snow. I don't want Stacy to have to get the girls out of bed. Could you follow me out and give me a ride back?"

The man climbing into the back seat of the Ford F-150 King Ranch pickup was the only reason Luke was still there. If that man was leaving, so could he. "Sure," he told Caden.

Caden opened the driver's-side door to the truck, and Max jumped in.

"Hey," one of the men slurred, "I agreed to let you drive me to the cabin, but I didn't say nothing 'bout no dirty mutt riding in my brand-new truck."

"That's fine," Caden said. He motioned for Max to get

out. "I'll call Sheriff Tedford, and he can drive you home instead. You can get the keys from him in the morning."

The man began to get agitated. "How'm I supposed to get back to town to get my truck?"

"Not my problem." Caden didn't appear at all fazed.

The man frowned. "Can't you leave the dog here?"

"Nope." Caden crossed his arms. "Max and I are a package deal."

"Fine, but I better not find dog hair all over my seat tomorrow." He moved around to the cab and got in.

Max jumped back in the truck again, and Caden nodded toward the back seat where the drunken man was. "I'd be more worried about him throwing up on the seat than a little dog hair."

Luke couldn't hear the man's response because Caden shut the door and started the engine. He waited for him to pull out onto the main road before following him in his SUV.

It was funny how things worked out. Stacy and Abbie had been adopted by separate parents from an orphanage in the country of Georgia. Stacy and Caden had traveled to Georgia, hoping to find information about her younger sister. While they were gone, Abbie had shown up in Coronado, looking for Stacy. Noah gave Abbie a job so she could afford to stay until Stacy returned from Georgia. By the time Stacy returned, Abbie and Noah had fallen in love.

When they were kids, Luke wanted to be part of a big loud happy family, but Noah wanted nothing more than his horse, an open pasture and a clear sky. Now Noah was the one who was part of a family, and Luke was alone. Yep. Funny how things worked out.

He slowed down to turn into Beaverhead Lodge. Caden drove the men to their cabin, then went into the main lodge and gave the keys to the night manager. Soon Noah and Max were in the front seat of Luke's SUV.

"Thanks for doing this," Caden said. "Stacy used to pick me up when things like this happened, but I didn't want to disturb the girls."

While Caden and Stacy were in Georgia, they adopted two young girls from the same orphanage where Stacy had lived. "What's it like? Going from newlyweds to a family of four in just a few months?"

Caden grinned. "It's been a crazy ride. I always thought I would have at least nine months to prepare for fatherhood. Instead, I had nine days."

Luke pressed his lips together. That was longer than he had, but he couldn't tell Caden that. "I imagine you had to give up a lot of your plans."

"Yes," Caden said. "But new ones have taken their place. I know better than most people how life can change in an instant, so I'm not taking any of it for granted."

His tone had a hint of sadness, and Luke fought the urge to ask him what he meant.

Caden rubbed Max's head. "What brings you back to Coronado?"

"I just needed to come home to take care of some things."

"By things, you mean Emily and Wyatt?"

Luke's mouth dropped open. "Does everyone in town know?"

Caden laughed. "I don't know about that, but Abbie told Stacy, and she told me."

Luke frowned. "I guess everyone will know soon enough."

"Have you told Noah?"

Luke grimaced. "No. Not yet."

"I'm sure you know him better than I do, but I don't think he'd appreciate hearing it from anyone else."

Luke pulled into the parking lot of the Watering Hole. "I'm going to tell him the next time I see him."

"Thanks for the ride." Caden got out of the truck and Max followed.

Luke scanned the parking lot, but Emily's car was gone. She must have gotten off work already. Still, he didn't relax until he drove by her house and saw her car parked safely in its spot. The lights in the house were off, so he kept driving and headed back to the ranch.

The snow had melted during the day, but it was below freezing now, creating patches of black ice on the road. Luke drove slower than he normally would. As he pulled up into the driveway to the house, his headlights fell on Noah's pickup. So much for getting home before his brother.

The porch light had been left on for him, and he opened the door as quietly as he could.

"Abbie told me you were here, but I didn't believe it."

Luke jumped. He should've known that Noah would wait up for him. "I didn't mean to wake you."

"You didn't. I haven't been to bed yet." Noah motioned for him to follow him to the kitchen. "Want some coffee?"

"At one o'clock in the morning?"

"Decaf." Noah topped his cup off and turned to lean against the counter. "When did you get here?"

"A little before noon."

Noah frowned. "Don't take this the wrong way, 'cause you know I'm happy to see you, but why are you home?"

Luke took a shaky breath. Might as well grab the cat by the tail. "I came to meet my son."

Noah's face remained blank. "So, Abbie was right. Wyatt is your son."

Luke nodded.

Noah set his coffee on the counter and crossed his arms. He gave Luke a long hard stare. Luke could feel Noah's anger from across the room.

"Is that why you ran off to Nashville? So you didn't have to face up to what you did?" The muscles in Noah's jaw were tight. "I never thought you would take after our father."

"Don't you dare put me in the same category as Karl." Luke's chest constricted as his own anger rose. "I wasn't running away from anything. I just found out, and I came as fast as I could."

He repeated the story to his brother about the lost letter.

"So all this time, Emily thought you knew and just didn't care?" Noah moved to the breakfast table. Luke followed him but didn't sit down.

"Yeah. And just like you, she had no faith in me, either." He gritted his teeth. "It's been a long day. I'm going to bed."

He didn't stand in the kitchen long enough to hear Noah's response.

EMILY TRIED TO concentrate on what the pastor was saying, but all she could think about was Luke. Why had he come to the tavern last night? He said he wanted to talk to her, but she couldn't help but wonder if there was more to it. She was probably overthinking things.

"Em." Her grandfather nudged her.

She pulled away from her thoughts to look around. Everyone was standing for the final song. She jumped to her feet.

"Where is your head, girl?"

"Sorry, Granddad," she whispered. "I'll tell you after the service."

As soon as the congregation was dismissed, she picked

up Wyatt from the nursery. As they walked toward the parking lot, she glanced around to see if anyone was close enough to overhear. Everyone was busy visiting with others, so she told him about Luke's unexpected arrival.

He looked skeptical of Luke's story. "So, all this time, he really didn't know?"

"That's what he said." Emily followed him out to his truck.

She'd hardly slept, thinking about Luke coming over today. Last night, he'd been protective of her. He even told a drunken stranger that she was his business. Her heart fluttered. Most likely he just meant that because she was the mother of his child, he worried about her. Not because he might be harboring some feelings for her, too.

Granddad held the door open for her. "I'm meeting George and Larry at the Bear's Den for lunch. Want to join us?"

"I better not. I don't know what time Luke is coming by." Emily buckled Wyatt into the car seat in the back of the pickup. "It's been a while since you've met your friends for lunch. Y'all don't want me tagging along."

He let out some sound that sounded suspiciously like a snort and walked around to get into the driver's seat.

She was glad that he was meeting his friends. After her grandmother died, he shut himself off from the world completely and rarely left the house. He was slowly entering the world of the living again.

Emily wondered if the outing had been arranged by Tricia. Because her aunt babysat for her on Friday and Saturday nights, she normally spent the night at Granddad's house and went to church with them on Sunday morning before going back to Springerville. This weekend, she'd gone home when she was finished babysitting. Tricia was always trying to get Granddad involved in more activities.

"Don't you let him off the hook," Granddad said suddenly. "Luke is that boy's father, and he needs to take responsibility for him."

Emily scrunched her face. "Money, right? Granddad, I'm not worried about money. I'm more concerned about his relationship with Wyatt."

"You should be worried about money." Granddad pulled out of the church parking lot. "Raising kids gets expensive. You make him pay his fair share."

She gave him a long look. "If he pays child support, he's entitled to spend time with him. That means giving Wyatt up for some holidays and weekends. Maybe weeks at a time. Did you think about that?"

His face hardened. "He can't take that baby all the way to Nashville."

She agreed. There was no way she was going to let her son go that far away without her. Yesterday, Luke didn't try to hold him or even talk to him, so she doubted that Luke would want to take him, at least not for a while, if ever.

"Well, you can't have it both ways," she told her grandfather.

Luke was parked in front of her house when her grandfather pulled into the driveway.

"Do you want me to stay?" Granddad asked as she unbuckled Wyatt from his car seat.

Yes. She shook her head. "We'll be fine. Have a good lunch."

As soon as Granddad drove away, Luke got out of his SUV. How did he always manage to look like a model right out of a Western-wear catalog? His dark denim jeans were crisp and his cowboy boots were polished. She sighed. The man always looked amazing. She glanced down at her waist. At least the dress she'd worn to church covered up most of her curves. Her oversize jacket hid the rest.

He walked over to her, his hands stuffed in the front pockets of his jeans. "Hi."

"Hi." She shifted Wyatt to her other hip. "Have you been waiting long?"

"Since about ten."

"You've been sitting out here in the cold for two and a half hours?" She started toward the front door. "You should have waited inside. The door was open."

"Never even crossed my mind." He stopped by the front door.

She opened it and went in. "I'm going to change out of this dress."

She set Wyatt on the floor next to his toys.

When she came back into the living room, Luke hadn't moved from where he was standing just inside the front door. Wyatt was banging a toy on the ground. As soon as her son saw her, he belly-crawled over to her.

"Do you want some lunch?" she asked Luke. She scooped Wyatt up and walked over to the kitchen to put him in his high chair.

Luke ventured a little farther into the house. "I brought pizza. It might be cold by now."

"From the market?" Coronado wasn't large enough to have a pizza place, but the deli at Coronado Market had some pretty good pizzas.

"We could put it in the oven for a few minutes." He looked uncertain.

Emily couldn't remember ever seeing him look unsure of himself. The hope she'd clung to slipped away. It was obvious he didn't want to be here.

She swallowed. "That's fine. That'll give me time to feed Wyatt and put him down for his nap. Then we can talk."

He stood there for another moment before turning and leaving. "I'll get the pizza."

Wyatt banged on the tray of the high chair, eager for his lunch.

"Hold your horses." Emily scooted a chair close to him. "Here you go. How about some peas?"

Luke came back inside and put the pizza in the oven. Even though he walked right by Wyatt, he didn't talk to him or engage with him. He went to the living room and sat on the sofa.

Wyatt wasted no time scarfing down the contents of the baby food jar. By the time he finished his dessert, he was beginning to yawn. She wiped his face and went into the bedroom to breastfeed him and then put him down for his nap.

When she came out of the bedroom, Luke had moved to the table. He'd taken his cowboy hat off, leaving an indentation in his thick brown hair. The ends of his hair stuck out in wisps all over his head. Emily had never seen him let his hair get long enough to display its curly nature. Maybe he was going to let his hair grow as long as his brother did. She couldn't imagine Luke with hair past his shoulders.

"It should be warm by now," she said. She grabbed a couple of paper plates from inside the cabinet and put them on the table.

As she set the pizza on the table, he pulled a chair out for her before sitting back down himself.

"I guess things are better with you and your grandfather?" He took a bite of his pizza.

She finished chewing her own bite. "Yes, thanks to Abbie and Wyatt."

"Abbie?" Luke gave her a confused look.

"She started helping Granddad at the store at the end of the summer. At the time, she didn't know she would be staying in Coronado, so she was trying to teach him to use his computer to do the books and keep up with inventory."

Luke's dark eyes widened. "Denny uses a computer?"

"Not exactly," she said. "Abbie and I had already become friends by that time. When she found out that he was my grandfather and I had experience with the system she was using, she hauled me into the store, told him I was his new employee and put me to work."

He didn't try to hide his amusement. "That sounds like Abbie. Your grandfather didn't fight her on it?"

"No." She sighed. "He wanted me there, but he was too stubborn to admit it."

"And that sounds just like Denny." He chuckled. "I'm glad things worked out. I know it really bothered you that he pushed you away after your grandmother passed away."

"Wyatt's given him a reason to live again." Emily got up from her chair and retrieved some ranch dressing from the refrigerator. "I don't think there's anything he wouldn't do for him."

After she poured some dressing on her plate, she offered the bottle to Luke. He took it and did the same. He had relaxed a little, but there was still tension between them. She couldn't eat until they settled some things between them. She pushed her plate away and leaned on the table.

"Let's address the elephant in the room," she said. "You're trying to figure out what you're supposed to do or say, and in the meantime, you look like all you want to do is run away. Let me make it easy. I don't expect anything from you. And I don't need anything from you. I am fine just like I am."

A spark of anger glinted in his eyes, and he started to speak, but she held up her hand.

"That being said, I'm glad you're here. I never wanted it to be a secret from you, and it killed me thinking that you knew but just didn't care. If you want to be part of

Wyatt's life, I would never try to stop you. But don't do it out of some overinflated sense of obligation you may feel because your father abandoned you. If you do, sooner or later you're just going to end up resenting us."

Luke slumped back in his chair. "I have no idea what I'm supposed to do."

She gave him a half-hearted smile. "I've felt that way for the last eleven months."

He returned her smile, but the dimples in his cheeks didn't show themselves, so Emily knew the smile wasn't genuine. Her stomach rolled, and she held her breath. This was where he was going to tell her that he wasn't ready to be a father, wish them a nice life and leave.

His brows pinched together. "I guess the first thing we need to do is set up child support."

Money. It shouldn't have surprised her, but it did. "There's also visitation."

Luke shook his head. "I don't come to Coronado very often."

"You want him to come to Nashville?" She couldn't imagine traveling that far with her son.

"No. I would never expect you to do that." His face was stoic.

Her eyes narrowed, and she pressed her lips together. "You want to set up child support. But you don't want to set up visitation?"

Luke lifted his chin, his jaw muscles tight. "Abbie expects me to move back to Coronado and work for Noah on the ranch. But I can't do that. I *won't* do that."

Emily stiffened. "I would never expect you to."

He gave her a pleading look. "I'm not father material. I'll do my part financially. Whatever you want. But please don't ask for more than that."

Her throat tightened, and for a moment, she couldn't

breathe. He didn't want to be part of their lives. He didn't want to get to know his son. He didn't want her. "Well then, it's a good thing I turned down your wedding proposal."

CHAPTER SIX

"ARE YOU SERIOUS?"

Emily looked around to see if anyone had overheard her friend's cry of astonishment. She was relieved to see that she and Abbie were still the only customers in the Bear's Den, despite it being breakfast time. Her grandfather's store wasn't the only business that was slow in winter.

"First, he proposed to you. Then basically, he says he won't do more than give you money."

"Pretty much," Emily said softly.

Across the table from her, Abbie dropped her fork onto her plate and leaned back in her chair. "Noah told me that Luke was really sensitive about working the ranch with him. I guess I didn't understand just how much."

"I don't think it was what you said to him about the ranch that made him change his mind." Emily stabbed a piece of fruit with her fork.

Abbie gave her a confused look. "What else could it be?"

"I think it was me." Emily sighed. "Do you really think he came all the way to Coronado just to tell me he wasn't cut out to be a father? If all he wanted to do was set up child support, he could have done that over the phone."

"You think there's something more to it?"

Her stomach churned. "Maybe he came here with good intentions but took one look at me and changed his mind."

Abbie gasped. "Why would you think that?"

She shrugged. Visions of female country music stars flashed through her mind. "There's no way I can compare to the women in Nashville."

Emily gave up on eating her fruit cup. What she really wanted was a big plate of biscuits and gravy. Which was exactly why she was feeling the way she was. "Let's face it. I was never exactly petite to begin with, and having a baby didn't help."

"So what if you don't look like Barbie? You're real. And you're beautiful inside and out." Abbie picked up a sausage link and bit into it. "You can't really believe that he changed his mind about being part of his son's life because you gained a little weight after having a baby?"

"I don't know. Maybe."

Abbie shook her head. "If he's that shallow, then good riddance."

"The thing that bothers me the most is that he hasn't even given Wyatt a chance." Anger was beginning to replace the humiliation. "Wyatt is an awesome kid, but Luke hasn't even held him. When I try to get close enough to hand Wyatt to him, he steps back like he's about to get burned."

"That's exactly what he's afraid of," Abbie answered matter-of-factly. "I don't know Luke very well, but I know he doesn't like confrontation. Whenever things get tense, he walks away."

Emily nodded. "You're right. Noah didn't even know he was going to Nashville until he was already gone. I think he was afraid that if he told him face-to-face, he wouldn't have been able to leave."

"Right. And every time Noah calls him and tries to talk to him about anything serious, Luke makes an excuse to get off the phone." Abbie shook her head. "I mean, honestly, who has that many meetings at just the right time?"

Emily laughed. “He sure had a lot of them when I called him to try to tell him I was pregnant.”

Abbie gave her a serious look. “Maybe he’s afraid that if he holds Wyatt, it will get too real for him to be able to walk away.”

“There’s not much I can do about that,” Emily said. “I’m not going to force him to hold his son.”

“So, what are you going to do?”

“Nothing.” Emily eyed the gravy-covered biscuits on Abbie’s plate while she bit into her dry toast. “We got along just fine before, and we’ll get along just fine now.”

As if on cue, Wyatt banged a spoon on the table and giggled at the sound. Emily stroked his curly hair. She was feeling a little better than she had when Abbie invited her to breakfast.

“What time are you leaving for Springerville?” Abbie pinched off a tiny piece of her biscuit and gave it to Wyatt.

Emily picked up her phone from the table and glanced at the screen. “Granddad’s appointment is at nine this morning. I’m hoping Wyatt’ll sleep all the way there.”

While most babies fell asleep on long rides, Wyatt usually did not. He hated being in the car. Emily suspected that he suffered from motion sickness like she did.

Abbie’s face brightened. “Why don’t you let me stay with him?”

“I couldn’t ask you to do that.”

“Breakfast with you is the highlight of my day. Noah’s going to be busy all day. He even put Luke to work. I’m tired of sitting at the house by myself.” She made puppy dog eyes at Emily. “Besides, I need to start practicing.”

Emily’s eyes widened. “Are you—”

“Not yet.” Abbie’s face turned red. “But we’re officially trying.”

“I’m so happy for you!” Emily reached across the table

and gave her friend a hug. "In that case, I'm happy to leave my car-ride-hating child with you while I take my grandfather to the doctor."

LUKE'S HEART WAS in his throat as he pushed the SUV to go as fast as he dared on the icy road. He pulled in front of Emily's house and jumped out of the vehicle.

Abbie opened the door before he knocked. "Thank goodness."

"What's wrong?" Luke willed his pulse to slow down. He scanned the tiny house. "Where's Emily?"

"She had to take her grandfather to Springerville." Abbie handed him a piece of paper that looked suspiciously like instructions.

When she picked up her purse and keys, Luke stepped in front of her. "Where are you going? You said there was an emergency."

"Yes," she said. "I forgot about a meeting with my Realtor, and I'm already late. So, I need you to watch Wyatt until I get back. It'll just take me a few minutes."

Panic clawed his chest. "I can't. I don't know anything about babies."

Abbie waved off his concern. "Don't worry. Wyatt's taking a nap right now, and I'll probably be back before he wakes up."

Luke glanced at the instructions. She wrote a lot of them down for someone who was only going to be gone for a few minutes. "Why are you meeting with a Realtor?"

"My father and I are going to open an accounting office in town. Hopefully, one with a kitchen so it can double as a bakery."

"Oh." He remembered Noah telling him that Abbie's father wasn't enjoying retirement as much as he thought he would. He glanced nervously at the closed bedroom door. "Hurry up, then."

Abbie nodded. "If you need anything, just text me."

With that, she was out the door. Luke sat down on the sofa and picked up the remote to the television. He turned it on and flipped through the channels trying to find something besides a snow-white screen. After a few minutes, he gave up. Emily didn't have cable, satellite or even a streaming device. She did have a large selection of DVD movies stacked neatly on the bookshelf next to the television set.

He picked a movie and sat down to watch it. As soon as it started, he realized he'd picked the same movie he and Emily had watched together on his last night in Coronado. That had been the first—and last—night he'd kissed her. He'd kissed a lot of girls, but a kiss had never affected him like hers did.

At that moment, there was nothing he wouldn't have done for her. If she'd asked him to stay, he would have. But she didn't. She told him how proud she was of him for following his dream. She even packed him some food for the road.

A cry pulled him from his memories of that night. He stared at the door to the bedroom as the cry got louder. His pulse raced. What was he supposed to do? The cry turned into a wail.

Luke stood up and pushed the door open with shaking hands. Blackout curtains hanging over the window kept the room dark, but the light from the open doorway illuminated the room enough for him to see Wyatt standing in the crib.

When Wyatt saw him, his wails turned into whimpers.

Luke walked over to the crib. "It's okay."

Wyatt reached for him with chubby fingers. Luke took a deep breath and picked the baby up. He was surprised at how light he was. The little boy buried his face in Luke's chest. "Ma-ma-ma-ma."

He patted Wyatt's chest, and the scent of baby shampoo and lotion filled his nostrils. "Momma will be home soon."

Wyatt cuddled up against him as Luke walked to the living room. With each step he took, his heart seemed to shift. When he sat down on the sofa, Wyatt lifted his head and stared at him with big brown eyes. Luke froze as Wyatt lifted one hand and explored Luke's face with his fingers.

Wyatt's face was serious as he studied Luke. A moment later, he grasped Luke's face between two chubby hands and pressed an open-mouthed sloppy kiss to his chin. Luke's heart swelled until he felt it was about to burst. Time stood still as he clutched Wyatt's tiny body against his chest.

At that moment, he knew his life would never be the same. How was it possible to feel like this about a tiny person he'd just met?

With Wyatt still cuddled against him, he reached for the list Abbie left him on the end table. Wyatt wiggled out of his arms and crawled across the sofa.

"Slow down there, buddy." Luke caught him before Wyatt fell headfirst off the couch.

He set the baby down on the floor like he'd seen Emily do. Wyatt took off, crawling on his belly to a basket of toys on the floor.

The list Abbie left him was long and detailed. It was almost as if she'd known she wouldn't be back when Wyatt woke up. He sent her a text, asking when she would be back.

Sorry! The Realtor is running late, too. I'll be a little while.

"Well, it looks like it's just you and me," he said to his son.

Wyatt looked up at him and grinned, showing off the

dimples in his cheeks. He crawled over to Luke and used Luke's legs to pull himself up to stand.

Luke's heart melted, and he picked his son up and bounced him on his knee. The baby erupted in a fit of giggles. "The list said to check your diaper when you woke up. I've never done this before, so you're going to have to help me."

With Wyatt on his hip, he walked around the house until he found the extra diapers. It took three tries before he got the new diaper on without it falling off, but he finally did it.

He smiled at his accomplishment. "There. That wasn't so hard. What else do we need to do?"

After two hours, he decided that he'd been had. Abbie wasn't coming back. What was more surprising was that he didn't want her to.

He sent one more text, this time to Emily.

When will you be home?

If she didn't respond, he wouldn't blame her. After all, he'd made it clear that he didn't want to be there.

In about an hour. Why?

He glanced at his son.

We need to talk. This time, I'll listen.

CHAPTER SEVEN

THE KNOTS IN Emily's stomach had nothing to do with the windy road up the mountain from Springerville to Coronado. Luke's message was burned into her brain, even without looking at the screen on her phone. What could he want to talk about? Hadn't they already said everything that needed to be said?

When Emily pulled up to her house, she was surprised to see Luke's SUV parked in the front. Apparently, he wanted to talk sooner rather than later. It would have been nice if Abbie had warned her that he'd shown up. Wait. Abbie's vehicle was nowhere around. She pulled her cell phone out of her purse and texted her.

Where are you? Is Wyatt with you?

Abbie's response was almost immediate.

I had to take care of a few things. Luke babysat. You're welcome. ;)

Emily stared at the winky face emoji. What did Abbie do?

She got out of the car and walked up to the house. As she approached the door, she heard Wyatt squeal. Her heart rate skyrocketed, and she rushed to open the door.

Luke was on the floor with Wyatt, playing peekaboo

with a baby blanket. He let Wyatt's blanket fall over his head and pulled the blanket off. Each time he did, Wyatt squealed louder.

Relief flooded through her, and she closed the door and leaned against it.

Luke glanced up and saw her. He gave her a crooked grin and scooped Wyatt up and walked toward her. "Look, Wyatt. Mom is home."

She held out her hands for Wyatt to come to her. The baby leaned over to her and planted a wet kiss on her cheek. She inhaled his sweet baby smell.

"Something came up, and Abbie had to leave."

Emily arched one eyebrow. "And you volunteered to babysit?"

"Not exactly." Luke shrugged. "You might say I was tricked into it."

Her heart dropped. That must be what he wanted to talk about. He probably thought she had something to do with it and wanted to make sure she didn't do it again. "I was going to take him with me, but Abbie insisted she wanted to babysit."

Wyatt leaned out and patted Luke's chest. Luke's gaze was warm, and he took Wyatt back into his arms. "I have a sneaking suspicion she may have set us both up."

At least he wasn't blaming her. "I'm so sorry."

"I'm not." Luke bounced Wyatt on his hip. He gave her a serious look. "Let's talk."

The knot in her stomach exploded into butterflies. She nodded and followed him to the sofa.

Wyatt wiggled away from Luke as soon as they sat down. Luke rubbed his palms on the legs of his jeans. He took a deep breath and lifted his gaze to look at her. "I owe you an apology."

His face was stoic, but his brown eyes swam with emotion. Emily waited for him to find the words he seemed to be looking for.

"I have been doing my best to avoid you and Wyatt." Luke's gaze drifted to Wyatt. "I thought he'd be better off if I didn't get close to him."

Emily pressed her lips together. "Why would you think that?"

"I don't know anything about being a father." Luke shook his head.

"No one really knows how to be a parent until they are one." She wasn't about to let him make excuses when the truth was that he just didn't want to be bothered. "Do you think I wasn't scared to death?"

Luke slumped back in his seat, and he dropped his gaze to stare at his hands. Emily took a deep breath. He was trying to be honest with her, and she was snapping at him instead of listening. She had to stop letting her emotions get the better of her.

"I shouldn't have interrupted," she said. "I'm sorry."

He lifted his head to look at her. "Do you know why my mother was never around after we moved to the ranch?"

She shook her head. Emily had heard lots of rumors about Luke's absent mother. None of them were very nice.

"Money."

She sighed. Everything always came back to money. "Was she trying to save enough money to move off the ranch?" Since Emily was trying to save enough money to buy a house, she could understand a mother making sacrifices to give her children a better life.

"No." He shrugged. "That's another story." His brow furrowed, and he took a deep breath. "I don't remember much about Karl, but I know he didn't help my mom take care of us. I never missed my dad, but I remember crying myself to sleep a lot because my mom wasn't around when

I needed her. So when I found out about Wyatt, I thought as long as I provided for you financially, that's all either one of you really needed."

Emily swallowed. She wanted to tell him that money wasn't the most important thing. Her mother and stepfather had lots of money. She'd never lacked for anything, except their attention. They'd given her everything money could buy, and all she'd wanted was their time.

He looked up at her, his eyes filled with uncertainty. "But now I know that's not what *I* need."

Her breath froze in her lungs. "What do you need?"

"I need to know my son."

She slowly let the air out. "I would really like that, too."

"I don't want to make promises I can't keep." Luke laced his fingers and tapped his thumbs together. "My life is in Nashville. I have some steady gigs, and I've made great connections. I have a great agent. What am I supposed to do? Give all that up and move back to Coronado to be my brother's ranch hand?"

She shook her head. "I never asked you to do that."

"I know that," he said. "But that's what everyone expects me to do."

Emily crossed her arms. "Stop worrying about everyone else. The only person you should be worried about is Wyatt."

"I am. Most of my gigs are on the weekends. What if I can only make it to Arizona a few times a year? He might end up resenting me more than if I just stayed away." Luke clenched his jaw.

"Who says you can only see him on the weekends?" She reached over and squeezed his hand. "We'll make it work. He won't resent you as long as you're honest with him. Seeing him occasionally is better than never being there at all. I only saw my dad a few times a year, but I never doubted he loved me."

"You've never talked about your dad." Luke frowned. "How old were you when your parents divorced?"

"They didn't. He died when I was eight," Emily said.

He let out a huge breath and leaned back into the couch. "I'm sorry. I didn't know."

"I don't think I ever told you. He was a Marine, so he was stationed overseas a lot." Emily cupped the back of her neck with one hand. "Mom married Clint less than a year later."

They sat in silence for a few moments. She could tell that Luke was trying hard to figure out what he was supposed to say, which was why she rarely talked about her father.

This conversation was about Wyatt, not her. She gave him a slight smile. "I can tell you from experience that I would rather have you here sometimes than not at all, and Wyatt will, too."

The tension seemed to melt away. "You're amazing, do you know that?"

She raised her eyebrows. "I thought you didn't drink."

He laughed at her teasing. "Seriously. Most women would have given me a list of demands in order to see my son."

"Maybe because we're friends, not lovers," she said. "We were friends before Wyatt came along, and there's no reason we can't remain friends. It's not like you made me any promises and then broke my heart."

He flinched slightly as if she'd pinched him. "You know you're going to be bombarded with questions when I leave. The gossip mill will be in full swing."

"I'm not worried about it. It can't be worse than all the

speculation and gossip that happened when people figured out I was pregnant."

Luke's brown eyes narrowed. "I'm sorry you had to face that on your own, too. Maybe this time it'll be more aimed at me."

She shrugged. "It's one of the dangers of living in a small town, I guess. People will always need something, or someone, to talk about."

Luke nodded. "I always admired the way you could shrug off other people's opinions, even in high school. You never seemed to care what people thought. What's your secret?"

"No secret. I just got pushed past the point of caring, but I don't recommend letting yourself get to that point." After her mother remarried, their lives revolved around what other people thought. For a while, it made Emily an angry, bitter person. "It's better if you have a few people whose opinions matter. Just be careful of who those people are."

That was a lesson her mother never learned. Her main priority became helping her stepfather advance his career. Every report card Emily received, every activity she participated in and every dinner party at their house was a reflection on their family. Emily resented it with every fiber of her being and went out of her way to do the opposite of what they wanted. It was almost a relief when she was sent to live with her grandparents.

"Speaking of," Emily said, "when are you leaving?"

"Sunday," he said. "I know six days isn't long enough to make up for almost a missed year."

"It's a start. What do you have in mind?"

He gave her a hopeful smile. "Do you have plans for the rest of the day?"

"No." Even if she did, she would cancel them so that she...so that Wyatt could spend time with Luke.

"So is it okay if I hang out here with you?"

"Sure," she said. "But I have to warn you, we lead a very dull life. I'm sure it's not nearly as exciting as Nashville."

He winked at her. "You might be surprised at how easily I'm entertained."

She couldn't help but smile as he turned his attention back to Wyatt. It was amazing how Luke's whole demeanor seemed to change. He was more relaxed and more like the Luke she remembered.

"He was born February 21?"

"Yes. He'll be one in a little over three weeks." She couldn't believe how fast time had gone.

Luke handed Wyatt a block. "He's not walking yet. Should he be? Is he behind?"

"No." Although, she'd worried about that herself. "The average is around twelve months. Some babies are earlier, and some don't walk until they're eighteen months."

Wyatt pulled himself up on the side of the sofa and walked to the end, using the sofa as a rail. He looked at her and hollered.

"He's getting close, though, isn't he?" Luke grinned.

"It'll be any day now."

Luke gave her a serious look. "I have some questions."

She tried to keep the tone light. "I may or may not have some answers."

For the next hour, Luke proceeded to ask questions about every aspect of their life. He asked everything from what time Wyatt got up to what cartoon characters he seemed to like the best. It didn't seem to be motivated by anything more than a true desire to know about his son, so she didn't mind answering the questions. More than once he reflected on how much he'd missed.

She curled her legs up beneath her and watched Luke playing peekaboo with Wyatt, and her heart felt as if it would burst. She knew it couldn't last. Luke was only there for Wyatt and had no interest in her, but she still wanted to hold the memory in her heart.

IT WAS GETTING late in the afternoon, but Luke wasn't ready to leave yet.

Emily walked out of the bedroom where she'd been folding laundry. "Would you like to stay for dinner?"

He couldn't help but grin. "If it's not too much trouble," he said.

"How do chicken enchiladas sound?"

"Sounds fantastic. That's my favorite dish."

"I know," she said. She gave him a sideways glance. "You used to tell Freddy he could pay you with his wife's enchiladas."

"Maria makes the best enchiladas." Luke licked his lips at the memory.

Emily smiled. "She's the one who taught me how to make them. Go entertain your son while I make dinner."

"Yes, ma'am!" He snapped a salute.

He went back to the game they had been playing. Luke had attached some large chunky Legos together, and Wyatt was trying to get them apart. Wyatt paused playing, and his face turned bright red, then he got a pained expression on his face. Luke started to panic. What was he doing? Was something wrong?

A few seconds later, Luke got a whiff of something and realized exactly what the problem was. "You didn't." He picked him up and took a tentative sniff. "Yes, you did."

Emily was busy in the kitchen, and he didn't want to bother her. How hard could it be to change a diaper? He looked around for the diaper bag.

Large hooks were hung on the wall close to the front door. Emily's jacket hung on one, and a diaper bag hung on another. He lifted it off the hook and looked inside. Clothes, diapers and wipes were all tucked neatly inside.

He had changed Wyatt's diaper after his nap, but it was just wet. This one was…not. And Wyatt was not very cooperative. Every time Luke tried to wipe, Wyatt tried to roll. Luke was struggling trying to contain the baby and the mess when he heard laughter behind him.

"Here." Emily squatted next to him. She held both of Wyatt's feet in one hand, lifted his bottom up and managed to wipe him in one swift movement. She tossed the used wipe on top of the dirty diaper before getting another wipe and cleaning him up good.

The new diaper was on before Luke even realized it was out. He shook his head. "How did you manage that so easily?"

"Lots of practice." She picked up the diaper and rolled it up. "I'm going to throw this in the dumpster outside."

"I'll do it." He jumped up and took it from her hand.

He didn't bother to put his coat on just to walk to the end of the yard. The snow crunched under his feet, and his breath came out in white puffs. The crisp air cleared his head like nothing else did.

Winter always did that. Even as a child, he loved to be outside during the winter. While most people saw dead plants, dormant trees and bare branches, he saw winter as a fresh start. Most people thought spring was the time of rebirth and fresh beginnings, but they were wrong. It was winter. Mother Nature wiped out all the overgrowth and got things ready to start anew. Just like him.

The sudden shock of having a child had worn off, and now he saw it as the opportunity to start new. New priorities. New responsibilities. Maybe a new family.

He walked into the warm air inside the house. He closed the door and went to lock the door out of habit. The dead bolt spun freely, so he looked at the inside of the door. The chamber where the lock should be was empty. He frowned. This wouldn't do. Emily needed a better lock than the one on the doorknob.

Wyatt looked up from his toys and squealed happily. Emily smiled at him from the kitchen. She pulled a pan from the oven and set it on the counter. The chicken enchiladas bubbled, filling the air with their aroma.

"Is there anything I can do to help?"

Emily nodded toward the living room. "You can put Wyatt in the high chair while I set the table."

"Hey, big man!" He tossed Wyatt in the air.

Wyatt giggled and smacked Luke's cheek.

He set Wyatt in the high chair, carefully pushing the tray into place. Emily put the last of the food on the table, and he pulled a chair out for her to sit down.

"Thank you." Her face turned red. She put a scoop of rice on Wyatt's tray and followed it with a spoonful of mashed-up beans. "Go ahead and start."

"You're not eating yet?"

"Honestly?" She laughed. "I rarely eat until after I put Wyatt to bed."

His stomach growled, reminding him that he hadn't eaten since breakfast, but he wasn't going to eat without her. He sat down but made no attempt to put food on his plate.

Wyatt picked up food with his tiny hand and shoved it into his mouth. He hadn't had time to swallow when he picked up more.

"He can eat regular food?" Luke tried not to sound as alarmed as he felt. "He won't choke?"

"As long as I cut it up small and keep an eye on him," Emily said. "He prefers real food, but I only give him a little."

She reached for the enchiladas, but Luke beat her to the spoon. He picked up her plate and scooped the food onto it, following it with the rice and beans before filling his own plate.

They ate in comfortable silence for a few minutes. Luke glanced at Wyatt every few seconds, still worried that he was going to choke.

Even though the enchiladas were wonderful, he couldn't relax and enjoy the meal. "What if he does start to choke?"

She smiled and stood up to open the cabinet on the end. On the top shelf was a plastic kit. She handed it to him. "It's an anti-choking device. Instructions are included."

Luke unzipped the container and looked inside. "I've never seen anything like this."

"I hadn't, either. As soon as Wyatt got a couple of teeth, Granddad started giving him little bits of food. It scared me to death, so Granddad bought this for me."

He reached out and stroked Wyatt's head. So many people had taken care of both Wyatt and Emily. He was grateful that she had a support system in place, but it should have included him. That knowledge weighed him down. He hadn't purposely avoided his responsibilities, but it was still his fault. He should've been there for her, and he wasn't.

"Your granddad is pretty attached to him, isn't he?"

"He is," she said.

Luke frowned. "I'm sure I'm not his favorite person right now. How mad is he at me?"

Emily took a bite of her enchiladas. "Until a few days ago, he didn't know that you were the one he was supposed to be mad at. It was me he was angry with."

"Why would he be mad at you?"

"*Mad* isn't really the right word." She shrugged. "When

I refused to tell him who Wyatt's father was, he came to the conclusion that I must not know."

Anger welled up in his chest. "He didn't accuse you of being—"

"Oh yes," she interrupted. "Among other things."

"Why didn't you tell him?"

She bit her bottom lip. "It's hard to explain."

He leaned back in his chair and crossed his arms. Was she embarrassed to admit that he was Wyatt's father?

She set her fork down and took a deep breath. "At first, I waited because I thought you should know first. After I didn't hear back from you, I was afraid people would accuse me of blaming you because you were gone."

"That's it?"

"Mostly." She avoided his gaze.

There was more to it than that. He arched one dark eyebrow. "Tell me."

She pushed some rice around the plate with her fork. "I don't want to."

"Why?"

"Because it'll make me sound like I'm trying to be altruistic."

"Well, now, you have to tell me." He winked and took a bite of food. He hoped teasing her would lighten the mood enough for her to be comfortable telling him. Even if she was afraid it would hurt his feelings.

When she kept her gaze averted from his, he reached over to reassure her. He covered her hand with his. "It's okay. You're not the first girl to be embarrassed about dating a Sterling."

Her mouth dropped open. "Embarrassed? That's not it at all."

He shrugged, secretly pleased that the thought enraged her. "Then what is it?"

"I didn't want to cause problems for your career."

The words were spoken so softly that Luke almost didn't catch what she said. "How would it cause problems?"

"I didn't want your name to be splashed across the front page of some gossip magazine." She raised her hands as if framing an invisible headline. "Up-and-coming country star hides a secret child."

The idea was so silly that he started to laugh, but when he saw the conflict on her face, he stopped. "I'm flattered that you believed I would be a big-enough success that a gossip magazine would care about me."

She tilted her head and gave him a confused look. "You haven't given up already. You're so talented."

After being in Nashville for over a year, he was starting to recognize the difference between talent and ambition. There were a lot of talented singers in Nashville, but only a handful had enough of both to make it to the top. Quint told him he had to be more aggressive. He'd planned on doing just that before he opened Emily's letter.

"Of course not," he said. "I have some steady jobs. And my agent is also pitching my songs to other artists."

She ran one hand through her curly hair. "Your songs are amazing, although I love hearing you sing, too."

"Thank you," he said. "But even if I did make it big, it's not your job to protect me. And I will never be ashamed to be Wyatt's father."

Her face turned red again, and she smiled. They ate in silence for a few more minutes.

"Do you know when you might be back?" she asked.

Was it just a few days ago that he'd thought about cutting back on his time at the HVAC company so he could devote more time to his music? So much for that idea. If anything, he needed to increase his hours so he could support his son.

"I have to talk to my agent and check my schedule," he said. "Maybe I can arrange to come back at least once a month. Maybe even every other weekend. If it's okay with you."

"It will give my aunt a little bit of a break." Her face flushed. "If you want to watch him while I work, that is."

"I'd love to." Although, he'd love it more if Emily was going to be there, too.

Wyatt banged the tray of his high chair and babbled loudly. He had mashed beans in his hair, and rice was stuck all over his face. Emily stood up and retrieved a washcloth from a drawer next to the sink.

"Are you finished?" Luke asked while she was washing Wyatt's face.

"Yes."

He gathered the dishes and stood up. The tiny home didn't have a dishwasher, so he started running water into the sink.

"I'll do that in a little bit," she said as she removed Wyatt from the high chair.

He waved her away. "It's the least I can do."

She balanced Wyatt on her hip with an uncertain look on her face. "I usually give Wyatt a bath right after dinner, and then he goes to bed. But it won't hurt him to stay up a little later than normal if you want to stay for a while."

He did want to stay, but he also didn't want to wear out his welcome. "I don't want to mess up his routine."

She nodded. "I'm going to go start his bath."

He reached his hands out to Wyatt. "Come here, son. Let Mama run your water."

Wyatt went to him easily enough, and Emily disappeared into the bedroom.

He carried Wyatt into the living room and sat on the sofa with him. He held Wyatt's chubby hands in his. "Pat-a-cake, pat-a-cake, baker's man." He sang the song from memory, clapping his hands together with Wyatt's.

A few minutes later, Emily returned. She didn't try to take Wyatt from him, she just stood to the side and waited for them to finish their game. He stood up and handed Wyatt to her.

"Tell Daddy good-night." She held Wyatt's hand in hers and waved.

The word sent a thrill through Luke that he hadn't anticipated. "Daddy," he murmured.

Emily's eyes widened. "I'm sorry. I should've asked you first. What do you want him to call you?"

"That's the first time I've heard that. I like it." He leaned forward and pressed a kiss to Wyatt's forehead. "Good night, son. Have a nice bath."

CHAPTER EIGHT

LUKE CREPT DOWN the stairs of the ranch house. He knew Noah would be up at this hour, but he had no idea if his sister-in-law was an early riser or not.

He heard music playing in the kitchen. Abbie must be up. It wasn't classic country music, so he knew it wasn't Noah. His brother didn't listen to anything that came out after the eighties. He peeked into the kitchen and saw Abbie rolling dough on the island. He shook his head. The woman baked more than anyone he'd ever known.

"Morning."

Abbie jumped. "You scared me."

He walked into the kitchen to pour himself a cup of coffee. "How did your Realtor meeting go?"

"Oh." Her face turned bright red. "I'm sorry. Are you really mad at me?"

"That depends." He leaned against the counter and took a sip of his coffee. "Why did you do it?"

She pursed her lips and looked him straight in the eye. "Because Wyatt deserves a father, not a financial donor."

Luke cocked his head. "And you thought tricking me into babysitting would turn me into a father?"

"Did it?" She raised one eyebrow.

"It takes more than a morning of babysitting to make someone a father," he said.

Her face fell, and she turned back to rolling her dough.

"You didn't come home after Emily got back. What did you do the rest of the afternoon?"

"I spent it getting to know my son." Luke set his cup on the counter and stepped over to his sister-in-law. He waited for her to look at him. "Thank you."

A grin spread across her face. "You're welcome. I knew you just needed a push."

Luke laughed. "I'm glad you were there to shove me. Are you and your dad really thinking about opening an accounting office?"

"Yes and no," she said. "Coronado is much too small to support a business like that full-time. We're still going to open a business, but it'll just be part-time, and it'll be in my dad's home office."

"Part-time? Between your part-time baking and your part-time accounting, sounds like you'll be busy all year long."

"Baking is more of a hobby than a business." Abbie pressed a round cutter into the dough. "Are you going to see Emily and Wyatt today?"

"This afternoon." He picked up his coffee cup again. "I'm going over when she gets home from the hardware store."

"Good." She nodded.

"I'm going to see if Noah needs any help in the barn." Luke downed the rest of his coffee and set the cup in the sink.

His jacket was hanging on the coat-tree next to the back door. He grabbed it and his hat and headed for the barn. The familiar smell of hay and horses infiltrated Luke's senses as he stepped inside.

Noah was brushing a large roan with a currycomb in the breezeway. "Good morning."

Jasper tossed her head and snorted, her gaze never leaving Luke.

He opened the gate to greet the horse. Jasper nicked his arm, causing him to jump. "Cut that out," he scolded her.

Noah laughed. "She missed you, but she's mad at you."

"I missed you, too." Luke stroked the horse's neck. Jasper leaned into him, rubbing her head against his chest. He glanced at Noah. "I know I should sell her, I just can't bring myself to do it."

"Don't you dare," Noah said. "She's the only horse that can keep Paddy under control. If you need the money, I'll buy her."

"It's not the money." Luke picked up a currycomb from the shelf and started brushing Jasper's coat. "I just feel guilty about giving you one more thing to take care of."

Noah picked up Paddy's back foot. "I have one hundred and fifty horses on the range and fifteen horses in the barn. One more doesn't make a difference."

"Most of those horses are wild. Jasper loves attention. There's no way you have time to give her that." He would be the first to admit that it was his fault Jasper was so needy. She was the first and only horse he'd ever bonded with.

"I don't, but Abbie does." Noah checked Paddy's hooves. "She was scared of horses until she met Jasper. Now Abbie spoils her worse than you did."

That made him feel better. When he left Coronado, he wanted to take Jasper with him, but he knew she'd never be happy being cooped up in a boarding facility. Jasper was used to roaming the fields, working cattle and riding fences.

"Need help with anything?"

Before he'd moved away, he would never have had to ask that question. He and Noah could work together all day, never exchanging a word, yet knowing what the other needed. Now everything was different. Instead of cattle, Noah managed wild horses.

Noah shook his head. "Not much to do today. I could use your help tomorrow, though."

"What's going on tomorrow?"

"I have to move the herd from the back pasture up to the east one."

Luke nodded. "Sure. Can't be much different than moving cattle, right?" Rounding up cattle had been a yearly event as soon as he was old enough to help.

"That's where you're wrong." Noah laughed. "Cattle are pretty cooperative for the most part. These horses are not. They resent being told where to move, and they will cause trouble."

Luke could almost sympathize with the horses. He'd never liked being told what to do, either. "Anyone else coming to help?"

"Caden will be here first thing in the morning, and Coy will be here later in the afternoon. He's coming in from a training camp in Florida." Noah opened Paddy's stall, and the horse entered on his own.

"Coy's coming? Is he still sore with me?" Luke hadn't seen his best friend in a few years, and other than one angry phone call right after he left Coronado, they hadn't spoken. He would like the opportunity to apologize in person.

Noah shrugged. "I honestly couldn't tell you. I was so busy the last time I saw him, we didn't have time to talk much. But if he hasn't reached out to you, I'm guessing he's still mad."

"Is Becky coming with him?" Coy and Becky had been a package deal since they were twelve years old, so Luke spent as much time with Becky as he did Coy. Becky was the more level-headed one, so if Coy wouldn't hear him out, he knew Becky would.

Noah shook his head. "Coy and Becky broke up. He's still on the rodeo circuit, and she's in Texas."

"What's Becky doing in Texas?" He followed Noah out of the barn and waited for him to close the doors.

"She got into veterinarian school at Texas A&M."

Coy and Becky had been the perfect couple. If something could come between the two of them, what chance did Luke have with Emily? Not that he was even sure he wanted a relationship with Emily. "Why did they break up?"

"Not sure." Noah shrugged. "They were still together when they came to help me at Whispering Pines in the fall. By Thanksgiving, they'd broken up."

Abbie was pulling the biscuits out of the oven as they walked in the back door. "Everything else is already on the table."

The small table in the breakfast nook was loaded down with food. Luke hung his hat and jacket up and sat across from Noah.

"You going to Emily's this afternoon?"

"Yes. As soon as she gets home from the hardware store."

Abbie set the platter of biscuits on the table and joined them. "Stacy and Caden are bringing the girls out this afternoon to go tobogganing. You should invite Emily to join us."

Noah nodded. "I'm putting a brisket in the smoker for dinner, so there will be plenty of food."

Luke spread butter on a steaming biscuit. "I'll ask her."

He would much rather spend the afternoon with just Emily and Wyatt. He didn't have a lot of time to be with them, and he wanted to make the most of it.

"What are your plans until Emily gets off work?" Noah got up to refill his coffee cup.

"I got some boxes in town yesterday, so I could finish packing up my room." If it went well, he'd be done before noon and could go to town and wait for Emily at the hardware store.

"Pack up?" Noah exchanged looks with his wife before turning his gaze back to Luke. "So you're really not planning on staying?"

"There's nothing for me here."

"Your son is here." Abbie gave him a pointed look.

Luke's chest expanded. "That doesn't change the fact that I don't have a way of making a living in Coronado. How can I take care of him if I can't support him?"

Noah took a bite of his eggs. "If you change your mind, you always have a place here. This ranch is half yours."

Luke shook his head. "I appreciate it, but you and I both know the Double S can't support two families."

Claiming that the ranch was half his would be an insult to all the hard work Noah put in to keep the ranch afloat.

Abbie tucked a strand of hair behind her ear. "Your music career must be going well, then."

"It's going okay. I have a second job to supplement my income."

This got Noah's attention. His brother cocked his head. "What do you do?"

"I work for an HVAC company."

"HVAC?" Abbie's gaze went from Luke to Noah and back.

"Heating, ventilation and air conditioning," Luke said. "I make good money, and my boss gives me time off for gigs and agent meetings."

"Well, there you go." Abbie's voice brightened. "Why can't you do that in Coronado?"

"Too small," Noah and Luke responded at the same time.

"You won't know unless you try."

It was Noah who rescued Luke from arguing with her. He held up a biscuit. "Why don't you sell homemade bread in town anymore?"

"Because I couldn't sell enough to pay for the cost of making it." She sighed. "I get it. But Nashville is so far away. When will you ever get to see your son?"

"I'll fly to Arizona whenever I can. I might even try to talk Emily into bringing Wyatt to visit me occasionally. When he's older, that is."

"Will that be enough?"

"It'll have to be," he said. "For now."

EMILY FOCUSED ON the computer screen in front of her. Wyatt was taking his midmorning nap in the nursery, so this was the best time to get caught up on the books. It was getting harder and harder to work and take care of Wyatt at the same time.

When he was first born, it was so easy. He slept most of the time. As he got a little older, he was content being in his swing or the bouncer that she could set next to her desk. But now, he was much more mobile and required more attention. She always felt like either her job or her son was getting shortchanged.

She heard the chimes from the bells hanging at the entrance to the store, but she rarely dealt with customers. Granddad took care of anyone who came in. Most of the time, it wasn't customers but friends who stopped by to chat.

Between the older men who stopped to talk to Granddad and the Reed sisters who stopped by to gossip, Emily knew everything that happened in the small town.

From her corner office, she couldn't see who had entered the store, but she heard her grandfather greet them, so she went back to her work. It was some time later that she heard her name and froze. The voices got lower as her grandfather and the customer walked farther away from her office.

She got up from her desk and walked to the doorway to see who her grandfather was talking to. Granddad was with Luke near the entrance of the store. Their conversation looked intense, but Emily couldn't hear what was being said.

Her grandfather's hunched figure straightened up, and Emily wondered if Luke had said something to make him angry. A moment later, her grandfather nodded enthusiastically, and the two men shook hands.

She stepped out of the office and waited for Luke to look in her direction, but he never did. He said something else to her grandfather and left the store.

Emily walked down the center aisle. "What was Luke doing here?"

"He wanted to know if I still carried toboggans and snow saucers."

"He didn't want to see Wyatt?"

Her grandfather shrugged. "He was in a hurry. Noah was waiting for him in the truck."

She narrowed her gaze on him. "He stayed and chatted for a while for someone in a big hurry."

He got a smug look on his face. "He did want to talk to me about a few things."

"Like what?" Her heart fluttered in her chest. Whatever Luke had said seemed to make her grandfather happy. Maybe Luke had decided to pursue a relationship with her and had asked for his blessing.

Granddad lifted his chin. "He thanked me for looking out for you and Wyatt, and he apologized for not being around."

Her shoulders slumped. "That's all?"

"No," he said. "He invited us out to the ranch for dinner tonight."

A tiny spark of hope swelled up again. Having dinner at the ranch would be nice.

"Did he say what time?" The ranch was almost thirty minutes outside town. If dinner was very late, it would be dark when she would be driving back home. Temperatures dropped fast when the sun went down, and the road to the ranch would get icy fast. She definitely didn't want to be driving back too late.

"Also, he said something about taking you and Wyatt tobogganing this afternoon, so he's going to pick you up a little after one."

Emily frowned. If she went out to the ranch with Luke that early, her grandfather would have no choice except to drive himself. He couldn't see very well at night.

She pulled her cell phone out of her back pocket. "I better call him and tell him I'm riding out with you."

"I'm not going." He shook his head.

"Why not?"

"I already have dinner plans for tonight. Now you better get finished with whatever you're working on so you can be ready when Luke gets back from Springerville."

"What's he going to Springerville for?"

"I don't know. My guess would be a toboggan or snow saucer." He gave her an exasperated look. "All I know is he's going to stop at your house this afternoon and pick you up, and you better be ready."

"Yes, sir." She gave him a mock salute and headed back to her office. Just before she got to the door, she stopped. "Wait. You have dinner plans? With who?"

"Don't you worry about me none," he said. "You worry about your own dinner plans."

"I'll find out." It felt good to tease him. Right now, everything felt good.

She felt as if she could float away with every step. It was one thing for Luke to come hang out at her house to spend time with Wyatt, but inviting her to his family's house was different.

It wasn't like he was bringing her home to meet his family. After all, she'd known Noah almost as long as she'd known Luke. And she was pretty sure she knew Abbie a lot better than Luke did. But by bringing her around them, he was acknowledging her to them. It wasn't much, but it was a start.

CHAPTER NINE

AT THE SPORTING goods store in Springerville, Noah picked out some toboggans big enough for the adults to ride on and some snow saucers for the little girls. Luke bought a snow saucer large enough for him to ride on with Wyatt.

Luke couldn't believe how much he was looking forward to the afternoon. The large hill behind the ranch house was the perfect place for tobogganing. He'd spent many hours trudging up the hill just to slide down as a kid. He hoped someday Wyatt would like it as much as he did.

When they got back to Coronado, he dropped Noah off at the Coronado Market so he could ride home with his wife. Then he went to Emily's house.

She opened the door and greeted him with a wide smile. "Hi."

"Are you ready?"

"Almost." She looked over his shoulder. "I thought Noah was with you. Did you go all the way back out to the ranch already?"

"I dropped him off at the market. Abbie was there, so Noah's riding out to the ranch with her." That hadn't been the original plan, but he was really happy when Abbie called Noah to tell him she was going into town to help Stacy.

She opened the door to allow him to come in. "What did you have to go to Springerville for?"

"We picked up some sleds for Wyatt and Stacy's girls, and Noah wanted some new ones to keep at the ranch."

"Oh," Emily said. "Are Stacy and Caden coming, too?"

"Yes," he said. "Stacy, Caden, their girls, Noah, Abbie and us."

He didn't miss the slight look of disappointment that flickered across her face. He smiled. Maybe she'd been looking forward to spending time just with him, too. He only had a few days left, and he didn't want to share his time with them. However, he wouldn't be around much, and he wanted to make sure Emily knew that his entire family knew about Wyatt and would be there to support her, no matter what.

Despite her claiming to be almost ready, it took almost an hour to get Emily and Wyatt's stuff loaded and ready to go to the ranch. He had no idea taking a child somewhere would be so much work. First, he had to move the car seat from her car to his rented SUV. Emily suggested they take her car, but he doubted her old vehicle would make it on the rough roads to the ranch.

He gave up trying to figure out how to secure Wyatt's car seat and had to stand back while Emily did it. Then they went back into the house while she packed a diaper bag, a large sackful of toys and another sackful of food.

"Is there room to put his high chair in the back?" Emily asked. "He could eat on my lap, but it might get messy, and he won't eat much."

"Abbie said she found a lot of baby stuff in the attic." Knowing Abbie, she had an entire nursery set up by now.

Emily frowned. "I hope she didn't go to too much trouble."

"She probably did. But there's no way either of us could stop her."

"Do you know that Abbie and Noah are talking about trying for their own baby soon?"

Luke didn't know that. "That explains why they were getting baby stuff out of the attic."

Growing up, he and Noah both swore they would never bring kids into a family as messed up as theirs. But meeting Abbie changed a lot of things for Noah. "Noah will make a great dad. He practically raised me."

"I have to admit I was a little surprised," she said. "Noah was as adamant about never having kids as you were."

Luke took the bags from Emily while she wrestled Wyatt into a heavy jacket. "Can you blame us? We don't have very good memories of our childhood."

"Neither do I." She slid a beanie onto Wyatt's head. "My mom basically picked my stepdad over me and shipped me to Coronado so I was out of her hair."

He waited for her to close the door and then followed her back out to the SUV. "Do you think anyone has a happy family anymore?"

Emily shrugged. "I don't know. I think Abbie's family was pretty happy."

"Hers didn't start out like that." Noah had told him that Abbie's biological mother died when she was an infant. Shortly after that, her father gave her and her sister up at an orphanage. By the time her adoptive parents got her to the States, she was very sick and spent most of her childhood in and out of hospitals.

Wyatt protested when Emily tried to buckle him into his car seat. His little legs kicked in the air as he tried to push her away with his hands. She seemed unfazed and patiently moved his arm so she could fasten the buckle. As soon as she plopped a pacifier in his mouth, he stopped squirming.

"He hates riding in vehicles." She closed the door. "That's why Abbie volunteered to babysit yesterday."

"Or at least that's what she told you." He opened the passenger side door for her. "I think we both know now it was a ploy."

Emily got an uncomfortable look on her face, and guilt hit him. She had apologized a couple of times for Abbie calling him. Was she worried that he thought she had something to do with it?

Before he closed the door, he touched her shoulder. "I already thanked her."

She rewarded him with a smile, and he closed the door. All the way to the ranch, Emily asked him questions about Nashville. Had he ever been to the Grand Ole Opry? Had he met anyone famous? Had he played onstage with anyone famous? She was a little disappointed when he told her he had never met, nor played with, anyone she would have heard of—yet.

"You can't believe how much talent there is in that town. Two weeks ago, I filled in for a guitar player. The singer was amazing, and I guarantee you he'll be on the charts within a year."

"What about you?" Emily tucked one of her wild curls under her own beanie. "When am I going to hear one of your songs on the radio?"

"I don't know," he said honestly. "I've got a lot of demos out. I'm just waiting to get a bite."

"I'd love to hear some of your new stuff."

"Don't have any." He pulled to a stop in front of the ranch house. "I haven't written anything new since moving to Nashville."

The admission worried him more than he wanted to admit.

Emily noticed it. "Don't worry. It'll come."

"Looks like everyone beat us." Luke nodded at the other vehicles parked next to the barn.

He turned off the engine and got out. By the time he'd gathered everything Emily packed, she had gotten Wyatt out of his car seat. Together, they walked up the steps onto the porch.

He paused before opening the door. Emily looked as nervous as he did. "I'm sure Stacy and Caden know about Wyatt. Are you okay with that?"

Her eyes narrowed, and she cocked her head. "Why wouldn't I be?"

He sensed that his question upset her, although he wasn't sure why. "It's just that people are going to ask a lot of questions. You know…about us."

She pressed her lips together and nodded. "And you don't want them to get the wrong idea about our situation."

"I don't really know what our situation is, to be honest." The last thing he wanted was for well-meaning friends and family to read more into their relationship than what it was. Or try to push them into a relationship they weren't ready for yet.

Emily smiled. "Don't worry. I'll make sure that they all know that we're just friends. Nothing more."

He flinched inwardly. Why did the thought of being nothing more than friends bother him so much? That was exactly what he wanted, wasn't it?

Luke pushed open the door and held it for Emily. Then he set her bags inside the entry before leading her toward the kitchen.

He paused at the doorway between the dining room and the kitchen. The room was a flurry of activity. Stacy was standing on one side of the island, stirring something in a giant mixing bowl. Opposite her, a small girl sat on her knees on top of a bar stool. Abbie stood behind her, helping her spread frosting on cookies. Noah sat at the table in the breakfast nook bouncing a smaller girl on his knee. Caden sat across from him munching on a cookie and laughing with the little girl.

Chaos. It was the only word he could think of to describe the scene. Never, in all his time growing up, had the kitchen ever been so full of activity.

Abbie looked up and saw him standing in the doorway. She pointed him out to the little girl in front of her. "Look. Uncle Luke is here."

The girl looked at him with wide eyes. Then her gaze slid to his left and she saw Emily. Immediately, she smiled. *"Gamarjoba."*

Emily brushed past him and walked over to the island. *"Gamarjoba. Rogor khar?"*

Luke frowned, but the little girl's face brightened, and she began talking quickly in a language he didn't understand. Apparently, Emily didn't, either, because she laughed and waved for the girl to slow down.

Both the girl and Emily looked at Stacy, who responded to the little girl, also in the same language.

Luke had known Stacy for many years, and until his mother's wedding, he had no idea she spoke another language. He'd briefly spoken to her at the wedding, but he hadn't met her girls. "How old are they?" he asked Stacy.

Stacy beamed. "This is Khatia. She's almost five. And the little one over there trying to get more cookies from her father is Marina."

Abbie helped Khatia off the stool. She held her hands out toward Wyatt, who reached for her. While Abbie cooed at Wyatt, Emily removed his jacket and beanie.

Luke stood stiffly, waiting for the bombardment of questions he was sure was coming. Something touched his leg, and he looked down. Khatia held up a cookie. He took it from her. "Thank you."

"You—" she scrunched her face in concentration "—welcome."

Stacy clapped her hands together and bent over to press a kiss to her daughter's forehead. "Very good."

Khatia's face turned red, and she hurried across the room to Caden.

"No more cookies," Stacy told her husband. "They're never going to eat dinner."

Caden laughed. "Sure they will. Especially if we go run some of this sugar out of them."

That seemed to be a cue. The two little girls raced out of the kitchen, and Caden and Noah stood up.

"The girls have been waiting for you to get here," Noah explained. "The toboggans are ready, and Jasper is hooked up to the wagon."

Emily raised her eyebrows. "Why do you need a wagon?"

"Toboggan Hill doesn't look that steep from here, but it is. We thought the girls would be better off getting a ride to the top."

A few moments later, the girls returned carrying jackets, scarves and mittens. Caden took one girl, and Stacy took the other. Before long, the girls were bundled from head to toe. The younger one, Marina, looked up at Noah from underneath the hood of her jacket. She held her hand out to him. "Go."

Luke glanced at Emily, who was putting Wyatt's jacket and beanie back on. "Are you ready?"

She laughed. "Ready to race you down the hill."

"I like the way you think." Abbie nodded. "Slowest toboggan has to do the dishes tonight."

Stacy joined in the laughter as she attempted to herd the little girls outside.

Luke paused and looked around the kitchen before stepping through the back door. This house had never felt like a home. It was always cold and empty. How different would things be if there had been this much laughter and energy while he was growing up?

EMILY WAS HALFWAY across the backyard when she realized that Luke wasn't following them. She looked back at the house as he emerged from the back door.

"Everything okay?" Was he having second thoughts about bringing her?

The lines around his face were tight, and he pressed his lips together. When he looked at her, the lines faded, and he smiled. "I was just thinking about the last time Noah and I went tobogganing."

"How long ago was that?" She shifted Wyatt to the other hip.

"I was twelve, I think." Luke walked slowly. "Our grandpa had died a couple of years before that, so Noah was running the ranch by himself. One morning, after breakfast, he told me to grab my sled because we were going to the hill."

He didn't talk about his childhood very often. Emily matched his pace. "That must have been a nice surprise."

"We spent the whole day running up and down the hill. It was one of the best days of my life." The lines around his face tightened again. "Then we got home."

Something in his tone put her on alert. "What happened?"

"It was a distraction." Luke nodded toward the barn. "When we got back to the house, my mom had packed up the last of her things and left."

Emily frowned. "I thought your mom wasn't around that much."

"She wasn't, but after Grandpa died, she had come home. She said she came home to help us, but all she and Noah did was argue about everything. When he found out the real reason she came back was try to sell the ranch out from under us, he kicked her out."

Emily didn't know a lot about the situation between the brothers and their mother, but they had started the path to reconciliation last year. Noah had even given his mother away when she remarried last October, and Luke had been the best man.

Rehashing bad memories was probably not a good thing for their delicate new relationship.

A palomino horse stood patiently with a small buggy hooked to her. Stacy and Caden had already loaded the girls into the back and were waiting for them. Emily let Wyatt stand up inside the buggy.

"Do you want to ride in the buggy with Wyatt?" Luke asked. He took Wyatt's diaper bag and placed it in the back of the buggy.

Wyatt let out a loud yell, and the two girls giggled, which made Wyatt do it again.

"Is anyone else riding?"

Abbie was standing on one side of the wagon. "Paddy won't pull a buggy, and Jasper can only pull two adults, max. Since you have the youngest, you get to ride in the buggy if you want."

She frowned. "That doesn't seem fair."

"It's not." Stacy laughed. "And that means you have to watch the girls and make them behave."

Emily glanced at the two girls. They sat calmly against the edge of the wagon, watching their surroundings with wide eyes. "I'm more worried about the horse. I weigh the most out of any of you."

The buggy was loaded down with blankets, baskets of snacks and thermoses of what she suspected held hot chocolate.

She wasn't going to be the only adult in the buggy. "I think I'll walk."

Noah took the lead rope. "Sit down, girls."

They did as they were told, and the buggy started to move forward. Luke walked beside the buggy with one hand on Wyatt. Stacy walked on the other side where she could reach the girls if they needed her.

At first, Emily was nervous about letting Wyatt sit in the buggy, but it moved slowly, and Luke was tall enough to reach over the side of the buggy and keep one hand on him.

It took a while for the buggy to make it up the trail to the top of what the brothers referred to as Toboggan Hill. From the top, the side of the hill facing the ranch was smooth. No trees or rocks jutted up to block the path of the toboggans.

Caden helped the girls down and carried their saucers for them. Stacy carried a large toboggan behind them. Emily held Wyatt close, waiting to see how this was going to go.

"I'll go first," Caden told the girls. "Watch Daddy."

He set his toboggan on the ground and climbed on. He leaned forward enough for the toboggan to start sliding on the snow. The little girls cheered. Khatia didn't have any trouble climbing on her saucer. She leaned forward and let out a shriek of delight as the saucer started to pick up speed.

Marina ran to Stacy and clung to her leg, so Stacy sat and put Marina in her lap. "Are you ready?"

Emily watched them slide down the hill. She glanced at Luke.

His foot was holding a large toboggan. "I think we should ride together the first time."

She nodded and moved over to him. He kept the toboggan from sliding while she got situated and held Wyatt on her lap. Luke sat behind her, nestling her against his chest.

"Are you ready?" His words brushed her ear.

Her heart thumped loudly in her chest, and she nodded.

Together they leaned forward, sending the toboggan into motion. The sled picked up speed, taking her breath away. As tightly as she clung to Wyatt, Luke clung to her. "I got you."

The words danced down her spine as the toboggan leveled out and slowed down. She looked at Wyatt who was still giggling. Luke got up and offered to take Wyatt from her arms before offering her a hand.

"He liked it," Luke said.

Caden had walked Jasper back down the trail and was waiting for them. Khatia was standing in the buggy, ready to go back up. Her brown eyes twinkled with excitement. Marina clung to Stacy's neck with tearstained cheeks.

"Uh-oh," Emily said. "Did it scare her?"

Stacy nodded and rubbed the little girl's back.

"Again!" Khatia pointed to the top of the hill.

They loaded all the saucers and toboggans on the buggy, and Noah led the horse up the trail once again. Stacy stayed at the bottom of the hill with Marina. This time, Luke and Noah raced each other down the hill. Emily followed Khatia down the hill, with Wyatt sitting in her lap again.

After a few more runs, Khatia ran over to her younger sister, pleading with her to try again. Marina would have none of it and refused to let go of her mother. Stacy appeased both of them with a snack.

"Didn't you challenge me earlier?" Luke gave Emily a wicked grin.

"I did," she said.

Abbie took Wyatt from her. "I better hold the baby for this one."

Both of them carried their toboggans up the hill. By the time they reached the top, they were huffing and puffing. She leaned over and rested with her hands on her knees.

A snowball hit her in the face. She wiped the snow away and searched for the source. Luke grinned at her. She scooped up some snow and hid it in her palm.

She held her hand over her face. "Something's in my eye!"

Luke rushed over to her. "Let me see."

She lifted her face toward him, keeping one eye closed like she had something in it. Luke gently tried to pry open her eyelid. Seeing her opportunity, she dropped the snow down the collar of his jacket.

"Whoa!" He jumped back. "You're gonna get it now."

Emily picked up her toboggan and ran a few steps. "You have to catch me first." She dove onto the board on her stomach and sped down the hill. Behind her, she could hear Luke's toboggan, but it wasn't anywhere close to her.

As her toboggan started slowing down, she glanced over her shoulder and saw Luke. He was sitting on his knees on his board. A second later, his board bumped her, and he tackled her, rolling her off the board and into the snow.

"Help!" she screamed between giggles as he straddled her and tried to rub snow on her face.

He was about to succeed when he started getting pelted with snowballs. Stacy and Abby were coming to her rescue and throwing snow at him as fast as they could.

"I give up!" He threw his hands in the air.

Stacy offered Emily a hand up and gave her a high five. "We got your back."

"Thanks." Her cheeks hurt from laughing so hard.

"Come get some hot chocolate," Abbie called. She'd already poured the girls a cup.

Emily sat on a fallen log, sipping her hot chocolate while Wyatt explored the snow. The men climbed the hill one more time for another race.

Stacy nudged Emily over and sat next to her. "I've never seen Luke like that. You're good for him."

"Like what?" Emily pretended not to know what Stacy was talking about, but she knew. Luke was usually reserved and didn't tend to show off his playful side. Emily had seen it a few times, but not very often.

"Mama, I'm cold." Khatia snuggled up to her mother.

Stacy picked her up and carried her to the buggy. She put Marina in the buggy, too, and covered both of them with blankets.

Wyatt's nose was starting to run, so Emily picked him and made sure his jacket was still tight around him.

Loud whoops echoed, and the men all headed down the hill at breakneck speed. Luke and Noah crashed into each other, so Caden won by default. When they saw the women had packed up the children, they realized it was time to go.

Luke walked over to Emily, his eyes twinkling, and the tip of his nose bright red. "Can I have a sip of that?"

She handed him the thermos she was holding. He took a long drink and handed it back to her. "Thanks," he said, wiping hot chocolate from his mouth.

"We better get back," Noah announced. "I need to check on the meat."

Wyatt leaned against her, resting his head on her shoulder. He was so tired. They started walking back to the house, and he quickly fell asleep.

CHAPTER TEN

AT THE HOUSE, the men disappeared into the barn while the women took the kids inside.

"So—" Stacy grinned at her "—Luke is Wyatt's dad? I didn't even know you two were dating."

"We're not. We weren't." Emily could feel her neck burning. "We're just friends."

"Are you sure about that?" Abbie nodded toward Wyatt.

Stacy touched her arm; her face was serious. "He didn't take advantage of you, did he? Play on your sympathies because he was leaving?"

"Not at all." While she didn't want to admit that she had been the instigator, she couldn't let them think badly about Luke. She took a deep breath. "The night before he left, he stopped by the house to say goodbye. I invited him in for coffee…"

"And one thing led to another." Abbie finished her sentence.

"Yes." To avoid having to say anything else, Emily picked up a cookie from the platter on the counter and took a bite.

Stacy touched her arm. "Why didn't you tell anyone it was Luke?"

"I thought Luke should be the first one to know, and I didn't want him to hear it through the rumor mill."

"I can understand that." Abbie bounced Marina on her

hip. "But after a year of not hearing from him, no one would have blamed you for admitting he was the father."

"I thought about it, but after a year, I decided it didn't matter anymore." Wyatt had woken up but lay against her chest.

"You wouldn't have been able to keep it a secret for much longer," Stacy said. "I can't get over how much he looks like Luke."

"I guessed it the first time I saw a picture of Luke when he was little." Abbie picked up dishes from the island and carried them to the sink. "I knew it all along," she said with a smug smile.

"That's because you didn't know him before he left," Stacy told her sister. "He's always been more interested in his guitar than girls."

Abbie nudged Emily with her elbow. "I guess he just needed the right girl."

Emily's face flushed again. "Don't try to turn it into something it's not."

"Don't you like him?"

Very much. Her heart skipped a beat every time she saw Luke, but he would never see her the same way she saw him. The uncomfortable look on his face before they walked into the house told her that he was not interested in anything more than friendship.

Was he embarrassed to admit that they'd been together, even if it was just one night? She glanced down at her bulky sweater. The cookie she'd been eating felt like sawdust in her mouth. She dropped the cookie in the trash can.

"I need to change Wyatt's diaper." She hurried out of the kitchen before they could ask her any more questions.

She picked up the diaper bag from where Luke had set it on the table and carried Wyatt into the living room. As soon as she was done, Wyatt rolled over to crawl away, eager to explore his new surroundings.

She sat on the sofa and supervised him to make sure he didn't get into anything he wasn't supposed to. It wasn't long before Abbie and Stacy joined her.

Emily decided to keep the conversation away from Luke. "You've done a lot to this place. The last time I was here, the house was so cluttered that you could barely see the walls."

"Not me," Abbie admitted. "Noah did it before we got married."

"Wow." Emily scanned the room. "Luke said Noah refused to discuss throwing stuff away."

"He didn't throw it away," Abbie said. "He sold most of it to antique dealers. The stuff that he didn't want to sell, he loaned to the Western Pioneer Museum."

"You mean that stuff was worth something?" Emily had only been in the house a few times, but she remembered that every available space seemed to hold something. Butter churns. Quilting racks. Washboards. All kinds of things that, while interesting, didn't seem very practical to have in the house.

Abbie nodded. "He made enough to pay off his loan with the bank."

Emily let out a long whistle. She'd worked with Noah for a while at the Watering Hole, and she knew how much effort he'd put in to holding on to the ranch. "I'm glad he's out from under that worry."

"Me, too."

Wyatt used Stacy's leg to pull himself up. He babbled and pounded his hand on her thigh.

"You're a handsome boy, aren't you?" Stacy scooped him up. "I didn't know you came out here with Luke."

"Not often. Sometimes, when he was short on time

because he had a show to get ready for, I would help him muck stalls or feed the animals. Things like that."

"Noah wouldn't do it for him?" This time, Abbie looked confused.

"He was out of town a lot," Emily said. "He was trying to get his trucking business going."

Stacy nodded. "That's while Luke was working at Whispering Pines?"

"Yes," she said. She'd forgotten that Luke worked at the campgrounds before leaving for Nashville.

Abbie laughed. "What is it with those Sterling boys? They both worked at the campground and the tavern and a few other places as well... All at the same time."

"Don't forget that they did it while running the ranch, too."

Abbie's face pinched. "I never realized how spoiled I was growing up until I moved here. I wasn't even allowed to have a job, and they worked two or three jobs at a time just to survive."

Stacy nodded toward Emily. "You fit right in with this family. How many jobs do you work?"

"Just two," she said. But she wasn't part of that family. Her gaze dropped to the floor where Wyatt was playing.

"You say that like everybody does it," Abbie said, laughing.

"Why do you work two jobs?" Stacy cocked her head. "Doesn't your grandfather pay you enough at the hardware store?"

"Yes," Emily said, "I make enough to pay all my bills, and he lets me bring Wyatt to work with me so I don't have to pay for a babysitter. But I really want to buy a house of my own. All the money and tips I make are going into a savings account until I find a house."

Abbie nodded. "How close are you? Wyatt is growing so fast. I know you want to find a bigger house soon."

"Didn't you live with your grandparents when you were in high school? I'm sure your grandpa would love to have you and Wyatt move in." Stacy gave her a hopeful look.

There might come a day when her grandfather would need someone to stay with him full-time. When that time came, she would gladly do it, but it would be because he needed her. Not the other way around. She had been uprooted too many times at the whims of other people, and she never again wanted to be in a position where someone else could control where she lived or what she did.

She lifted her chin. "For now, I'd really like a place of my own."

"Did you move around a lot when you were little?" Stacy asked her.

Emily nodded. "Both my dad and my stepdad were military, so moving was a regular part of my life."

Wyatt rubbed his eyes and reached for her. Normally, she didn't put him down this late in the afternoon, but he had been fighting a cold, so he probably needed an extra nap. She picked him up. "Luke said you might have a pack-and-play?"

"I can do better than that," Abbie said. "Come see the nursery."

Emily followed Abbie down the hall to a room right across from the master bedroom. When Abbie opened the door, Emily's mouth fell open. "Is there something you need to tell me?"

The last time she'd been inside, the desk was piled high with papers and a large sofa took up most of the room. Now, the desk and sofa were gone and had been replaced by a crib. A rocking chair sat in the corner.

"Not yet." Abbie's face turned red. "We were cleaning

out the attic and found Noah and Luke's crib. Since we want to start trying for a baby soon, Noah brought all the baby stuff down to see what condition it was in, and I got a little carried away."

"It looks amazing." Emily touched the dark wood of the crib.

"The crib's in a lot better shape than we anticipated. We're planning to replace the mattress, but it should do for now."

"It'll be perfect." She sat down in the rocking chair, and Wyatt squirmed to get into position to eat.

By the time she got herself situated and Wyatt started to feed, Abbie had slipped out. Emily heard Abbie and Stacy talking in the living room.

She closed her eyes and stroked the top of her son's head. Abbie and Stacy had both been adopted by different parents and raised across the country from each other. They hadn't found each other until a few months ago, but they already acted as if they'd known each other their entire lives.

As an only child, Emily dreamed of having a sister. A built-in best friend. She was happy that Abbie and Stacy had found each other. She glanced at her son. At least he now had an aunt and uncle, and probably cousins soon.

Was he doomed to be an only child, like she was? At this point, she couldn't imagine having more children. Not that she didn't want more. It was just that there weren't a lot of marriage prospects in Coronado. There weren't many single men in town, and none of them were interested in her. At least they weren't now that she had a child.

Maybe Luke would get married someday and give Wyatt some half siblings. A sharp pang of jealousy stabbed her middle. She had been in love with Luke since she was sixteen, and seeing him with another woman would rip her apart. Still, if it meant Wyatt could have a real family, she would hide the pain and be happy for him. Or she would at least try.

Wyatt must have sensed her tension and wiggled against her. She took a deep breath and forced herself to relax. "Hush, little baby, don't say a word," she began singing to him. She rocked and sang and prayed that everything would turn out okay.

LUKE BRUSHED JASPER down while Caden fed the rest of the horses. Noah put the buggy away and went to check the meat in the smoker.

Luke scanned the barn. The last time Emily was here, they'd climbed into the hayloft to escape an angry rooster. He could still remember the smell of her shampoo as they hid under the hay. He'd desperately wanted to kiss her that day. In the end, he decided against it, not wanting to jeopardize their friendship.

The night he left, he wasn't worried about ruining their friendship. Leaving town gave him the courage to kiss her. Where was that courage now? Playing in the snow with her had felt good. Being with her felt right. But how did she feel?

"Daddy!" Khatia ran into the barn with Noah right behind her.

"Slow down, pumpkin," Caden said. He knelt next to her and explained that the horses might get scared. "Do you understand?"

She nodded, then started telling him something in her native tongue.

"Did you catch all that?" Luke asked him when the little girl ran back out of the barn.

"Not a word." Caden shook his head. "I'm not learning Georgian nearly as fast as she's learning English, but

I don't want her to think I'm not listening and stop talking to me."

Luke tsked in sympathy. "That's got to be hard, not being able to understand what's being said."

"For both of us." Caden nodded. "But what about you? What's it like to suddenly find out you're a dad?"

"Yeah. It's going to take some getting used to."

Noah entered the barn, the smoky smell of meat clinging to him. "Food's almost ready."

Luke followed Caden toward the entrance of the barn.

Noah stopped him. "Have you checked your tack for tomorrow?"

"Not yet." Luke fought back the irritation that sprang up. He knew what he needed to do to prepare for the next day. Why did his brother find it necessary to remind him?

"When were you going to do that?"

He straightened up and looked at his brother. "Later. Right now I'm going to spend some time with my son."

With every step he took toward the house, he became more and more irritated. He knew Noah didn't mean anything by it. Noah's life revolved around running the ranch and everything on it, including Luke.

Abbie was pulling rolls out of the oven when he entered the back door. "Emily's in the office."

Luke nodded and walked through the dining room and down the hall. The door to the office was partially shut, and he paused outside. He could hear Emily singing. He stuck his head inside, careful not to make any noise.

The curtains were drawn, darkening the room, but he could see Wyatt cuddling against Emily's chest. The rocking chair creaked in time with the lullaby. The sight of them drew him into the room like a magnet. The baby looked so peaceful. Luke couldn't remember the last time he had slept like that. He was still a little in awe that Wyatt was his son. How could he have made something so beautiful and perfect?

His gaze drifted to Emily. Her short curly hair stuck up all over her head. Her hair was as carefree as she'd always been. Even in high school, she'd never been obsessed with hair and makeup like a lot of the girls he knew. Sometimes it seemed that she went out of her way to prove she didn't care. Oversize sweaters and baggy pants seemed to be her clothing of choice.

Not much had changed, he noted, looking at the gray sweater that hung loosely on her shoulders. Little did she know it was her personality that made her so attractive, not her clothes.

She looked over and caught him staring at her. "What?" she whispered.

"I was just thinking—" He caught himself. She'd been pretty clear that they were just friends. Telling her he thought she was beautiful would do nothing but make her uncomfortable.

Wyatt shifted and let out a slight cry. Emily started singing again. Soon he drifted back to sleep. She stopped rocking and stood up, still singing softly as she lay Wyatt down in the crib. He made a small sound of protest, but she continued to sing as she rubbed his back.

Emily looked around. She caught Luke's eye and pointed to a blanket that had fallen on the floor next to the rocking chair. Luke picked it up and brought it over to the crib. He covered Wyatt's tiny body with it. She lifted her hand and backed slowly away from the crib.

Luke followed her into the living room, where she paused. "Did you need something?" she asked.

"I just wanted…" What did he want? Right now, he wanted to kiss her, but he didn't dare. He sighed.

"Hey, guys," Abbie called from the entryway, "dinner's ready."

"We'll be right there." He nodded toward the dining room. "Are you ready?"

Emily stared in the direction that Abbie had gone. She sighed. "I guess."

Luke rubbed the back of his neck. "I'm sorry. When I invited you out here, I wanted to prove to you that I'm ready to accept full responsibility for Wyatt. And I wanted to show Noah that you and I were going to be able to be friends and work together."

Emily's brow furrowed slightly. "You don't have to prove anything to me. Or Noah for that matter."

He took a shaky breath. "I know. But I still felt like I needed to make some type of effort. I'm not always going to be around, and I wanted to make sure you know that they are your family, too."

She touched his arm. "I appreciate the effort."

He covered the hand on his arm with his. She tried to pull away, but he held tight and laced her fingers through his. "I'm glad you came."

Her blue eyes clouded. "I'm glad you invited me."

Luke didn't move. Her eyes were the pure blue color of the Arizona sky on a warm spring day. He could get lost in them.

"We better get in there," Emily said, pulling her hand from his.

Luke wanted nothing more than to continue talking to her. He'd forgotten how easy it was.

Luke followed her to the dining room. His grandmother's china was set on the table, and candles were lit in silver holders. He glanced at Noah, who was standing at the head of the table. For as long as he could remember, meals had been served at the small table in the breakfast nook in the kitchen.

He frowned. "Did I miss something? Why are we eating in here?"

Abbie smiled. "We decided that since this is our first time eating together as a family, it was a special occasion, and we should sit in the dining room."

Noah nodded toward the table. "Abbie thought it was a waste to have a large room like this that never gets used, so she started a new tradition. All family meals are now served in here."

Luke pulled out a chair for Emily. She looked uncomfortable. After she sat down, he sat next to her. Noah said a blessing over the food, another first for Luke to witness, and then they started passing the food around.

He waited for the dishes to make it to them. "So what's your favorite food?"

"This," Emily said as Abbie slid a casserole of baked macaroni and cheese in front of her.

"Macaroni and cheese?"

"Not just any macaroni and cheese." Emily plopped a large spoonful onto her plate. "Abbie's homemade green chili macaroni and cheese. It's to die for."

Luke put a small spoonful on his plate. The only kind he'd ever had was from a box. He tasted it. "Wow. This is really good."

"Did you doubt it?" Emily took a large bite and winked at him.

Halfway through the meal, Wyatt cried from the nursery.

"I'll get him," Luke said.

He was eager to escape the dining room. Emily fit in better than he did. At least she had a lot in common with Abbie and Stacy. Caden and Noah talked about the horses that were coming through the wild horse management program. Occasionally someone noticed that he wasn't talking and asked him a question, but for the most part, he didn't contribute much to the conversation.

Wyatt was standing in the crib. His chubby hands held on to the rail, and he bounced up and down and hollered. When Luke stepped over to the crib, Wyatt reached for him. He picked him up, and Wyatt buried his face in his chest. Luke rubbed his back and soaked in the feel of his little body.

He carried him back to the dining room.

Abbie was scooping something into bowls. "We have peach cobbler for dessert. Noah's getting ice cream to put on top."

"Sounds good," he said.

Emily stood up and walked over to him with a napkin in her hand. "None for me, thanks."

She wiped Wyatt's nose with the napkin. He grunted and tossed his head from side to side to avoid his mother's attempts to clean his face.

"Sorry." Luke averted his gaze from her. "I didn't realize how runny it was."

How did he not notice that his son's face was covered with mucus? It was the first thing Emily saw.

She clapped her hands together two times very fast and held them out to Wyatt. Instead of going to her, he leaned on Luke's chest and wrapped his arms around his neck.

"Guess he wants to stay with you," she said. "I'll fix him some food. Do you want me to get the high chair?"

Luke's chest swelled, and he pressed a kiss to the top of Wyatt's head. "No. He can sit in my lap for now. If he's too distracted, you can put him in it."

Emily went to make a plate for Wyatt, and Luke sat at

his chair. Wyatt leaned back against his chest and rubbed his eyes.

Abbie placed a bowl of cobbler in front of him with a large scoop of ice cream on top. Luke offered a tiny bite of ice cream to Wyatt.

Wyatt tasted it and smacked his lips, causing everyone at the table to laugh.

"He likes it," Khatia said between bites.

Luke gave him another taste, and Wyatt tried to grab the spoon from him. "No, you better let me do that."

Wyatt's hand reached out and grabbed the bowl, knocking it off the table and onto the floor. Emily rushed over and picked up the bowl before Luke had time to react. She used the spoon to put as much of the food back into the bowl as she could.

Luke stood up to get a paper towel to wipe the floor, but Stacy was already handing him one. "I'm sorry," he said. "He's faster than I am."

"Babies always are," she said. "I'll fix you another bowl."

"I can get it," he said. "Enjoy your cobbler."

Emily tried to take the paper towel from him, but he shook his head and handed Wyatt to her. "It was my fault. I'll clean it up. You feed Wyatt. Turns out, I'm not very good at it."

She gave him a sad look but took Wyatt to her chair.

By the time he finished wiping the floor, everyone else was almost finished eating, including Wyatt, who didn't seem to have as much interest in regular food as he did ice cream.

Luke leaned close to Emily. "Are you ready to go?"

She nodded. Luke started gathering Wyatt's things while Emily helped clean off the table. Or at least, helped as much as she could while holding Wyatt. This time, it didn't take as long to pack up.

After buckling Wyatt in his car seat, Emily got into the front and leaned her head back against the seat with her eyes closed.

"You okay?" Luke asked. Did she regret coming? The only thing he really accomplished was proving that he wasn't a very good father.

"Yes." She laughed softly. "But I'm going to be sore tomorrow."

He let out a sigh of relief. "I probably will be, too, but I'm helping Noah move horses tomorrow, so I'll work it out."

"Sounds like fun." She gave him a pointed look. "How did you get roped into that?"

"I figured it was the least I could do." He navigated down the dirt road. "He almost lost the ranch because of me, so if I can do something to help while I'm here, I should."

Wyatt fussed in the back seat, and Emily reached over to calm him. "Why do you think you had anything to do with Noah almost losing the ranch?"

"I left." He swallowed, the weight of past decisions hitting him. "If I had stayed, Noah wouldn't have had to sell off the rest of the cattle and work three jobs. If I'd stayed, you wouldn't have had to raise Wyatt for almost a year by yourself. If I'd stayed—"

"Stop it," Emily snapped. "If you had stayed, both of you would still be working three jobs each, just to keep the ranch afloat. The reason he got the contract with the wild horse management fund was because he'd sold off all the cattle. And if you'd stayed, he never would've met Abbie. And we wouldn't have Wyatt."

Her words made him pause. Maybe things had worked out better because he left.

CHAPTER ELEVEN

LUKE WAS SITTING at the kitchen table drinking coffee, when Noah walked in.

"You're up." His brother's eyes widened. "And you made coffee."

"You said to be ready to leave by five this morning," Luke said.

"It's only four." Noah poured a cup of coffee.

He sighed. No doubt his brother was thinking about all the times that he didn't get out of bed until fifteen minutes before they needed to leave the house. It didn't matter that Luke was always in the truck or at the barn on time, his grandfather would grumble about how lazy and irresponsible he was.

Noah, to his credit, tried to defend him by pointing out that he was always ready on time, but that didn't matter to their grandfather.

Noah sat across from him and took a sip of his coffee. "I'm glad you don't feel it necessary to hide in your room from me."

Luke raised one eyebrow. "You knew?"

"Of course I did," Noah said. "You were an early bird from the day you were born. I don't know how many times you bounced on me while I was trying to sleep because you were up and ready to play."

"I don't remember that," Luke said.

A hint of sadness crossed Noah's face. "You were pretty

young. After we moved to the ranch, I waited for you to come get me out of bed, but you didn't. I finally figured out you were hiding in your room so you didn't have to deal with Grandpa."

"It seemed easier. No matter what I did, I could never please him, so it was better to just avoid him."

Luke got up and poured himself another cup of coffee. He had avoided their grandfather, while Noah, on the other hand, followed him around like a puppy.

"He was a hard man," Noah agreed. "There were times I hated him as much as you did."

"I didn't hate him." Luke leaned against the counter. "I just didn't understand him. The two of you were joined at the hip, and maybe I was jealous."

"I had to be. When Mom left, she told me to watch out for you. Grandpa didn't understand you were too little to do some of the jobs he gave you, so I volunteered to do them. I didn't realize it just made you feel left out."

"I thought you did it because you loved it so much." He'd never considered that Noah had another reason for being the first one to jump up when their grandpa wanted something done. "After Grandpa died, you even quit school to work the ranch."

"I didn't have much choice." Noah shrugged. "If the ranch failed, what would have happened to us? Dad was gone. Mom was gone. I had to keep a roof over our heads and food in the house."

The wistful tone of Noah's voice made Luke see his brother in an entirely new light. Running the ranch was all Noah ever talked about. He never imagined that there was anything else Noah would want to do.

"Have you told Mom yet?" Noah asked.

Luke groaned. "No. With everything that happened, I didn't even tell her I was in Arizona."

Noah's eyebrows raised. "You're going to be in trouble." He stretched out the last word in a singsong way.

"I know." Luke glanced at the clock. "What time does she get up?"

"How would I know?" Noah shrugged. "You were always a mama's boy. Don't you two talk all the time?"

Luke had always had a better relationship with their mother, at least when he was younger. By the time he was in high school he'd grown as bitter toward her as Noah was. Still, he never shut her out of his life completely the way that Noah had for a while. Last year, all that changed.

"Not anymore." Luke shook his head. "You're the golden boy now."

His tone was teasing, but in truth, he was happy that Noah had mended fences with their mother. Their grandfather had done everything in his power to make them hate her. And it almost worked. It was still going to take some time to build trust back up, but now that they knew the truth about why she'd left them with their grandfather, it was a lot easier to forgive her.

Noah sighed. "She gets up at six."

Luke started laughing. "Who's the mama's boy now?"

Noah rolled his eyes and finished his coffee. "Let's get those horses moved."

Luke suppressed a smile and stood up to rinse his cup in the sink. He grabbed his jacket from the coatrack by the back door and followed Noah to the barn.

The icy wind burned his lungs, and the snow crunched under his boots. Despite the bone-chilling air, he still loved winter. His grandfather would have said Luke was lazy and liked winter because there wasn't as much work to do.

He fished his gloves out from his jacket pockets as they walked. "Do you ever wish you could talk to the old man? Find out what made him the way he was?"

Noah shook his head. “There are a lot of things I would like to do to him. Talking is not one of them.”

Luke had always been the one to look for motives behind every action. Noah just took everything at face value. “I remember him telling stories about when he was a kid. His dad was even worse. At least that’s the way he made it sound.”

“Then I’m glad I never met him.” Noah slid the double doors to the barn open and hurried inside.

Most of the horses ignored them, but Paddy and Jasper sensed that this was not a regular day and began pacing in their stalls. As soon as Noah opened the door to the tack room, Paddy tossed his head and snorted, ready to get to work. Jasper seemed almost as eager.

“I took one of the new ropes from the supply closet,” Luke said. “Mine had some dry rot on it.”

He didn’t have to tell Noah he’d taken a rope, but it was his way of letting Noah know that he checked his gear last night when he got back from dropping off Wyatt and Emily.

A vehicle pulled up to the barn, and Luke heard the slamming of a door. A few minutes later, Caden came into the barn, hardly recognizable under his heavy coat and wool hat. He wrapped a scarf around his neck as he came into the barn.

Luke laughed. “Are you cold?”

Caden glared at him. “I hate winter.”

Noah gave Luke a pointed glance. “Caden is a desert rat.”

“The valley?” Luke asked, using the nickname for the Phoenix area.

“No.” Caden shook his head. “Tucson.”

“You’ll get used to it.”

“I’m going to have to,” Caden grumbled.

It didn't take long to have the horses groomed and saddled. Luke led Jasper outside where Noah's gooseneck trailer was already hooked up to the beat-up truck. He loaded Jasper into the trailer with Caden and Noah's horses and opened the door to the cab of the truck. Caden slid to the middle.

"Thanks for helping me out today." Noah turned the key in the ignition. "I need to get those horses moved to the upper pasture so I can reinforce the fences again."

"You have to do that a lot, don't you?" Luke had heard Noah and Caden talking at dinner the other night about how many fences the wild horses knocked over.

"Keeps me busy, that's for sure." Noah cast him a sideways glance. "I know you wanted to spend time with your son before you leave."

"No problem," Luke said. "Emily is working at the hardware store all day, so I wasn't going to be able to see them until this afternoon anyway."

Noah shifted the truck into gear, and they headed away from the ranch house, deeper into the pastures. Ice crunched under the tires, and the truck lurched occasionally as it lost traction on the snow.

The horizon was bright gold, and streaks of pale pink stretched across the sky. The sun would peek over the mountains soon, and by midday, the ice would melt, turning the road into a muddy mess.

In the distance, Luke could see horses milling around. "It's so strange to see horses out here instead of cattle."

"I agree. I'm hoping to start building a herd back by next winter." Noah nodded toward an old windmill. "If they don't destroy the place before then."

Luke squinted in the dim light. The fence that surrounded the windmill lay on the ground. Pieces of the fence posts were strewn about. "They did that?"

"Yep." Noah stopped the vehicle. "Hang on."

Luke waited in the truck while Noah walked around surveying the damage. Using his phone, Noah took pictures before getting back in the truck.

"Why is he taking pictures?"

Caden took another drink from his coffee thermos before answering. "The Wild Horse Management program reimburses him for damage done to existing structures."

Luke looked at the fences. "Why do the horses do that?"

"They don't like fences, I guess." Caden chuckled. "Most of the time, there's something on the other side of the fence they want. They have no problem destroying whatever gets in their way."

Noah jumped back into the truck, and they continued down the road. Noah talked about some of the horses on the ranch and the damage they'd caused. With each story, Luke's chest grew tighter. The repercussions of the decisions he'd made started to weigh on him again.

"Luke." Noah reached over and nudged his shoulder. "Luke."

He started. "Sorry. I was..."

"Lost in your own thoughts," Noah finished. "I've seen that look before. Got another song swimming around in your head?"

"No." He hadn't written a new song since he left Coronado.

Despite what Emily had said last night, he still wondered if he'd made a mistake in leaving. "I was wondering how different things would be if I hadn't run away to Nashville. I should've stayed to help you get back on your feet."

"I'm sure glad you didn't." Noah lifted his left hand and pointed at his wedding ring. "If you stayed, I never would have met Abbie. And I'm willing to bet you wouldn't have a son, either."

Luke frowned. "That's what Emily said, too."

"Things have a way of working out for the best," Noah said. "Stop worrying about the past and move forward."

"When did you become so philosophical?"

Noah grinned and held his ring hand up again. "Love changes a lot of things, brother."

Luke relaxed against the seat. Maybe he hadn't burned as many bridges by leaving as he thought he had.

THE HARDWARE STORE had been slow all morning, which was a good thing because Wyatt was unusually fussy. Emily had just put him down for a nap, earlier than usual, when the bells on the front door rang.

From her office, she saw a woman approach the counter and speak to her grandfather. She looked vaguely familiar, but Emily couldn't place her. Her grandfather nodded his head toward the office, and the woman smiled. As soon as she did, Emily knew who it was. Only someone related to the Sterling boys would have dimples like that. This had to be Luke's mother. She stood and met the woman at the door.

"Hello, Emily," the woman said. "I'm Colleen Thomas, Luke's mother."

"I thought that's who you were," she said. "I see now where Luke gets his dimples. It's nice to meet you, Mrs. Thomas."

"Please, call me Colleen."

Her smile was genuine, and despite the negative things Emily had heard about her, she immediately liked her. She could only assume that Colleen had found out about Wyatt, but who had told her?

"I'm sorry for showing up like this, but when Luke called me this morning and told me the news, I couldn't wait one more minute to meet my grandson." She looked over Emily's shoulder into the office. "Is he here?"

"Yes," Emily said. "But he's taking a nap right now. Would you like some coffee?"

Colleen's face fell slightly, but she nodded enthusiastically. "I'd love some. Our coffee maker broke, so Gerald took it as a sign that we needed to quit. The only time I drink coffee now is at work."

"How do you like it?" Emily walked over to the counter where the pot was.

Her grandfather kept a pot of fresh coffee in the store all day long, especially in the winter. He claimed he didn't drink that much, but it was always empty at the end of the day, even when they didn't have any customers.

"Sugar, no cream."

Luke told Colleen about Wyatt, so he must be okay with her coming to see the boy, right? Maybe Emily should text him to double-check? No. He was moving horses and wouldn't have service.

Emily poured the coffee and handed it to her. "Where do you live, Colleen?"

"Snowflake."

The town of Snowflake was almost two and a half hours away from Coronado. "Luke must have called you pretty early."

"Not too early." She shook her head. "But then again, I get up before most people. Always have. Luke gets that from me."

Luke was an early riser? Emily tucked that information away for later. She was a night owl herself. "The chairs in my office are more comfortable than these stools. Wyatt just went down, so it might be a while before he's up."

Colleen followed her into her office where Emily and her grandfather sat down on the sofa. "How are you, Denny?"

"Not too bad, not too bad." Grandpa poured himself a cup of coffee. "How's Gerald?"

"He's fine. Although his lack of caffeine in the morning is causing some issues."

Emily sat in the chair at her desk. "Does he get grumpy without his coffee?"

"No," Colleen said, "but I do."

Granddad laughed. "Have you tried one of those newfangled single-serve machines?"

"I just ordered one," she said. She looked at Emily. "I ordered some stuff for Wyatt, too. I hope you don't mind."

"Depends on what it is," Emily joked. *And why you did it.*

Every time her mother came to visit, she brought lots of stuff for Wyatt and liked to make a big deal of what she got and how much it was. She'd done the same thing to Emily after sending her to Coronado to live with her grandparents. As if buying expensive gifts could make up for picking her new husband over her daughter.

"I wasn't sure what size he was or what he needed," Colleen said. "I also stopped in Show Low and Springerville on my way here. My car is full of stuff for him."

Emily stiffened. "That wasn't necessary."

"I know, but I wanted to. He's my first grandchild, and I can't wait to spoil him rotten!" Excitement radiated from her.

Emily pressed her lips together and took a deep breath. She searched for words to say that wouldn't upset her.

Colleen's head tilted, and she stared at Emily for a moment. She clutched her folded hands to her chest. "What is it? You're upset. I upset you."

Irritation gave way to guilt, and Emily shook her head. "It's okay. I'm just not big on the whole gift-giving-for-no-reason thing."

"No reason?" Colleen raised one eyebrow. "He's my grandson. Isn't that reason enough?"

"Of course." She swallowed the sour taste in the back of her throat. "Thank you."

She didn't want to ruin Wyatt's chance at having a relationship with his grandmother. Maybe Colleen was just excited, and this was a onetime thing. If not, she'd ask Luke to talk to her about it.

A sound came from the nursery, and Colleen jumped up.

"He probably needs changing. I'll be right back." Emily went to get Wyatt from his crib.

A fresh diaper later, she carried him into the office. As soon as Colleen saw him, her eyes glistened with tears. She stood up and approached slowly, as if she was afraid she was going to scare him.

"Hello, Wyatt," she said softly.

Wyatt leaned his head on Emily's chest, but he wrinkled his nose and smiled at Colleen.

"He looks just like Luke." Her voice was full of emotion. "He's so beautiful."

"Would you like to hold him?" Emily asked.

Colleen held her hands out to Wyatt. "Hello, sweet boy. Can Grammie hold you?"

Wyatt didn't reach for her, but when Emily handed him to Colleen, he didn't cry. Instead, he stared at her with fascination. Colleen kept talking to him and moved to sit on the sofa. She bounced him on her knee, causing him to giggle.

"He loves to play giddyup horsey," Granddad said.

Emily noticed the way he hovered protectively over Wyatt, and it warmed her heart. He had never had to share Wyatt before.

The bells on the door rang, and he left the office to wait

on a customer, but not before pausing at the doorway to watch Colleen and Wyatt for a moment.

After a couple of games of horsey, Wyatt had warmed up to Colleen and was giggling and playing with her. Thank goodness he seemed to be feeling better. His grumpiness this morning and his stuffy nose all night had Emily worried that he was getting sick.

Wyatt pressed a sloppy kiss to Colleen's chin, and she burst into tears.

"What's wrong?" Emily jumped up from her chair and rushed to her. "Did he bite you? He does that sometimes when he's trying to give kisses."

"No." Colleen wiped a tear away. "I'm just so happy. I never thought I'd get to be a grandmother."

"You didn't think Luke or Noah would ever have a family?"

Colleen sniffed. "I always knew they would have a family someday. Or at least I prayed they would. I just wasn't so sure they'd allow me to be part of it."

The pain in her voice banished all Emily's fears. This was a woman who bought gifts *because* she loved, not *to be* loved. That was the difference.

She squeezed Colleen's hand. "I think that Wyatt is very lucky to have you for a grandmother."

This made the tears flow again, and Colleen wrapped Emily in a hug, sandwiching Wyatt between them. "Thank you," she whispered. "Luke is so lucky to have you."

Emily bit her lip. Luke must not have told her the whole story. Her brow furrowed. "Luke and I aren't together. We…we're not a couple."

Colleen blinked. "What do you mean?"

"We're just friends. We've been friends for a long time." She rubbed one hand to her chest. "It was just a onetime thing. He was leaving for Nashville, and we… Well, it was…"

"I understand." Colleen squeezed her hand and smiled. "That doesn't mean I'm not going to pray it turns into more."

Emily's face flushed. Who was she to tell Colleen it would never work? She'd been praying the same thing for the last ten years. "Would you like to take Wyatt into the nursery? He has some toys in there."

Colleen bounced Wyatt on her lap. "Do you want to go play?" She stood up and followed Emily into the nursery. "What a lovely playroom!"

Emily looked around the room, trying to see it with new eyes. It was large enough that Wyatt's crib fit against one wall, and there was plenty of space for toys and playing. A small playhouse sat in one corner, and a slide stood in the middle of the room. The shelves were stacked with toys, mostly wooden ones and stuffed animals, and the floor was covered with a foam puzzle. "Grandpa remodeled his workroom for Wyatt before I started working here."

"Your grandfather is a very talented man." Colleen set Wyatt on the floor and walked over to look closer at the toys. "Did he make the wooden ones himself?"

"Yes." It made Emily sad to think that they were probably the last things he'd ever make. "It took him a long time to finish them because his arthritis was so bad that he could only work in short spurts."

Colleen nodded her head in understanding. "Yes. Gerald has that issue, too. He used to love team roping, but his hands don't cooperate anymore."

"How long are you going to be in town?" Emily asked.

"If Noah and Luke don't have any objections, I'd like to stay overnight and spend some time with my entire family." Doubt laced Colleen's voice.

"I'm sure they won't mind. Do you have any idea what time they'll be done moving horses?"

"I'm going to call Abbie right now and see if she's heard from them." Colleen pulled her phone from her purse and stepped outside the playroom.

Luke had asked Emily if he could come over after he finished, but he didn't have any idea what time it might be. If his mother was staying over, would he still want to come into town to see Emily? Should she offer to go to the ranch instead? She didn't trust her old car to make it that far and back.

Colleen entered the playroom with a big smile on her face. "Abbie had the best idea! Why don't you ride out to the ranch with me? We can spend the day together, and after dinner tonight, Luke can take you home. He told me this morning he would like for us all to have dinner together when I came down. Of course, he had no idea it would be today!"

Emily's heart fluttered just like it did every time she heard that Luke made plans to see them. She really needed to get a grip on that reaction. "That would be nice, but I don't get off work until three. I'm sure you don't want to wait around here that long."

"Go ahead." Granddad stood at the entrance to the nursery. "Things are pretty slow, so I might close up early anyway."

"It's settled then." Colleen clapped her hands. "Before we head out there, maybe we can stop at your house. I need to unload a few things to make room for the two of you in my car."

CHAPTER TWELVE

"HEADS UP!"

Luke looked up just in time to see a black mustang racing toward him. He pulled his cowboy hat off and waved it in the air, yelling at the top of his lungs.

The mustang veered and tried to go around him. Jasper was a born cutting horse and moved on instinct to stop the mustang's escape.

The two horses faced off against each other, and Luke tensed, waiting to see what the mustang's next move would be. The horse's eyes rolled back, and he flattened his ears, baring his teeth to take a bite out of Jasper.

Luke urged her out of the way in the nick of time, and the mustang turned and headed for the other end of the pasture. It took several minutes for his heart rate to slow down. He patted Jasper's neck, as much to comfort himself as to comfort her.

He glanced across the herd to see Coy weaving back and forth behind the horses. Coy glanced in his direction, and Luke tipped his hat. Coy returned the gesture and went back to working the herd.

Except for that one defiant mustang, the horses had been fairly cooperative. How long would they remain that way? The pasture they moved the horses from was a mess. Luke had never seen a poly stock tank destroyed, but the one in the bottom pasture had been. If these horses could destroy a water tank like that, what else were they capable of?

Luckily, Noah had already reinforced the fences in the pasture where the horses were being moved to, and the water tanks were galvanized steel.

It was almost dark when the last horse was ushered into the pasture, which meant Luke and the rest of the men would be riding their horses back to the trucks in the dark. As soon as the sun went down, the temperature dropped quick, so they rode as fast as they could.

Several times, Luke glanced at Coy, but he didn't say anything. For one thing, it was too cold to talk. For another, he hadn't spoken to his former best friend in a year and a half. As much as he wanted to clear the air, he didn't want to do it in front of his brother and Caden.

He counted back in his head. This was February, so two years and one month ago, he'd told Coy he was moving to Nashville and that he needed to find someone else to work as the groundskeeper and maintenance man at Whispering Pines Campground. Coy's cousin, Stacy, managed the campground, but technically it was Coy's responsibility. Months passed, and Coy was too busy riding bulls on the rodeo circuit to look for a replacement. Every time they talked, Luke reminded Coy that he was leaving.

When May rolled around, an agent called to set up a meeting, and Luke couldn't wait any longer. He gave Stacy his two weeks' notice, and as soon as the two weeks were up, he left. Stacy called Coy to come home and help. In turn, Coy called Luke, furious that he had actually split. That was the last time they'd spoken.

Once they reached the trucks, Noah loaded Jasper into the trailer with Noah and Caden's horses and walked around to where Coy stood next to his truck. He nodded at Luke. "Want to ride with me?"

"Sure." He looked at Noah. "See you at the house."

He walked around to the passenger side of Coy's truck

and got in. The first minute was filled with awkward silence. They had known each other since kindergarten, and there had never been a strained moment between them until now.

"I'm sorry." They both spoke at the same time.

Coy laughed. "Me first."

Luke shook his head. "No, man. I should have waited for you to hire someone before I bailed. I put you in a tough spot, and I'm really sorry."

Coy reached across the cab to clap him on the shoulder. "I'm the one who's sorry. You told me you were leaving, but I didn't believe you. That's why I never hired anyone. The truth is, I'm proud of you. You finally got the guts to chase that dream."

A weight lifted from Luke's shoulders. So many times, he'd wanted to call Coy and tell him about Nashville, but he felt like he couldn't.

"What about you? You're one of the top bull riders in the country." Luke may not have been talking to Coy, but he'd kept up with his career. "That bull you rode in the national finals was a tough one. I thought for sure you had him."

Coy cocked his head. "You were there?"

Luke nodded. "I was playing in a club right off the strip."

"Why didn't you tell me?"

He laughed. "Coy Tedford, you are one of the most hardheaded and stubborn people I've ever met. If you wouldn't answer my phone calls, I'm pretty sure you wouldn't want to see me in person."

Coy frowned. "You're probably right."

"So what happened with Becky?"

"She wanted me to quit riding and move to Texas," Coy said. "I said no, so she said bye."

Luke suspected there was more to the story, but he

didn't ask. Coy changed the subject by asking about Nashville. The remainder of the ride to the ranch house was spent catching up.

Coy parked next to Noah's truck at the barn. Caden's truck was already gone. He must've been in a hurry to get home to his wife and girls. Luke knew the feeling. As much as he enjoyed talking to his old friend, he was anxious to go see Emily and his son.

"You staying? I'm pretty sure Abbie's made enough food for an army."

"Nah," Coy said. "I promised Dad I'd meet him at the Bear's Den for dinner. I sure hope I get to see that kid of yours before I leave."

"Me, too." Noah opened the truck door. "Maybe we can meet up tomorrow before you leave."

He got out of the truck and went inside the barn to help put the tack away and feed the horses.

Noah looked him over. "I don't see a black eye or a bloody nose. Does that mean you two worked things out?"

"Yeah." Luke took the saddle off Jasper and carried it to the tack room. "I can't believe he and Becky really broke up."

"I know. It's weird not seeing them together." Noah started brushing Paddy's coat. "Did you know Mom was here?"

"No." Luke's heart jumped. He hoped she didn't come down to meet Wyatt before he had a chance to talk to Emily about it. "I told her that maybe she could come down later this week and meet Wyatt."

Noah laughed. "Well, she didn't listen."

Luke finished his chores as quickly as he could and hurried to the house.

No one was in the kitchen, but he heard laughter coming from the living room. He walked across the foyer and saw his mother sitting on the sofa with Abbie and Emily on either side of her. A large photo album was open in her lap, and the women were going through the pictures.

Emily looked up and saw him. “Hi. How did it go?”

Abbie jumped up. “I lost track of time! I better get dinner on the table.”

“It went well. No trouble.” Luke looked around. “Where’s Wyatt?”

“Asleep in the nursery,” Emily said. “He’s been really fussy today.”

His mom closed the photo album and came over to him. “Your son is beautiful.” She threw her arms around him and hugged him so tight he could barely breathe. “Thank you for telling me about him.”

He wrapped his arms around her and hugged her back. A steel band of guilt tightened across his chest. He should have called her earlier and told her about Wyatt. Why hadn’t he? Shouldn’t calling his mother with big news be one of the first things he did?

Noah was right. He was a mama’s boy. When they first moved to the ranch, Luke had been too young to work, so he spent all his time with her. He went everywhere she went. One of his fondest memories was singing to her at the beauty salon after she got her hair cut. All the women in the shop made a big deal over him and gave him candy. That was probably when he’d been bit by the performing bug.

Without their father around to make her cry, his mom finally seemed happy. And that made him happy. But less than a year after they moved to the ranch, something changed. She started leaving for longer and longer stretches. By the time he was in high school, she was gone more than she was at home, and Luke didn’t care anymore. At least, that was what he told himself.

He had no idea at the time that her own father was pulling strings and manipulating her as well as them.

His mother finally let go of him and stepped back. "Abbie has a roast keeping warm in the oven, and I made a lemon meringue pie."

He smiled. "Your pies are the best."

She left to go to the kitchen, leaving him and Emily alone. Emily set the photo album on the coffee table.

"I'm sorry if you got bombarded today," Luke said as he sat down beside her. "I started feeling guilty because I hadn't told her about Wyatt. So I called her this morning."

Emily ran one hand through her blond curls. "It's okay. We had a nice time together."

Luke shook his head. "I told her I would set up a time for us to meet later. Maybe have dinner or something. I should've known she wouldn't be able to wait."

She touched his leg. "Stop apologizing. She's been great. And unlike my mom, she really seems to care about Wyatt and wants to get to know him."

There was a hint of bitterness in her voice, and he realized that she never spoke about her mom. He looked down at where her hand was still on his leg, and he squeezed her hand. "That's her loss. You've done a great job. Wyatt is a wonderful little boy."

As if on cue, the baby started to cry. Emily started to get up, but Luke waved at her to sit down. "I'll go get him."

By the time he pushed the door open to the room where Wyatt had been sleeping, his cries had escalated. "Hey," Luke said as he flipped on the light and walked over to the crib. "Have a good nap?"

He picked Wyatt up from the crib and pressed a kiss to his head. Then he frowned and cupped the back of his son's head with the palm of his hand. Was he supposed to feel that warm? Wyatt cried and snuggled deeper into

Luke's chest. Luke rubbed his back and hurried back to the living room.

Emily caught his eye as soon as he appeared in the doorway. She was at his side in a few steps. "What's wrong?"

"He feels really warm to me," Luke told her.

As soon as Wyatt saw Emily, he reached for her. Emily cuddled him into her arms and pressed her lips to his forehead. The corner of her eyes crinkled. "He's got a fever."

"I'll warm up the truck. You get his things together." Luke's chest tightened.

He pulled the keys out of his pocket and nodded at Noah in the dining room. "We've got to go—Wyatt's running a fever. Sorry about dinner. Tell Mom I'll see her later."

When he came back to the house after starting the SUV, Emily already had Wyatt's things piled by the door. Luke picked up her bags and held the door open for her, every inch of his skin tingling. Was his son going to be okay? Had he done something wrong while babysitting him earlier to make him sick? Abbie never should have asked him to watch the baby.

He opened the back passenger-side door for Emily, waited for her to buckle Wyatt into his car seat and then opened the door for her to get in. His stomach was tied up in knots, and he had to remind himself not to speed down the dirt road leading away from the ranch.

"Where are you going?" Emily asked when they got to the main road and he turned right instead of left.

"Springerville," he said.

"Why?" Emily's voice held a touch of panic.

He looked at her. "That's the closest emergency room."

She rolled her eyes. "Turn around and take us home. He doesn't need to go to the ER."

He pulled over to the side of the road. "Does Coronado have an urgent care now?"

Her face softened. “Relax, Luke. Babies get sick. Right now he’s running a slight fever—it’s nothing to be alarmed about. When we get home, I’ll give him some medicine, and he’ll be fine.”

“Are you sure?” His heart was still pounding.

She reached over and touched his arm again. “Trust me. He’ll be fine.”

CHAPTER THIRTEEN

EMILY YAWNED AND waited for the coffee to be ready. It had been a long night. After getting home, Luke refused to leave until he saw that the medicine worked and Wyatt's fever went down. What would he have done if he'd still been there when Wyatt started throwing up?

After having to change Wyatt's clothes and the sheets in his crib, she'd been afraid to lay him back down. What if he threw up, and she didn't hear him? What if he choked on his vomit? She'd spent most of the night holding him in the rocking chair, which meant very little sleep for her. Around 6:00 a.m., Wyatt's fever broke, and he finally fell into a deep restful sleep. She put him in his crib, but she didn't dare go to sleep herself. He hadn't thrown up in several hours, but she kept a close eye on him through the camera on the baby monitor.

After calling her grandfather and letting him know she wouldn't be coming into the store, she texted Freddy and told him Wyatt was sick, so she wouldn't be at work tonight.

She set her coffee on the table and opened her laptop. She took a sip and went straight to the listings on her favorite real estate website. She'd hoped to own her own home before Wyatt's first birthday, but time was running out. She had a Realtor who was on the lookout for a home, but Emily knew the only way to get a good deal on a house was to be fast. And she doubted if her Realtor was browsing through the MLS listings this early in the morning.

Her phone dinged, and she suppressed a smile. Luke had either called or texted half a dozen times and it wasn't even seven o'clock. If she took more than a few minutes to answer his texts, her phone started ringing. It was one of the reasons she didn't dare try to catch some sleep after putting Wyatt down in his crib.

Still no fever and he's sleeping.

Luke's concern for Wyatt last night had been touching. She remembered how she felt the first time Wyatt ran a fever. Scared. Worried. Helpless. She'd seen all those emotions on Luke's face the night before. It had surprised her. The Sterling brothers weren't exactly known for their sensitivity. She'd worked with Noah at the Watering Hole after Luke moved away, and he was the epitome of the strong silent type. But maybe it shouldn't surprise her about Luke. She'd heard some of the songs he had written. There was a poignant sadness to many of them, suggesting that the old saying "still waters run deep" was true.

A light rapping let her know someone was at the door. Someone who didn't want to be too loud and possibly wake up her son. Was Luke there already? She'd just texted him.

She opened the door to find her grandfather standing at the door. "Hi, Granddad. What are you doing here?"

He held up a brown paper bag. "I thought you might want some breakfast."

She stepped to the side to let him in. He set the bag on the table, next to her laptop.

He glanced at her computer screen. "Why are you looking at houses?"

"I've been looking for a while now," she said. Had he forgotten already?

"I know that," he said. "I mean, why are you looking and not Meghan? I thought she was your real estate agent."

"She is. I just like to look for myself." Meghan Simpson had promised to have her at the top of her list, but she was a popular agent. What if she was so busy with other clients that something good slipped by her? Emily wasn't about to sit back and let that happen.

"How's Wyatt?"

"He was up all night." Emily opened the bag. Donuts. Still warm. The Candy Shoppe had struck a gold mine when they decided to add donuts to their menu.

She spotted a few small boxes inside the bag, too. "Granddad, you didn't have to get more medicine. I have plenty."

"Better to have too much than too little." He walked into her kitchen and poured himself a cup of coffee. "How are things going with Luke? He's willing to take responsibility?"

As if on cue, her phone dinged. She picked up the screen and showed it to her grandfather.

On my way. I stopped to get medicine for Wyatt. Have you had breakfast?

A smug smile crossed her grandfather's face. "Glad to hear that he's stepping up. What kind of child support is he going to give you?"

"We haven't talked about it yet." If she had her way, they wouldn't talk about it at all.

There was something about asking him to give her money each month that bothered her. She shouldn't feel that way. Luke was Wyatt's father, and he should shoulder some of the financial responsibility. But she'd spent the last seven years ensuring that she was financially independent from everyone. Her parents. Her grandfather. No one would have control over her life. Taking money from Luke gave him some power. It didn't matter that he had a right to be concerned about Wyatt's upbringing.

She texted Luke back and told him she had already had breakfast.

"I'll go then." Her grandfather started toward the door. "I'll call later to see how Wyatt's doing."

Her grandfather had barely pulled out of the driveway when Luke pulled in, so Emily waited at the door. He got out of the SUV, a grocery bag looped over his arm and a white Styrofoam box in his hand.

As he strolled up the path to the front door, she thought he was the perfect picture of a cowboy. His slow, purposeful gait was lightly bowlegged, bordering on a strut. She almost expected to hear the jangling of spurs as he made his way to her door.

She glanced down. Her robe hung open, revealing the flannel pajamas she wore. She pulled the robe closed and tightened the belt. One hand went up to her head to tame her curls, even though she knew it would do no good.

He gave her a crooked grin, deepening the dimples in his cheeks. "Wyatt still asleep?"

"Yes. Finally." She held the door open for him. "You didn't have to bring breakfast."

"I doubted if you'd have time to make anything." He walked over to the table and paused.

He set the box down and peeked in the bag. His eyes narrowed. "I'm not the only one who thought you might need breakfast."

"Or medicine." Emily picked up the bag and removed

the small boxes. “Between you and my grandfather, I’m set for a couple of years.”

The lines on his face softened. “Your grandfather brought you donuts?”

“Who else?” Did she detect a hint of jealousy in his voice? The thought made her feel warm all over. “What did you bring for breakfast?”

“Biscuits and gravy.” He pulled a donut out of the bag. “Where did he find jelly-filled donuts in Coronado?”

“The Candy Shoppe added donuts to their menu.” She closed her laptop and moved it to the kitchen counter. “You want them? I’d much rather have biscuits and gravy.”

“Only if you’re sure you’re not going to want one later.”

She grabbed a couple of plates from the cabinet and put them on the table. “Help yourself.”

His donut was gone by the time she scooped a gravy-laden biscuit onto her plate. She slid the bag of donuts closer to him.

Luke sat down and selected a second donut. “How can you pick biscuits over donuts?”

“This—” she held up a forkful of biscuit “—is my comfort food. When I used to go visit my granny in the summer, she made this for me every morning.”

“Your mom didn’t make your biscuits and gravy?”

“Maybe when I was little. When I got older, she wouldn’t allow it in the house. It was too fattening.”

“Fattening? Was she one of those women who was always on a diet?”

“No.” Emily swallowed. “I was. Or rather, she was always putting me on a diet.”

His brown eyes widened. “Why?”

She laughed. “Look at me.”

“I am.”

His brown eyes were full of warmth as he gazed at her,

sending ripples of pleasure down her spine. Heat flooded her cheeks. "I'll never be mistaken for Barbie, that's for sure."

"Why would you want to?" He pressed his lips together. "How old were you then?"

"Mmm." She took another bite of food. "I think the first time she mentioned my weight was when I was ten."

"Something like that would've given most girls a complex." He frowned. "It's a wonder you're not anorexic or something."

She bit her lip. *Or something* was more like it. She rebelled against her mother's efforts by hoarding food and binge eating. Not exactly the healthiest choice, either. It wasn't until she came to Coronado that she stopped using food as a source of control and learned to actually enjoy it. Along with making healthier eating choices.

"We'll probably get invaded by my mother before she goes back to Snowflake." Luke bit into his second donut. "I thought we could escape by going shopping in Springerville, but with Wyatt being sick, that's probably not such a great idea."

"What do you need there?" She scraped the last of the gravy off her plate with her fork.

He cocked his head. "Not for me. For Wyatt."

"Why?" Her back stiffened. "He doesn't need anything."

His face fell, and she realized her words came out harsher than she intended. She took a breath. *He's just trying to help*, she reminded herself.

She tried to lighten the mood and pointed to the stack of boxes on the other side of the living room. "Whatever I don't have is probably in that stack of things from your mother."

His gaze followed. "Wow. She went a little overboard."

"Just a little." Emily frowned. "I hope it's not going to become a habit. By either of you."

He flinched. "You've had to provide for him by yourself for almost a year. Surely you can indulge me and my family by letting us buy him some new clothes and toys."

She nodded. "I'm sorry. It was a knee-jerk reaction. I'm just not really into getting gifts."

He frowned. "I don't think I've ever heard anyone say that."

He didn't ask for an explanation, but Emily could see the curiosity on his face. She sighed. "Gifts were my mom's way of trying to buy love and forgiveness. Whenever she came home with a gift, I knew something was wrong. And now that I'm a single mom, I worry that if people offer to buy him stuff it's because they feel sorry for me."

"I don't feel sorry for you. I feel sorry for me." He arched one eyebrow. "And I promise, I don't have an ulterior motive for buying him things. I do it because I want to, not because I want something."

She swallowed. "Thank you. I'll try not to be so sensitive about it."

"Good." He took another bite of donut. "How was Wyatt's night?"

"His fever broke early this morning, and this is the longest he's slept all night, so I think the worst of it is over."

A gruff cry came from the bedroom, and Luke jumped up. "Can I get him?"

She nodded.

When he didn't return immediately, she glanced at the baby monitor, but Wyatt was no longer in his crib. She crept to the bedroom door.

Luke had laid Wyatt on the bed and was changing his diaper. He was speaking in a soft voice to their son, who kept trying to roll over and escape.

To his credit, Luke didn't lose patience with him and turned it into a game. It took a few minutes, but the diaper was finally changed. "There." Luke gave Emily a triumphant look. "We did it."

His smile went straight to her heart.

LUKE PICKED WYATT up off the bed and carried him to Emily. "I probably didn't do that right."

"You did great," she said. She pressed her lips to Wyatt's forehead. "Still no fever. That's good."

"How can you tell?" Wyatt had felt a little warm to him, but nothing like last night.

"I don't know how to explain it. Practice, I guess?" Her brow puckered. "I need to feed him."

"Okay." He wasn't sure why she hesitated. Then he noticed Wyatt rooting at her chest. "Oh. You mean *you* need to feed him."

She nodded.

Was she embarrassed to breastfeed Wyatt in front of him? Or was she worried that he was the one who would be embarrassed? "I'll wait in the living room."

He sat on the sofa and picked up a real estate magazine off the end table. As he flipped through it, he saw that some of the houses had been circled with a red pen. Some of the circles had *X*'s through them. Was Emily looking for a house?

By the time Emily came into the living room, he'd flipped through the magazine twice. He put it down when she sat on the end of the sofa.

She set Wyatt on the floor, where he made a beeline to a small basket of toys.

Wyatt scooted across the floor on his tummy and pulled himself up into a standing position when he reached the basket. "How long before he starts walking?" Luke asked.

"Not long." Emily's eyes never left Wyatt. "He's close now. You should see him at the hardware store. I put him in his walker, and he zips all over the place."

Luke scanned the small room. "Don't you have a walker for him here?"

"No," she said. "There isn't enough room for him to use it."

That was true. He couldn't imagine how much more could fit in the trailer.

Emily shrugged. "Besides, we spend most of our day at the store anyway."

"I'm glad things are better now between you and your grandfather." When he left Coronado, they hardly spoke.

"For the most part." Emily clapped her hands together and held them toward Wyatt, coaxing him to her. "Is your mom still in town?"

Luke got the distinct impression that she was trying to change the subject. "Yes, but she's heading back this morning. She was planning to stay all day, but since Wyatt is sick, she said she'll wait until he's feeling better."

"Your mom is really nice." She bounced Wyatt on her knee. "She really wants to be part of Wyatt's life. Yours, too."

He frowned. "Now that Noah and I know the truth, we both feel really bad about shutting her out for so long."

Wyatt wiggled down to play with toys in the middle of the floor.

"There's usually more to things than we know. What happened?"

"Grandpa made us believe that she dumped us off at the ranch because she didn't want to be bothered with us. I also suspected she just wanted to get away from him. Goodness knows Noah and I wanted to get away from him often enough when we were kids.

"Turns out, my dad had borrowed a bunch of money from him. Then my dad split with the money, and Grandpa wanted my mom to pay it back. He was holding it over her head. She had no choice except to go back to work as an airline stewardess to make enough money to pay him back. By the time she was able to pay him back, Grandpa had basically poisoned us against her."

Luke slipped off the sofa to sit on the floor. Would Wyatt be as bitter toward him as he and Noah were toward their mom because she wasn't around all the time? The thought made his chest ache.

Emily slid to the floor next to him. She touched his forearm and looked straight into his eyes. "Just so you know, I will never do that to you. Wyatt will never be told you're not here because you don't love him or want him around."

How had she known what he was thinking? Relief surged through him. "Thank you." His gaze dropped to her lips, and he suddenly wanted very badly to kiss her.

Emily squeezed his arm. "You're welcome."

She stood up and went to the kitchen to get coffee, and the moment was lost.

Luke held one hand out to Wyatt. Wyatt grasped his hand and took a step before falling on his bottom. He crawled into Luke's lap. The little boy's eyes looked droopy and dull, and his nose was runny. "He still doesn't feel good, does he?"

"No." Emily walked back to them and felt the back of Wyatt's neck with her hand. She reached over to the side table and got a tissue to wipe his nose. "But I don't think his fever is back, so that's a good sign."

Luke's heart turned over at the sight of the tired little boy cuddled on his lap. The last time he was here, Wyatt was crawling all over, playing with toys and making lots of sounds. Today, he was a totally different child. "Are you sure you don't need to take him to the doctor?"

She nodded. "If it's a viral infection, there's not much that can be done other than let it run its course."

"How do you know if it's a viral infection?" He leaned against the sofa so that Wyatt was in a more reclined position in his lap.

"For one, his fever never got really high. For two, his snot is clear, not green."

His throat tightened. There was so much he didn't know. The weight of his inadequacy pressed down on him.

Emily's face pinched, and she moved from the floor to sit beside him. Her leg brushed his, and he could feel the heat from her body.

"I've learned through trial and error," she said. "The first time Wyatt got sick, I panicked completely. I would have called for an ambulance if Millie hadn't stopped me."

"Millie Gibson?" Luke didn't know Millie very well. She was a few years behind him in school, but her brother had been a classmate of his.

"Yes. She just finished nursing school. She still works at the market on her breaks, and she was there when I went to look for medicine for him. I felt like such a failure. I didn't know what to do for my own baby, and here comes Millie, three or four years younger than me, with no kids of her own, and calms me down and tells me what to do."

That made him feel marginally better. Wyatt shifted and wrapped his arms around Luke's neck, leaning against his chest. Luke's heart raced, and he cuddled the little boy tighter. Wyatt let out a sigh, and his tiny body relaxed.

Emily's blue eyes clouded with emotion. "I think he knows."

"Knows what?"

"That you're his dad." She reached over to rub Wyatt's

back. "He doesn't usually go to people so quickly. Noah is always trying to get him to come to him, but Wyatt never does."

"That's probably the first time I've had something over on my brother."

Emily laughed at his teasing tone. He liked the sound of her laughter. She was so much more easygoing than a lot of people he knew.

"Speaking of Millie—" she picked up her phone from the end table "—I better let her know I don't need her to babysit tonight."

Luke flinched. Why didn't Emily ask him to babysit? Did she not trust him? Or did she doubt his commitment to their son?

Wyatt reached up and touched Luke's face, exploring his nose and his mouth. When his hand got to Luke's mouth, Luke pretended to eat his fingers, and Wyatt giggled. The giggles went straight through his heart.

He waited for her to finish her text and put her phone down before clearing his throat. "Why didn't you ask me to babysit?"

"Um..." Emily pinched her lips together and shifted uncomfortably.

Luke's heart stuttered. He didn't say anything but waited for her.

She shrugged. "To be honest, things have happened so fast, I never thought about it."

He nodded. "I understand."

She sighed. "Since we're on the subject, would you mind watching him for a little while right now?"

He let out a sigh of relief. "Of course not. Do you need something? Or do you want me to run to the store for you?" Not that he would rather run errands than be with his son, but he wanted to do whatever he could to help her.

"Last night, Wyatt threw up all over my bed and his. Twice. If I wait too long to wash the quilts, it might stain. I don't want to risk taking him out in the cold and him getting sick again."

"I'm here all day," he said. "Or at least until you kick me out."

"Thanks."

A few minutes later, Emily had loaded all the dirty bedding into her car and left, headed for the town's only laundromat. As a bachelor, Luke only had to go to a laundromat once a week. He couldn't imagine how often Emily needed to do laundry with a baby in the house.

He bounced Wyatt in his arms as he walked the length of the home. It only took about twenty steps. There was no place to put a washer and dryer. If there had been, he would've been tempted to buy her a set.

Luke sat down on the couch, and Wyatt wriggled out of his lap and to the floor where he crawled over to the basket of toys. Luke moved to lie on the ground next to him, content just to watch him play and explore around him.

As he watched his son, a melody started to run through his head. The more he tried to ignore it, the more insistent it became. He gave up and began to hum the tune.

Wyatt turned his head to watch him with big brown eyes. He crawled across the floor and climbed back into Luke's lap. Soft brown curls stuck up all over his head in a million directions. Was his hair going to be as curly as Emily's?

Luke hummed a few more bars. The tune was good, better than anything he'd written in a while. He sat Wyatt on the floor, got up and walked into the kitchen to look for a piece of paper. He found Emily's junk drawer, which had a notepad and a pen. He scribbled the notes down before he could forget. His phone dinged and he glanced at it.

Sorry it's taking so long. How's Wyatt?

He snapped a picture of Wyatt in his lap and sent it to her.

He's fine.

Wyatt started chewing on his toys instead of banging them, and Luke glanced at the clock. He opened his wallet and pulled out the list of instructions that Abbie had left him when she tricked him into babysitting. He stared at the list. It was past the time Wyatt normally ate lunch. "Are you getting hungry?"

He carried the boy into the kitchen and put him in the high chair. It took three tries to find the cabinet that housed the baby food jars. A spoon was easy to find, thank goodness. Wyatt banged his hands on the tray of the high chair and kicked his legs wildly when Luke opened the jar of peas. His mouth opened and closed like a little baby bird's.

Luke scooped a bit of baby food out of the jar and fed it to Wyatt. Half of it dribbled out of his mouth and down his chin. After a few minutes, Luke got good at catching the food before it fell all over him. He scooped it off Wyatt's chin and pushed it back into the baby's mouth. By the time the jar was finished, Wyatt's clothes and face were a mess.

Luke got a wet paper towel and cleaned him up the best that he could, despite Wyatt tossing his head from one side to the other. Luke started singing, and Wyatt stopped fighting him. His chest swelled. It seemed his son liked music as much as he did.

Wyatt was getting fidgety, so Luke stood up to walk around with him. He bounced the baby in his arms and stopped to look at the calendar hanging on the wall. A few things were jotted down in some of the squares. Denny's doctor's appointment. Due dates for bills. The twenty-first was circled with a heart.

He glanced at Wyatt. "That's your birthday, isn't it?"

The circled number on the calendar seemed to mock him. If he went back to Nashville when he was supposed to, he would miss Wyatt's first birthday. He had already missed out on so much, he wasn't willing to miss any more. But how could he be there for his son when he lived fifteen hundred miles away?

CHAPTER FOURTEEN

EMILY CHECKED HER hair one more time. She'd put extra mousse on her curls so that they hung in soft ringlets around her face instead of poking out in all directions. She tugged the long sweater farther past her hips, ran her hands over the thighs of her soft denim jeans and smiled. It had been over a year since she'd been able to button her favorite pair of jeans. Would Luke notice?

She hadn't heard from Luke since early this morning. He was going to help his brother on the ranch and wouldn't have service, but he promised to be at her house before she needed to leave for work at the tavern. The Mississippi pot roast she'd put in the slow cooker before going to work at her grandfather's store was ready. The warm meaty aroma of the food filled the house and made her mouth water.

Wyatt pulled on the leg of her jeans, and she bent down to pick him up. "Mamamama," he babbled as he patted her cheek.

She picked him up and checked one more time for a fever. None. Thank goodness. Other than a few cranky spells the day before, he was back to his usual self.

After Emily got home from the laundromat the day before, Colleen had stopped by on her way out of town. She ended up staying most of the afternoon. Between Luke and Colleen, Wyatt hadn't lacked for any attention. Emily had been able to get the laundry done and even do some cleaning she'd put off for a while.

While she appreciated the help, it was nice to have a few moments of peace and quiet. She needed to get used to it, though. Wyatt had a family now. It had been just her and Granddad, and her aunt Tricia, of course, for so long that she never considered asking anyone for help.

Now, she had almost too much help—at least for a little bit longer. Luke was going back to Nashville on Monday. That only gave them three more days together. Would he forget about Wyatt once he returned? She had the feeling that Colleen was going to become a regular fixture in their lives. Already, she'd volunteered to take over Millie's Thursday night babysitting duties, but tonight Luke was going to watch Wyatt for her.

She scanned the small house. She'd never had more than one person at her house before, so she couldn't imagine having family over. Hopefully, that would change soon. Meghan had called her this morning and asked her if she was interested in looking at a fixer-upper. The home wasn't on the market yet, but the sellers were willing to let Emily come see it first. Her body hummed with excitement every time she thought about it.

She carried Wyatt into the living room and sat on the floor with him. She was helping him stack blocks together when Luke knocked on the door.

"Come in," she yelled.

The door opened slowly. He looked around the room, but didn't seem to spot her on the floor right away.

"I'm down here," she said.

"You should really keep the door locked."

"Not you, too!" She laughed. "Have you been talking to Granddad?"

"Yes. And we're on the same page." Luke hung his hat on one of the hooks by the door. "You work at a hardware store—don't tell me you can't find a better lock than this one."

"Only every day. I have three of them sitting in a drawer in the kitchen."

"They don't do much good there." His teasing smile showed off his dimples. "You have to put them on the door."

"Yes, I know," she said. "I tried, but I can't get the dead bolt to line up with the thingamajig in the knob."

Luke laughed, and the sound of it even made Wyatt stop and look. "Why doesn't your grandfather do it?"

She grimaced. "He has such bad arthritis in his hands that he can't hold tools anymore. I couldn't ask him to do it."

Wyatt handed her a block and grunted.

Luke nodded at him. "What are you doing?"

"We're playing a game." She placed a yellow block on top of the tall stack. "I build it. He destroys it."

Wyatt immediately knocked the entire structure over and giggled.

"Looks like a fun game." Luke joined them on the floor. His eyes swept over her. "You look nice."

Her heart fluttered. He noticed. She averted her gaze from his. "Thanks. Are you hungry?"

"Are you kidding?" He inhaled. "Even if I wasn't, I'd still eat."

Wyatt handed her another block, and she handed it to Luke. "Here, Wyatt. Go play with Daddy."

Emotion swam in Luke's eyes, and he gave her a smile that sent shock waves running through her body. She stood up and tugged her sweater down again. "I'll set the table."

Her pulse was still racing as she put the food on the table. The blocks crashed as another tower was toppled. Wyatt giggled. Luke giggled. And her heart swelled even more. He had no idea how much his smile affected her. She couldn't let him know, either.

The noise in the living room stopped, and she turned around in time to see Luke putting Wyatt in his high chair. She cut up Wyatt's dinner while Luke fixed his own plate. He waited until she sat down before starting to eat.

There were so many things she wanted to ask him. She'd already asked him the most generic questions. How was his music career going? Had he found a new band to play with? Had he written any new songs? But there were other questions she was more interested in asking. Did he have a girlfriend? Was he seeing anyone?

She steered clear of the questions because she wasn't sure that she really wanted to know the answers. Instead, she asked him about the ranch. They chatted about the possibility of a storm moving in over the weekend. By the time she finished eating, she was exhausted. She had no idea that small talk could be so draining. She sensed that he was selecting his words carefully, too, although she doubted if he did it for the same reasons she did.

After dinner, she went over Wyatt's schedule with Luke. After she explained the bedtime routine for the third time, Luke rubbed the top of her arm with one hand. "I got it. If I have any problems, I have your number. And Freddy's number. And your granddad's. And Millie's and Stacy's and Abbie's. I think I'm covered."

She nodded. Maybe she should call Freddy and tell him she couldn't come in. No. If she didn't go to work, Luke would leave as soon as she put Wyatt in bed. At least if she left, Wyatt would get more time with Luke.

"I probably won't be home until at least midnight. Earlier if it's really slow. Freddy is good about letting me leave early on Thursdays, but I close on Fridays and Saturdays."

"Why Thursdays?" Luke picked Wyatt up and walked with her to the door.

"Millie works at the hospital in Springerville on Friday mornings, so I don't want her to have to be up too late babysitting."

"And your aunt usually babysits Friday and Saturdays? Does she go back to Springerville when you get home or does she stay the night here?"

"I work until closing on those nights. Tricia goes to Grandad's when I get home and spends all day Saturday with him. Then she stays Saturday night and goes home after church on Sunday."

He nodded. "You've got a good system worked out. I guess my being here has thrown everyone off."

"Actually, your timing is perfect. Tricia couldn't come tonight because she has a workshop tomorrow morning for school, so Abbie was going to watch Wyatt." She paused. "I don't go in until after Wyatt's asleep."

She added the last part because she wanted him to know that Wyatt wasn't being neglected because she worked two jobs.

She opened the door to leave and paused. "Can I ask you a favor?"

"Anything."

Her words came out in a rush. "Would you go look at a house with me tomorrow?"

"Are you thinking of moving?"

She nodded. "I've been saving up money to buy a house for a long time. That's why I still work at the tavern."

"That's great. Where is it? Here in town?"

"Yes. It's not officially on the market yet because it needs a lot of work. The owner is willing to let me look at it first. If it's not in too bad of shape, and if it's something

I can fix myself, I'd like to put in an offer before it gets snatched up by an investor from out of town."

He smiled. "What time is the appointment?"

"Ten o'clock in the morning." Her insides quivered with excitement every time she thought about it. "It's that big house at the end of Cous Lane. I've never been inside, but it's surrounded by trees, and it has a yard."

"The one Justin Long lived in when we were kids?"

Emily frowned. "I don't know who that is."

"That's right," he said. "You didn't move here until high school. Justin was gone by then. If it's the same house, I've been inside. It's nice. Big rooms. A fireplace. Wyatt would love the backyard."

Excitement welled up in her chest. "Really? Meghan said it needs a lot of work—that's why I asked you to go with me. I don't know a lot about repairs, so I don't want to get in over my head. Plus, someone else is coming to look at it tomorrow afternoon, so if it's not too bad, I'd like to make an offer first."

Luke's brow furrowed. "I didn't know you were looking to buy a house. I've got some money saved up—"

"No." Emily shook her head. "I won't take your money."

His face pinched. "Why not? Consider it back pay for child support."

"No. I don't need your help." Her heart pounded in her chest. "I mean, except for your opinion. I'd like your opinion. Not your money."

"I don't get you. Most women would demand that I pay my fair share. I'm trying, but you're shutting me out. Don't you think I should have some say in where my son lives?" His brown eyes flickered with anger. "If I can afford to help you find a better place to live, why would you turn that down?"

"I'm not trying to shut you out," she said. "I'll never stop you from spending time with Wyatt. If you want to buy things for him, knock yourself out. But a house wouldn't just be his. It would be mine, too. And I refuse to be beholden to anyone regarding my living arrangements ever again."

Luke nodded, his face more somber than usual. "Okay. I get it. Have a good night."

"Thanks." She leaned in and kissed Wyatt's cheek. "Good night, little man. Be good for Daddy."

"See you in a few hours," Luke said. His words were clipped.

Emily nodded and closed the door behind her.

His tone bothered her. Was he upset because she didn't want to take money from him for a house? He, of all people, should understand. He wasn't content working on the ranch because it was his brother's passion. He wanted something all his own.

That was all she wanted. Something all her own. Before her dad died, they moved every time he got transferred, but it didn't bother her because they were still a family. After he died, she and her mother stayed put for a couple of years. But then her mother married another military man, and they started moving again. But this time, it didn't feel like a family. It felt as though she was being dragged along as an afterthought.

When she came to Coronado, she had a stable home and the family she needed. She stopped worrying about moving all the time. Then cancer took her beloved grandmother, and her granddad was too overwhelmed with grief to deal with anything else. He demanded that her mother take her back. So once again, Emily's world was upended, and she was at the mercy of her mother and stepdad.

Did she really think Luke would try to control where she lived if she accepted his money? No. But she never thought her granddad would kick her out of his house when Grandma died. It wasn't a chance she was willing to take.

"How did babysitting go last night?"

Luke glanced up from his coffee. Abbie placed a plate of homemade biscuits on the table. He shrugged. "It was good."

Across the table from him, papers rustled as Noah turned a page in the newspaper. "Emily got off pretty early, didn't she?"

He spread butter on a steaming hot biscuit. "She was home by ten. The Watering Hole was pretty slow."

"Usually is this time of year." Noah set the newspaper down and grabbed two biscuits for himself.

Abbie pushed a bowl of scrambled eggs toward Luke. "You must have left as soon as she got home then."

He shrugged. "Why wouldn't I? There was no reason to stay."

Not that he hadn't wanted to. But after the way they left things before she went to work, he wasn't sure if she would have wanted him to stay.

Abbie and Noah exchanged glances.

"Humph." Abbie went back into the kitchen.

Luke turned to his brother. "What did I do wrong?"

Noah chuckled and spooned gravy over his biscuits. "I think she was hoping that you and Emily might end up getting back together."

Back together. They had never been a couple. "It's not like that with Emily."

"Are you sure about that?" Noah laughed. "Wyatt wouldn't be here if it wasn't."

"It was a onetime thing." Luke paused between bites of food. "I stopped to say goodbye, and we both got a little carried away."

"Can I ask you something?" Noah stared at him for a moment. "Of all the people in this town, why did you stop to tell *her* goodbye on your way out of town?"

"I don't know." Luke stared at his coffee. But he did know. Of all the people he worked with at the tavern, of all the people he played music with, of all the people he knew in Coronado, she was the one he would miss the most.

"Maybe you should figure that out." Noah finished his coffee and stood up. "You going to Emily's this afternoon?"

Luke frowned. "I was supposed to meet her at ten this morning."

Noah leaned back in his chair. "Supposed to? But not now?"

"I don't know. We got into an argument." Was it really an argument? No. More like they didn't see eye to eye. "She asked me to go look at a house with her."

Abbie had just walked back into the room. She gave him a hopeful smile. "You're house shopping together?"

"No. She's looking at a house that might need some work and wanted my opinion on it."

Abbie plopped down in her chair and gave him a sharp look. "What did you do, Luke?"

"Nothing," he said. "I told her I would be happy to go look at the house with her."

"And?" Noah gave him the same look that he did when they were kids and he knew Luke was skirting around the truth.

He sighed. "I told her if the house needed too much work, I would be happy to help her buy a different one."

Abbie snorted. "I bet that didn't go over well."

"No." Luke stirred his eggs with a fork. "Why is she being so stubborn about me giving her money? All I want to do is make sure my son has a safe place to live."

Abbie's mouth dropped open, and she leaned forward with her elbows on the table. "You didn't word it like that, did you? That makes it sound like you offered to help because you don't think she's capable of doing it on her own."

"Of course not." Luke tapped his fork on the table and replayed the conversation in his head. He was sure he hadn't insulted her in that way. "I wasn't trying to take over. I just offered to give her enough money for a down payment on a house she wanted. How she uses that money is up to her."

Abbie's green eyes held a hint of sadness. "You know the reason she wants to do it on her own, don't you? Because her entire life she felt like she had no say in where she lived. When she finally felt like she belonged, her grandmother died and her grandfather kicked her out.

"She wants a place of her own. A place that no one can ever take away from her. If she lets you pay for that, even if your name isn't on the deed, it's still not completely hers."

Luke scratched his head. "Why do women have to be so complicated?" He looked at Noah.

Noah laughed. "If you figure it out, let me know."

Abbie balled up a napkin and threw it at him. "Like you men are so much easier to figure out!"

Noah laughed and leaned across the table to kiss her.

Luke stood up and carried his plate to the kitchen. Watching Noah get goo-goo-eyed while talking to his wife was odd. It didn't fit with the tough, no-nonsense brother he'd known for all of his twenty-six years. There was a time when Luke would have sworn that Noah would rather get punched in the nose than show any emotion.

He rinsed his plate in the sink and put it in the dishwasher. Noah walked past him on his way out to the barn. Luke followed him. "I'll go check the fences," he volunteered.

He didn't have anything else to do until meeting Emily's Realtor. He might as well help his brother.

Dark clouds hung over the mountain, blocking most of the light from the morning sun, and the bite of the wind was colder than normal. A storm was moving in. Luke had planned on riding Jasper to the pasture to check on the fences, but one more look at the sky, and he decided to take Noah's truck instead.

The snow was coming down hard by the time he made it back to the ranch house. He stared at the dark gray clouds. It wasn't going to let up soon. He should head into town before it got too bad. He might have to get a room in town tonight—that is, if Emily still let him babysit Wyatt while she went to work.

He stomped the snow and mud off his boots before opening the back door to the kitchen.

"Luke, is that you?" Abbie called.

He walked into the living room where she was dusting the fireplace mantel.

"Emily called. She said that you didn't need to come to town this morning."

His stomach knotted. She must be really angry with him. "I guess she wants to meet the Realtor by herself."

"No." Abbie shook her head. "She canceled the meeting. She also said to tell you that you don't have to babysit tonight. She's not going to work. She caught Wyatt's stomach bug."

Emily was sick? She must feel awful if she wasn't going to look at the house. He went up to his bedroom and grabbed a change of clothes and his toiletries and headed back downstairs.

"Where are you going?" Abbie asked.

"To Emily's."

"But—"

Luke shut the door before Abbie could try to convince him not to go. He glanced at his phone. Why didn't Emily call and tell him herself? A message flashed on the screen: No service. He had forgotten to connect his phone to the ranch's wi-fi. If Emily had tried to call him, it wouldn't have gone through.

Oh right. There was no cell phone service at the ranch. That was why Emily had called the house phone. But why tell him not to come? If she was sick, at least he could take care of Wyatt so she could rest.

He pushed the SUV as fast as he dared on the dirt road. The snow was melting on the road as fast as it landed, making it a slushy, slippery mess. He would be no good to Emily if he slid off the road.

As soon as he hit pavement, he picked up speed and pulled up to Emily's house in record time.

He knocked on the door and waited. No answer. Her car was in the driveway, so he knew she was there. He knocked again. Nothing. Finally, he checked the doorknob. It was unlocked.

He pushed the door open and stepped inside. A kid's television show played on the TV, and toys were scattered all over the living room floor, but there was no sign of Emily or Wyatt. His heart pounded. Where was she?

The bedroom door was partially open, and he peeked inside. Emily was sprawled across the bed with her head lying close to the edge. Wyatt sat up in his crib when he saw Luke.

Luke picked Wyatt up and carried him to the living room. He set the little boy on the floor and went back to close the bedroom door. Just as he started to close the door, Emily rolled over and retched into a trash can on the floor.

He rushed in and sat on the side of the bed, rubbing her back.

"Tricia?"

"No," he said. "It's me."

She wiped her mouth with the back of her hand. "What are you doing here?"

"Abbie said you were sick, so I came to help."

"Where's Wyatt?" She tried to sit up.

"Wyatt's fine." He reached up to touch her forehead. "You're burning up. Have you taken any medicine?"

She shook her head and lay back on the bed. He searched the medicine cabinet in the bathroom and returned with two acetaminophen tablets, a glass of water and a wet washcloth.

"Go away," she murmured. "You'll get sick, too."

"Don't worry about me." He pressed the washcloth to her forehead. "Here. Take this."

She sat up long enough to take the tablets before falling back on her pillow.

The cell phone on her nightstand began to ring. He picked it up and glanced at the screen. "It's your aunt Tricia. Do you want to answer?"

She had already fallen asleep. He thought about ignoring the phone. But what if Emily already told her she was sick? He didn't want Tricia to worry too much.

"Who is this?" Tricia's voice had an alarmed tone.

"This is Luke Sterling," he said.

"Thank goodness you're there," she said. "Is Emily okay? How's Wyatt?"

"She's got a fever and is throwing up. I gave her some medicine and she's sleeping now." Luke went into the living room as he talked, closing the bedroom door behind him. "Wyatt's fine."

"I'm so glad you're there," Tricia said again.

"Tricia—" Luke hesitated for moment. "Who is Emily's Realtor?"

"Meghan Simpson. Why?"

"Emily was supposed to meet her this morning, but she canceled. I thought maybe I should go in her place and take pictures for her."

"That's very sweet of you," Tricia said. "She'll appreciate that. I have a workshop this morning, but I'll head over there as soon as I get finished."

Luke sat on the sofa, and Wyatt crawled over to him and pulled himself up. He stroked Wyatt's feathery soft hair. This was *his* family. *His* responsibility. "There's no need. I'll be here until Emily gets better."

"Are you sure? A sick mama and a baby is a lot to handle."

"Yes." He'd never been more sure of anything in his life. No one else should be taking care of his son. Or Emily. She meant as much to him as Wyatt did.

CHAPTER FIFTEEN

EMILY FORCED HER eyes open. Her head still pounded, but her stomach wasn't cramping any longer. She glanced at the nightstand and saw a glass of water, a folded-up washcloth and a bottle of acetaminophen. The last thing she remembered was Luke wiping her forehead with the cloth and giving her water.

Luke. She sat up in bed. Was he still here? Wyatt wasn't in his crib. Where was he? What time was it? She reached for her phone, but it wasn't there. She rolled out of bed and walked to the living room.

The only light came from the television set. Luke lay on the sofa with Wyatt snugged to his chest. Both of them were sound asleep. She looked around for her phone and found it on the kitchen table. It was a few minutes before midnight. What happened to Tricia? She checked her text messages. Nothing.

Tricia wouldn't have just decided not to come. She checked her call log. No missed calls. She looked again. Tricia had called this morning. Emily stared at Luke. The only explanation was that Luke answered the phone. Had he told Tricia not to come? Or had she been here and left?

Emily scrubbed her face with her hand. She must have slept all day. Well, when she wasn't throwing up. She walked back to where Luke and Wyatt were cuddled together. They looked so content. Her heart swelled.

Wyatt's head was pressed against Luke's chest, his

mouth open. Drool had made a wet spot on Luke's shirt. His arm was wrapped protectively around Wyatt.

She opened the camera app on her phone and snapped a picture.

Luke opened his eyes. "Hey," he whispered.

"Do you want me to put him in his crib?"

Before she could reach for Wyatt, he shook his head. "I don't want to wake him up."

"It won't," she said. "He could sleep through a herd of buffalo."

Luke glanced down at the sleeping child before moving his hands so Emily could slide her arms under Wyatt. She inhaled Wyatt's sweet baby smell.

When she laid him in his crib, he stirred a little but settled down as soon as she patted his back. She picked up the bottle of medicine on the nightstand and the empty glass and carried it into the kitchen.

The lights were on now, and Luke was waiting for her. "How are you feeling?"

"Like I got hit by a truck."

He gave her a sad smile. "Are you hungry? Do you want some broth?"

She shook her head, and the slight movement caused her head to pound more. She took two tablets from the medicine bottle and swallowed them with some water. "Thanks for coming to help. Wyatt should sleep all night, so I'm going back to bed."

She trudged her way back to the bedroom, checked to make sure Wyatt was warm and crawled under the covers.

When she opened her eyes, sunlight filtered through the curtains. She yawned and stretched, reluctant to crawl out from under the warm blankets. Sitting up, her gaze drifted to the crib. Wyatt wasn't there. She tossed the covers back and got out of bed.

Wyatt was in his high chair, eagerly shoving scrambled eggs into his mouth. Luke sat at the table eating breakfast, too.

He smiled. “You look better.”

“I feel better.” She bent down and kissed the top of Wyatt’s head. “Did you stay all night?”

“Yes.”

“I’m sorry. My aunt was supposed to come after her workshop yesterday.”

“I told her not to,” Luke said.

“Why?”

“There was no reason for her to drive all the way from Springerville. I was already here. Besides…” He stopped talking and pressed his lips together as if he was trying to keep from saying something.

She arched one eyebrow at him. “Besides what?”

He sighed. “A storm was moving in yesterday, so I didn’t want her to risk it.”

“A storm?” She frowned. “That’s right. Freddy said something about it the other night.”

“If Tricia had come, she would’ve been driving right in the middle of it and been stuck here all weekend.” He stood up and put his plate in the sink. “Do you want some breakfast?”

She should be starving since she hadn’t eaten anything in more than twenty-four hours. But with Luke’s brown eyes focused so intently on her, all she could think about was that she hadn’t showered. Or brushed her teeth. Or changed clothes. She glanced down at her crumpled pajamas.

“No,” she said. “I’m sure you’re ready to go home, but would you mind staying long enough for me to shower?”

“I’m not going anywhere.” He got Wyatt out of his high

chair. "The snowplows haven't cleared the roads yet. Go ahead and shower."

The way he looked at her made her heart flutter. She pushed the butterflies down. "I'll hurry."

The hot water from the shower did a world of good. By the time she got out, she felt almost normal. Before leaving the bathroom, she checked her reflection in the mirror one more time. She scrunched her curls and checked her sweater for stains. It was as good as it was going to get.

Luke was sitting in the middle of the floor, coaxing Wyatt to come to him. Wyatt stood next to the sofa, holding on to the edge. He reached for Luke and grunted.

"Come on." Luke wiggled his fingers at Wyatt. "Show Mommy."

A second later, Wyatt took a couple of wobbly steps toward Luke.

"Oh my gosh!" Emily rushed over to them, knelt on the floor and planted kisses on Wyatt's cheeks. "You walked! What a big boy you are!"

Wyatt wrapped his arms around her and climbed onto her lap.

Luke beamed. "He did it twice yesterday."

A twinge of sadness stamped out some of her excitement. "Twice? And I missed it."

His face grew pensive. "Don't feel too bad. You missed one milestone. Think about how many I've missed."

Emily had learned early in life to question the motives of everyone. Her mother never did anything out of the goodness of her heart. Every action was motivated by how it would make her look. This obsession with appearances affected every part of Emily's life. She had to dress a certain way, act a certain way and participate in certain activities. When Emily hit her rebellious teenage years, she refused to comply any longer. Her mother worried that

Emily's behavior would ruin her husband's chances for a promotion, so she packed Emily's things and sent her to Coronado to finish high school.

Emily had told herself that Luke was only there out of obligation, but the pain etched into the lines on his face told her differently. He wasn't there because he was afraid that people would accuse him of shirking his responsibility. He hadn't stayed all night because he was afraid people would judge him if he didn't. He was there because he was truly concerned about the welfare of his son.

She bit her bottom lip. She hadn't really given Luke the benefit of the doubt. "Thank you for staying," she said. She squeezed his arm. "I hope you know that I would never neglect Wyatt, no matter how sick I was."

"It wasn't Wyatt I was worried about." His hand covered hers. "Besides, I didn't want anyone else taking care of you. That's my job now."

His words sent her heart racing. She closed her eyes and tried to think logically. Was it an overinflated sense of obligation to the mother of his child that made him say that…or something else? She swallowed.

"In that case—" she forced a laugh "—it's a good thing I got sick when I did. A few days later, and I'd be on my own."

At the not-so-subtle reminder of his upcoming departure, his face fell. Was he dreading it as much as she was?

She tried to keep her tone light. "What time does your plane leave tomorrow?"

Luke's brow furrowed. "Ten o'clock."

"In the morning?" She knew this was coming. She just wasn't ready yet.

Wyatt crawled back to his toys, and she moved to sit on the sofa. Her head was starting to ache a little, and she rubbed her temples with her fingers.

"At night," he said. "Looks like you're stuck with me all day Monday."

He didn't look any happier about it than she felt. The longer he stayed, the harder it would be for her to pretend she was okay with them being just friends.

He stood up and moved to sit behind her. He began massaging her temples with his fingers. "I did something."

She closed her eyes, his fingers relieving some of the pain from her headache. She waited for him to finish his thought, but he didn't. "Are you going to tell me what it was?"

His fingers moved from her temples to her neck. He was quiet for another moment. "I met with Meghan yesterday and looked at that house."

She snapped her head up. "Why?"

"Because I knew how excited you were about it." He handed her his phone. "I took some videos, as well as pictures of the areas that need the most work."

Emily scrolled through the pictures. Her heart wrenched. It was everything she wanted in a house. She handed the phone back to him. "Thanks for doing that."

"That's it?" Luke gave her a confused look. "It's not what you were looking for?"

She wrapped her arms around herself. "It is. But she was showing it to an investor yesterday afternoon. I'm sure he's already made an offer."

"Actually," he said, "the owner really wants to sell it to a local family and not someone who just needs a vacation home."

Her heart leaped. "Really? How do you know?"

He shrugged. "That's what Meghan told me. Why don't you call her?"

She picked up her phone and scrolled through the contacts for Meghan's number.

"Dadadada!" Wyatt's loud voice jolted her from her task.

Her mouth dropped open, and her gaze darted from Luke to Wyatt and back. "Did he just call you Dad?"

His face broke into a huge grin. "I think so."

Emily threw her phone on the sofa before she scooped Wyatt up and tossed him in the air. Luke wrapped his arms around Emily with Wyatt sandwiched between them. Wyatt squealed in protest and wiggled to get out from in between them.

"I guess he's not a fan of bear hugs," she said.

"I guess not." He laughed.

For a moment, they both watched Wyatt playing with his toys.

Luke took a deep breath. "It's amazing how fast the world can change."

"By the end of the week, he'll be walking everywhere. Next time you see him, he'll probably be running." Emily scooted back to lean against the sofa.

She picked up her phone again to call Meghan.

"Before you do that—" Luke moved closer to her and took one of her hands in his "—I want…"

She glanced at the hand holding hers. It was shaking. She rubbed the back of his knuckles with her thumb. It was as much of an attempt to soothe her own nerves as his.

"I don't want to miss out on anything else." He took a deep breath. "And I think Wyatt deserves to have a real family. A *whole* family."

Emily's breath caught, and her chest swelled. She would never ask him to give up his dream and move back to Coronado, but if he made the choice on his own, she wouldn't try to talk him out of it.

He peered into her eyes. "Would you consider moving to Nashville with me?"

The hope that had been welling up in her chest crashed like a meteor hitting the earth.

LUKE HELD HIS breath as he watched a range of emotions flicker across her face. The sparkle in her blue eyes dimmed and a tiny V formed between her eyebrows.

His heart began to race. Maybe she wasn't interested in anything besides friendship. He felt as if he was standing on the edge of a cliff. There was no backing down now.

He took both of her hands in his. "I know it's a big step, and I understand if you're not ready for it yet. If you just want to be friends, I understand that, too."

"I thought..." Her face turned red, and she took a deep breath. "What exactly are you asking? What do you want from me?"

Hadn't he made that clear? His heart pounded so hard he couldn't hear his own breathing. "I'm saying I want to give our relationship a chance."

She bit her bottom lip. "I didn't think you thought of me as anything more than a friend."

"Friendship is the best foundation for a relationship, don't you think?"

Her breath hitched, and she lifted her gaze to look at him. "You want a relationship?"

"I do," he said. He hooked one finger under her chin and lifted her face to his.

He pressed his lips to hers, softly at first, but as she moved closer to him, he stopped being careful. He wrapped both arms around her and pulled her closer to him, reveling in the scent and taste of her.

When he finally broke the kiss and pulled away, he smiled. "Does that mean yes?"

The twinkle was back in her eyes, and she smiled. "I would like to give our relationship a chance. But..."

His chest swelled, and he cut off her words with another kiss. She tasted of spearmint, and she smelled even better. He could spend all day with her in his arms. He squeezed her tighter just in case he started to float away.

"There's so much to do," he said. "Do you think a week will be long enough to pack everything up? My apartment is really small, but it will do until we find someplace bigger."

His mind buzzed with ideas. "I'm thinking we should look for a place on the outskirts…"

"No." She turned away.

"Okay. I can try to get another week off work. It's slow right now, so it shouldn't be a problem."

She ran one hand through her hair and pressed her lips together. "I can't move to Nashville."

He frowned. "Why not?"

"Because I can't." She went into the kitchen.

His shoulders dropped. "You don't even want to discuss it?"

"No." She opened the bottle of medicine and shook a couple of tablets into her hand.

He noticed that her hands were shaking. "Is your headache coming back?"

She nodded and swallowed the pills with a cup of water. She came back to the living room and stood in front of him. "Why?"

He was a little taken aback by her aggressive stance. She seemed angry. "Why what?"

She crossed her arms. "Why do you want a relationship with me? You never did before."

"That's where you're wrong," Luke told her. He stepped closer and trailed one finger up her arm. "I think I've been in love with you since you knocked Matthew Price off the bleachers for booing at me during our senior talent show. I was just too scared to do anything about it."

"But..."

He could see the doubt in her eyes. "Don't you know how amazing I think you are?"

Her blue eyes glistened, and he couldn't help but kiss her again. This time she didn't kiss him back.

"I can't go to Nashville with you." Her voice cracked. "There are too many things here."

"What do you mean?" He made a broad sweep of the tiny trailer. "You don't want to leave all this?"

She lifted her chin. "I mean my job, my grandfather, my aunt, my future."

His nostrils flared as his own anger bubbled to the surface. "You can find a new job. We can come back and visit your family as often as you want. And I'm sorry, but I thought your future might include me."

"It does. As long as it's in Coronado." Her arms dropped to her side. "I'm sorry, but I can't leave my grandfather."

"I can't move to Coronado, you know that."

Her eyes were full of sadness when she looked at him. "Then I guess we're stuck being friends."

CHAPTER SIXTEEN

THE KNOCK ON the door sent Emily's heart pounding. She took a deep breath. Maybe if she didn't answer the door, Luke wouldn't leave.

He had to leave. He had a life to go back to. A life that could include her, but wouldn't.

She paused with her hand on the doorknob and took a deep breath before opening the door.

Luke stood in front of the door with his hat in his hands. A touch of relief flashed on his face. "You're here."

She opened the door farther to let him in. "Your text said you were coming over to take us to breakfast. Was I supposed to be somewhere else?"

"I thought you might have gone to work at your granddad's store." He shrugged.

"No. He gets sick easier than he used to and is worried that I might still be contagious, so he told me to stay home today."

Luke rocked back and forth on his feet. "I'm sorry I got angry with you yesterday."

"I'm sorry I snapped at you."

Luke stepped close to her and wrapped his arms around her waist. "Leaving is hard enough. I don't want to argue, too."

"I know." She could hear his heart. She closed her eyes and enjoyed the feel of his strong arms around her.

"Just so you know, I'm not giving up." He pulled her closer. "We're a family."

She lifted her head from his chest. "I would be lying if I said I wanted you to."

He pulled away but kept his arms wrapped around her. Arm in arm, they walked into the living room. Wyatt saw him and crawled over to him.

She did the math in her head. He needed to check in one hour before his flight and it was a four-hour drive from Coronado to Phoenix. "So you can stay until four thirty."

"More like five." He picked Wyatt up and tossed him in the air. "Hi, son."

Wyatt giggled and smacked Luke's face with his hand. Luke caught his hand with his mouth and pretended to eat his fingers. They played that game for a few more minutes.

"Did you call Meghan?"

"Not yet," she admitted.

"Why not?" Luke gave her a puzzled look. "I thought it had everything you wanted."

"It does." Emily bit her bottom lip. The house was perfect…in theory. She sighed. "If the repairs are too costly, I won't be able to get a loan. I'm scared of falling in love with it and then it falling through."

"Emily Beck, I'm shocked. You've never been scared of anything." He shook his head and handed Wyatt to her. "You get Wyatt ready to go. I'm calling Meghan."

"No," she said. "I'll call her later this week."

"Later may be too late." He gave her a pointed look and picked up his phone. "The owner wants to sell it to someone local, but he still wants to sell it. If you wait too long you'll miss the opportunity all together."

She nodded. "You're right. I'll call her after breakfast."

"We're going now," he said and held up his phone. "Meghan will meet us there in fifteen minutes."

Her hands shook as she put Wyatt's coat on. She felt as if she was teetering on the edge of a giant cliff. If she got her hopes up about the house and the bank said no, it would hurt too much.

And it wasn't just the house. It was him, too. Luke said he wanted a relationship, but would he still feel that way when he returned to Nashville? She didn't want to let the wall down around her heart only to be hurt.

Luke carried Wyatt to his SUV while she transferred the car seat. Despite the cold air, her palms were sweaty. She wasn't sure if it was from excitement or nerves. Luke buckled Wyatt in and got in the driver's side.

After driving through the main part of town, he turned onto Cous Lane, a gravel road on the outskirts of town. Emily's heart thumped as they neared the house. When Luke turned down the driveway and pulled in front of the cabin-style home, she thought her heart might burst.

Snow lay on top of the roof like a layer of frosting on a cake. The front yard was mostly bare, except for a couple of small pine trees. Weeds had overtaken the flower beds that hugged the front of the wraparound porch, but Emily could envision them bursting with flowers.

Luke parked under an awning on one side of the house. "It would be easy to block this in, if you ever wanted to turn it into a garage," he said.

She laughed and unbuckled Wyatt from his car seat. "My old car doesn't need much."

A few minutes later, Meghan pulled in behind them in her shiny Cadillac Escalade. "Have you been waiting long?" she called as she got out of the vehicle.

"Just got here," Luke told her.

Emily followed Meghan up the front steps onto the porch. A few of the boards creaked when she stepped on them, and she noticed several broken planks.

Wyatt reached for Luke, and she let him take the baby. Wyatt wiggled to try to get down, but Luke entertained him by tossing him in the air. Was Wyatt going to miss Luke as much as she was when he left?

Meghan unlocked the front door, and Emily stepped into the great room. A rock fireplace took up one corner, and the wood beams in the ceiling gave everything a rustic feel.

"The house is older," Meghan said. "There is no central air or heat, but the last owners began the ductwork for it, so it could be added. If you didn't want to do that, the fireplace works great."

The kitchen was spacious, although most of the cabinets needed to be replaced, and the dining area was big enough to fit all of Luke's family.

Emily's face flushed. She shouldn't be thinking like that. Not yet.

As they walked through the rest of the house, she tried not to envision Luke in every room. The house wasn't large, but it would be big enough for a family.

"I didn't show you this area when you were here," Meghan said to Luke as she unlocked a narrow door off the kitchen. "This is the basement."

Emily followed Luke down the steps into the unfinished basement. The single light bulb in the center of the room didn't put out a lot of light, but the floor was dry, which was a good sign.

Luke touched the cement wall. "This would make a great music studio!"

Was he imagining it as his home, too? She swallowed. Her heart was beating so loud that she didn't hear the things Meghan was pointing out.

Next, Meghan led them upstairs, where the majority of

the repairs were needed. "The roof leaks in a few places, and the wiring needs to be redone."

Emily immediately thought of Caden. He was an electrician, and she was sure he would give her a fair price. She glanced at the ceiling where dark circles marred the paint. A roof could be mended. At least the walls were solid, and the floor wasn't rotten.

Hope swelled up in her chest. The house didn't look as bad as she'd thought it might.

"What do you think?" Luke nudged her. "Do you love it?"

She looked around the bedroom they were standing in and walked over to the window. Acres of forest stretched out behind the house, belying the fact that they were still only a few minutes from town.

"I do," she said.

She followed Meghan down the stairs and waited on the porch for her to lock up. "I'll call the lender that I'm prequalified with this afternoon and get the ball rolling."

Meghan smiled. "So you're ready to make an offer? I can have the papers drawn up by noon."

"Yes," Luke said, just as Emily said, "No."

Emily pressed her lips together. "I can't make an offer until I talk to my lender about the repairs."

"I understand." Meghan nodded. "But don't wait too long. I've already had a few offers from out of town investors who are ready to buy it sight unseen."

Emily's chest deflated. "I'll have an answer for you today, if I can."

Wyatt started to cry, and Luke gave her an alarmed look. "What does he want?"

"He's probably hungry," she said.

"That I can fix." Luke walked over to the SUV and opened the door for her.

"Are you sure you would rather stay here than move to Nashville with me?" He was joking, but only partly. "Nashville has a lot to offer. Besides great music, it has lots of things for kids to do and great food. It would be a great place to raise a family."

She gave him a pointed look. "Why don't you stay here and work for your brother?"

"Touché," he said. "Are you ready to go eat?"

She buckled her seat belt. "I'm starving."

There were only a few people at the Bear's Den. Most of them were locals. When Luke and Emily walked in together, several people stopped and stared at them.

Kimberly, their waitress, had gone to school with both Emily and Luke. She smiled at Luke and welcomed him to Coronado, but she barely acknowledged Emily. When Kimberly tried to hand him a menu, he nodded toward Emily. "Ladies first," he said.

Kimberly's gaze shifted from Luke to Wyatt and back again. A soft gasp escaped her, and Emily coughed to cover a laugh.

"What was that about?" Luke asked as soon as Kimberly walked away.

Emily got Wyatt situated in a high chair and handed him a bottle. "She just realized that you are Wyatt's father. I'm pretty sure that gasp was from shock."

"What's so shocking about that?"

Emily's face turned pink. "Really? Of all the girls at Coronado High School that had a crush on you, I'm the last one they would guess you would have a child with."

He gave her a long stare. "Why? You're beautiful. And funny. And caring. And amazing." It angered him that she couldn't see herself the way he did. "Any man would be lucky to have you."

"Thanks," she mumbled and averted her gaze to the menu.

He cocked his head to stare at her. "You had a crush on me in high school?"

"Of course I did." She laughed. "I used to write your name all over the back cover of my history book."

"You did a good job of keeping it a secret. I had no idea. And no one in town suspected either because they're all surprised to see us together."

Her eyes narrowed. "And what would have happened if I told the whole town you were Wyatt's father? Did you really want to find out about it from the rumor mill?"

"No," he said. "I guess I just don't want it to be a secret anymore."

Emily glanced at the door. "You just got your wish. Here come the Reed sisters. The entire town will know it before your plane leaves today."

Margaret and Edith Reed, identical twin sisters in their seventies, made a beeline across the restaurant to their table. Each sister had her signature hair color. Margaret's hair was bright pink while Edith's hair was so blue it was almost turquoise.

"Hello, Emily. Nice to see you, Luke." Margaret was the first to speak.

Edith gave Emily a knowing smile. "I see you finally told Luke about his son. It's about time."

"Yes, dear," Margaret agreed. "We thought we would never see the two of you together again. I always told Edith that of all the couples we've set up, you two had the most potential."

Emily's face turned red the second the two women walked away.

Luke leaned closer to her and whispered, "What are they talking about? They never set us up."

"Yes, they did," she said. "Or at least they tried to. They asked you to fix their gate one time. When you got there, you took one look at me, figured out what was going on and took off like a shot."

He frowned. "I don't remember that, but if I ran away, it wasn't because of you. Those women are terrifying."

Her phone chimed as she received a text message. She pulled it out of her purse and checked the message. "Granddad is closing the store for the rest of the week. The furnace is out."

"Why a week? Your granddad has fixed lots of furnaces."

She dropped her phone back inside her purse. "Remember, he can't do things like that anymore because of his arthritis. How could he hold the tools to fix a heater?"

"Did he call someone to fix it?"

Emily nodded. "He called a company out in Springerville, but they can't make it until next week. Grandpa will probably bundle up and try to tough it out, but it'll be too cold for Wyatt, so it looks like I'll be out of work until they can come fix it."

Luke waved Kimberly over to the table. "We need to put our order in to go. And we need it quickly."

Emily cocked her head but didn't question him until they'd both given Kimberly their order. As soon as she walked away, Emily asked, "What are we doing? Why do you want to get the food to go?"

"Because I'm going to drop you off at home and go fix the heater for your grandfather."

"I appreciate that, but do you know how to fix a heater?"

Luke gave her a slight smile. "How do you think I make a living in Nashville?"

"I don't know," she said. "I assumed it was with your music."

"No. I work for an HVAC company. I discovered I'm

actually pretty good at it. I'm as good at that as Noah is at being a cowboy."

Her eyes widened, and she sat back in her chair. "So you aren't pursuing a music career in Nashville?"

"Yes. But playing part-time gigs doesn't bring in a lot of cash. And they're usually at night. I need something to do during the day." He gave her his lopsided smile. "Besides, I kind of like not having to live in my truck."

Their breakfast arrived in take-out boxes, and they hurried back out to his vehicle. When he dropped her off at the trailer, he leaned over and brushed a kiss across her lips before she got out of the SUV.

"Be back as quick as I can." He fought the urge to kiss her again.

"Don't you want to eat your breakfast first?"

He shook his head. "I don't want your grandfather sitting alone in that cold store for too long. I can heat up my food when I get done."

She squeezed his hand. "Thanks for helping Granddad. I know he'll appreciate it, too."

AS MUCH AS Luke hated to miss out on the last few hours with his son, he couldn't go back to Nashville knowing that he could've helped Emily's grandfather but didn't.

"I sure appreciate this," Denny told him for the tenth time. "I hate not being able to do it myself."

Luke could understand the man's frustration. The entire time he was working, Denny watched over his shoulder, offering guidance and advice. Luke found the issue right away but gave Denny credit for helping.

"You've got a knack for this," Denny said. "Did you ever think about opening up your own business?"

"I can't say that I have," Luke told him. "There are a lot of companies in Nashville, so it would be hard to compete."

"Nashville? I'm talking about right here in Coronado."

"It's tempting, but I don't think there's enough of a demand for a full-time business." Luke picked up the tools and carried them back to the storage room.

Denny followed him. He pointed out a section of the storage room. "Those shelves right there are for Caden Murphy. He's a good electrician, but he said the same thing. There's not enough demand for a full-time business. So he works at the market with Stacy, but he has his contractor's license and does the work whenever it's needed."

Luke raised his eyebrows. He didn't know that Caden was a certified electrician. "That's great. But he also has another business to support him and his family. I don't."

"What about the ranch?" Denny's frown deepened.

"The ranch belongs to Noah. It can't support both of us."

Denny nodded. "Well, you think about it. If you ever decide you want to pursue it, you're welcome to the use of the store. I got a lot of wasted space nowadays."

"I appreciate that."

Luke stayed long enough to make sure the temperature was comfortable before leaving. He mulled over what Denny had said on the drive back to Emily's house.

"Did you fix it?" she asked when she opened the door to let him in.

"Piece of cake," he said. "I have one more thing to fix, though."

He walked into the kitchen and found the drawer with all the locks. Emily held Wyatt, and they watched him assemble the dead bolt and fix the door.

"There," he said. "Now I won't lie awake at night worrying about your safety."

Emily laughed. "Your daddy's silly," she said to Wyatt.

"Dadada," Wyatt babbled and reached for him.

He took Wyatt in his arms and held him close. His heart ached knowing he was going to have to say good-bye soon.

"Can I ask you something?" Emily's face was serious.

"Anything."

"Why didn't you tell me you had another job in Nashville?" Her blue eyes were somber.

Taking Emily's hand, he walked over to the sofa and sat down.

"I wasn't trying to hide it from you. It never came up, and I didn't think about it." He paused. "Wait. Is that why you don't want to take any money from me? Did you think I was barely scraping by on my music?"

"Well, I know it doesn't pay much when you're getting started." She shrugged. "But regardless, I don't like taking money from anyone. Still, you should have told me."

"You're right," he said. Then he laced his fingers through hers. "I've been thinking about something. In May, I'll have been in Nashville for two years. If I don't have a record deal by then, I think I might move closer to Coronado."

"What do you mean, closer?"

"There's no way for me to make a living in Coronado," he said. "Your granddad even suggested I start an HVAC company and run it out of his store. But a company like that would never make it here. And even if I was willing to be my brother's ranch hand, I don't think the ranch can support two families. But Springerville isn't that far away. What do you think? Could we compromise?"

Emily nodded. "Yes, Springerville is close enough for me to still be able to help Granddad. But as much as I would like for you to come back, I can't let you give up your dream. Not for me. Not even for Wyatt."

"That has been my dream." He lifted one hand and let his fingers play with one of her wayward curls. "But maybe it's time to have a new dream. I had another dream once, too. I dreamed of having a real family. That's one dream that I can control."

She reached up and cupped his cheek with her hand. "I'll support you no matter what you do, but if you give something up, make sure it's for the right reasons."

"Three more months." He clasped her hand and kissed her palm. "If nothing happens by May, then I can come home knowing that I gave it my all."

"Fine." She let out a deep sigh. "Three more months."

Luke glanced at his watch and stood up. He reached into his back pocket and pulled out an envelope. "Don't tell me you can't accept it, because I'm not giving you a choice."

Emily scowled. "I told you, I don't need your money."

"I don't care," he said. "Wyatt is my son, too. Whatever you don't use, put in a savings account for him, but please, take it."

"Fine." She accepted the envelope from him and dropped it in her purse.

Luke caught her eye and smiled. "I gotta go."

"I know."

"I'll call you every night." He kept hold of his son.

"I know you will."

His brown eyes searched hers. "And I'll be back in two weeks, I promise."

"Don't," she said. "Don't you dare make promises you may not be able to keep."

"But—"

"No. My dad promised me he would be home for my eighth birthday. He didn't make it. He never came home again. If this is going to work, we have to trust each other. I know you will do everything you can to be here, but you never know what might happen. So tell me you'll do your best to make it back for the weekend, but please don't make me any promises."

He nodded. "I will do everything I can to make it to you in two weeks."

"Thank you," she said and kissed him.

CHAPTER SEVENTEEN

THE NEXT TWO weeks crawled by. Even though Luke called every night, it wasn't the same. How had he become so ingrained in their lives in the two weeks he'd been here? Not even two whole weeks. She glanced at the calendar on the wall. May couldn't get here fast enough.

She tucked her phone into her back pocket. She doubted she would hear it ring over the loud music in the tavern, but she would most definitely feel it vibrate. Her last two phone calls with Luke had been cut short, so she didn't want to chance missing a phone call altogether.

Millie knocked on the door at exactly five thirty on Thursday. Emily could set a watch by her. She opened the door.

"Hi." Millie breezed inside. "Oh my goodness! He's walking!"

Emily laughed as Millie rushed over to pick Wyatt up and tickle him. "That's right. You haven't seen him in a couple of weeks."

Wyatt's fist got tangled in her bright red hair. Millie was the only person Emily knew who had curlier hair than she did. Emily kept hers short, but Millie's hair hung almost to her waist. Most of the time it was in a messy bun on top of her head, but occasionally, she wore it loose. Doing that while babysitting a soon-to-be-one-year-old was probably not the best idea.

"Thanks for coming tonight. I know I told you I

wouldn't need you on Thursdays anymore, but Colleen called this morning and said her husband wasn't feeling well."

"That's okay," Millie pressed a kiss to Wyatt's cheek. "I'm glad his grandma wants to be involved. But I'm going to miss him, so call me anytime you need backup."

"You know I will. How are things at the hospital?"

"Didn't I tell you?" Millie removed Wyatt's fingers from their death grip on her hair. "I quit."

"Why on earth would you do that?"

"One of the nurses I work with told me that the home health agency needed more nurses. A lot of their patients are in Coronado, and they don't have any nurses who want to travel this far."

Emily frowned. If someone needed an in-home caregiver, she would've heard about it at the hardware store. "Who would need home health here?"

"More people than you think. It's not just hospice patients or the elderly." Millie set Wyatt down by his toys. "Randon's dad is one of my patients."

Randon was Millie's brother's best friend. Emily always wondered why Millie and Randon had never dated. Randon was crazy about her.

"I heard that he had lung cancer," Emily said. "How's he doing? Has he stopped drinking?"

Millie shrugged. "The drinking will get him before his cancer does."

"I thought you really liked working at the hospital. And it pays so well, too." Emily shook her head. "I don't know why you don't just move to Springerville and work there full-time. They've offered you a job a dozen times."

Millie gave her a sharp look. "For the same reason you don't just pack up and move to Nashville."

"You've been talking to Stacy."

"You know how small towns are. You told Abbie. Abbie told Stacy. Stacy told me. And we all agree that you're an idiot."

Tactfulness was not one of Millie's better-known qualities. Emily sighed. "Part of me agrees. But I can't leave Granddad."

"I know." Millie squeezed her arm. "I can't leave my parents, either. Being there for them is more important than making money."

Millie's father was in the early stages of Alzheimer's, so her mother had her hands full. As the youngest of five children, and the only girl, Millie was close to her mother, but she'd always been a daddy's girl. It had to be hard to watch her father deteriorate. It was one of the reasons Millie became a nurse.

"I'm glad someone understands." Emily bent down to kiss Wyatt's head. "Go ahead and lock the door behind me. I have a key."

"Lock the door?" Millie's brow wrinkled, and she looked at the door. "It's about time you got a new lock."

"Luke installed it." She felt a rush of warmth every time she thought about it. No one had ever worried about her like that.

As she drove into the Watering Hole's parking lot, a black SUV pulled in behind her. The doors opened, and Emily groaned. She recognized Shane Nichols emerging from the vehicle. The Mogollon Hotshots must be in town for a training exercise. That meant it was going to be a long night.

While most of the members of the elite wildland firefighting crew were quiet, Shane was not. And the other crew members he brought with him to the tavern were usually just as rowdy as he was. One of these days, his loud mouth was going to get him into trouble. Emily sighed as she walked inside. At least they tipped well.

As expected, the men with Shane got louder with every beer. She wished Freddy would shut down the bar for the night and make them leave, but business had been slow, so as long as they weren't causing trouble and kept spending money, Freddy would let them stay.

"Expecting a call?" Freddy asked her when she pulled her phone out of her pocket and checked it. "You've done that at least three times in the last thirty minutes."

"Luke was supposed to call me back, but he hasn't." He had called around three o'clock that afternoon, but he had to get off when his agent called him on the other line.

Should she call him back? No. He said he would call back, and he would. He was probably really busy. That was okay. He would be there tomorrow night. She probably wouldn't see him until Saturday morning since he wouldn't get to town until really late, but she would sleep better just knowing they were in the same state.

A loud commotion came from Shane's table, so she hurried over to see what had happened. One of the guys had knocked over an entire pitcher of beer. Not because the man had had too much to drink, they told her about five times, but because he was telling a story and he liked to use his hands when he talked. *Yeah, right.*

Emily wiped the table down and went to get the mop bucket. There was so much noise and chaos that she never heard or felt her phone ring. She frowned at the text message.

You didn't answer, so you're probably busy at work. Hope you have a good night.

Luke didn't ask her to call him after work. Last weekend, he had asked her to, despite it being after 2:00 a.m.

in Tennessee. Maybe he was really tired. Or maybe he'd already started losing interest in her.

THE FIRST THING Luke did when he woke up that morning was to check his messages. Nothing. Why didn't Emily call him back? Maybe she was mad because he had to cut their phone conversation short twice this week. It couldn't be helped. His agent, Kirby, had never called him as much as he had this week. There was a showcase coming to town that needed opening acts, so Kirby had arranged for him to audition.

If she was mad that his phone calls were cut short, she really wouldn't be happy when she found out he wasn't going to make it to Coronado until Saturday.

No. She might not be happy about it, but she wouldn't be mad at him. He had worked too hard to let any opportunity pass him by. Emily understood that. Or at least, he hoped she did.

He opened his messaging app and saw the last message he'd entered:

Call me when you get off work.

Only he'd forgotten to hit Send. He scrubbed his face with his hands. How had he not sent the message? He already knew the answer. He'd fallen asleep.

There were so many new song ideas floating around in his head that he couldn't sleep until he'd written them all down. He was so excited to be writing songs again that he'd stayed up much later than normal.

Jay was glad to have him back at work, but work had been slower than normal. He had gotten off work by three o'clock every afternoon, which gave him plenty of time for the additional auditions Kirby sent him on.

Luke had never minded coming home to an empty apartment before, but now the silence was deafening. One good thing about spending so much time alone was that he had ample opportunity to work on his new songs. In all the months he had lived in Nashville, he hadn't written one new thing. In the last two weeks, he'd written two new songs and started on another.

Of course, Kirby was thrilled to hear that his dry spell was over. But it wasn't because he had finally adjusted to life in Nashville; it was because of Emily and Wyatt. They inspired him in a way he hadn't felt in a long time.

It was still too early in Arizona to call Emily, so he sent her a text instead.

Good morning. Sorry I missed you last night. Did you have a good night?

Almost immediately, his phone rang. "Good morning," he said.

"I'm sorry," she said.

He wanted her to be sorry. But he felt bad for wanting that. "That's okay. You must have had a busy night."

"Yes," Emily said. "One of the hotshot crews was in town for a training exercise, so the tavern was full, and they stayed late."

Luke frowned. "It wasn't Shane's crew, was it?"

He didn't like Shane. Not only was the young man full of himself, he didn't know how to take no for an answer. Freddy had threatened to kick him out of the tavern for harassing the waitresses more than once.

"Yes. But he was actually pretty decent last night. They brought some rookies with them, and those guys made Shane look like a choirboy."

His chest grew tight. There was nothing he could do

about that from where he was. He knew Emily could take care of herself, and he knew Freddy would never allow anything to happen to her. But the thought of someone else bothering her was almost more than he could bear.

"What time does your plane land tonight?"

"About that." Luke took a deep breath. "I guess it's a good thing you wouldn't let me promise. I won't be there until tomorrow."

"Oh. Is everything okay?"

"I guess that depends on how you want to look at it. I got a callback for a showcase I auditioned for, and my agent arranged for a record producer to come listen."

"That's great! I'm not sure what the downside of that is supposed to be."

He bit his bottom lip. Here was the part she might not like. "If I make it into the showcase, I'll be performing most of the summer."

"Oh." She was quiet for a moment. "Every day?"

"No. Just the weekends. I could fly down during the week." That would mean missing some rehearsals, which would probably be frowned upon.

What was he thinking? He didn't even have the job yet.

"I was thinking that Wyatt and I could fly up there sometimes, too," Emily said.

Luke's chest swelled. "You would do that?"

She sighed. "I think we have to address how we're going to juggle this, because I don't think you're going to move here in May. Actually, I forbid it."

"You forbid it?" He raised his eyebrows and laughed, imagining her facial expression when she said those words. "I don't think you can do that."

"Too late," she said. "I already did. Tell me more about the producers coming to hear you play."

Luke couldn't help but get excited thinking about it.

"It's a pretty big deal, I guess. Kirby says he's only done it for two other artists in the past."

"And how did it work out for them?" Emily asked.

"They both sold platinum records."

"That's awesome! We'll have to celebrate. So what time will you be here Saturday?"

"I have good news and bad news," he said. "The bad news is that I won't be there until past Wyatt's bedtime."

Her response was soft. "Oh. What's the good news?"

"The good news is that I'm staying for the whole week. I don't want to miss Wyatt's first birthday."

"That is good news." The warmth returned to her voice.

"Have you heard back from your lender yet?"

"Yes," she said. "They want an estimate of what the repairs will cost before they can give me an answer."

"Why?"

"Because that would determine what kind of loan I'll need." Frustration laced her voice. "I know it needs a lot of work, but it has so much potential. What if it needs so much work that I can't qualify for a loan?"

"When do you have to have a repair estimate turned in?"

"Yesterday," she grumbled. "They said it doesn't have to be an official estimate and for me to give them a ballpark figure, but I wouldn't even know where to begin."

He laughed. "Have you asked your grandfather?"

"My grandfather?" There was a pause on the line before Emily let out a gasp. "My grandfather! He does home repair estimates for customers all the time! Why didn't I think of that?"

Luke walked over to the counter in his kitchen and picked up a pencil to take notes. "Maybe the owner will finance it himself? Have you talked to him about carrying the loan?"

"No," she said. "I didn't think about that. He would probably charge a really high interest rate, don't you think?"

"Maybe, maybe not." He wrote on a piece of paper, *Call Justin Long.* "You said it needs a lot of work, so maybe he'll carry the loan while you make enough repairs for it to qualify for a traditional loan."

Emily sighed. "And in the meantime, I'll use all my savings on house repairs and not have enough for the down payment required by the bank."

Luke laughed. "Since when did you become such a negative Nellie?"

"Since I fell for a musician."

He couldn't help but smile. That was the closest she'd come to admitting that she had feelings for him, too.

CHAPTER EIGHTEEN

THE PINE TREES were nothing more than dark shadows by the time Luke got to Coronado on Saturday night. He knew Wyatt would be in bed. He'd hoped to get to Emily's house before she went to sleep, but it seemed like everything was conspiring against him.

First, there was a mechanical issue with the plane, and they sat on the tarmac for almost two hours. Then it took them over an hour to find the rental SUV he'd reserved. He could've gotten a sedan, but the chances of a two-wheel drive being able to make it to the ranch weren't great.

It was almost eleven o'clock when he pulled up in front of Emily's house. The porch light was on, but her car wasn't there. For a split second, he worried that something was wrong. Then he realized that Emily was at the tavern. The car parked in front of her house was probably her aunt Tricia's. He thought about knocking on the door and peeking in on Wyatt, but he decided against it.

What he should do was go to the ranch and get a good night's sleep before coming back in the morning. He kept telling himself that as he drove to the Watering Hole and parked next to Emily's car.

There were more cars than usual in the parking lot. Loud music flowed out of the bar. Luke recognized the music and searched the parking lot until he saw Dan Tippetts's pickup. He got out of the SUV and went inside.

The dance floor was crowded, always a good sign for

the band. He stood next to the bar and scanned the crowd looking for Emily.

"What can I get you?" a tall woman asked from behind the bar.

He recognized the woman but couldn't remember her name. "Just a soda."

When she handed him the drink he dropped a couple of dollars on the counter as a tip. He turned around and leaned against the bar while he continued to look for Emily. He finally spotted her delivering drinks to a table in the corner. Her wild curls added to her unconventional beauty. She smiled and chatted with the customers but never lingered at a table long enough to encourage too much conversation.

Her blue eyes turned toward the bar, and she saw him. A giant smile spread across her face, and she hurried over.

He met her halfway. Without thinking, he pulled her into his arms and kissed her. Emily kissed him back. She tasted of spearmint gum and strawberry lip gloss. Nothing had ever tasted so good.

"Why, Emily Beck," the tall woman commented, "you've been keeping a secret from us."

Emily's face turned bright red, but she kept her arms wrapped around Luke's waist. "Caroline, this is Luke Sterling."

Caroline. Luke remembered. He had seen her handle a rowdy customer with ease a few weeks ago. He reached out and offered his hand. "It's nice to meet you officially."

She smiled and shook his hand. "I've heard a lot about you. You're kind of a legend in these parts."

Luke laughed. "Don't believe everything you hear."

The grip of her hand on his got firmer, and her eyes glinted like onyx stones. Her face grew colder, and she pulled him closer to her. "Just so you know, I don't care how much people around here like you. If you hurt Emily, I'll hurt you."

He returned her grip and looked her in the eye. "I would never do that, but I appreciate that you're looking out for her."

The woman's face broke out in a smile. "Good."

"Sorry about that," Emily said as they moved away from the bar.

"I meant what I said. I'm glad she's looking out for you. What time do you get off?"

She scanned the tavern and gave him a sheepish grin. "Probably not until closing time."

"Do you mind if I hang out for a while?" He didn't want her to think that he was there to spy on her or anything. He just missed seeing her.

She smiled at him. "I would like that, but we're pretty busy. I may not be able to chat much."

"That's okay," Luke said.

He went to find a table to sit down at, and Emily went back to work. He chose a small table in the far corner.

"Hey, mister," a man at the next table said as he leaned toward him. "Just so you know, she has a kid."

"I know," Luke said. "It's my kid."

The man nodded with wide eyes and turned back to his own table.

Luke leaned back in his chair and watched the band, though he knew where Emily was at all times. Dan caught his eye and waved him over.

"Want to play something for us?" Dan asked him. "I could use a break."

Luke nodded. "I actually have a new song I would love to try out."

It was the song he'd played yesterday at the showcase audition. While Kirby assured him that the small group of people he played for had liked the song, the best way to gauge a song was to play it for a crowd.

Dan introduced him and handed him a guitar.

"I'd like to play a new song for you tonight if y'all don't mind." Luke strummed a few chords on the guitar. "This is about being lost until you find what you didn't know you were looking for. Emily, this one's for you."

The crowd cheered, and he took a deep breath. A hush fell over the bar when he began to sing. He always loved being onstage, but a feeling of euphoria overcame him that he'd never felt before. When he looked up to see the reaction of the crowd, he could tell that they were feeling it, too. A few couples leaned into each other. A few more swayed on the dance floor. He knew the song was a winner.

He scanned the crowd, looking for the one person whose reaction mattered the most. Emily was leaning against the bar, one hand covering her mouth. Even from across the crowded room, he could see that her eyes glistened with tears.

After the last note died, the crowd roared. He took off the guitar, and Emily practically ran across the floor, jumping into his arms right there onstage. He kissed her with everything he had, and the crowd cheered even louder.

"That was the most beautiful thing I ever heard," she whispered in his ear.

He cupped her face. "Not as beautiful as you."

"More! More! More!" the crowd chanted.

"You better give them what they want, Music Man," Emily said breathlessly. "Or else they might tear the place down."

He played three more songs and then handed the guitar back to Dan.

"How am I supposed to follow that?" Dan asked, laughing. "You're sounding better than ever."

"Thanks." He shook Dan's hand, then the hands of the rest of the band members before returning to the small table in the corner.

Caroline approached him with a beer. She set it down in front of him. "I hope you're thirsty. Practically every table here has bought you a beer."

Luke frowned. Rule number one for musicians was don't disappoint the fans.

He looked around to see several patrons watching him anxiously with their glasses raised. The first drink would be easy to fake. But what about the rest? His heart rate rose slightly.

He'd seen a singer turn down drinks bought by the customers once. They turned on him almost immediately, accusing the guy of thinking he was better than them and creating a scene.

Caroline leaned closer to him and whispered, "It's nonalcoholic."

His chest deflated like a balloon, and he relaxed. "How did you know?"

She nodded across the room to Emily. "Don't worry. We got your back."

He held up the mug and nodded at the table watching him. When he took a long sip, they cheered, but then turned back to their conversations.

Emily stopped by the table a minute later to give him a glass of water. "To help wash down that beer."

"Thanks." He leaned back in his chair, content to watch her work.

Her face was flushed, probably because she never slowed down for a second. She buzzed between tables like a bee in a field of flowers. If she wasn't delivering drinks, she was cleaning tables.

The bass player in Dan's band said something to her as

she walked by, and she laughed. Luke's eyes narrowed. What had the man said? And since when was he the jealous type?

As the night wore on, Emily seemed to lose some of her sparkle. A couple of times, he caught her looking in his direction with a sad expression on her face. Something was bothering her.

Freddy rang a large bell hanging over the bar, and people at the neighboring table groaned.

Emily stopped by their table. "You heard the bell. Last call. What'll you have?"

An hour later, the last patron had been ushered out, the band had left, and Caroline and Emily started cleaning up.

Luke trailed behind them. As soon as a table had been wiped down, he picked up the chair and put it upside down on top of the table.

"Someone trained you well," Caroline commented.

"He used to help me clean up before he ran off to Nashville to get famous," Emily joked.

Caroline shook her head. "Well, if Nashville doesn't want you, you got a job here."

Before Luke could think of something clever to say, Emily spoke up. "I don't think we're going to have to worry about that."

That was when it struck him. She knew he was going to stay in Nashville. Wait. She *knew.* He hadn't made a decision yet. He had until May to do that. Or had he already made up his mind?

DESPITE THE HEAT inside the bar, Emily was chilled. Her chest felt like a truck was parked on top of it, and she couldn't seem to catch her breath. Earlier today, she couldn't wait to see Luke again. Now she dreaded going home because she knew he would be there. And she knew she had to let him go. She trudged to the cleaning closet to get the broom.

Caroline stopped her. "I got this tonight, honey." She jerked her head toward Luke. "I think you've got bigger plans tonight."

"That's okay. It's my turn to close up," Emily said.

Caroline snatched the broom from her hand. "I insist. You can do it next time."

Emily looked at the door to see Luke waiting for her. She glanced at the back. No. She wasn't going to sneak out the back exit like a coward. She took a deep breath, thanked Caroline and walked toward the door.

Luke held the door open for her and took her hand as he walked her to her car. "What's wrong?"

"Nothing." She dug her keys out of her purse and turned to face him. "Wyatt is already in bed, and I'm really tired. I'll see you in the morning?"

He winced as though she had kicked him. "Yeah. Sure. See you in the morning."

Emily watched him got into his rented SUV and drove away. She knew she had hurt his feelings, and he was probably confused. Especially after the way she kissed him earlier. She couldn't help herself. The song was so beautiful it had swept her away in a tidal wave of emotion.

Everyone in the bar had told her how lucky she was to have Luke in her life. Some of the women asked what her secret was. Others wanted to know where they could find a musician like him. The more they gushed over the song and Luke, the worse she felt.

Standing up on that stage, it was obvious Luke was born to perform. And he was willing to give it all up for her and Wyatt. Their deal was that he would wait until May to give up on his dream and come back home. But contract or not, she couldn't let him walk away, no matter what it cost her.

When she unlocked the door and let herself in the house, Tricia sat up on the sofa.

Her aunt could tell immediately that something was wrong. "What happened?"

Emily sank down on the couch and leaned her head on Tricia's shoulder. She didn't want to get into the whole story. Tricia would tell her to stop making mountains out of molehills and let Luke make his own decisions. But Tricia had never heard him sing. She didn't know how he could mesmerize an entire bar with his songs and his voice.

"What is it, baby?" Tricia rubbed her back.

"I don't think things are going to work out with Luke after all," she said.

"Don't give up on him yet. I have a feeling he may surprise you." She stood up and got her purse. "I promised Evan I would come home tonight. It's his anniversary tomorrow, and I'm taking the kids for the day. Are you sure you're okay?"

"I'm fine," Emily said. "Or at least I will be. Tell my cousin I said hello."

After checking on Wyatt, she climbed into bed to cry herself to sleep.

Her phone buzzed, and she picked it up from the nightstand next to her bed.

What's wrong? What did I do? Talk to me.

She sighed. How could she tell him she was mad because he deserved to have his dreams come true?

It's nothing. I'm sorry. We'll talk tomorrow.

Before he could respond, she turned her phone off. She couldn't help but feel cheated. She had been in love with

Luke from the first day she saw him. Their friendship had grown, and now that they had a chance for a future together, she was going to give it up.

But there was no way she could let him choose between them and his music career. She knew, without a doubt, he would pick his son. If the choice was just between her and Nashville, she wasn't sure what his decision would be. Either way, it didn't matter. She wasn't going to let him choose at all.

He could still be Wyatt's father even from Nashville. For a while, they could go through the motions of a long-distance relationship. Sooner or later, though, it would come down around them. It would hurt a lot less if she just bit the bullet.

WYATT WOKE HER UP, ready to play. If he hadn't, she wouldn't have even gotten out of bed. All she wanted to do was curl up in a ball and wallow in her own misery. She lifted Wyatt out of the crib and changed his diaper. Then she trudged into the living room.

She happened to glance out the window and froze. A white SUV was parked in front of her house next to her car. She moved back the curtain for a better look. Sure enough, Luke was sitting in the front seat of the vehicle. She opened the door and waved at him.

He jumped out of the car and walked up the snowy path to the front door. He stopped in front of her. "Whatever I said or did to you last night, I'm sorry."

"It wasn't you." She held the door open for him.

When Wyatt saw him, he broke out into a huge grin and toddled his way over.

"Wow! Look how well he's walking!" Luke picked up his son and hugged him. "Do you think he remembers me?"

She nodded. "I don't think he would have rushed over here if he didn't remember you."

"I missed you so much." He pressed his cheek to Wyatt's. His brown eyes found hers. "You, too."

Her resolve to stay tough crumbled. "I missed you, too," she admitted.

"Do you want to tell me what's really bothering you?" He gave her a pointed stare. "You seemed happy to see me last night. At least at first." He cocked his head and raised one eyebrow. "Didn't you like my song?"

He was teasing. If nothing else, the kiss she'd given him onstage in front of the whole bar told him she did.

"I loved it," she said. A lump formed in her throat, but she swallowed it. She had to say it before she chickened out. "I was right. You belong on that stage. You belong in front of people, singing your songs. You'll have a contract before May, I'm sure of it."

He licked his lips and crossed his arms. "So you're upset with me for something I haven't done yet?"

She let out a half giggle, half sob. "I know it sounds crazy."

"Yes, it does." He took her face in his hands. "Let's not worry about that now. Can we just enjoy the time we have?"

She blinked the tears away. "Of course."

She couldn't, though. She would go through the motions and pretend, but in the back of her mind she knew he belonged in Nashville. As long as she kept that in mind, she would survive the week.

CHAPTER NINETEEN

LUKE PLAYED WITH Wyatt on the floor while Emily cooked breakfast. While things were more relaxed, an undercurrent of tension was still there. Both of them avoided talking about the future. Luke suspected Emily was having doubts that things could work out between them. And honestly, so was he. Music was part of him, and he was fooling himself if he thought he could give that up. Turned out, Emily knew it all along.

He played onstage all the time in Nashville. So why was last night different?

He glanced at Emily, who was humming in the kitchen.

Her. Last night was different because he was playing for her. He wasn't worried about a record producer watching him in the crowd. Or if the bar owner was going to invite him back to play again. He played for her.

He groaned inwardly. What was he supposed to do with that? He couldn't have her if he wanted a music career. But he couldn't have a music career without her.

Is that what happened with Coy and Becky? He had never met two people more suited for each other, but they broke up because of Coy's dream. He sighed. Did that mean any chance of having a relationship with Emily was doomed?

She caught him staring at her. "I'm not hungry yet, and neither is Wyatt. There's still a lot of snow on the ground. Let's build him a snowman."

"Should he be outside?" Luke asked. "The last time we played outside with him, he got sick."

Emily nodded. "I don't think that's why he got sick, but he's fine now. I think it'll be okay. Besides, I need to get out of the house."

Luke couldn't agree more. He jumped up and grabbed Wyatt's jacket. As soon as Emily had him all bundled up, they went outside.

The snow in the front yard had been trampled down, but on the side of the house it was still soft and fluffy. While Luke packed some snow in his hand, Emily made a snow angel.

Wyatt plopped on the ground and tried to imitate her.

Luke had added enough snow to the ball in his hand that he needed two hands to hold it. He put it on the ground and rolled it to pick up more snow. Wyatt noticed what he was doing and toddled over to him.

Together, they pushed the ball around the yard until it was almost the same size as Wyatt. Luke picked him up and stood him on top of the giant snowball. Wyatt squealed and stomped it.

Emily rolled her own snowball over to him. Luke set Wyatt on the ground and picked hers up, placing it on top of his. It didn't take long to make one more, smaller, snowball.

The snowman was almost as tall as Emily. She ran inside to get some things to decorate the snowman with.

"Here." She appeared with a plastic shopping bag full of items.

Strawberries were used for the eyes. A carrot for his nose and blueberries for his mouth.

"Couldn't you find any nonfood items for him?" Luke poked a stick into the snowman for an arm. "I'm afraid a bird or a squirrel will run off with his face."

Emily shrugged. "These were about to go bad anyway. Might as well feed the animals with them."

"What do you think?" Luke picked Wyatt up so he could see.

Wyatt tried to take the strawberry from the snowman.

"He's probably getting hungry," Emily said.

They came back inside, and Luke put Wyatt in his high chair. After Emily set his food in front of him, she pulled a folded piece of paper out of her purse and handed it to Luke.

"What's this?" He stared at the list of names and phone numbers.

"I promised Granddad I would give this to you. They're all people who want you to fix the furnace at their house."

He stared at the list. "All these people? I didn't know there were this many people in town."

"Oh yes," Emily said. "Probably more. Grandad can't seem to stop telling everyone how great you are."

He folded the paper in half. Was this her grandfather's way of trying to convince him to stay in Coronado and open an HVAC company?

"I'll talk to him tomorrow and see who needs it the most," Luke said. "I don't mind helping, but I'm here to see you and Wyatt. I don't want anything to interfere with that."

"I'm sure Granddad will appreciate that." She got a worried look on her face. "I hope he doesn't put too much pressure on you to open a business out of his store."

He tucked the list of phone numbers in his pocket. It was a crazy idea. An idea he wished he could entertain, but while the list was long now, he knew it wasn't sustainable. There just weren't enough people in Coronado to keep a business like that afloat. At best, it would be a part-time job.

The rest of the morning went smoothly, and soon Wyatt was rubbing his eyes. Emily went to put him down for a nap, so Luke drove over to the Coronado Market to get some snacks to eat while they watched a movie.

Coy's truck was parked outside. Luke frowned. Was Coy still in town? Or was he back? He walked into the store and saw Coy standing behind the counter.

"Are you working here now?" he asked, half-joking.

"No. I just stopped by on my way out of town to buy an energy drink for the road." Coy's expression was tight. "While I was here, Millie came in, very upset, and Stacy asked me to watch the front for her. They're in the back now."

Luke frowned. "Any idea what happened?"

Coy shook his head. "What are you still doing in town? Don't you need to get back to Nashville?"

"I just got in last night. I'm here for the week. Wyatt's birthday is Wednesday."

"Becky's birthday is next week." Coy's eyes held a far-off look. "I think it's great that you and Emily are working things out. At least she supports you."

Noah's eyes narrowed. "Becky always supported you, too."

Coy shook his head. "I thought so…until she gave me an ultimatum. Now I'm footloose and fancy-free."

He didn't look it. He looked like he'd lost his best friend, which in reality was true. Becky had been his other half for so long that Coy probably didn't know how to function without her. Noah wondered how Becky was faring.

Coy glanced to the door that led from the store to Stacy's apartment. "I guess she's not coming right back. What did you need?"

Luke selected a couple bags of chips and some beef

jerky and checked out. On the drive back to Emily's, he thought about Coy and Becky.

Becky had always supported Coy's dream to be a professional bull rider, so what changed? If Luke and Emily pursued a relationship like he wanted, would there come a time when Emily would stop supporting him, too? Would she end up giving him an ultimatum?

When he walked back into the trailer, Emily was sitting on the sofa, her legs curled up underneath her and tears in her eyes. She was on the phone, so Luke went into the kitchen and poured two bowls of chips, then grabbed a couple of sodas from the fridge, not wanting to interrupt.

When he walked back into the living room, Emily disconnected the call.

"What's going on?"

Emily let out a sigh. "Do you remember Randon Farr and Brian Gibson?"

"Yeah. Millie's brother and his best friend." Both of the boys had joined the military a couple of years ago. The air in his chest froze. "Did something happen to them?"

She nodded. "They were ambushed while on a mission."

"Oh no. Are they..." He couldn't even bring himself to say the word.

"They're alive," she said, "but they're both badly injured. Randon is the worst off. Apparently, he pushed Brian out of the way and shielded him."

"Why doesn't that surprise me? Randon was always watching out for Brian." Both men were a couple of years younger than him. "Man, I hope they're going to be okay."

Emily nodded and took one of the bowls of chips from him. "Let's just watch the movie and forget about everything else for a while."

Luke agreed. He needed to do something mindless for a while. The movie started, but he found he couldn't focus. He kept thinking about Coy and Becky, and Randon and Brian.

Randon had been in love with Millie since grade school. He never acted on his feelings, though. Now it might be too late.

He glanced at Emily, who was staring at the television screen. Was he like Randon? He'd known Emily for ten years. He'd been half in love with her for most of that time but would never have admitted it to anyone, even himself.

Didn't they owe it to each other to try to make things work? Not just for Wyatt's sake, but for their own?

His phone rang, and he declined the call without even looking at the screen. It was probably his brother, wanting to know what time he would be home. A few minutes later, the phone rang again.

"Aren't you going to answer that?" Emily asked.

This time he looked at the screen. "It's my agent. What could he want?"

Emily sat up and moved away.

"Hello."

Kirby immediately started talking, and Luke could hardly keep up.

"What's going on?" she asked when he hung up the call.

He stared at her with disbelief. "I think I'm in shock."

"Why?"

"First of all, I didn't make it into the showcase. They liked my music, but I guess they didn't like me."

Emily touched his hand. "I'm so sorry. I know you were really hoping for that."

"I have to fly back to Nashville, right now." His voice shook.

Confusion clouded her blue eyes. "But you…but you said you didn't get the spot."

"Not in the showcase, no. But remember the record producer who came to watch the audition? He loved my songs and took them back to some of his artists." Luke stopped talking and tried to gather his thoughts. "One of the top artists in the country wants to record 'Emily's Song.'"

"That's good, right?"

He nodded. "The only problem is he's very picky and refuses to record a song before he meets the songwriter. He's sending his private jet to Phoenix to pick me up."

"Right now? Can't he meet you next week?"

Luke's breath caught in his chest. "Right now. He's under contract to have the album cut by the end of the week. He's planning to record the song on Wednesday."

"Wednesday is Wyatt's birthday."

"I know," he said. "That's why I said I would go today."

Emily squeezed him tight. "Congratulations! I knew you could do it!"

"A contract." He shook his head. "I still can't believe that he wants to buy the exclusive rights to my song."

"I can." Emily took a deep breath. "Your music is fantastic. Soon, the whole world will know it."

The joy subsided as he realized what this meant. A steel band seemed to wrap itself around his chest, and he suddenly had to fight for air. "I guess this means I'm not leaving Nashville."

Didn't he all but make that decision last night? Somehow, saying it out loud made it official.

"Isn't that what I've been trying to tell you?" she said.

Luke cupped her face with his hands. "This doesn't change anything. I'll fly down there, meet the guy and be back in time for Wyatt's birthday. I promise."

"What did I tell you about promises?" Tears glistened in the corners of her eyes.

He kissed her gently. "I promise."

Excitement warred with sadness as he gathered his

things. Emily walked him to his SUV, but his shoulders got more tense with every step. He was about to get everything he ever wanted. So why did he feel like he was losing what he needed most?

THE NEXT MORNING, Emily went through the motions of getting ready for work and pretending that everything was okay. The other night, while listening to Luke sing, she knew she was going to lose him. He was too good to give up his dream. Finally, someone in Nashville had realized that, too.

She had survived without Luke Sterling in her life for over a year. She had been just fine without him, and she would be fine again. The first time he left, she got Wyatt out of the deal. At least this time, Wyatt got his father in his life. It made up for the giant hole in her heart.

By lunchtime, her grandfather knew something was up.

Concern was written across his weathered face. "What's going on? Is Luke coming by the store today?"

Her cell phone rang, and she glanced at the screen. It was her Realtor. "Hi, Meghan. What's up?"

A few minutes later, she hung up the phone. She turned to her grandfather. "Do you want to close the store for a little while and go for a ride with me?"

"Where to?"

"I went and looked at a house recently. It's a fixer-upper so the bank won't approve a traditional loan on it, and the lender wants an estimate of what it will cost to repair it. Luke wants me to ask the owner if he's willing to finance it himself. But he's already knocking some money off the asking price to make repairs, so I don't know if he's willing to do that. I'd appreciate it if you would come look at it and tell me what you think the repairs will cost."

Granddad grinned. "I'd better grab my price books. They'll help us determine the cost of supplies."

It had been a while since Emily had seen her granddad excited about much. By the time she grabbed Wyatt and all his stuff and walked out to the car, Granddad had gathered a big stack of books to take with them.

They spent the rest of the morning walking through the house. Grandad checked every wall and support beam. Every so often, he stopped to take notes or to look something up in one of the books he carried around.

Meghan waited patiently for Granddad to finish in one room before moving on to the next.

"Do you think the owner is willing to finance?" Emily asked Meghan.

"It's funny that you ask that," Meghan said, tossing her long dark curls. "I just spoke with him this morning, and he said he'd be willing to carry the loan if necessary."

Emily couldn't help but be a little suspicious. "Isn't that unusual? Especially in Coronado? I mean, any investor from Phoenix would pay more than his asking price. And he wouldn't have to wait on the money."

Megan nodded. "Normally, you would be right. However, the owner doesn't want this to be a vacation home. He wants it to be a family home, and he knows that in order to do that, he's going to have to make some accommodations."

"What do you think, Granddad?"

Granddad slapped the wall closest to him. "It's a solid house. Most of the repairs are minor. The roof leaks—that's the biggest thing. The floors need to be redone, and a little paint wouldn't hurt, either, but overall I think it's a good deal."

"I do, too." She turned to Meghan. "How long will it

take to draw up the paperwork? If my lender doesn't work out, how much of a down payment does the owner want?"

Meghan opened up her folder to review her notes. "I believe he was asking for twenty percent."

"Twenty?" Emily's heart dropped. "I was hoping for ten. I might be able to swing fifteen."

But not twenty. There was no way she could come up with that much money.

"She'll take it," her grandfather said.

"Didn't you hear what I said? I don't have that much money."

"You don't, but I do."

"Granddad, I can't take your money." She would rather accept money from Luke than take money from her grandfather.

"I'm old," he joked. "What else am I going to do with it? Besides, I'm not doing this for you. I'm doing it for my great-grandson."

"I still can't let you do that."

Granddad shook Meghan's hand. "You draw up the paperwork, and I'll take care of this one's stubbornness."

Meghan laughed. "Yes, sir. I'll have it ready in the next couple of days, Mr. Morgan."

Emily rolled her eyes, but she didn't want to continue arguing with Granddad in front of Meghan. It was important to her that she did this on her own, though.

Wyatt fell asleep on the way back to the hardware store, so as soon as they got there, she went to lay him in his crib. When she came out of the nursery, Granddad patted the stool next to him.

"Sit down. We're going to talk."

She groaned. "Not another come-to-Jesus meeting."

He nodded. "Luke came down this week for Wyatt's

birthday. Why isn't he helping you make this decision? Where is he?"

She pressed her lips together to keep them from quivering. "This is my house, not Luke's. He had to go back to Nashville."

His brows drew together. "He just got here! Why did he have to go back already?"

She pasted on a bright smile, not wanting Granddad to know there was anything wrong. "He sold one of his songs to Matt Spencer."

"The country singer?" Granddad's mouth fell open in disbelief. "He knows Matt Spencer?"

Emily nodded. "He does now. Matt wanted to meet him, so he sent his own personal plane to pick him up."

"When's he coming back?" Granddad said. "Will he be back in time for Wyatt's birthday?"

Her throat tightened, and she pushed the lump back down. "He said he would be."

"Then he'll be back." Granddad seemed sure. "I've seen the way he looks at you and Wyatt. You're his family. He'll be back."

A tear trickled down one cheek, and she quickly wiped it away. "I'm sure he'll be back for Wyatt's birthday. But he'll probably have to go back right after that. He got a contract for his music. All kinds of doors will open up for him now."

"Is that what's bothering you?" He pulled a chair up and sat down next to her. "You wanted him to crash and burn so he would have to come back to Coronado?"

"I didn't want him to fail," she said. She bit her bottom lip. Maybe she did. No, even subconsciously, she hadn't wanted that. She sighed. "I just wanted him to want to be with us more than he wanted to be in Nashville."

Her grandfather gave her a long look. "How do you know he doesn't?"

"He's not here now, is he?" She couldn't keep the sarcasm from her voice. "I'm in a no-win situation, Granddad. I don't want us to be his second choice, but I also don't want him to give up his dream for us."

Grandpa laughed and shook his head. "You realize you make absolutely no sense."

"I know." She scrubbed her face with her hands. "What am I supposed to do?"

"Do you love him?"

She took a deep breath and held it. "I do."

"Let me ask you another question. And I want you to tell me the truth. Has he asked you to move to Nashville with him?"

Her throat felt so thick she could barely swallow, so she just nodded.

"You told him no, didn't you? Because of me."

Again, she nodded her head.

"Why?"

"Because I made a promise to Grandma."

The frown lines on his face deepened. "I think you'd better explain that. Start at the beginning."

She shrugged. "You already know Grandma encouraged me to enroll in bookkeeping classes at the junior college in Springerville while I was still in high school. She did that because she thought I might want to take over the business someday."

It made her heart ache to talk about her grandmother. When Emily came to Coronado, she was a bitter, angry teenage girl who took her frustration out on everyone around her. It was her grandmother who taught her the real meaning of family and love.

"When she got cancer, she told me she wasn't afraid

of dying, but she was afraid of leaving you alone. She knew my mom would never be around, and Aunt Tricia's husband was going through cancer treatment at the time, too, so she made me promise that I would always be here for you."

Granddad sniffed. "That's why you came back to Coronado when you graduated? Even though I sent you away just like your mom did?"

Emily nodded. "You sent everyone away, not just me. You had a reason—you were grieving. My mom sent me away because I was a nuisance to her."

Granddad squeeze her hand. "Can you ever forgive me?"

She hugged his neck. "I forgave you the moment the words came out of your mouth."

"You know," he said, "you can live in Nashville and still be there for me."

She shook her head. "I'm not okay with being that far away from you."

"Just promise me something," he said. "Don't give up your happiness for a grumpy old man like me."

CHAPTER TWENTY

LUKE WAS IN awe of the recording studio inside Matt Spencer's home. The live booth was big enough for an entire band, and the control room had a state-of-the-art mixing console with more buttons than Luke had ever seen. Gold records decorated one wall, and pictures of music legends decorated the other.

Matt Spencer, the Grammy award–winning singer, walked over to greet him. "You must be Luke."

Adrenaline shot through him. "Yes, sir. It's an honor to meet you, Mr. Spencer."

He laughed. "Call me Matt. Thank you for coming on such short notice. I'm sure Kirby told you we're in a time crunch."

"He did. He said you need to finish cutting the album this week."

Matt nodded. "I'm due in London on Monday morning, so I have to get this finished up by the end of the week. I'm pretty picky about the songs I record, and I have to tell you, this one really spoke to me, man."

Luke's chest swelled. "Thank you. The song means a lot to me, too."

Matt led him to a leather sofa outside the studio and motioned for him to sit down. "So why sell it to me? Why don't you record it yourself?"

Luke rubbed his hands on the legs of his jeans. "I'd be

lying if I told you that I didn't think about it. But I love 'Emily's Song,' and I want it to have the best singer available."

"You don't aspire to be a singer?" Matt handed him a water bottle before sitting across from him.

Luke smiled. "I guess I wouldn't be in Nashville if I didn't. But I've discovered I'm a lot better at writing songs than singing them."

Matt nodded. "We all have one thing we're better at. I envy your ability to put words together. I can't do that." He jerked his head toward the sound booth. "See that dude with the long blond hair?"

"Yes."

"He came to Nashville to be a singer, only he can't sing. But he can play the guitar better than anyone I've ever heard." Matt grinned. "You gotta find what speaks to you and stick with it."

"I'll remember that."

"I have an ulterior motive for telling you that story." Matt leaned back.

Luke opened the water bottle and took a drink. "Which is?"

"I like your music. Your songs have something in them I haven't heard in a while." Matt opened a folder that was on the coffee table.

Luke found himself looking at a list of all of his songs. More than half were highlighted.

"I want to buy these songs, too. I don't know when I'll record them, but I want them."

Excitement welled up in Luke's chest. He thought he was coming here to sell one song; he never dreamed it would turn into something more.

"I have a condition, though. And this is why I wanted to meet you in person."

The seriousness of Matt's tone tamped down Luke's

spirits. He'd heard horror stories of songwriters who were forced to sign exclusive contracts with a singer, making it impossible for them to work with anyone else. For some, it turned out fine. But for others, it was a career death sentence, stifling their ability to work in Nashville.

"What is it?"

"Don't look so scared." Matt laughed. "I want first dibs on the next ten songs you write."

Luke relaxed. "So, you want the chance to buy my songs before anyone else."

"Exactly." Matt leaned forward, his face serious. "That means you, too. You can't record a song until I have a chance to hear it."

Luke thought about the rush he got from playing his song in front of the crowd at the Watering Hole. "You said record it. But I could still play the song in public, right?"

Matt nodded. "I know how you songwriters are. You need to play it in front of people to see if it's any good."

Luke ran one hand through his hair. A deal like this could establish him as one of the most sought-after songwriters in Nashville. But it could also ruin any chance he had to become a star himself.

"My agent is going over all the details with your agent right now, so you don't have to give me an answer yet," Matt said. "Take some time. Look over the contract and talk it over with your family."

Family. Images of Emily and Wyatt popped into his head. What would Emily tell him to do? "When do you need an answer?"

"We've already agreed on 'Emily's Song,' so that's a done deal. I'd like an answer on this contract by the end of the week."

"I think I can manage to have an answer by then." Luke's insides were shaking.

"Good." Matt stood up and offered him his hand. "I'm cutting 'Emily's Song' on Wednesday morning. You're welcome to join us and watch."

Luke shook his hand. "I'd love to, but unfortunately, I have to get back to Arizona. My son's first birthday is on Wednesday."

Matt grinned. "You can't miss that then. What part of Arizona?"

"Coronado. It's small, I'm sure you haven't heard of it."

Matt laughed. "It's right outside Springerville. I know where it is."

EVEN THOUGH WYATT's birthday wasn't until Wednesday, Emily and her grandfather were already getting prepared. Her trailer was much too small for more than a couple people, so Granddad had agreed to have the party at the hardware store.

All morning, she and Abbie had moved empty shelves to the sides of the store, opening up a large area in the center.

"Is Luke going to make it back for the party?" Abbie set up a folding table in the middle of the floor.

"I think so." Emily covered the table with a red tablecloth. "I haven't really talked to him, although he did send me a picture of him and Matt Spencer."

"Matt Spencer?" Abbie held out her hand. "Let me see."

Emily pulled her phone from her back pocket and opened the picture.

Abbie squealed. "I can't believe he got to meet Matt Spencer!"

"Exciting, isn't it?" Emily kept her voice light. "Matt is going to be singing one of Luke's songs on the radio."

She wondered how Luke really felt about that. Wouldn't he rather be singing the song himself? She tapped the screen and closed the picture, but not before seeing the text message he had sent with the photograph.

Miss you. Don't give up on us yet.

She stared at the screen. She missed him, too.

"Earth to Emily." Abbie snapped her fingers.

"Sorry. I was just thinking."

"About Luke?" Abbie wrapped one arm around her. "Why don't you just admit that you love him?"

"What good would it do me?" Emily shoved her phone in her back pocket. "Luke's life is in Nashville, and mine is here."

"Is it, really?" Abbie tucked a strand of hair behind one ear. "What's so important here that you can't be with the man you love?"

Emily rubbed the back of her neck. She couldn't say her job. Abbie was the one who'd trained her for the job and could probably do it twice as fast. Her house...now that Grandad promised to help with the down payment. Oh, how she wanted that house. But was it worth giving up Luke?

The only real tie holding her in Coronado was sitting on the stool next to the counter. "I can't leave Granddad."

"Humph." Abbie walked to the counter. She lifted up her hands and shrugged her shoulders at her grandfather. "You're right. She's as stubborn as a mule."

Granddad laughed. "I told you she wouldn't listen to sense."

Emily's gaze narrowed, and she put her hands on her hips. "What are you two talking about? And why are you talking about me behind my back?"

Abbie crossed her arms and glared at her. "We're talking about the fact that you think you have to stay here, when your heart is in Nashville."

"I can't leave Coronado." How many times did she need to say that?

"I know," Abbie said. "You promised your grandmother you would watch over your granddad. You didn't promise to give up your entire life for him."

"How am I supposed to watch out for him from Nashville?"

"I don't need a babysitter," her grandfather huffed. "I've made it on my own for seventy-five years."

Emily sighed. She hadn't meant to insult her granddad. "I know you can take care of yourself. But whether you want to admit it or not, you're no spring chicken. What happens if you slip on some ice and fall? Lose your glasses again? Someone needs to be able to help you."

Granddad shook his head. "I can see that between you and Tricia, I'm never going to have a moment to myself."

Emily laughed. "I only harass you if you need it. And lucky for you, Tricia lives in Springerville, so you only have to put up with her on the weekends."

"Until June," he said.

She wrinkled her brow. "June? What are you talking about?"

"Tricia's retiring at the end of this school year and is moving back to Coronado." Granddad gave her a smug look. "So you see, there's nothing to stop you from moving to Nashville."

Emily crossed her arms. "Why didn't she tell me?"

Granddad shrugged. "She just told me on Sunday after church. If you'd gone with us, you would know that."

Emily pinched her lips together and shook her head at him. "Luke was here. I couldn't go."

Abbie gave her granddad a smug look. "You hear that? She wanted to spend time with Luke."

Granddad nodded. "If she was around him all the time, she wouldn't feel like she had to skip church to see him."

Then the two of them broke into a fit of giggles and Emily realized the entire conversation had been a setup.

"You two are impossible." She went to the nursery to see if Wyatt was awake.

He was standing in his crib, bouncing up and down. "Dadadada."

"Not you, too." She picked him up. "Are you all conspiring against me?"

She laid Wyatt on the changing table to put a fresh diaper on him, and her heart pounded in her ears. Were they right? Should she go to Nashville?

She set Wyatt on the ground, and he ran out to the main area of the store where Abbie was setting up another table.

"Where did Granddad go?" Emily asked her.

"I don't know." Abbie snapped the legs of the table in place. "He got a phone call and disappeared to the back."

"Probably a supplier needing inventory," Emily said. "I've shown him how to find it on the computer a million times, but he prefers to go to the back and look it up himself."

Abbie laughed. "You can't teach an old dog new tricks."

"Especially not that one."

"Are we okay?" Abbie asked her. "You know we just give you a hard time because we love you, right?"

"Of course we are." Emily walked over to her friend. "I know. And I appreciate it. Sometimes we don't know what's best for us until someone else points it out."

"Does that mean you're going to go to Nashville with Luke?" Her eyes widened.

Emily took a shaky breath. "Yes. If he asks me again."

Abbie folded her arms across her stomach and cocked her head. "We may have a problem. Luke is a Sterling, after all. What if he's afraid to ask you again? I mean, how many times does a person need to hear no before they give up?"

"Oh," Emily gasped. "Abbie, what am I going to do?"

"Ask him, of course!"

LUKE HAD HAD all night to consider Matt's offer. As he sat outside Kirby's office, he still didn't know what to do. If he accepted the contract, what did it mean for his career? Would he still have a career?

"Good morning, Luke." Kirby motioned him to come into his office. "How are you feeling? You've made your first sell, so that's something to celebrate."

"It's pretty exciting," Luke admitted. "Did you go over Matt's offer?"

"I did." Kirby sat down behind his desk. "He said he invited you to the recording session."

"He did, but tomorrow is my son's first birthday. My plane leaves at 7:30 tonight."

Kirby laughed. "You've got it bad, don't you? A few weeks ago you didn't even know you had a kid. Now look at you. I know you're anxious to get back to Arizona for your son's birthday, but I think you need to be at that recording session."

Luke's breath froze in his chest. He closed his eyes and took a breath. Was this where his agent was going to try to make him pick between his family and his music career?

Suddenly, everything he'd been feeling came into laser-sharp focus. His music was important to him. But not as important as Wyatt and Emily. He was prepared to walk out of that office right then and never come back.

"Sit down," Kirby said. "What do you think about Matt's offer?"

Luke rubbed the palms of his hands on his jeans and cleared his throat. “Honestly, I don’t know. On the one hand, it’s a great opportunity to establish myself in Nashville. But on the other hand, I have to wonder if I’m shooting myself in the foot and ruining any chance I have at my own singing career.”

Kirby tapped his fingers together. “I’ve known you for over a year now, and I feel like we can be pretty frank with each other, don’t you?”

“Of course.”

“If I didn’t think you had talent, I would never have taken you on. When you first came to me, I fell in love with your music. But I have to admit, you’re just an average singer.”

Luke should have been upset. This was the one person who was supposed to have his back. The person who could make or break his career. But to his surprise, hearing Kirby say out loud the one thing he’d always suspected himself felt liberating.

“So, you think I should give up any aspiration I have of being a singer and concentrate on writing music.”

“That depends.” Kirby’s face was somber. “I expected more from you after a year. I kept waiting for you to bring me new music, but you never did. After a year of nothing, I’ll admit I was starting to lose confidence in you. As a matter of fact, I was considering letting you go.”

Luke’s stomach dropped. Of all the things he expected to hear, that was not it. A knot formed in his stomach. How could he go from the biggest high in his life last night to fearing he was about to be dropped by his agent less than twenty-four hours later?

“Then last week, you show up in my office with the best songs I’ve heard in a long time.” Kirby shook his head. “What do you think happened?”

Luke shrugged. “I’m not sure.”

“I know. And so do you.” Kirby leaned forward, his elbows on the desk. “You tried to force it. And music doesn’t come that way. You went back to what you knew and, dare I say it, back to the girl you love, and the music started flowing again. Am I wrong?”

“No.” Luke realized the truth of Kirby’s words. Music was part of him, but so was Coronado. And now, so were Emily and Wyatt.

“I’m not sure if it’s that small town, becoming a father or seeing his mother again, but something’s changed in you. Something for the better. I’d hate to see you lose that.”

“What are you saying?”

“I think you should take Matt’s offer and sign the contract.” Kirby slid the papers across the desk. “I think we’re going to make some beautiful music together—and a lot of money. But I don’t think you’re going to be able to do that here.”

Luke’s mouth dropped open. “What do you mean?”

“One of the perks of being a songwriter and not a performer is that you can write music where it comes to you the best.”

Luke narrowed his gaze. “You think I should go back to Coronado?”

“Yes.” Kirby nodded. “But first, you’re going to that recording session in the morning.”

CHAPTER TWENTY-ONE

EMILY LOOKED AROUND the hardware store. Balloons and streamers hung from empty shelves. Red-and-blue tablecloths covered the tables and pictures of construction vehicles were everywhere. While she and Abbie had moved shelves and set up tables, she had no idea who put up all the decorations.

"Did you do all this?" Emily asked her grandfather. "This place looks amazing."

"Nothing's too good for my great-grandson." He shrugged. "Colleen did most of the decorating, though. I was a little busy."

Wyatt tugged on her grandfather's leg, and he hoisted him up. "Let's go get you some cookies," Granddad said.

She bit the inside of her lip as she watched him walk away. If she went to Nashville with Luke, Wyatt wouldn't grow up here. He wouldn't come to love the store like she had. Panic shot through her. He wouldn't know Granddad like she did. If she moved away, chances were that Wyatt wouldn't remember him.

Noah walked over to her with Colleen and another man. "Emily, have you met my mom's husband, Gerald?"

"It's very nice to meet you." Emily reached out her hand. "I've heard a lot about you, but I don't think we've met before. And, Colleen, you did such a good job with the decorations!"

Colleen squeezed her hand. "Thank you. It was so much

fun! Now, I don't want you to get upset with how many presents we brought for Wyatt. He's my first grandchild, so I hope you will forgive me if I spoil him a little."

"Get in line, Colleen," her grandfather said. "I get to spoil him first."

"This place looks great!" Tricia appeared next to her. "I'm going to have to hire you to throw my retirement party."

"I'll give you my number." Colleen laughed. "I love to throw parties."

"Hey." Emily turned to her aunt. "Why didn't you tell me you were planning to retire this year?"

"It was kind of a last-minute thing." Tricia popped a potato chip into her mouth. "I've been eligible for several years, but I was still trying to adjust to the idea of being a widow and needed something to keep me busy. I finally decided I'd better retire before I get too old to enjoy it."

"Well, congratulations," Emily said. "Granddad says you're moving in with him."

"Yes." Tricia arched one eyebrow. "You're not the only one who made a promise to my mom. Besides, if I'm here, you can concentrate on raising your own family."

Emily nodded. Her family might end up consisting of just her and Wyatt. She still hadn't heard from Luke. All last night, she'd expected him to show up at her door.

He promised he would be there for the party. What if he got to Nashville and decided to stay?

She took a deep breath and looked around at all the people who had come to celebrate Wyatt's birthday. Stacy and Caden and their girls were there. Noah and Abbie, of course. Freddy, Caroline and several other members of the community she had known for years. Even the Reed sisters were there.

The only person missing was Luke. Emily had managed to get through the entire morning without worrying too much, but it was almost noon, and he still wasn't there. Maybe he really wasn't coming, after all.

While the adults helped themselves to punch and snacked on chips and pretzels, the kids took advantage of the large open area to run around as fast as they could. Wyatt had already progressed from walking to trying to run and did his best to chase Khatia and Marina around the store.

"Are you okay?" Abbie gave her a look of pity.

"I'm fine. Or at least I will be." She kept glancing toward the entrance of the store.

He had promised her. He promised her that he would make it back in time for Wyatt's birthday. But he didn't. Just like her dad hadn't. She prayed his reasons for not showing up were selfish ones and that nothing bad had happened to him.

By one o'clock she decided that Luke wasn't coming. He'd made his choice, and it wasn't them.

"I think it's time for birthday cake," Emily announced. She glanced at Abbie. "You want to help me get the kids rounded up so Wyatt can blow out his candle and we can sing 'Happy Birthday'?"

Abbie put her phone in her back pocket with a guilty look on her face. "Actually, I think we should open presents first."

"Before blowing out the candles?"

Abbie and Stacy exchanged glances.

"I agree with Abbie," Stacy said. "Let's open the presents before giving the kids a sugar rush."

Emily was too miserable to argue with them. Without Luke there, she didn't care what order they did things in.

They gathered the children around, and Stacy's girls were only too happy to help Wyatt open presents. Wyatt was much more interested in crumpling the paper than he was in what was inside the boxes. As he was opening his last gift, Colleen whispered something to her husband. Gerald nodded and walked past the party toward the back of the store.

Once the presents were done, Colleen stood in the middle of the floor and called for everyone's attention. "In honor of Wyatt's first birthday, we have a present for Emily."

"Me?" Emily pointed at herself in confusion. "That wasn't necessary." Emily was flattered that Luke's mother wanted to give her something, but it was completely unexpected. "There's nothing I need, really."

"You're wrong."

Emily's heart almost stopped. She turned around and saw Luke. She faked her best smile. "You made it."

"I promised you, didn't I?"

"You did." It was hard to talk with the lump in her throat, but she managed to get the words out without sobbing. "How long do you get to stay?"

"Not long," Luke said. "Only forever."

"What?" Her hand flew to her mouth. "You're not serious. What about your contract?"

"Oh, I'm very serious. As a matter of fact, my agent threatened to drop me if I didn't."

Emily choked back a sob. "Why would he do that?"

"Turns out, he likes my music better than he does my singing. And I write a lot better music when I'm around you." He stepped closer and slid his arms around her. "So, I'm afraid you're stuck with me."

"I don't understand. How are you going to make music from here?"

"All I do is write the songs. I can do that from anywhere. I'll just have to fly to Nashville a few times a year."

She wrapped her arms around his waist. "Are you sure? Because if we need to live in Nashville, we can do that, too. I love you, and I want to be with you, no matter where you are."

He wiped a tear from the corner of her eye. "You know, that's the first time you've said you loved me."

She sniffed. "I've loved you since the first time I saw you. I just kept it a secret."

"No more secrets," he said. He pulled an engagement ring from his pocket and dropped to one knee. "I love you, and I want the whole world to know. Will you marry me?"

"Yes." Her heart felt as if it would burst, and she kissed him.

Everyone cheered. Noah clapped Luke on the back.

"Congratulations." Abbie hugged her tight.

Wyatt saw Luke and toddled over to him. "Dadada."

Luke kissed him and tossed him into the air. "That's right, son. And I'm not leaving you again!"

"Son, where is the rest of her present?" Colleen patted his cheek.

Emily looked at him through tear-filled eyes. "What are you talking about?"

"Actually, I have two presents." Luke pulled a key from his front pocket. "I hope you don't mind sharing your house with me."

"My house?" Her mouth dropped open. "The one on Cous Lane?"

"I know you wanted to do it on your own, but the day I went and looked at it, Justin had already had two offers. As soon as I saw it, I knew you would want it."

She pursed her lips. "So...the entire time Meghan was showing me the house and telling me the owner would only sell it to someone local, she was lying to me?"

"No." Luke wrapped his arms around her waist. "Technically, I was the owner by then, and I told her I would only sell it to someone local. And only if it was you."

She couldn't help but laugh. "Were you really going to make me pay you twenty percent down?"

"No. I just told her to tell you that to see if you wanted it badly enough to let me help you. Or marry me."

"Hey!" a loud voice called from the back room. "Can I come out now?"

"Oh!" Luke's eyes widened. "I almost forgot your second present."

Luke waved his hands to get everyone to quiet down. "Ladies and gentlemen, may I present, singing my song in public for the very first time, the one and only Matt Spencer!"

The country music star strolled out of the back room and began playing his guitar, although he wasn't able to start singing until everyone stopped screaming.

As Matt sang the song Luke had written for her, Emily leaned against Luke's chest and listened.

"I like the way you sing it better," she whispered in his ear. "How did you manage this?"

"Did you know there's an airstrip in Springerville?" he murmured in her ear. "He flew me here himself and wanted to meet the inspiration behind what he is sure will be his next number one hit."

When the song was over, Emily's grandfather came over and pulled her in for a hug. "Congratulations." He shook Luke's hand. "Welcome to the family."

"Well, sir," Luke said, "I'd like to be a little more than that, if you don't mind."

"What do you mean?"

Wyatt squirmed in his arms, so Luke set him down. The little boy ran to the pile of wrapping paper still on the floor.

"I'd like to take you up on your offer. As it turns out,

I'm going to have some extra time on my hands when I'm not writing music. I was thinking that if I'm a part-time writer and a part-time service technician, I might make enough money that I can give you a dozen or so more great-grandkids."

"Sounds like music to my ears," he said, grinning.

Luke pulled Emily closer to him. "What do you think? Music to your ears?"

"No. Music to my heart." She kissed him again.

* * * * *

Keep reading for an excerpt of a new title
from the Intrigue series,
COLD CASE INVESTIGATION by Nicole Helm

Chapter One

Anna Hudson was no stranger to mistakes. She was an act first, think later type of person. Because more often than not, that worked out for her.

And if she was being bracingly honest with herself—which her current situation seemed to call for—it tended to work out because she had five overbearing, determined and with-it older siblings to help her clean up her messes.

The fact that she'd spent most of her adult life—which wasn't a huge amount of time considering she was only twenty-five—trying to create some distance, some independence from her family was something she'd been proud of. She certainly didn't *want* someone always sweeping in and cleaning up her messes. She wanted to prove to the people who'd raised her from the time she was eight and her parents had disappeared that she could take care of herself.

Too bad she'd finally gotten herself into a jam no one could save her from. She took a deep breath of the cold, invigorating air. Winter held the Hudson Ranch in its grips and for the first time in her life Anna wasn't wishing for spring. Or summer.

Especially not summer.

She closed her eyes, willing the nausea away. Her

doctor—not her *normal* doctor, because even doctor-patient confidentiality wasn't safe in Sunrise, Wyoming, but the doctor she'd found the county over—had told her "morning" sickness could hit at any time and last possibly her whole pregnancy.

Three months in was definitely enough for Anna, but her baby didn't seem to be getting the memo.

So far, she'd been able to keep everything on the down-low, but the more unpredictable the nausea and food aversion got, the harder it was to hide.

She couldn't conceal it forever. Realistically, she understood that. In practice? She'd given herself three months. She considered that fair. Lots of women waited to announce their pregnancy until they were into their second trimester.

The problem was her secret was getting harder and harder to keep. She lived with too many people, had too many friends. And the three-month mark had come and gone.

Surely she could wait until she started to show? That seemed fair. Her family would be upset, but…

"You okay?"

Anna jerked. She hadn't heard Cash approach. She turned to face him and forced herself to smile. She couldn't throw up in front of him. That would be too much. Someone would insist she see a doctor, and then…

"You aren't…pregnant, are you?" he asked very, *very* carefully, and out of nowhere to Anna's estimation.

Of all the people she'd expected to call her out on it, her brothers had been at the bottom of her list. Particularly Cash, who didn't even live at the main house and kept his nose out of her business the most out of any Hudson—

though that was still pretty nosy. Still, Cash didn't butt in, for the most part. He had his own daughter to raise.

She supposed it made sense, though. Since he *was* a dad. Izzy was eleven, and her mom hadn't stuck around for long, but once upon a time, Cash had been the attentive husband to his pregnant wife. So of all the people in her life, he'd been the closest to the signs of pregnancy the most recently.

"Hell in a handbasket, Anna," he muttered when she didn't answer.

She swallowed down all that wanted to come up. "I don't see what business it is of yours." Bravado was often the best response to her overbearing siblings. Or had been.

Cash rolled his eyes. "You wouldn't." He adjusted his hat on his head. "Who knows about this? Certainly not Jack or we'd have had a shotgun wedding by now." His frown deepened. "You're not even dating anyone."

She smiled at her brother, because an off-putting offense was always the best defense. "I know you're a monk and all, but there is this thing called a *one-night stand*."

He swore again, taking off his hat and raking his hand through his hair. "Who is it?" he demanded, all furious and older-brotherly.

Anna didn't shrink in on herself, though she kind of wanted to. Pregnancy was making her weak. She sniffed and lifted her chin instead. "None of your business."

"Why not?"

Anna had always considered Cash the most reasonable of her brothers. Jack and Grant were the upstanding stick-in-the-muds, Palmer was more like her—or had been before he'd decided to go fall in love with her best friend—and Cash was…the reasonable one. The single dad who kept an even keel no matter what went wrong. His typical response to anything was to hunker down.

But the look on his face was decidedly unreasonable and bloodthirsty.

"I don't need you wading in to fix my problems, Cash. I can handle this."

Cash's expression changed. She realized he might be the calm one, but he was also the worst one to find out about this. Because he'd been in an accidental pregnancy situation himself. As the father of the baby.

"You told the guy, right?" he said. Very carefully. All cool and detached while his eyes were hot with his own issues.

Anna decided silence was her best weapon. But that only made Cash swear even more.

"Anna, you gotta tell the guy."

She shrugged jerkily, because anyone telling her what she had to do grated. Especially when they were right. "Why?"

"Because it's his kid, too."

There was no argument to be had here. First, Cash wasn't the audience. Second, she knew she had to tell the father. Every night she told herself tomorrow would be the day.

And every morning, she chickened out. Not her usual MO, but Hawk Steele was a *problem*.

"He isn't local."

"So take a trip," Cash replied. Firmly.

And she had to blame it on pregnancy hormones. Because she was not a soft woman. She'd learned to be hard. She'd lost her parents at eight, and though her sister had tried to fill in as a kind of maternal influence, Mary was only two years older than she was. So Anna had learned how to be tough, how to be a Hudson.

She'd done the rodeo. She was a licensed private investigator. She'd fought people, shot people, been shot at.

She didn't cry.

But there were tears in her eyes now, even if she managed to blink them away. "Cash, I can do this on my own. Well, not my *own*. But I have you guys. We'll be all right."

Cash inhaled, then pulled her into a hug. Because he had a little girl, and he was a good dad, and he knew how to comfort better than any of them. "We will be, Anna. No matter what." He pulled back, fixed her with a stare that made her wonder if her parents would just despair of her if they were still around. "But he has to know. You've got to give him a chance to be all right, too."

"I know. I do. I just..." Well, bottom line was she just didn't want to. She had always handled guys easily. She had four older brothers, plenty of family trauma. Guys had never scared her, never gotten the upper hand on her. She enjoyed the ones she wanted, then discarded. And had lived that way quite happily and carefully...

Until she'd met Hawk Steele's dark blue gaze across the room at a bar. She'd been handling a private investigation case, away from Sunrise and away from her family, and he had...

She'd *never* felt that way. And as tough girl as she liked to pretend, she'd never had a one-night stand before. They hadn't even exchanged last names at the time. There'd just been something elemental. *Necessary.*

And she'd been foolish enough to forget all her rules. To forget *everything*. Until she'd woken up in his bed, wrapped up in him, knowing she had to get the hell out before…something.

She hadn't been surprised when he'd shown up in her life a little while later. Because of course she'd looked him up after that night. It wasn't hard to track down a guy named Hawk in Bent County, Wyoming. Especially when, it turned out, he *worked* for Bent County as a fire investigator.

So when her friend Louisa's family home burned down before Christmas, Anna had figured she'd end up running into Hawk Steele. She'd practiced her casual, flirty smile. Her unwavering *I don't care about you* bravado. And it had worked. When they'd run into each other, she'd been calm and cool.

He had been shocked. For a second. But a second of shock on Hawk Steele *was* something.

"I can come with you," Cash offered, bringing her back to the present.

It was a sweet offer. She wouldn't take it, but for the time being, she'd let him believe she might. "Thanks. I'll… He kind of travels around, so I'll see if I can pin him down for a meeting." She pulled back from Cash's hug, flashed him a smile. "Promise."

"Look, if you need me to, I can cover your chores. Izzy can help out a little more with the dogs. Then I can—"

"No. I'm good."

"You don't want to overdo it."

"I know. I listen to all my doctor's many instructions." She looked up at the gray winter sky. The Hudson Ranch had been in their family for generations. Though all of them worked on their pet project—Hudson Sibling Solutions, solving cold cases for people like them who didn't have answers—the ranch was their foundation. The six of them worked together to keep it going.

Because her parents had. And her grandparents. And so on.

"Mom handled all this stuff when she was pregnant with me, right?" Anna said, waving her hand around the stables and the cows and the mountains that made up her life, her roots. "That's the memory. Supermom doing ranch work and taking care of all of us and… I bet she never…" Anna couldn't finish the sentence. She rarely thought of her mother, only remembered odd flashes of a strong, warm woman who'd always made her feel safe.

Until she and Dad had just been…gone one day.

"She was supermom," Cash agreed. "But, first of all, we were kids and she was an adult, so we don't really know what she had going on or didn't. Second, and take it from someone who spent a lot of years trying to be Dad, you don't have to be the parents ours were. You just have to be the one that's best for your kid."

Kid. She still really didn't quite think of whatever was growing inside her as a *kid.* Or herself as a parent. Maybe that was just another thing she was putting off.

"I've got chores to do. Then I'm heading out of town for a few days," Anna said firmly. Because she'd already decided that, and she wasn't changing any plans just because Cash had found her out. "And before you lecture me, it's just research. Nothing dangerous."

Cash's frown was epic, but she was used to big-brother admonitions over her side job.

"I don't think you should keep doing your private investigation work."

"And I don't recall asking your opinion. I told my boss

I'm taking a break from the bounties and stuff like that for a while, and that I didn't want to travel as much. This is a simple gathering of some adultery evidence over in Wilde. Take some pictures. Hand them over to the PI office. The end."

"I don't like it."

"Didn't ask you to."

Cash blew out a breath. "Fine, but for the love of God, tell Jack about this before you go. I do not want to be the secret keeper."

"But you're so good at it!"

He groaned as she walked away, laughing. Because… Well, Hawk was a multilevel problem, sure, but Cash was right. She'd be okay. She always was.

ANNA DIDN'T LIKE to admit that pregnancy had an effect on her body. But after a day of driving around trying to catch some salesman cozying up with his pretty lawyer, and coming up empty, Anna was exhausted. And since Wilde was too small to have even a nearby B and B, she'd had to drive over to Fairmont to find a place to stay.

Since she was going under the radar, she stayed at a run-down little motel a few miles outside of Fairmont. Not her first choice, but it was one night and she could sleep one night anywhere, especially as exhausted as she was.

She thought dimly about calling up Hawk. She didn't have his cell or personal number, but she had his work number. After watching him handle Louisa's fire case, she knew he was enough of a workaholic to probably answer even after hours.

But she was too tired. Maybe she'd wake up early and call him.

She crawled into the dingy bed, not even bothering to shower. She'd handle it all in the morning. She was always a good sleeper, so it was no shock when she fell into an almost immediate sleep.

She woke up to a coughing fit. When she blinked her eyes open, they started to sting. It was dark, but something was wrong. Her throat burned. It was too warm. And… it smelled like fire.

She leaped out of the bed in the same motion she swept the phone on the nightstand into her hand. She didn't know where the fire was coming from, but there was one. She ran for the door, grabbed the handle and pushed, thinking it would give, because of course it would. But it didn't, so she just rammed right into it. She twisted the dead bolt, then tried again, but nothing happened. The door was stuck.

The knob wasn't hot, though, so the fire was coming from…somewhere inside. Smoke was filling the room, so she crouched, trying to find some better air to breathe.

She didn't panic. Couldn't. She dialed 911 on her phone while still turning the lock and knob. There was no window in this room. There was one in the bathroom, but she was afraid that was the source of the smoke.

Someone picked up, but before she could even get out a word, something hit her head. Hard. So hard she only had a moment to try to brace her fall before the world went dark.

When she woke up, she was in a hospital bed.

She blinked at all the blinding white. Everything was fuzzy. Groggy. Had the fire been a dream? Was *this* a dream?

She didn't know how long she existed in this odd in-between state before it felt like she was really with it. Before she understood and started to remember.

Panic slammed into her. The fire. Her baby. She put her hands on her stomach, but she didn't know if it was any different. She didn't know…

She looked wildly around the room, expecting to see the familiar face of one of her siblings or at least a doctor.

Instead, standing at the foot of her bed was the one person she didn't want to see.